Her Beautiful Life

OTHER TITLES BY BRIANNA LABUSKES

Raisa Susanto Novels

By the Time You Read This

The Truth You Told

The Lies You Wrote

Dr. Gretchen White Novels

See It End

What Can't Be Seen

A Familiar Sight

Stand-Alone Novels

Her Final Words

Black Rock Bay

Girls of Glass

It Ends with Her

PRAISE FOR BRIANNA LABUSKES

What Can't Be Seen

"The book's well-constructed plot matches its three-dimensional characters. Psychological-thriller fans will be eager for more."

—*Publishers Weekly*

A Familiar Sight

"A horrific brew for readers willing to immerse themselves in it."

—*Kirkus Reviews*

"A strong plot and unforgettable characters make this a winner. Labuskes is on a roll."

—*Publishers Weekly*

"*A Familiar Sight* has everything I crave in a thriller: a shocking, addictive female lead; unexpected twists that snapped off the page; and an ending that made me gasp out loud. I never saw it coming, but it was perfectly in sync with the razor-sharp balance between creepy and compelling that Labuskes carries throughout the novel. This is a one-sitting read."

—Jess Lourey, Amazon Charts bestselling author

Her Final Words

"Labuskes skillfully ratchets up the suspense. Readers will eagerly await her next."

—*Publishers Weekly*

"Labuskes offers an intense mystery with an excellent character in Lucy, who methodically uncovers layers of deceit while trusting no one."

—*Library Journal*

Girls of Glass

"Excellent . . . Readers who enjoy having their expectations upset will be richly rewarded."

—*Publishers Weekly* (starred review)

It Ends with Her

"Once in a while a character comes along who gets under your skin and refuses to let go. This is the case with Brianna Labuskes's Clarke Sinclair—a cantankerous, rebellious, and somehow endearingly likable FBI agent with a troubled past. I was immediately pulled into Clarke's broken, shadow-filled world and her quest for justice and redemption. A stunning thriller, *It Ends with Her* is not to be missed."

—Heather Gudenkauf, *New York Times* bestselling author

"*It Ends with Her* is a gritty, riveting roller-coaster ride of a book. Brianna Labuskes has created a layered, gripping story around a cast of characters that readers will cheer for. Her crisp prose and quick plot kept me reading with my heart in my throat. Highly recommended for fans of smart thrillers with captivating heroines."

—Nicole Baart, author of *Little Broken Things*

"An engrossing psychological thriller filled with twists and turns. I couldn't put it down! The characters were filled with emotional depth. An impressive debut!"

—Elizabeth Blackwell, author of *In the Shadow of Lakecrest*

Her Beautiful Life

BRIANNA LABUSKES

This is a work of fiction. Names, characters, organizations, places, events, and incidents are either products of the author's imagination or are used fictitiously. Otherwise, any resemblance to actual persons, living or dead, is purely coincidental.

Published by Thomas & Mercer, Seattle
www.apub.com

EU product safety contact:
Amazon Media EU S. à r.l.
38, avenue John F. Kennedy, L-1855 Luxembourg
amazonpublishing-gpsr@amazon.com

ISBN-13: 9781662527456 (paperback)
ISBN-13: 9781662527449 (digital)

Cover design by Alan Dingman
Cover image: © ALICIA BOCK, © Vera Lair / Stocksy; © Iurii Vlasenko, © javarman / Shutterstock

Printed in the United States of America

To all the women I've been lucky enough to call friends

CHAPTER ONE

Det. Jamie Alvarez

The locals called the farmhouse on the hill The Orchard.

Detective Jamie Alvarez called it an eyesore. The rich couple who owned the place had refurbished it to within an inch of its life, and then had paid other people to work the land while they made pretty videos of themselves posing with the apple trees.

Jamie flashed her badge and was waved through the security gates, which had always struck her as excessive. As did the rest of the fancy fencing that surrounded the entire property.

She wasn't 100 percent sure anymore how to define *irony*—except that her daughter had told her that Alanis Morissette's song was all wrong, ironically—but she thought maybe this counted. The Bouchards had spent hundreds of thousands of dollars protecting themselves from the monsters who lived outside their walls, and yet what they'd ultimately had to fear had come from within.

After winding her way up the drive, past the pretty rows of apple trees, Jamie parked by three other cop cars, all with their lights still going. She checked her watch. Five minutes past midnight.

This was terrible business, and that kind of thing always happened in these hours.

Before getting out, she took a moment to catalog what she knew about the couple.

Catriona and Kristopher Bouchard.

They were rich, beautiful, and mysterious enough that they were mainstays of the locals' chatter at the bar on Sunday afternoons.

The wife, Catriona, was a social media influencer, one of those women who pretended it was 1950 while ignoring the fact that, in 1950, she wouldn't have been allowed to have a career making a spectacle of herself for the public to consume.

Kristopher had some kind of lofty title, like *financier*, which Jamie had long ago realized just meant that he had been born rich and had successfully invested in that trust fund. He was also very French in a way that delighted some in their small Vermont village and had others questioning his masculinity with outdated slurs.

Not that Kristopher would have heard them. The couple almost never went into town, except on Sundays, when they attended church and ran a few errands. Their children were homeschooled, their groceries were delivered. A man named George St. James ran the business portion of the orchard, and he prioritized a national audience rather than trying to sell the goods at the local farmers' market.

The choice to keep to themselves—and more importantly, to hoard their money—had not endeared them to the locals.

When Jamie could delay no longer, she hefted herself out of the driver's seat, regretting that third glass of wine she'd had with dinner. Normally, it wouldn't have mattered much—she was no lightweight—but she wanted to be on steady ground for what she was sure awaited her inside.

"Detective." A uniform was on her almost immediately. He was sweet, adorable, and at least twenty-five years her junior.

"Is Keller here?" Jamie asked, even though she could plainly see his car.

"In the study."

With the body went unsaid.

Jamie had worked homicide cases before, and she never liked them. Detectives were supposed to crave the high stakes, so she wouldn't admit that fact to anyone. But if she'd wanted to see bodies violently ripped apart, she would have taken a job in a city a long time ago.

The rookie hovered at her elbow, as if he expected to be invited along. *O'Connor,* she thought. *Josh O'Connor.* A newbie, straight from the academy. What a way to start your career.

She dismissed the rookie with orders to watch for any other newcomers, and then jogged up the steps to the porch. She took one last look over the land. Truman Capote would have shit his pants to be able to describe this scene. A gorgeous New England landscape tinted by the scent of a decomposing body, so strong she could smell it all the way out here.

A shiny red apple, rotten at its core.

She snorted to herself, and stepped into the farmhouse.

It felt strange even calling the place that. Her parents' home—that was a farmhouse. There, the paint could always use a fresh coat, the piles of dirty boots stank up the mudroom, and the floor creaked in an annoying, not charming, fashion.

This, on the other hand, was a set straight out of a Nancy Meyers movie, the kind Jamie's daughter, Maria, made her watch.

The Orchard, she thought again, and decided that was a much more apt name for it than *The Farmhouse* would have been.

Prestigious, but with a hint of malevolence.

Noise tumbled out of the study a few doors down, and Jamie just prayed no one was messing up her crime scene.

Toby Keller should be in there already. He might act too much like he was on *Criminal Minds: Burlington*, but he had meticulous standards in practice. She was glad he'd gotten to The Orchard as quickly as he had.

She headed toward the sound of his voice. Or really, she headed toward the smell of blood, of flesh.

Of death.

Maybe it was a procrastination technique, but she took a moment to stop by the pictures that hung outside the study. The hallway acted as a gallery wall, with dozens of photos all coming together perfectly to form the image of a loving, beautiful family. Jamie paused by one that included the whole family—Catriona, Kristopher, and their six children.

They were so pretty it almost hurt to look at. But what had grabbed Jamie's attention in this particular picture was that the photographer had caught a moment in between poses. The adorable twins were laughing with each other, the oldest girl was pouting, the boys looked about two seconds away from tussling, and Catriona and Kristopher were staring at each other as if to say, *Can you believe this is our life?*

For better or worse.

Jamie sighed. It was so easy to fake a picture.

She hustled the final few steps to the study.

"Detective Alvarez," Keller said when he spotted her, his face lighting up.

She should probably pull him aside and talk to him about being too excited while standing over a corpse.

"What do we have?" Jamie asked, though she had a fair guess as to what had happened.

She had listened to the 911 call enough times to have it memorized.

"He . . . Oh, God. Oh my god. He's dead. I think he's dead."

Although now, staring at a body that was missing a good portion of its head, she couldn't understand how anyone would have expressed any doubt on the state of Kristopher Bouchard.

CHAPTER TWO

Holland

Three days earlier

I had watched plenty of horror movies in my life, certainly enough to know that driving down an isolated dirt road toward a compound—or orchard, if we're being sticklers—where I would be required to surrender my phone for the entirety of my stay was a sequence of events that had a solid chance of leading to my death.

In fact, if I were watching this play out, I would be screaming at the screen, telling the stupid girl behind the wheel of her little rented Nissan that she should turn her ass around.

But starving because I had run out of money to pay for food also had a solid chance of leading to my death. A slasher-film-type murder would at least be quicker.

That's why I decided to view the towering trees on both sides of the road as beautiful instead of atmospherically claustrophobic. And I decided to find it funny that the local who'd pointed me in the right direction when my GPS adopted a *Jesus take the wheel* mentality had asked me three times if I was sure I didn't want to stop at the gun shop to pick up a weapon.

This was fine, I was fine.

I did pull to the side of the road right before I got to the thick steel gates guarding the compo—orchard, the orchard—to take a few calming breaths.

Because I was as obsessed as anyone else with social media, I scrolled through my favorite apps for one last hit, then reread the article pitch I'd sent to my editor to remind myself this was a great idea, actually, and not something I would regret as soon as the doors closed behind me.

Catriona Bouchard is one of the Founding Mothers of the "tradwife" movement—made up of people who extol the value of "traditional" gender roles where women are wives and mothers, while the men work outside the home to "provide" for their family. (The premise of the trend is inherently ridiculous for many of the most popular tradwives, who are likely the breadwinners in their relationship due to their social media success.)

The rise in popularity of the movement stems in part from reactionary backlash to the #MeToo campaign as well as intersectional feminism gaining a foothold in popular culture.

Social media influencers in general make money in several different ways: with affiliate links where they get paid when their followers click through to an item from their stories; partnerships where a brand pays them to talk up their product; and the miscellaneous opportunities, such as book deals, that come with having built up a large, devoted audience. Attention is currency these days, after all.

The tradwives are a subgenre of these social media influencers. Like the rest of them, they are selling a lifestyle, one where women are subservient to men. Notably, they often also shun any institution that might challenge their belief system, such as public schools that teach evolution and require vaccines to ensure the safety of all students.

Catriona Bouchard is the perfect tradwife. Her eleven million followers are captivated by her aesthetically pleasing life, with her postcard-perfect apple orchard, six children all under the age of ten—who never seem to throw tantrums or fight among themselves—and kitchen that would make Martha Stewart weep with joy. Her husband, French financier Kristopher Bouchard, fits surprisingly well in the cameos he makes in the backgrounds of her videos, dressed in cozy knit sweaters and work boots that don't have a speck of dirt on them. She makes her own fresh mozzarella that she serves on homemade sourdough bread, picks apples for pies straight off the trees, and does it all while looking fit and elegant.

That's who the world knows. I know Catriona Bouchard as Cat Vandale, from Bakersfield, California. We met in Savannah eleven years ago, when she was a pastry chef and the brightest star on Savannah's culinary scene.

That Cat would have laughed at women like the one she has now become.

So what happened?

I had a pretty good idea of what had happened. It was the same thing that had led me to sitting on the side of the road in my tiny rental car, ready to spend three days with a woman I hadn't talked to in ages.

It was money.

Even if it was the truth, that answer would not get this article to go viral—which was pretty much required these days, when it seemed like a minor miracle that anyone was paying for long-form pieces that actually took time to write. I'd been with *Profile Magazine* for nearly a decade now, had won awards for several of my pieces, and yet still felt like I was on the verge of being laid off with every slight dip in clicks on my stories.

I needed a big splash to remind the C-suite I was worth my paycheck, and Catriona Bouchard was going to be my ticket for employment for another year.

My editor had gotten a gleam in his eye during our video call about my pitch, usually a good sign that he also sensed an opportunity to drive unprecedented traffic to the site and create demand for collectors' copies of the actual magazine, something usually reserved for former boy band members turned triple-threat entertainers.

We both knew a few things were working in my favor to make this one huge.

Even though Cat "shared her life" with her eleven million followers, she was otherwise an incredibly private person, almost to the point of being called a recluse. Neither she nor Kristopher was ever caught candidly on camera outside their social media pages. They didn't speak to the press, and they interacted with fans in incredibly sterilized ways that reeked of someone else doing the actual chatting.

Their entire public footprint was limited to the videos they decided to share.

Which meant there was high demand for content about them that went beyond that.

Also, there was the simple fact that Cat was mesmerizing. Though she wasn't particularly bubbly or sexy or funny, that never seemed to matter. People were fascinated by her—and that tendency predated social media. I couldn't count how many times we'd sat down at a table full of strangers and one by one they would shift toward her like sunflowers seeking the warm rays.

She had never seemed to realize it—though she probably did now. Obscene popularity had a way of pounding even the most stubborn self-doubt out of people. Eleven million followers was not something that happened by accident, or to everybody.

So this profile was almost certain to attract a wide audience.

I didn't want to just phone this article in, though. That seemed like a waste of an interesting person.

I didn't have free rein, of course. I would be working within the constraints Cat had dictated just two days ago, when she'd accepted my request for a visit. A photographer from *Profile Magazine* would be joining us Monday morning for a planned shoot, but I wasn't allowed to take any pictures myself.

In fact, my phone was going to be confiscated at the front gate and returned to me only upon my departure. I was allowed a voice recorder, but nothing else.

Obviously, I'd balked at the stipulation. I had been interviewing people for ten years in this job and had never had to surrender my phone.

I had been told, in response, that it was a deal-breaker for Cat. And both sides knew I was getting more out of this than they were. I had no leverage.

I told myself I was used to interviewees' eccentricities—people who were intriguing enough to warrant a profile usually were a little weird. But it did give me a moment of pause, just long enough to hear the voice screaming in my head to turn around, go home, get out before whatever bad thing could befall me when I drove through those gates.

It felt like an overreaction on my part in response to being forcibly separated from my phone, but considering those stupid things represented safety, security, and connection, maybe it wasn't all that irrational.

On the flip side, the bizarre rules, the guardhouse, and the privacy that came with both would benefit me. It made it seem like the Bouchards had something to hide, and people would want to see if they did.

Even with all that potential, I still hadn't settled on the angle I was going to take with the profile.

If I wrote about how Catriona Bouchard's image was all fake and she was putting on a performance to sell her branded cake batter and kitchen utensils, I would lose all those built-in readers immediately.

I could write that piece before I even walked through the door. Everyone knew the image was fake—to at least some extent. That was a deal we already made with influencers: They gave us videos to watch while we sat on the bus or waited in line for groceries, and we pretended we were getting real glimpses into their lives.

That was a take so cold it could've chilled the cosmos the *Sex and the City* gals were all drinking on the first go-round.

People only wanted to see how the sausage got made if they were trying to make sausage themselves—the rest of us just wanted to gorge on the fatty end product knowing it wasn't good for us but not caring all that much anyway.

What I needed to do was find a different way in. A crack, not in the facade that everyone knew was a facade, but one in the foundation.

Cat's relationship with Kristopher.

"Don't go in with the story already written, Holland," I told myself.

I didn't know anything about them as a couple, really, because Cat had met Kristopher after I'd left Savannah for New York. But I'd watched all her videos.

And they made me curious about whether the two of them were as happy as Cat often said they were.

"Holland," I whispered again. "You're writing the story."

Before I could travel any further down *that* path, I turned my car back on and traveled forward on the path that would take me to a story that I wasn't inventing in my head.

An older gentleman in a rent-a-cop uniform was waiting for me at the gatehouse—he'd probably seen me coming long before I'd taken my last social media break on the side of the road.

"Hi, I'm Holland Tate," I said, digging out my ID. "With *Profile Magazine*."

I had always loved that the magazine's founder hadn't tried to be too clever with that name. The reader knew exactly what they were getting.

"We've been expecting you," the guard said in a four-packs-a-day voice. I wondered at the contrast between the frail old man and the rest of the security measures. I could've easily taken him out if I were feeling frisky—and I wasn't exactly an Amazon or the serial killer the Bouchards apparently thought might try to break into this compound.

Orchard, I corrected myself, so I wouldn't accidentally imply to *Cat* that this whole setup gave me Waco vibes.

The guard toddled back into his little house, with one hand on the gun at his waist. I wanted to ask him about his setup. What exactly was he doing with my ID in there? Was everyone who came through checked? Was there just one button that opened the gate? How many cameras were around to catch intruders?

Was it as hard to get out as it was to get in?

Holland, I snapped at myself. This *wasn't* a horror movie.

. . . said every girl ever who blithely waltzed to her death in an old haunted house.

That was okay; I wasn't scared of ghosts.

Except maybe I was. I was scared of the ghost my former best friend had become of herself.

I reached over to jot that down in my notebook. A little dramatic, maybe, but it wasn't a terrible lede.

I wasn't yet sure of how much of myself—and our past—I was going to include in the profile. It was my foot in the door, obviously, but would anyone care about the year and change we lived together in Savannah?

Maybe they would—plenty of interesting things had happened. Tragic things, too.

But that would open me up to questions I wasn't sure I wanted to answer.

Scratch that. It would open me up to questions I *knew* I didn't want to answer.

Like why we hadn't talked in ten years.

The guard was back.

"Now I just need your phone," he said, after returning my ID. "And to do a quick search of your luggage."

"Is that really necessary?" I asked, despite having been warned about both.

"House rules," the guard said with the tone of someone who had to defend something he knew was ridiculous.

I pressed my phone close to my chest for a moment, then reluctantly handed it over. His search was embarrassingly thorough—including riffling through the tampon box I'd stuffed in there—but he was a professional the whole way through, which I appreciated. When he was done, he punched in a few numbers on the box attached to the guardhouse.

No biometrics or anything fancy. That was interesting.

After I drove through, I couldn't help but watch the gates slowly close behind me.

The rest of the way to the farmhouse was just as idyllic as the long road leading in. While Cat filmed all over her property—and I'd watched most of the videos she'd posted, a somewhat daunting task—she never showed this area. Probably smart, in terms of security.

Her fans were *devoted.*

Maybe those gates with the passcode were necessary. Wouldn't it feel like a movie set to one of those fans? If they could just take a quick jaunt up north, they'd get to meet their favorite celebrity—even if that person would be considered E-list by real movie stars.

It would only take one mentally unwell person to rupture this perfect world for good. In that light, the security measures made sense.

Except the one where I'd had to give over my phone. That seemed more designed to keep me from taking any videos that would damage Cat's perfectly curated image.

My fingers tightened on the wheel as the road crept upward to a view that, in the very literal sense of the word, was breathtaking.

Neat rows of trees swollen with fruit marched at the feet of a pristine white farmhouse perched atop a hill. The red barn next to it could have been lifted out of a Winslow Homer painting, while the pond in the distance offered a sense of depth and pastoral sprawl.

That wasn't what had my pulse racing, though.

It was the fact that it all seemed so familiar.

Although I had never been to The Orchard before, I could easily remember Cat's six children playing with the goats that bleated in their pens outside the barn area.

I could remember afternoons in the summer spent by that pond on a picnic blanket that probably cost more than the current value of the car I was driving, and a basket full of food that would be more appropriate at Versailles. Always finished off by one of Cat's fabulous cakes, the ones that made her famous in the first place.

I could remember Cat, cradling her coffee in a perfectly beautiful mug, talking to the camera during a sleepy morning on that wrap-around porch, in one of the rare times she actually addressed her audience.

Honestly, it felt like I was part of that family, like I really knew them.

Like I had a *right* to them, a right to have opinions on their choices, a right to get updates on their lives, a right to see even their most private moments.

It was an odd sensation, like I'd stepped into *The Truman Show.* With the caveat that I'd actually known Truman before he became a commodity to be consumed.

What must it be like for Cat?

No one was supposed to feel bad for people who made entire jobs out of posting to social media, but I did. It came with a downside that I, personally, would have found terrifying.

I knew that I didn't actually have a right to any of those things just because I'd followed along with their videos, but there were plenty of people out there who couldn't or wouldn't acknowledge that.

Part of me thought that Cat and her brethren could simply stop posting. If they couldn't handle the parasocial relationships that inevitably came from the job, then they could stop doing the job. But another part of me wished we could, as a society, make sure there were fewer of those vultures to deal with.

In preparation for this story, I'd scanned the comments on her posts, simply picking ones at random to get a sense of what the responses to her were. Plenty of them were kind and uplifting messages. But way too many were from entitled followers who were either "concern-trolling"—masking critiques under the guise of being worried for the health or safety of someone in the family—or straight up rude and intrusive.

I'd once heard internet behavior compared to basic hygiene. In this analogy, we were in the pre-handwashing days, where we simply had to cut off limbs because we didn't understand infection. And Cat was exposed to the worst kinds of germs on a daily basis.

To still post videos letting people into her life was, to me, equal parts brave and foolish.

I finally reached the end of the drive, pulling to a stop beside a gleaming Range Rover. Almost the second I put the car in park, the farmhouse door opened.

Out stepped Catriona Bouchard, slim and elegant and tastefully beautiful, a warm, practiced smile plastered on.

I thought back to the first time we'd met each other. She'd hated me the moment she'd seen me. It had been obvious. She'd never been able to keep her thoughts off her face—something that, back then, she definitely had thought she'd mastered and now clearly had.

But it hadn't taken me long to figure Cat out and wind my way into her heart. She was insecure and arrogant at the same time; she was mean and judgmental; she was a total pain in the ass more often than not. God, she'd been fun, though. And quick, and clever and loyal and fierce and courageous. She'd been terrible and brilliant and . . . *real.*

Being next to her had been like flying too close to the sun, exhilarating and terrifying all at once.

As I stared at her now, all I could see was a placid, empty shell.

I wondered then if I was being honest with myself about why I was here.

Although being honest with myself wasn't my strong suit. My sister had said I liked to live in stories of my own creation; while a particularly angry hookup buddy had deemed it lying to myself.

Either way, it wasn't always easy to grasp my underlying motivations when there were easy answers skimming along the surface.

Yes, if I wrote a killer article that got a million clicks, it might help my ever-dwindling bank account, as well as add another win to my résumé. That was true.

Maybe, though, maybe I was curious to see if any part of my friend was still in there.

Just waiting to be freed from a beautiful cage of her own making.

CHAPTER THREE

Cat

Then

I wanted to kill my roommate.

Former roommate, to be accurate.

I had the knife skills to make it painful. I'd trained with the CIA, after all.

New York's Culinary Institute of America, of course, but still just as useful in that regard as the alphabet agency.

"How crazy could they be?" asked Michi, the hostess at the bistro I was single-handedly turning into Savannah's hottest restaurant. I put the phone on speaker as I buzzed the next applicant into the building.

I thought about the one I'd just shown the door. "She had seventeen cats. Not one, not two, seventeen."

"Yikes," Michi said, appropriately appalled. "Remind me why Mark isn't moving in?"

I hadn't told Michi about the lamp Mark had thrown against the wall during our last fight. I had a feeling that relationship was doomed in the exact same way too many of the rest of mine had been. Thankfully, I was saved from answering by the knock on the door.

"Next one's here," I said. "See you tonight, babe."

"Text me when it's done so I know they didn't chop you up and feed you to their cats," Michi said.

I would have laughed except this was now my sixth interview for someone to take over the second room in my apartment—abandoned by she-who-shall-not-be-named without any warning whatsoever two days before rent was due. So instead I offered a dry "ha," and hung up.

I breathed out, rolled my neck, like I did before starting any competition, and pasted a smile on my face.

My first impression of the girl on the other side was that she was drop-dead gorgeous. She had thick auburn hair she wore in a messy ponytail that signaled she didn't care about her own beauty, and that just made her more appealing. She had the kind of freckles that looked like someone had spilled a container of them all over her face, and eyes that tipped up so it seemed like she was perpetually thrilled about life. Her lips were the kind of naturally bee-stung that girls paid hundreds of dollars to replicate—I could always tell when they were fake, and hers weren't.

I wanted to slam the door in her face. I didn't like the idea of having this person around me. I was . . . pretty. But it was in a subtle aristocratic way, with fine features and thin lips and eyes that gave me a resting bitch face. I knew the score. Hot boys flocked to girls like this, while wealthy men married women like me.

Still, I was desperate, and hate it though I might, her attractiveness wasn't enough to make me turn her away. It certainly wasn't a seventeen-cat-level red flag.

"Hi," she said, in one of those sexy, husky voices. "I'm Holland. Holland Tate."

She even had a cool name.

I smiled wider, constantly fighting my own face's tendency toward revealing what a cunt I was. "Hi. Oh my gosh, it's so nice to meet you. I'm Cat. Come in, come in."

"It smells so good in here," Holland said, and I tried not to smirk with pleasure. It was well known in the real estate world that throwing some premade cookie dough in the oven made people like a home better. I would literally rather die than touch one of those garish yellow tubes, but it did inspire me to whip up a batch of pumpkin spice cookie bars that I hadn't even bothered offering to the last five applicants. They had not deserved them.

Holland gratefully took a bar, and flushed pink after the first bite. "Holy shit, you made these?"

Again, I tried not to preen. It was an unattractive quality, I'd been told. No one at CIA, or anywhere in the culinary field, would ever mind. We were all arrogant bitches, just like surgeons. But with the normal folk, I did at least attempt to come off as humble.

"They're nothing fancy."

"If I could bake like this, I'd be seven hundred pounds," Holland said, eyeing my lean frame with an appreciation *I* appreciated. Of course, I'd rather have her curves, but that was womanhood, wasn't it?

At some point, my shoulders relaxed in a way they hadn't all morning. "Do you want to know a secret?"

Holland's eyes practically sparkled. "Of course."

"I don't even like desserts," I confessed.

Her lips parted in delighted surprise. "What? That's wild."

I shrugged. "I know what flavors taste good together, but I'd much rather have cheesy fries if I was going to have a cheat day."

"I will eat all the cookies and cakes and brownies you ever feel like making," Holland said on an amused rush, before shoving the rest of the pumpkin bar in her mouth.

"Well, considering I'm a pastry chef, that'll be plenty," I said. I always enjoyed people's reaction to my occupation. I'd been to plenty of parties and experienced friends trying to look impressed when meeting lawyers and teachers and even doctors. It wasn't that those careers weren't worthy—probably more worthy than mine, to be honest. But they were pedestrian.

I was unique.

People loved unique.

Holland didn't disappoint.

"You should tack on an extra couple hundred bucks in rent," she said, and then pressed a laugh back with her hand. "I should *not* have said that."

I grinned. "Right, don't give me ideas."

It was almost shocking how quickly she'd won me over, but I wasn't exactly a complicated person. That was why I'd been so annoyed by the five previous applicants. My ego needed a little petting, sure, but how much of a hardship was that, really? And you would get plenty of sweets for your efforts.

Beyond that, as long as someone didn't cringe at my casual use of profanity, and the sometimes mean thoughts that made it past my usually tight filter, then I could become their fast friend.

During the tour of the apartment, Holland dropped a few curses and said something cuttingly cruel and scarily accurate about the It Girl pop star of the moment that actually got me to laugh.

I was sold.

"What about you?" I asked, right before an offer for the room passed my lips. I should at least make sure she was employed. "What do you do?"

"I'm an MFA student. For writing," she said, with the same casualness I'd used when dropping that I was a pastry chef. People in her life had been impressed with her, too. And I was. The difference between us was that I would never show it.

"You're going to pen the Great American Novel?" I teased, because even if I was bitter that she was nearly as interesting as I was, I wasn't going to let that derail this successful interview.

She laughed, all whiskey and tumbled rocks. "Hardly. But I do have a stipend from the university for housing, so you won't have to worry about me missing rent."

It was interesting how easily she shrugged off discussion about her work. Not even a modest *Well, it's not Hemingway, but . . .*

It soothed my few remaining ruffled feathers.

I smiled, more pleased than I could have ever imagined at the start of this morning. "How soon can you move in?"

CHAPTER FOUR

Holland

Now

By the time I got out of my car, Kristopher had come up behind Cat, sliding an arm around her waist. They watched me from the porch, the king and queen awaiting the scribe, wishing she could get her shit together a little faster, probably.

Maybe I would have, had I not had to dump half the contents of my entire duffel bag out for the guard at the gate to search.

"Holland, welcome," Cat said when I made it to them. She wrapped her arms around me, and all I could think about was how sweaty my back was. "It's been far too long."

And whose fault was that?

That wasn't a rhetorical question, if I was being honest. I didn't know. Hers? Mine? A little of both, probably.

Mostly, though, I was pretty sure it was Kristopher Bouchard who was at fault.

"So long," I agreed, before turning to the man who had married my best friend and hidden her away in the middle of Nowhere, Vermont.

"I've heard so many things about you," Kristopher said with the barest—and most perfect—hint of a French accent.

I almost laughed at that, because usually people would say—even if they were pretending—that they'd heard *good* things. But not Kristopher. I wondered if the misstep was language-based or if he'd deliberately wanted to unsettle me.

"Only good things," Cat hurried to add, which made it all the more awkward. That should have been my line, delivered playfully. But now it seemed like they were covering for the fact that they had been talking shit about me.

Quite an auspicious start.

"Obviously," I said, trying to smooth it all over, and Cat laughed, though it was a second too late to come off as natural.

I shook off the moment and turned my attention to Kristopher.

As I'd already known, he was objectively handsome, if you liked his type. He wasn't much taller than Cat's 5'8", but he wore his frame well, draping his slim muscles in cashmere and tailored jeans. He had thick, dark hair that he wore in a bun, and olive skin that was aging like fine leather. His brown eyes reminded me of a cow's, but somehow that worked for him.

"This is Kris," Cat finally said.

"I gathered," I said dryly, knowing that it must be strange to both assume everyone knew everything about your family and realize it was odd to act that way.

She stared at me for a beat, then two, before laughing.

Cat was nervous.

Kris seemed to realize that at the same moment, because he squeezed her hip. My gut read it as too hard, a warning sign rather than a comforting check-in; my mind told me to stop seeing bruises in harmless gestures.

Did Cat flinch, though? Or was that just a trick of the light?

We all stood there in a moment so painfully uncomfortable I wanted to sink into the ground. I was good at easing the way, usually. It was a large part of my job, even. But for some reason my tongue was heavy and clumsy in my mouth, my charm gone in the face of Cat's clear anxiety.

She had never been the nervous type before. Was it just because she wasn't used to being interviewed? It probably was scary to feel out of control when she'd been so careful with her content for so long.

That thought unlocked me from my own paralysis. I had to un-fuck this moment. "Thank you so much for inviting me out here. I can't wait to get to know your beautiful family better."

It was only after I said it that I realized the *better* might have come off as a sour note—maybe I should have pretended I didn't know anything about them to put her more at ease. But that was an obvious lie that wouldn't help the situation.

Cat finally fully smiled. "We're so thrilled to have you."

Just then a young boy shot out of the door, his mop of curls bouncing as he hurtled toward Cat. In one smooth move, she scooped him up, resting him on her hip.

Louis, I knew.

All six of her children had French names, like she was building out a little royal court for herself.

Louis's twin sister was called Céline, and they were three years old.

Then there was Fleur, the oldest at nearly ten.

Gabriel, at seven.

Guy, who was about to turn six.

And the baby, Vivienne, which was such a big name for such a tiny creature.

Objectively, it was strange that I knew all of them and how old they were despite the fact that I was a complete stranger who hadn't spoken to their mother during their lifetimes. It was strange that I knew what ice cream flavor was Louis's favorite and that Fleur loved the goats and hated the chickens.

Still, it was nice going in with some details. The article wouldn't be about the children except in broad strokes, but having the basic foundations would make finding the *real* story easier.

"Mama, Mama, Mama," Louis babbled.

Cat's face was pure joy as she stared into his eyes. "What is it, baby?"

"Celly hit me," Louis said with the sweet lisp of a toddler.

I had watched hours of videos of this family, and this was the very first time I had ever heard of even the hint of bad behavior from the children. I pressed an amused smile away only to find Kris watching me.

At first his expression was cold, but in the blink of an eye, the warmth rushed back in.

"I guess they are human," I said.

Kris winked. "We bring in the robots to swap them out when they're in really bad moods."

I snorted. I was curious to see how Cat would handle this situation—I didn't have kids, but I did know that gentle parenting was en vogue these days. Would Cat sit the twins down for some introspective chat about nice hands and big feelings?

Before she could do much of anything, a woman darted out of the house, a little flushed and out of sorts. "I'm so, so sorry, Mrs. Bouchard."

At first, I barely noticed her, in that way that sometimes happens with strangers on the periphery of your attention. I caught details. Young. Thin. Blond.

That was enough to get me to actually look—if there was something Cat did *not* like, it was young, thin blond women standing around making her appear inferior in any way.

And when I looked, when I actually looked, I nearly took a half step back.

The young woman was a dead ringer for Cat.

Not in that *oh, if you squint at a distance* kind of way. No, they were nearly identical.

Sure, the woman's edges were a little softer than Cat's, her face rounder, with a hint of curves beneath her matching yoga set.

But if this woman had been waiting for me on the porch, I would have, at least for a second, thought it was Cat.

"He just got away from me," the woman explained. "I'm so, so sorry."

"It's quite all right, Anna," Cat said. Ten years ago there would have been more bite in her voice. Given the effusive apologies, Anna must have been told in no uncertain terms that Cat and Kris were not to be disturbed in front of the reporter.

This Cat was more forgiving, it seemed.

Anna reached for Louis, who clung briefly to his mother before relenting. Then the young woman turned and rushed back inside without once acknowledging me.

It wasn't surprising that Cat had never mentioned a nanny. That would undercut the perfect-mother image she wanted to embody. But it did feel like I'd missed a step, a swoopy feeling in my stomach that signaled I was unbalanced in a nonthreatening way.

Because even though I knew Cat's videos were a fantasy, they still *felt* like reality. I knew I was being sold something fake, and yet my brain was not immune to buying what she was selling.

I wondered how many other people I'd encounter this weekend who never made it in front of the camera.

"I'm sorry for the scene," Cat said, turning back to me.

It was odd seeing her off-kilter. The Cat I knew had been a lot of things. Unsure of herself, though? Never.

"You know, little ones," she continued.

"Not so much, actually," I admitted, and Kris laughed softly.

"You will soon," he said, slipping his arm around Cat's waist again. He waved toward the open door. "Please, leave your bag here. We'll have it taken up to your room."

My fingers curled around the straps, just as they had my phone when the guard asked me to give it up. I liked my privacy, and though this was ostensibly a nice-host thing and not a we're-constantly-digging-through-your-possessions thing, it did actually seem like it could be both.

Separately, these small things were hardly remarkable. Together they added up to something that had me on edge.

I dropped the bag, because of course it wasn't worth a fight.

"Oh, Mia," Cat greeted someone I couldn't yet see, the relief in her voice palpable.

In the next moment, a woman rounded the corner. She was short and plus-size, with dark hair that she had pulled back into an ultra-sleek bun at the nape of her neck. She was dressed impeccably in a tailored suit, a high-buttoned shirt, and impossibly sharp black designer stilettos. Her glasses were oversize and stylish, and she looked like she could absolutely plan my murder without breaking a sweat.

I wondered if one of the unspoken job requirements for being hired on at the Bouchards' was to be gorgeous. Cat had always loved making things beautiful, even when all she could afford in her effort to do so was a pretty little cupcake holder.

"You must be Holland Tate," the woman said. "I'm Mia Preston."

Ah.

Of course, this was Cat's manager.

I had originally contacted Cat directly with my profile request. It had taken her several months to get back to me, but on Wednesday she finally had. We exchanged a few emails, but she quickly directed me to this woman, who had arranged the actual logistics.

Mia charged ahead without waiting for me to respond. "You'll get a tour of the house first, but afterward, I'd like us to go over our plans for the weekend so that we're all on the same page."

Kris laughed and turned to me. "With these two running the ship, you better get used to being bossed around and kept on a tight schedule."

He was such a host—friendly and welcoming but in a polished way that set my radar to *suspicious*. If someone was as slick as this, it made me think they were hiding something beneath all that oil.

I hadn't been sure what to expect with Kris. I realized I was biased against him—he was an easy person to blame for the fact that Cat and I had never healed the rift between us. Beyond that, I didn't know much about him. In Cat's videos he was about one step above a prop, and I tended to notice his absence more than I noticed the times he showed up at the end to eat whatever she'd been baking.

Now he was trying to land funny little asides with me, winking, smiling, and laughing. He came off as warm when he knew I was looking at him. And then I would catch tiny flashes of cool calculation in his expression when he thought I wasn't.

He was also a multimillionaire many times over, and those guys didn't tend to be *nice*. That was not how you made that much money.

At the same time, I realized I was, kind of desperately, hoping I'd like him. It would mean that I might be able to repair my relationship with Cat—something I rarely let myself acknowledge could be a lovely perk of writing this article.

If I let myself want it, it would become my main focus, and that wasn't professional or acceptable. Hope was a seed, though, that had planted in the softness of my heart. And if I didn't get along with Kris, any kind of reconciliation would be a nonstarter.

So I smiled and laughed, probably a second too late, just like Cat had on the porch.

"We haven't even offered you refreshments or checked if you need the lavatory," Cat said. "I'm so sorry."

"Worst hosts in history," Kris said, slapping his forehead with his open palm. "We are a bit rusty—you'll have to forgive us."

I seized the opportunity to pry. "You guys don't host much, but you don't go into town, either? Doesn't that get lonely?"

Cat's expression went plasticky.

This was the same woman who'd thrown parties at our apartment every week. National Cookie Day? Party. Take Your Daughter to Work Day? Party. An ironic one, of course, because we loved irony back then. But, still, a party. Cinco de Mayo, a.k.a. National White Girls Drink Margaritas Day? The biggest party you've ever seen.

Yet here she lived like a hermit.

Mia cleared her throat and exchanged a look with Kristopher.

It was quick, but there, in that way you meet your friend's eyes across the room when someone you both hate says something ridiculous.

Cat and I had perfected that look.

What did it mean when Cat's manager did the same with her husband?

Don't write the story . . .

"I don't think that's possible with so many little ones running around," Cat finally said, with her content voice. Melodious, feminine, yet empty of any emotion.

"And, of course, we have plenty of staff working at The Orchard," Mia added on. "At our busiest we have a dozen people in and out every day."

"We're also fairly self-sustaining, so we don't have to rely on local stores," Cat said, as if that were a good thing. "I can tell you all about what we do to limit our carbon footprint and—"

I tuned her out a little bit, I'm not afraid to admit. I'd watched this spiel, not only from her but from other tradwives of the homesteading-farming variety. The deeper you went down the tradwife rabbit hole, the more you could identify the different subgenre of influencer. There were the Mormons, who dominated their little slice of the internet. You had the cosplayers, who mostly liked the outfits and hairstyles of the fifties. You had the hippie mamas and the wellness mamas, who thought modern life was the root of all evil. You had the women I liked the most, the ones who were the genuine article, or as close to it as possible—the ones who were steeped in Appalachia, who ran their homes with an iron fist and made moonshine and cookies with too much vanilla extract in them for their bearded blue-collar husbands.

And then you had women like Cat.

The prairie girls. The homesteaders. The ones who drank goat milk straight from the teat and had to dodge their free-range fowl every time they went to feed the cows.

They all intersected, of course, tied together by what they sold as "traditional" norms.

"Do you live here?" I asked Mia, possibly interrupting Cat.

Mia's brows twitched, which seemed to signal that I *had* just cut off the woman whom I'd come to profile.

"Yes," Mia said. "We find it easiest, considering the lack of appropriate real estate available in town."

Again, I watched her eyes flick to Kris's as quick as anything.

"How cozy," I murmured, and this time it was Cat's gaze that crashed into mine. It had been ten years, but we could still hear the layers in each other's voices.

Or she could hear the ones in mine.

Hers were harder to parse out nowadays.

I did notice that during all this Cat had stepped away from Kris, who'd let his hand fall back to his side. She wouldn't look at him or Mia.

And the children were nowhere to be found.

One big happy family.

CHAPTER FIVE

Holland

Now

I thought I was going to have to beg, borrow, or steal one-on-one time with Cat, but my first opportunity came almost immediately. Apparently Cat, and Cat alone, was going to give me a tour of the house. Quickly after this was announced, Mia and Kris made their excuses and peeled off. Though, notably, they went their separate ways.

When I was sure Cat and I were actually by ourselves, I tapped her elbow. "Hey."

Cat offered up a small, confused smile. "Hi."

I grinned at her, letting my genuine affection shine through. "It's legit so good to see you."

Something complicated flashed in and out of her expression. The last time we'd talked before all this had been at a funeral, where we'd fought like banshees. And we'd only been friends for about a year before that. Most people would consider us little better than strangers.

Most people weren't us, though.

For a second, I thought it was just me who thought that, but then everything about Cat softened and she took me in her arms in a fierce hug. I sank into her embrace, missing not so much her but that time in my life, when it had felt like we ruled the world.

"It's *so* good," she said. She smelled of lavender and yeast from perpetual bread-making. I was pretty sure I smelled of McDonald's french fries and my cheap peach deodorant. "I wouldn't want anyone other than you writing this article."

The proof of the statement was my presence here, but it also felt a bit like a lie. Not only had we not talked for ten years, but I'd known her before she adopted whatever this persona was. This nice, unassuming, pretty but not movie-star-beautiful character. I could tell her devoted fans stories that would floor them, maybe even leave them appalled. Certainly, it would cost her followers if I spilled what I knew about her, in all her terrible, fascinating, mean, and funny glory.

People on the internet, as a whole, didn't like nuance or flaws. They wanted this version of Cat, and I was supposed to give it to them, only maybe an inch deeper than what they already saw.

I wasn't sure if I would indulge them or not, which meant that Cat shouldn't be so excited that I was the one writing the article.

Still, I cared about her, which was more than she would get from some other journalist just as hungry for their next viral article as I was for mine.

Ten years hadn't erased that. Our last fight hadn't erased that.

"I want people to see you," I said after a moment. "I'm hoping I'll be able to accomplish that."

For whatever reason, that made her re-don her plastic mask. It was different from the warm one she wore in her videos, that she'd *just* been wearing, which also seemed fake. But this one made her look like someone who thought of emotions as foreign concepts. She cleared her throat. "Well, let me tell you about the house."

I made interested sounds because I thought it might help her relax—and it did. It quickly became apparent, though, that it was going to be the most soul-crushingly boring thing I'd had to listen to in recent memory. And I'd recently sat through a half-hour-long subway train breakdown with a man who'd thought it a good idea to read the birthday section of a local newspaper out loud to keep everyone entertained.

"We really like the pop of color this gives us," Cat said, pointing to a green-but-nearly-black wall feature that could slide back to reveal a television. The rest of the room was all neutrals. People could say what they wanted about our shabby apartment back in Savannah, but it at least had character. This was beautiful and empty of any kind of life.

I hoped that wasn't going to be the headline for my profile.

"And this is one of my favorite light fixtures in the house."

The polite part of me wanted to ask why, and every other part of me told that part to shut the hell up. "Hmm."

So it went, as this carefully curated Interior Design Barbie showed me around the farmhouse.

I guessed that she hadn't completely lobotomized her personality, but there was only so much she was willing to show the world at large.

Right now, that included me. Even if there had been a tantalizing point in time when I'd gotten to see the real her.

I had to get back inside somehow. I'd promised my editor I'd get back inside.

Honestly, I also missed her. She had been so funny, so cutting and clever and vulnerable and *interesting*. *Boring* was definitely subjective—there were people out there who cared deeply about the exact shade of green-but-nearly-black that she'd used for her pop of color and would have been fascinated by this tour. Part of this disconnect was on me. But *my* Cat had never once mentioned a sconce or wainscoting, and it seemed like that had been for the better.

I didn't tune her out as she gave me the tour—I was here to profile her, after all. But my mind did wander a little bit, circling back to the question I couldn't shake.

Why had she finally agreed to let me come here, especially if she was just going to talk at me about couch fabrics? And laugh nervously and speak in platitudes. She was popular and famous enough that she didn't need whatever exposure my profile would bring.

The respectability, though? That might've been enough to win her over. We didn't tend to profile influencers in our magazine—it wasn't exactly highbrow, but people had to bring a certain level of *interesting* to the table. That didn't have to be fame and fortune, either. They just had to be compelling.

Getting on the cover? That could be a huge ego boost for someone who probably was self-conscious about their true status in society.

Maybe it was all as simple as that.

We were just about to head up the stairs to the next floor when I stopped. A piano melody slid beneath the crack in the nearest door—a haunting, beautiful piece from someone who was clearly talented.

Cat had walked by without pausing, but now she glanced back to see what was keeping me.

I pointed to the closed door. "Who's the musical talent in the family?"

Her hand flew to the delicate necklace she wore, a nervous gesture that I recognized even after a decade. "Oh, you know."

"No?" I said, confused as she grabbed my hand in an effort to keep me moving toward the stairs.

I didn't resist completely, but I didn't make it easier on her to pull my body weight. The few extra seconds I dragged behind paid off when the door to the room opened.

I turned, gleeful to find out what had made Cat panicky, and came face-to-face with an angry teenage boy.

The shadows in the hallway were thick enough to obscure some of his features, but I was able to put him at about sixteen years old, with the acne to prove it. He had floppy dark hair and olive skin and brown-cow eyes.

This was what Kristopher must have looked like as a teenager.

Not that I needed the similarities to know exactly who this was. I had recognized him immediately from the articles detailing his mother's freak accidental death.

This was Stefan Moreau. Cat's stepson.

I just hadn't realized he was living with the family—though of course he was. His mother had died six months ago, so it made sense his father would become his full-time guardian.

But he hadn't made an appearance in a single one of Cat's videos, even ones that showed the whole family as they got ready for church or sat down for dinner.

"You're the journalist," he said, his stare unblinking. I imagined he probably had a fairly fraught relationship with the press at the moment. They should've been leaving him alone, but tabloids rarely cared about *should*.

"I am," I said. "But I just write profiles. Not news."

His face twitched at that, surprise or derision, maybe. "If you really want a story, you should ask what actually happened to—"

"Steffie," Cat cut him off. He dropped silent, but watched me, wanting to see if I was going to bite, probably.

"What actually happened to whom?" I asked, though I imagined he must've been talking about his mother.

Stefan—Steffie?—finally looked at Cat. "No one important, apparently."

He said it like the words were a dagger aimed straight at Cat's heart, and I knew in that moment that this scene had played out exactly as he'd wanted, as part of an argument that must have started long before I got here.

Without waiting for a response, he pushed past me so aggressively that I fell back against the wall, banging my elbow in the process.

Cat rushed over, dismayed. "Are you okay?"

"Of course," I said, mostly embarrassed to have been knocked off balance by a scrawny teenager.

"I'm sorry." Her hand flexed against my shoulder even as she stared down the hallway after the boy. "Steffie just lost his mother about six months ago. He had been living with her full-time, and it's been quite an adjustment."

Cat was used to everyone knowing all the details of her life—or thinking they knew all the details. Once upon a time, I *had*. We'd lived in each other's pockets, known every secret, known about the weird rash on the underside of a boob, or what our faces looked like after waking up, hungover, next to the toilet.

But I got the impression that she didn't think Steffie—or the circumstances that had brought him to her house—was common knowledge.

From what I could tell, her followers realized that Kris had been married before, but he wasn't interesting enough to a US audience to garner coverage of his private life pre-Cat. French tabloids, on the other hand, were enamored with him and his drama.

Cat had a large presence online, so it took some digging to find those society blog posts, as well as the articles about Odette Moreau's death, but they were there. To uncover them, you simply had to be incredibly devoted . . . or a journalist writing a profile about the topic.

Research was something I prioritized, and I was as certain as I could be that I knew any tidbit that existed in the wild about Catriona Bouchard. I even kept track of the silly rumors that circulated about their family every once in a while—one of the more pernicious ones was that she'd worn a fake baby bump through all six pregnancies.

I was positive that Cat could tell me stuff this weekend that would surprise me, but it wouldn't be anything that was available *somewhere* online. I'd found it all.

Still, I decided to play dumb for two reasons. One, research was always going to buttress a profile, but it could never be the heart of it. Cat's story had to come from her in her own words. And—more importantly—I wanted the recorder to pick up the answer. So, despite already knowing, I asked, "He's Kristopher's son?"

"Yes," Cat said. And then after a beat rushed to add, "From his first marriage."

I nodded, but then thought about how Steffie simply never showed up in her videos. The nanny and the manager, I could understand. But a member of the family, hidden away like Mr. Rochester's wife?

That crossed into kind of odd.

"He doesn't like social media?" I asked.

It made sense that he didn't, of course. He'd been thrust into the spotlight in such a horrific fashion, even if he didn't live in the country where he was being talked about. He was a teenager who had internet access; he was going to read the stories.

It did surprise me he didn't even get a mention in a video or two, though. I would have thought it would be the kind of story that tugged on heartstrings and gained followers.

"He's had a rough few months," Cat said, leaning on the easiest excuse there was. "I don't want to expose him to scrutiny."

I nodded because even if that wasn't the full truth, I wasn't here for Steffie.

"What was he talking about back there?" I asked.

Cat smiled too wide, then seemed to realize it and course corrected to a deep frown. This was such a strange, glitchy version of her, I wasn't sure what reactions I should take seriously.

"He's just angry at Kris," she said.

"So . . . he wants me to look into what happened to *Kris*?" I asked as if I didn't know what she'd meant. Again, forcing her to be explicit.

I desperately wanted to know how Kris and Cat had reacted to Odette's mysterious kayaking death. I had done a deep dive, but for once the internet conspiracy theorists had let me down. There was hardly even a hint of foul play, despite the fact that the woman who had died had been the ex-wife of a multi-multimillionaire. And she'd died in such a strange way.

It all seemed right out of a *Lifetime* movie script—or at least would act as catnip to hungry true crime aficionados.

"Honestly, it's too much to get into at the moment," Cat said, clearly closing the door on a discussion that made her uncomfortable. "Suffice it to say, he has some misplaced anger. Toward me, of course, but mostly toward Kristopher. It's understandable—his therapist said it would be stranger if he wasn't acting out. That kind of roller coaster has been hard to deal with, though, if I'm being honest. Kristopher prides himself on being a good father."

"Does he?" I tried to keep the doubt out of my voice. Obviously, I wasn't going to have an accurate view of Kristopher's involvement in his kids' lives. The tradwife aesthetic was all about, well, traditional gender roles. The women in charge of the kids, the men in charge of the work. Kris wasn't ever going to be shown in Cat's content as someone who I personally would call a good father, just by virtue of what they were selling.

But I'd already acknowledged what they were selling was fake, so I also had to acknowledge that, in reality, maybe he was the world's best dad.

"Yes. He is," Cat said, with a note of defiance.

She really shouldn't have cared what I thought, but I added, "That's great. You deserve a good man."

That didn't get her to relax. In fact, she seemed to tense further, her fingers toying with her necklace again.

"I love Steffie dearly," she eventually said. "But you can only try so hard until the person themselves has to make the choice to be included."

"Is that how it works?" I asked beneath my breath. Because I was pretty sure it was incumbent on the parents, step or not, to make sure the kid felt a part of the family.

Cat's lips pinched in tight. "I'd appreciate if you don't include him in your piece. He's . . . troubled. And I don't want to put him through any more stress."

Yet she'd invited me here. Apparently, the exposure had been worth the risk to his mental health. Or maybe she just knew that if she asked me something—genuinely asked as a favor to her—then I would do it.

That was how it had always been between us.

And to be fair, I had never had any plans on including Steffie in the profile. If people were interested in him, he would have made bigger news six months earlier, when his mother died.

So it was easy to agree. "I won't put him in the article."

She hugged me in spontaneous gratitude and relief.

It wasn't soft, like our hugs had always been. Instead, it was as if she hadn't touched someone outside her family in quite some time. She was awkward, bony too, and didn't quite know what to do with her hands.

I patted her shoulder blade and stepped back, because the embrace was an unsettling reminder of how much this wasn't my Cat.

She ran a nervous hand down the front of her blouse.

We were uneasy with each other, which we had never been. From the very first time we'd talked, it had always felt like we'd known each other decades.

My main goal wasn't to revive our friendship, but that secret hope that we would was withering away beneath our dually strained smiles.

Cat opened her mouth like she was going to say something, maybe to try to bridge this gap between us. But then her eyes slid over my shoulder and the mask slipped firmly back into place.

CHAPTER SIX

Cat

Then

I met Benji in the emergency room, having been put there by my boyfriend.

This time Mark had broken three ribs along with my wrist, and blamed it on the fact that I'd talked too long to another guy at a club. It didn't matter that the guy had been gay. That never mattered.

I hated waiting in that stupid gown on that stupid bed, where I could hear someone vomiting just outside the curtain.

I'd been there an hour by the time Holland arrived. She rushed in, past everyone trying to stop her, practically shaking in righteous indignation as she looked me over.

She had never liked Mark. To be fair she'd only known him three weeks—I'd only known *her* three weeks. But she'd sized him up almost immediately.

"He doesn't seem to actually like you," she'd said in her offhand but piercing way the weekend she moved into the apartment. Mark and I had hosted a party to welcome her, and he hadn't liked that I'd spent most of the night mingling instead of by his side.

"He's insecure," I'd said, because it was true and it made sense to me. I was so much more successful than he was, I was more attractive and more charming. I was smarter and had more friends and a brighter future than he did. All the things that guys cared about—except for money, and that would be coming—I one-upped him on. Not that I cared. Mark was handsome and well socialized. He fit in anywhere I took him, and he didn't complain too much about the hours I needed to spend perfecting my craft.

For me, that was a win. Add in great sex, and well . . . I was willing to put up with a lot.

But I did need to draw the line somewhere.

That was probably at broken ribs.

"Cat," Holland said, all serious, as she sank into the chair beside my bed. "You can't let him treat you like this."

Some part of me knew this wasn't my brand. I was not the type of girl to be put in the hospital because of her boyfriend. I was an exacting, demanding perfectionist when it came to baking. I carried myself in the world that way. To be sitting here now, in this open-backed gown, with my roommate of three weeks staring at me with pity—it was mortifying, to say the least.

But part of me also knew that beyond my appearance, men didn't tend to like me.

Men liked girls like Holland. She was fun, flirty, quick to banter and tease. She smiled easily and often, and wore makeup that looked like she wasn't wearing makeup.

I had to work to get men like Mark, ones who wouldn't embarrass me as I tried to get a foothold in Savannah society.

I didn't have the luxury of being picky.

"I *can* let him treat me like this, but I won't," I said.

Holland laughed, some of the worry dropping out of her features. She found me funny, which I liked. Not everyone appreciated my sense of humor.

"I had a whole speech prepared," she said. "About you leaving your abusive boyfriend."

"And I bet it would have fit in beautifully in a *Lifetime* original movie," I assured her.

She wrinkled her nose. "Maybe they have openings for a starving writer."

I gasped. "You shut your mouth. You better not be going around telling people you're starving, that doesn't reflect well on me."

Holland laughed again, and it hit my bloodstream like fizzy champagne.

That was the moment that Benji "knocked" on the curtain and then stepped into the little triage room. His eyes tracked immediately to Holland, despite the fact that I was the patient.

My mood soured.

It took him five seconds too long before he shifted his attention to me. When he did, I glanced at Holland, who was now pinker than she had been before. She had clocked his appreciation just as I had.

"I'm Benji Croft," he said, grabbing the rolling chair and sitting near my knees. He was handsome enough, though not like Mark, who was old-money beautiful. Benji's nose was too big for his face, and he had fairly pedestrian hazel-green eyes. He had ordinary—though *thick*—brown hair, kissed a little blond by the sun, and he was maybe only an inch or two taller than me.

There was something magnetic about him, though. Maybe that was because after he'd *finally* turned his attention to me, he was all in. He listened, hardly blinking, though his eyes softened as I told him about "tripping" down the stairs. Holland had scoffed at that, but even she had to realize that I wasn't about to press charges against Mark, not if I ever wanted to work another private party in Savannah. And considering how many weddings took place at the plantations around the city, I could make that my full business if I ever needed to. Not that I would, of course. But it would be nice to have the option.

Benji allowed the lie to pass, too. And soon after, I was drugged up and released into Holland's care.

"He was cute, huh?" I asked, testing it. I couldn't be too clever, as the painkillers were already dulling my thought process. I didn't want to expose too much, or imagine I was being subtle only to act like a jackhammer instead.

"The doctor? Yeah, I guess," Holland said, though she was distracted, ordering a ride for us, while juggling my bag of prescription drugs and instructions on how to help me recover.

What if I'd been forced to give the room to the lady with seventeen cats? *She* would not have been here, gently shoving me into the back of a Toyota, while the lights and sounds all blurred around me.

I leaned over and smacked a kiss to Holland's forehead. "You're the tops."

"Okay, painkillers." Holland laughed, but she didn't push me away when I snuggled into her side. "I didn't realize they made you sound like you stepped out of a 1950s movie."

"Oh my god, noooo, that's my nightmare," I said. "Was there a worse time period to live in than that?"

"Hmm, dinosaurs?" Holland offered, and I giggled. She was *so funny*. But not as funny as me.

"I'd take the dinosaurs over ten kids with their dirty diapers, and a life stuck in the suburbs," I said. All my *s*'s were blending together, though, so I figured I should stop talking to maintain my dignity.

Holland rested her head against mine. "You never have to worry about that, babe. You're going to be a fucking star."

"Honestly . . ." I said and then paused, liking the feeling of the word in my mouth. I was too distracted by that pleasure to continue until Holland nudged me.

"Honestly, what?"

"Oh, right," I said, closing my eyes, ready to let myself sink into the abyss. Holland would take care of me—I didn't have to worry. "Honestly, I'd kill myself first."

CHAPTER SEVEN

Holland

Now

"Ladies," Mia Preston called, interrupting us from a distance as if she'd sensed we were having a moment that could get revealing. "I know you might not be finished, but I did want to grab Holland before dinner."

Cat, of course, all but sighed in relief. "The rest isn't all that interesting. I'm sure you've seen a bunch of the house, anyway."

I had, of course, along with her eleven million followers. It hadn't seemed quite this large, but that was probably on purpose. If I had to describe the way Cat portrayed their life on her social media page, it would be *quaint*. Only people who knew what to look for would be able to pick out just how expensive everything was. It actually cost a lot to make an oven that looked like it could have been salvaged from a late-1800s prairie house.

"I'll see you at dinner, Holland," Cat said. And then, without acknowledging Mia at all, she sailed off down the hallway.

I slid a glance toward Mia, who was fussing with the tablet she carried. I wasn't sure what her relationship with Cat was like, but so far their interactions had mostly been like two satellites that never actually intersected. It was an odd way to deal with one's manager.

Or . . . perhaps they just knew each other so well, they didn't even need to directly talk to know what the other was thinking.

Mia touched my elbow and I realized I'd zoned out there for a second, imagining all of us caught in some silly soap opera. "Let's go sit in the kitchen."

We'd just passed through the room a few minutes ago, so I easily led the way back. It was gorgeous, like the rest of the house, filled with pricey items designed to look rustic.

"So," I said, when I sat down across from Mia at the expansive farmhouse table. "I'm going to have free rein over everything, access to anyone I want to talk to, and no limitations placed on my time, right?"

Mia snorted. "Yeah, and we'll send you home with a gift basket containing a check for one million dollars."

I batted my eyes, all innocence. "My ethics wouldn't allow me to accept that, but I appreciate the generosity."

"Ah, your ethics. That's the flaw in the plan," Mia said, snapping her fingers. "Well, I suppose then we should talk about your schedule. To be honest, I don't have a ton on the books. You'll simply follow Catriona as she goes about her life from now until Monday morning."

"And that entails?" I asked, despite the fact that I had a fairly good idea. Cat had done enough "get ready with me" videos throughout different times of day for me to figure out her normal routine.

Which, when put like that, sounded kind of creepy.

Mia tilted her head back and forth, considering. "You know, meal prep, eating, and relaxing—outside on the patio if the weather permits, inside by the fire if it doesn't."

"And you'll be filming content?" I wasn't incredibly interested in watching the sausage get made, nor in writing about it. There was a niche audience for that kind of thing, for sure. But I wanted something more human than a behind-the-scenes look at creating social media videos.

"No, we decided to prepare posts ahead of time," Mia said, and I guessed the reasoning was twofold. They probably didn't want to shatter the mystique, and also I would absolutely get in their way.

"There would be too much downtime for you to sit through if we carried on as normal. You'd be surprised at how many hours go into a thirty-second reel."

I actually didn't think I would be, but I was grateful for the decision.

"The kids will, of course, poke their way into the schedule, I'm sure. It's hard to plan anything to the second when there are six children involved, but that will give you a good sense of Catriona's days," Mia said. "And, of course, there will be church on Sunday."

I nodded. None of that really seemed to require a private meeting between the two of us.

My curiosity was sated a moment later, when Mia leaned forward, her face serious.

"Oh, you're giving me the shovel talk," I said out loud, mostly by accident.

That threw her. "What the hell is that?"

"Like the father tells the groom the morning of the wedding, *You better treat my girl right, or else* . . . and then there's the threat of a grave, and the shovel it takes to dig one," I said, and when she just stared at me blankly, I shook my head. "I'm sorry, I distracted you. Deliver your warning."

Mia blinked like she wasn't quite sure what to make of me.

"If it were up to me, you wouldn't be here," she said after a moment.

And . . . that was odd. It would make sense if the decision was coming from Cat, who liked her privacy. But why wouldn't a manager leap at the opportunity when her publicity-shy client actually said yes to some good coverage? If I had been in Mia's shoes, I would've been relieved that Cat had agreed to *something*, especially if I was making a percentage of whatever she brought in. "Why's that?"

"I don't trust you," she said simply, clearly not confrontation-averse. "I think you probably have an agenda, and I don't think it's a good one."

"Huh," I said, somewhat at a loss for words. I'd dealt with my fair share of Mias, and while they were generally a nervous breed, few had been outright hostile to the idea of more attention for their client. There was no such thing as bad publicity, and all that. "Is it me specifically? Or just media you don't trust?"

Or was there something here she didn't want me to find? An affair, perhaps, with the husband of the house? That would certainly put a blight on the image of the picture-perfect family they were selling.

"Both," she admitted. "Long-lost friends who come crawling out of the woodwork after someone gets rich and famous rarely have good intentions."

"Oho," I said, impressed with the fact that she didn't pull punches. "Well, Cat's been rich and famous for a long while now, so that doesn't really hold up."

"You've been biding your time," Mia said with a shrug. "She's hit her stride now and is at the peak of her success. You think, might as well cash in."

"The world runs on networking and favors," I said. "This will help both of us out."

"Will it?" Mia asked, but I knew the question was rhetorical. "Anyway, it doesn't matter how I feel. Catriona has given you the green light. So. We obviously aren't about to make you sign an NDA, as that would defeat the purpose of you being here. And your magazine has a policy against us reading a draft of the piece. So all I'll say is that I would advise you to present Catriona in a truthful light."

"Is that a threat?"

Mia smiled, but it would probably be more accurate to say she flashed her teeth. "Now, why would that be a threat? Isn't that your goal as a journalist? To show your subjects in a truthful light?"

"Sure, normally. But in this particular case, I wonder if you see the truth as subjective," I said. "I don't, for the record. But . . . you have an image crafted for Cat, one that might not be . . . as *truthful* as you might want her followers to believe."

"They're not stupid and neither are you," Mia snapped. "Of course Catriona has a brand image. She's the CEO of a multimillion-dollar business."

"A business that's built on the idea that women shouldn't be CEOs of multimillion-dollar businesses," I couldn't help but point out. When Mia's brows rose, I waved it away. "Sorry. I promise, I'm not here to write that story—it's been written."

Mia folded her arms on top of her binder. "What story are you here to write?"

I didn't know yet, was the *truthful* answer. I was good at my job, and that was usually because I could see a sculpture in a block of marble. I needed to start chipping away at the thing before I got a good sense of what that figure actually was. Still, I could sense the shape of it already.

"Change," I finally said. "I want to write about change."

That apparently was the correct answer, given the new appreciation in Mia's expression.

So I elaborated. Off the cuff. "I want to write about how we become different people in the different seasons of our lives, how love can shape us into something that would be unrecognizable to our younger selves, how children can. How we make the decision to jump off a cliff, and what would have happened if we didn't. I think any reporter coming in here could tell the story of who Cat is now. I want to tell the story about how she's changed from who she used to be."

Some of the walls went back up. "For the worse?"

"No." Just because *I* didn't recognize the Cat I had known, that didn't mean it was bad that she'd become this version of herself. Not everything in the world was for me or needed my approval. "Look, people who don't like her are going to go into this wanting to be proven right. But imagine how powerful it is for the women who do love her, to see that she was once so different. It almost makes the lifestyle switch even more compelling and authentic."

I could see Mia's brain working. *Compelling. Authentic.* Those were incredibly weighty terms in her business. Dollar signs were flashing in bright neon behind those shrewd eyes.

"Well, you've already convinced Catriona, and that's what matters," Mia said again. After that, though, I could tell Mia was more relaxed as she ran me through the ground rules.

I was not to wander anywhere by myself.

If, by some strange circumstance, I did wander away by myself—she said this with the pointed look of someone who could predict journalists' nosy impulses—I was, through threat of death, to stay away from the outbuilding where the orchard machinery was kept.

The third floor of the farmhouse was completely off limits, as well, as it was the Bouchards' bedroom.

"The whole thing?" I asked, picturing the gigantic footprint of the mini-mansion.

"The whole thing," Mia confirmed. I was also to stay out of Kris's office on the first floor, which Cat had already told me as we'd passed by his closed door.

"And Kris is the only one of us with the security code for the gates, which changes daily," Mia said, in an almost offhand manner as she wrapped up her spiel.

At that, I pressed my hands flat on the table so they wouldn't shake.

"None of the rest of you have the code?" I asked, not because I expected a different answer, but because I hoped it would make the absurdity of that fact sink in.

"The guard does." Mia was already on her feet, her mind clearly elsewhere. "But, otherwise, no."

The guard, who knew exactly who wrote his paychecks. That was essentially the same as only Kris having the code.

"Isn't that dangerous?" I asked. "What if Kris has a heart attack? What if he's incapacitated?"

"We would call down to the guardhouse," Mia said, like it was obvious. "This isn't an embassy or the TSA. It's simply easier for one person to have it since it changes daily."

"I'm sorry, no," I said. "Not only is this wild to me, but it's wild that everyone is fine with it."

Mia, for the first time, clued into the fact that I was serious. "There's no need. It would be a hassle to distribute the code to everyone on the property, especially since we rarely leave. And, honestly, it would undermine the fact that there is a code and that it's ever changing."

I stared at her. "And the people who work here, the ones who don't live here? How do they get in?"

"They're on a list, and check in with the guard," Mia said slowly, obviously confused by my confusion. "They have to show ID each time they enter, just as you did, but honestly it's the same people every day, so it's not that complicated."

I didn't even know how to make her realize how strange this was. "Why does the code change daily?"

"Well, we had some security incidents early on." Mia studied me for a moment, trying to decide whether to divulge what those were, I guessed. "Someone tried to kidnap Fleur when she was a baby. Thankfully, it wasn't successful, but it did make the Bouchards extra careful about security. They hired the top experts in the world, and that, my dear, is why you have to go through a few minor inconveniences to get in here."

"Jeez," I said, though of course I'd known about it. Because it was what I should ask if I were hearing about it for the first time, I said, "For ransom?"

"They weren't successful, so we don't know their motives," Mia said. "But it did not seem like it was for money, no."

The children were part of the whole tradwife aesthetic. In fact, Cat had gone viral in the first place because of the outrageous cakes she'd made for her babies. I knew some influencers, even of the tradwife ilk, were reeling it in, only showing the backs of heads or the hint of their kids.

But Cat put all of hers in her videos.

"Listen, I'm just looking out for you guys. When the zombie apocalypse happens and Kris is one of those dudes who pretends he wasn't bitten and eats you all because you don't have the security code to get out of here, don't come crying to me," I said, mostly trying to defuse whatever tension I might have created.

Mia's lips twitched. A victory.

She sobered quickly, though, her eyes drifting out the window before sliding back to me. "There's . . . there's probably one more thing you should know."

I straightened, because she sounded serious. "Okay . . ."

"No one is worried," she assured me, to which the only response was, of course, to worry. "Catriona has received an uptick in, how should I put this, *obsessive* messages recently."

My pulse kicked up. This was a side effect of playing the game, everyone knew that. It didn't make it any less scary, though. "How obsessive?"

"Nothing threatening," Mia rushed to say. "But messages that make it clear someone has been watching on the rare occasions she goes to town. 'That coffee looked good,' things like that."

"About coffee she didn't post on her public account?" I clarified.

"Correct," Mia said. "Again, there's nothing threatening—"

"Uh, making sure Cat knows she's being watched is inherently threatening," I said, once again amazed by these people's risk-assessment abilities. "Have you contacted the police?"

"We've been working with a digital security person for quite a long time," Mia said. "We've handed the matter over to her, and she's been monitoring it. The account changes, but it's clearly the same person."

I swallowed hard. No one would call me overly anxious, but I didn't like this situation. "So you haven't contacted the cops?"

"Not yet," Mia said, studying me. "It's all taken care of. I just wanted you to know. Plus, as you've experienced, our security is incredibly tight."

I laughed, though it was without much humor. "Yeah it is."

And for the first time since I'd been warned I would be searched upon arrival, I actually appreciated that fact.

CHAPTER EIGHT

Det. Jamie Alvarez

Jamie's car was blocked by too many cruisers in The Orchard's driveway, so she left her keys with Keller and talked a uniform into giving her a ride back to the station.

"What do you think about that place?" she asked the kid. He was the same one who'd met her in the driveway a few hours earlier. Josh O'Connor. Eager to impress.

His knuckles tightened around the steering wheel, which he held at the perfect ten and two. "Don't want to leap to any conclusions."

Jamie suppressed a smile and made a note to find out more about him. "You're not on the record."

He shot her a quick glance, as if to check if this was a test. Then he drummed his fingers on the wheel, thoughtful rather than tense now.

"I think you can start seeing things in a different light once tragedy strikes," he said finally. "What might first appear eccentric now looks shady as hell." He glanced at her again. "Excuse me."

"I can handle 'shady as hell,'" Jamie assured him. "Especially when it's accurate. Keep going."

"Well, there was the kidnapping attempt on Fleur Bouchard," he said, squinting a bit into the distance. "That was seven years ago? About then."

"So you would have been five?" she teased him because that was a language they all spoke fluently. O'Connor almost relaxed at the gentle jibe, the familiarity of the banter a comfort in these trying times.

"Har har," he said, good-naturedly. That boded well for his future with the department. "Were you here for that?"

"Yeah," she said, though she hadn't worked the case. The baby had been kidnapped, but then less than an hour later, she was found outside a church in town, wrapped in a blanket—the villain having apparently gotten cold feet.

The FBI—which had jurisdiction over kidnapping cases involving minors ever since Charles Lindbergh's baby had been abducted—had sent a forensic psychologist along with their crew. He'd spoken in sentences that only rarely included monosyllabic words, and walked like he'd had a stick shoved up his ass a few decades earlier.

He'd come to the conclusion that Fleur had likely been taken by one of Catriona Bouchard's overeager followers. Either someone who thought she wasn't raising Fleur correctly or someone who just wanted to be closer to the family they viewed as their own.

Once reality set in—and apparently it had quickly—she'd dropped the child off at the church without ever once having woken her.

It never failed to amuse Jamie that all those moms out there who plastered every detail of their children's lives all over the internet were more worried about serial killer vans from the eighties than what their online stalkers would do.

"It made sense the security fence went up after that, right?" O'Connor asked. "Of course it made sense."

"Yeah," Jamie agreed. It had been a little weird, but understandable.

"And then the family stopped coming into town," O'Connor said.

Some people would consider this area of the state Burlington, but really they were a little bit too far out for that. There was a local village, though, and the Bouchards' absence had been felt.

"Which I guess you can see making sense," O'Connor continued. "Right after. But now, seven years later? It feels a little . . ."

He trailed off and she patiently waited.

"Cult-y," he finally finished. "I'm studying up on them."

"Looking to join?" she asked.

"I mean," he said, licking his lips, "I wouldn't hate to specialize someday."

She appreciated that, she did. But wanting to specialize in something meant he saw cults in every shadow, just like a new resident doctor started diagnosing themselves every time a fart smelled weird.

He wasn't wrong in what he was pointing out, though. He was just jumping to cults instead of something a little bit more common.

When Jamie got back to her desk, she dropped the bag she'd been carrying onto it. The memory cards jostled and then settled. They were Holland Tate's, handed over to Jamie by one of the crime scene techs.

Much of the seventy-two hours and change leading up to Kristopher Bouchard's death had been recorded word for word. How many investigators stumbled into that kind of luck?

Jamie went searching for a recorder that could play them back.

Once she got set up properly, she popped in a pair of earphones and hit play. The first hour was mostly uneventful, although Stefan Moreau made an angry appearance that she marked the time stamp on.

Her pen hovered throughout Mia Preston and Holland Tate's first lengthy conversation.

"And Kris is the only one of us with the security code for the gates, which changes daily."

"None of the rest of you have the code?"

"The guard does. But, otherwise, no."

"Isn't that dangerous?"

Jamie stopped the recording, a chill that could only come from realized premonition skittering over her skin.

She marked the time before once again pressing play.

So you haven't contacted the cops?

Jamie shook her head and rewound the recording. She must have missed something, her fingers too slow.

Obsessive messages, she scribbled this time. *Not threatening.*

She sat back, tapping her pen against the desk. Mostly, she sided with Mia on this. The reason the whole *influencer* thing worked in the first place was because these people had the ability to mesmerize an audience. There were side effects that came with that.

But Mia had made it sound like the messages were coming from someone in Jamie's district. It probably didn't have any bearing on this case, but it wouldn't hurt to try to track that person down, whoever it was.

She sighed. This wasn't a TV show starring detectives with a seemingly endless budget and resources only the US Army and maybe NSA had at their fingertips.

It was just a crappy police station north of Burlington with fewer than ten full-time employees on staff.

Who even did that kind of work? On TV it was always some cool nerd with dyed hair and a hacker background who had gone straight because of some traumatic personal reason. In real life, though, was that a job now? It must be.

No one on her staff had those capabilities, though.

The last time they'd had anything close to that was when a forensic psychologist had helped out with the Fleur Bouchard kidnapping.

Jamie swiveled to wake up her computer. She pecked at the keys until she brought up the case file for that investigation—never closed, because they hadn't caught the person who'd done it.

What the FBI psychologist might not have known was that the priest at the church where the woman had left Fleur always arrived extremely early for his morning run. Most villagers could set their clocks by when he ran by their houses.

That meant the baby had only been left outdoors and unprotected for a few short hours at most.

Maybe it had been a coincidence. Or maybe the woman had known that was the safest option.

And if that was the case, didn't that mean she might be a local?

This obsessed fan Mia and Holland had talked about only three days before Kristopher Bouchard's death had also likely been a local, given the messages they'd sent.

What if . . . what if . . .

Jamie shook her head, and with a few keystrokes, her computer was black again. Now, who was playing at *Criminal Minds: Burlington*?

CHAPTER NINE

Holland

Now

Mia was waiting for me as I stepped out of my room on the way to dinner.

"Afraid I'll wander into Kris's office while 'trying to find the bathroom'?" I teased.

"Of course not," she said. "I'm simply being a considerate host."

"I think it's pronounced 'guard,'" I said, drawing out the word, and I swore she almost laughed.

"Come on," she said, tilting her head toward the stairs.

The weather was deemed just the right side of crisp, so we were having dinner outside, under the setting sun. Fairy lights were strung overhead, though they weren't quite needed yet, light jazz music played from hidden speakers, and the table was set with placements fancy enough for a wedding dinner. Or at least the rehearsal.

Steffie was notably absent.

When we walked out, Kris paused from where he was pouring wine and met Mia's eyes.

"You two are close?" I murmured beneath my breath, and Mia flushed, averting her gaze.

Caught out.

"He's mentoring me," she said. And then louder, to actually include Kris, she added, "He has a sharp mind for business."

Mentoring—is that what they call it? "I would imagine. You've built quite an empire, Kris."

Men like him always took that at face value as a compliment, and he didn't disappoint.

"Luck, timing, and a little talent," he said with a wink. "And a phenomenal partner in crime."

He'd made sure to add that part just as Cat walked out of the carriage house behind the patio carrying a maroon Le Creuset. Mia, meanwhile, excused herself to sit at the far end of the table with Anna and the children.

Kris watched her go, though the shadows were deep enough that I couldn't tell if he was checking out her ass in front of his wife.

If I'd had to put money on Kris cheating with someone, it would have been with the look-alike au pair, but I might have lost that bet.

Interesting.

There were three open seats at the head of the table, and I took the one that had probably been meant for Kris just to see what kind of reaction it would provoke. His mouth went a little tight, but he recovered well, taking the spot at my right, leaving the one at my left elbow open for Cat.

"We're really so pleased you're here, Holland," Kris said. "Catriona hasn't kept in touch with many friends from Savannah. I've been eager to meet you and hear stories from her wild days."

I didn't bother to point out that Cat hadn't kept in touch with me, either.

"Those stories are locked in a vault," I said, only half joking. More than anything, the stories were *ours*, not meant for Kris's consumption.

"She must have been so busy at The Bistro, anyway," Kris said lightly. There was no way he actually wanted to hear about her life as a young, hot lady in Savannah.

"She always pushed herself to be the best," I said. "So, yes, that kept her busy. We still managed to get into a bit of fun along the way, though."

"That sounds like Catriona," he said, with a grin. "She always wants to be the best at anything she does."

My eyes drifted to Cat, who was serving the children, the baby wrapped on her chest. He was right: When her goal had been to take over the Savannah culinary scene, she had accomplished way more than anyone would have expected from someone so young. When she'd set her mind on social media, she'd garnered eleven million followers and become one of the most talked about influencers in the country. When she'd set her heart on marrying, she'd found herself an impossibly handsome man with over a hundred million dollars in the bank.

It didn't even matter that she used her husband's money to buy her success—at least through the trickle-down effect of being able to create a beautiful, envy-inspiring life for herself—she'd still accomplished it.

And now she had her own money.

"How does the Catriona Bouchard business work?" I asked, turning back to Kris, who lounged in his seat with an indolence that bothered me. A king surveying his kingdom.

"Do you want the details on how we pick each season's colors, or . . . ?" he asked, seeming amused by my open-ended question. But I loved open-ended questions, which let you see where someone's mind was pointed.

"You're that involved?" I asked. "In the pots-and-pans side of things."

"And in her content," Kris said, as if it were a given. "I help with everything from her 'get ready with me' videos to deciding if we should add a new frying pan to the line."

"What about your own business? And the orchard."

"We have a busy life," he said, with a benign smile.

I shook my head, trying to imagine Kristopher Bouchard standing in Cat's gorgeous walk-in, setting up her ring light and getting her best angles. That seemed like something a personal assistant would do.

"So are you fifty-fifty partners in all your businesses?" I asked, even though that was probably more blunt than you would normally expect from a dinner guest.

"We're fifty-fifty partners in life," Kris replied, and I tried not to roll my eyes at that. "But I make the ultimate decisions. 'The head of every man is Christ, the head of Christ is God, and the head of a wife is her husband.'"

I took a deep swallow of my wine. "So, what does that mean in practical terms? She doesn't have control of the money she makes off her brand?"

The question came out sharp, but Kris just studied me impassively. "You're not religious, are you?"

"What do you think?"

"I think you likely view religion with the disdain of the modern woman," Kris said.

I refrained from pointing out just how modern a woman his wife was, considering she benefited from all the advances they pretended to hold in contempt.

"I think out of the two of us," I said, letting the irritation bleed into my voice, "you're the one who butchered a passage from Corinthians, so you might want to ask yourself what reaction you're reading as disdain." These types of men had all told themselves stories about women like me, and I was tired of it. "Because that seems like a projection from you, not me."

The silence between us went taut. I might have said he wasn't used to being challenged by a woman, but that would've been falling into the image they were selling. Cat might be putting on an act for me, but the real her must have slipped out during ten years of marriage. Even Mia, though she was an employee, seemed the type to push back against Kris.

I didn't think he liked being challenged by *me*.

Finally, he huffed out a breath, seeming to shake off the tension. "I can see why you and Catriona were friends."

I ignored that because, no, he really couldn't see why we were friends. He didn't know me and he hadn't known the Cat from back then. "So, I'm sorry, did you answer if she has access to the money she makes off her business?"

"The business I founded?" he parried almost lazily. Like he'd had this conversation thousands of times. I wondered if that had been with Cat or in his own head because he felt guilty about keeping her money from her. "Ms. Tate, I don't actually think you understand how financial arrangements work within marriages."

"I understand perfectly well," I said. "I understand that a reason so many women don't leave their husbands is because they don't have their own financial security."

I wasn't about to enlighten him, but women Cat's and my age had grown up with constant lectures about the importance of our own bank accounts and opening cards in our own names to build credit if we got divorced.

He tilted his head. "From what I understood, you are a respected journalist."

The tone in his voice suggested that he now thought he'd heard wrong. Was I being aggressive? Probably. But I could do far worse than poking at the business side of their marriage. "Oh, I'm getting plenty of information for my article."

His mouth pinched, but in the next second, Cat swanned up to us, ladle in hand. Her plasticky smile was back, her knuckles white against the handle. "What are you two talking about?"

"About how you guys met," I said before Kris could offer anything. I rested my chin on my fist. "But he hasn't actually gotten to the story yet."

Kris grabbed Cat's arm when she finished serving him a pumpkin-colored soup. He kissed the inside of her wrist, and I tried to remember that I had no reason to dislike him.

No real reason—my own personal grudge aside.

"Charmer," Cat chastised, but then dropped a kiss on his upturned mouth.

It was all very sweet, but I couldn't help remembering a video from a few weeks back. Cat had been ravaged by the flu or COVID, and she'd made a video about how she'd just wanted to lie in bed all day. But as a wife and mother, that wasn't an option. She'd gotten up, put on makeup, and made the family an elaborate dinner that they'd eaten without her. Kris had made a brief cameo espousing how amazing she was.

Maybe she hadn't actually made him dinner. Maybe she hadn't even been sick. But they had *chosen* to post that video. Whatever they'd been trying to portray about their relationship had struck me as incredibly sad.

Strength was a crucial part of the tradwife concept. The women were strong because they didn't take meds to give birth; they were strong because they got up at dawn to milk the goats; they were strong because they maintained their patience at each "Mama, Mama, Mama"; they were strong because motherhood was the world's hardest—though most rewarding, don't forget that part!—job.

And yet it all felt like they were protesting a bit too much. Because at the end of the day, no matter how "strong" they thought themselves, they would always consider themselves weaker than any man.

"You tell the story," Cat said now, nudging Kris before rounding the table and taking her seat across from him.

"I was traveling for business," he said, as he settled into the clearly well-told tale. "And my secretary had fumbled reservations at some place . . ."

He glanced at Cat for help, and she grinned. "It doesn't matter, it wasn't as good as The Bistro."

"No, never," he said, eyes locked on hers. "I was supposed to be entertaining a client, but I show up at this other place, no table, no way to get us in."

I raised my eyes at that. He struck me as the type who would have been given a table even if they had to kick someone out to do it.

"I'm panicking," he said. "And I look across the square, and hand to God, the single ray of light from the setting sun was aimed directly at The Bistro's sign."

"Fate," I murmured.

"Fate," he said, without any of my sarcasm. "The meal was . . . so-so." He tilted his hand back and forth. "But the cake. The cake. I would have given my life to the woman who had made it."

"And you did," Cat said, a rehearsed line if ever there was one.

"And I did," he agreed. "The rest, as you say, was history."

"So you wooed her away from The Bistro, huh?" I asked, because I was still having trouble imagining my Cat meeting this man—at such a time, right after the funeral—and deciding to give up everything she'd worked so hard for for years.

And as I had the thought, I realized that maybe the funeral *was* the key to it. She'd been emotional, unstable. And here came this gorgeous, wealthy man willing to sweep her away from a city with too many raw, painful memories.

"Can you blame me?" Kris asked, bringing her hand up to his lips once more. "Once I had a taste, I couldn't walk away without her."

"I'm surprised you didn't try to open a pastry shop in town here," I said.

Cat shrugged. "I get to design our cake mixes. My own place sounds nice in theory, but that would just mean waking at four a.m. and leaving my kids behind."

What she said made sense, but I also couldn't help but mourn my Cat, the one who'd had dreams different from this life, no matter how comfortable it was.

I was probably supposed to comment with something encouraging here, but I couldn't manage it.

"I get the sense you don't approve," Kris observed.

Sometimes I marveled at the fact that people with wealth and power seemed to be obsessed with social approval from the masses. If I had as much money as Kris did, I would tell someone like me to go fuck myself if they didn't like how I lived. "I'm not here to approve or disapprove. I'm here to tell a story."

It probably wasn't the right thing to say—it likely confirmed that I didn't approve, even though that wasn't where I stood. I was, like so many women my age, trying to reconcile someone I'd known like the other half of my soul ten years ago with the person who sat in front of me now. People changed, it wasn't that strange. But Cat had always had a stubborn personality, one that didn't morph with the trends or the company she kept.

She'd been who she was, for better or worse. You could love her or hate her for it, but you were never going to walk away feeling nothing.

This woman—she just seemed so generic.

And it was . . . odd. Disturbing, if I was being honest.

"Well," Cat said now. "I think it's time we eat."

"Grace," Kris called, and all the kids snapped to attention.

The rest of the table joined hands, and I let Kris take mine. His palm was warm, a bit too damp to be pleasant; it was soft too, especially considering he technically owned a working apple orchard.

Cat had her head bowed.

There was a saying I'd heard: In Washington, DC, people asked what you did for a living; in LA, they asked who you knew; in the South, they asked what church you went to.

But despite the fact that it probably would have helped her career in Savannah, Cat had never been religious enough to be able to answer that last one truthfully. I wondered how serious her conversion was—when she closed her eyes, was she actually praying? Or did the aesthetic of it just fit her new lifestyle?

When they finished up, Cat smiled at everyone. "Eat, please. Before anything goes cold."

"Does Stefan not join the family for dinner?" I asked, as I shamelessly dug in. One thing that hadn't diminished was Cat's talent.

Cat toyed with her necklace. A gesture she now seemed to reserve for when she worried about her stepson.

"He prefers to take his meals inside," she said after a quick glance toward Kris, who'd given her a subtle nod.

"I know a lot of teenagers who would prefer that," I pressed. "But you don't force him?"

"Gentle parenting," Cat said, with just a hint of amusement to signal that she was in on the joke. "We don't force our children to do anything."

I nodded. "It's important to teach bodily autonomy."

"No means no," Cat said, and my body twinged with the muscle memory of this, of understanding each other's humor.

Kris looked between us, befuddled, though pleasantly so.

"You two must have been a riot back in the day," he said.

Cat met my eyes. "We were something."

CHAPTER TEN

Cat

Then

I had never had a friend before.

If someone heard me say that, they would immediately protest. Of course I must have had friends—growing up, perhaps? Maybe. Sometimes they came attached to whatever loser boyfriend I was dating at the time; I distinctly remember in high school there were three girls I would ride around in cars with, blasting emo music too loud with the windows down; in New York, my CIA peers had felt like comrades in arms, at times, considering how grueling both the city and the institute had been; and the staff at The Bistro invited me places and enjoyed parties I threw.

So maybe the world would say I'd had friends, but I had never viewed them that way. I never told them about my life or let my guard down or even cared very deeply about them at all. They were people to pass time with, that was it.

Lovers weren't friends, and neither was family. Those fell into their own categories.

Which meant I felt fairly confident that Holland Tate was the first person I would ever call an actual friend.

That, of course, was—objectively—a bit of a sad fact. I was twenty-three years old and had never had a friend? The thing was, I had never known what I was missing. I had never known you could show someone all the messed-up shit in your head and they would like you, not in spite of it but because of it.

Holland sat in my bed now, cradling both a cup of coffee and her pounding head.

"I definitely made out with someone last night," she said, squinting against the light pouring into the room.

I hadn't been there—like most people in the restaurant business, I never had my "weekends" on Fridays and Saturdays.

When she'd told me she was going out, I'd gotten snappy enough with her that I was almost surprised she wanted to share a morning debrief with me. But she didn't seem to mind my jagged edges—or at least she had been able to recognize my jealousy for what it was.

"I'm guessing he wasn't any good at it if you can't remember for sure," I pointed out, and she groaned.

"I shouldn't have gone out mad." She had been angry at a professor who'd called her writing pedestrian and she'd wanted to get drunk about it.

"Or sad," I said with a sympathetic pout.

Holland shot me a rueful look, because even if she wanted to pretend it was all rage, it wasn't. There were some professions out there where it probably didn't feel like you were cutting your chest open every time someone consumed something you produced, but the two of us would never know them.

"Fair point."

I preened. "Shall we get some hair of the dog in you?"

Holland brightened. "Shasta's?"

It was our favorite brunch place in the city. "Where else?"

We spent most of our time there skewering Holland's asshole professor while the waiters brought us an endless supply of tapas and mimosas. I didn't mind not talking about myself, considering the fact that Holland more often than not was the one having to soothe *my* feathers.

I liked the reciprocity of our relationship. Again, it was unique. To me, at least.

We were just about to ask for the check when our waiter quietly informed us it had been taken care of.

"By the owner's daughter," he said.

As if she had been waiting for her cue, Annabelle Allen swooped over to our table.

Belle had been a year younger than me at the CIA. She had specialized in food studies and sustainability, so our paths had thankfully not crossed often. But if people in this day and age could have nemeses, I would've called her mine.

She had excelled at everything naturally and been beloved by everyone. All I ever saw when I looked at her, though, was a spoiled princess who'd never struggled a day in her life.

I stood to kiss her on both cheeks in greeting, because that was how things were done.

"Catriona," she cooed.

I had a love-hate relationship with my name. My mother had taken inspiration from the Scottish Gaelic variation of Katherine, which was fine until you asked Americans to say a name with an *o* in the middle that was useless except for confusing people.

There was a bit of a fancy air to it all, though, which I had always liked.

Holland called me Cat, which I also liked.

"Annabelle," I said, because she'd always been strictly Belle and I had the sense that she also had a love-hate relationship with her full name. Of course she did. If you could be called Beauty as your name, why wouldn't you embrace that?

"I'm so thrilled to see you here," she said, dimpling prettily, her sweetheart face flushed nicely from the kitchens. "We're so honored you like our restaurant."

"I don't think we said anything about 'liked' yet," Holland interjected, her light tone keeping the words from splatting to the floor between all of us. But just barely.

Belle's warm demeanor dimmed, slightly. Just enough for her to look like a puppy who'd been scolded. "Was there something amiss?"

"We loved it all," I rushed to reassure her. I hadn't put together that Annabelle Allen of the CIA and the Allens of Savannah were one and the same, but now that I had, I realized I couldn't piss the heir off. Shasta's wasn't the only restaurant they owned, and they had a prominent voice in the culinary scene in the city.

I gasped and grabbed her hand, mostly to distract her. "You're engaged! Was this the iceberg that sank the Titanic?"

She giggled, pleased. "I know, it's so embarrassingly big."

Holland caught my eye.

Can you believe how gaudy that thing is? she seemed to say.

I tried not to smirk, pleased with not only being able to read her thoughts but also because she'd had the same one as me.

I'd never before been able to look at a friend like this and immediately know precisely how and why we were judging someone else.

"And, I'm sorry. We haven't met," Belle said, staring at Holland. I wondered if she'd caught the shared moment.

"I'm Holland, Cat's roommate," Holland answered.

"Roommate," Belle said, as if she'd never heard the word before. She had been born rich and now was clearly marrying rich. The concept probably *was* fairly foreign to her. "How . . . quaint."

"Right," Holland drawled, before grabbing her purse and standing. "Well, I have no interest in anything else you have to say, so I think it's time we take our leave."

With that, she looped her arm in mine and tugged me toward the door. I grabbed my wristlet and mouthed "Sorry" to Belle even as I let myself be pulled away.

I couldn't help but laugh as we spilled out onto the sidewalk, though. "Oh my god, you're terrible."

"You didn't like that person *and* she was a bitch," Holland said with confidence, as she pulled up her rideshare app. "A fake bitch, at that. Who the hell cares what she thinks?"

I grabbed Holland right then, pulling her into a hug so tight I could feel her heart beating against my rib cage. She put up a token fight, but mostly leaned into it. It didn't matter that Belle Allen could potentially tarnish my reputation. I had never had someone who was so immediately and completely in my corner as Holland had just been.

"I'm going to start wearing a bracelet, What Would Holland Do," I said, sighing happily when she finally pushed me away and went back to her phone.

"The key is not giving a shit about people you don't care about or know," Holland said, gruff as anything. She was so interesting—she could be as sweet as honey to someone she'd just met. She might have been to Belle, even given the obvious stress that had been pouring off me in waves. But insult her, or insult something she cared about, and the gloves came off immediately. That was when she showed just how hard she could punch.

"You know, I used to think I didn't care what people think, and then I met you," I said, as we loitered by the curb, waiting for our car.

She stared at me for a good thirty seconds, and then she started laughing. She laughed so hard that I swear tears ran down her cheeks—I couldn't be sure, though, because she was all but doubled over.

"Oh, babe," she said finally, taking big gulps of air to calm herself down. "I have never in my life met someone who cares more about what people think than you."

That put my back up because it sounded like an insult. "That can't possibly be true."

"Maybe not," Holland said, her outright amusement fading into something softer, more fond. "It's a good thing, you know?"

"No it's not," I snapped, still annoyed.

"It is," Holland said. And poked a finger into the soft spot below my shoulder. "Babe, if you didn't care what people thought, you'd be a menace to society."

A car pulled to the curb, and Holland opened the door for me. Before she shepherded me inside, she said, "Actually? I'm pretty sure you would have killed someone by now."

"No need to butter me up," I said, as I slid in. "You're forgiven."

CHAPTER ELEVEN

Holland

Now

"You're not supposed to be out here."

I spun toward the voice in the darkness. "Jesus."

"No. Jeremy," the man said. "But I get that a lot."

"Har har," I muttered, though I didn't relax quite yet. It was dark, and we were outside alone behind the carriage house–type structure Cat had emerged from earlier—where I assumed she kept a real working kitchen.

I let my eyes rove over the man. His hair was two inches too long, but he held it back with a headband that somehow worked really well on him. He had the touch of summer on his skin despite the fact that we were deep into fall. His vibe was grungy—he wore a basic T-shirt that looked like it really had come out of a six-dollar three-pack rather than the $4,000 one Kris would pretend had been cheap.

He was the help.

And he was . . . hot. My attention lingered on his thick forearms, his beat-up knuckles, and the stretch of fabric over his shoulders.

He patiently let me appraise him, clearly aware of his appeal.

My fingers curled around the recorder in my pocket and flipped it on.

"So, I'm not supposed to be out here?" I asked. "Who exactly are you to tell me that?"

I made sure it came off as flirtatious instead of hostile.

"Jeremy," he said with a pleased grin. "I thought we'd established that."

I rolled my eyes and took a hit of my vape.

He reached out a hand, silently asking for a go.

"These are terrible for you," he said as he blew smoke from the side of his mouth.

"So is talking to strange men in the middle of nowhere in the middle of the night," I pointed out. It was fully dark now—the fairy lights had turned off on the patio. We'd lingered at dinner, but Cat and Kris had gone to bed not long after the look-alike had hauled the kiddos out of there. They'd cited a 5:00 a.m. alarm, and parental life in general. I knew I would be up with them because I couldn't squander my time, but I also didn't think I was physically capable of going to bed at 9:00 p.m.

Mia had walked me to my room, and I'd all but expected her to lock me in for the night. She hadn't—though she had strongly implied that I would be eaten by bears if I was caught wandering the grounds. Too bad she didn't realize the puny black bears of the east read to me as no more dangerous than squirrels.

I didn't have my phone, the books in my room had been decorative, and they hadn't even put a TV in there to entertain their poor guests who were going through technology withdrawal.

What was a girl to do but find some entertainment?

"You're worried about me even when we're behind a fence and Stan?" Jeremy asked, and I laughed.

"Stan the guard?" I asked, delighted at how perfect that name was for the old man who'd pretended not to see the tampons in my bag.

"Stan the guard," Jeremy confirmed. "You'd be surprised, he can hang."

I took my pen back. "I'm not surprised at all. He looked like a baller. I'm guessing he's got girls all up and down Vermont."

"They call him Casanova," he said. "And you're Holland, if word on the street is correct."

I only realized just then I hadn't introduced myself. *Raised by wolves,* Cat had teased more than once about my lapses in manners. I had always had a reporter's personality, though. I liked being in charge of conversations, and I was always going to ask more questions than I answered.

I was an observer, but one who liked to push buttons to see what I could make happen.

"You're going to be taking my job next," I said.

He leaned against the back wall of the carriage house and brought out his own vape pen. I gaped at him, and he just grinned at me, completely unrepentant for stealing a hit when he had his own.

I quickly realized, though, that he was indulging in a much mellower substance than I was.

"No, thanks," he said. "I like my current job just fine."

"Which is?" I asked, mostly expecting him to say *gardener*.

He blew out some sour smoke, then eyed me. "I don't think I can tell you."

"Oh, jeez," I said. "There's literally no better way to make sure I'll never drop this topic."

"Yeah, I walked into that one," he admitted with a cheeky grin that suggested he'd done it on purpose. "Off the record? Is that what I'm supposed to say?"

"Sure." I didn't bother turning my recorder off. It seemed like that was enough for him to convince himself he'd done his due diligence to protect his employers, which was what I was guessing his hesitation had been.

"I'm the chef," he said, mischief in his eyes, in his voice, a little boy getting away with something.

I blinked at him, my brain sluggish from the long day. And then I pictured Cat, coming out of the carriage house, carrying the soup like she'd had it simmering on some stove for hours.

She'd accepted my compliments for it without a single blush of shame.

"What the hell?"

He lifted a shoulder. "Turns out running a business actually takes a lot of time. Catriona needs help making dinner most nights."

I grappled with that and, genuinely thrown, landed on probably the most pointless argument. "She posts pictures of everything as if she made it."

"That was all part of the contract." He leaned in. "But I haven't used my best recipes on her yet."

"Smart." Everyone was trying to hustle someone. I should have known that by now, but the depths to which people would sink on social media continued to astound me.

The wild thing was that I didn't resent her for having a chef. As with every part of the Bouchards' life, I had to admit I would've done something similar if I had their type of money. It was the fact that she lied about it to her audience, one that had been told that women really could have it all if they just worked hard enough, if they sacrificed enough, if they were just *perfect* enough. They could raise a family of six—seven!—and make their own bread from scratch and homeschool their kids and put elaborate meals together every day and keep up with the cleaning in their house that was big enough for a ginormous family and do all the laundry and pack picnic baskets so that the kids could have fun and come up with enrichment activities and have their own business and prioritize their gorgeous husbands and and and and and . . .

I was exhausted just thinking about how any one person could do that without an army of help.

And Cat had that army. She just told other women she didn't.

There hadn't even been a camera rolling when she'd brought that soup out tonight. There had been no reason to lie. Except that I supposed *I* was the camera. If Jeremy had served us, that definitely could have made it into the article.

What must it be like to live life like that? Constantly judging each action and reaction for how an audience would perceive it.

"Does she still make the desserts, at least?" I asked, because I wasn't about to spill all that out to Cat's private chef, whom I'd met five minutes ago.

"Oh, yeah, those are hers," he said, his head tipped up to the sky. "For better or worse."

"Bitchy much?" I asked. I was annoyed by Cat right now, but at a foundational level, I would always be *more* annoyed on Cat's behalf if anyone trash-talked her.

He laughed. "I don't think I've been called a bitch since sixth grade."

I raised a brow. "If you don't want to be called one, don't act like one."

"Ohhhh," he teased, a mocking callback to the school playground. "Nah, you're right, she's a genius when she gives a shit. Problem is she mostly doesn't give a shit."

"That is not the Cat I knew," I said, which was essentially becoming the tagline of the entire weekend.

He lifted one shoulder. "That's what happens when you're loaded on Valium more often than not."

I inhaled softly. "That's quite an accusation."

"Is it?" he asked, looking surprised. "Don't all the Stepford Wives eat them like candy?"

Maybe, but Cat had never liked to be out of control like that. She'd partied as much as the next person, but day-to-day, while doing her work, she'd always been stone-cold sober.

"It sounds like you don't like her very much."

He stared at me from hooded eyes. "She's talented. It sucks that she's wasting it."

I looked around. "She got all this with her talent."

Jeremy grunted. "Was it with her talent? No matter what kind of cute story they tell, I don't think it was what she could do in the *kitchen* that got her all this."

I knew he was implying that what she did in the bedroom had bought her this life, and I didn't like it, didn't like him thinking about Cat like that, even if I'd had thoughts that weren't so different.

"What exactly are you doing with your *talent*?" I asked. "Because ghost-cooking for a social media influencer doesn't exactly sound like setting the culinary world on fire."

"Yeah, but I'm not as talented as she is," he said, and I realized he really was a creative type who hated to see unfulfilled promise. For a second there, I had been wondering if he was some jilted lover who was bitter about being upstaged.

I took another hit, then tried to surprise a genuine reaction out of him. "So what's up with the look-alike?"

"I know, right?" he asked, unfazed by the non sequitur. "I thought I was tweaking when they first introduced her."

"That was some kind of freaky *Twilight Zone* shit," I said, matching his scrubbed-down tone.

"You know why they do it, right?" he asked, sliding me a look. I shook my head. "It's in case she's caught on some B-roll video for their content. It'll look like Cat, and they don't have to edit her out or do it over."

I tried to recall some of the videos I'd watched, attempting to spot Anna in my memory, as if such a thing were possible. There were always a few from a distance, in a golf cart headed out to the orchard, the kids playing in the pond, a baby wrapped to Cat's chest as she watched from shore.

But that had just been a blond ponytail, hadn't it? And a figure, a silhouette. I thought about what Anna had been wearing all day and realized it could have been out of Cat's wardrobe.

It probably wasn't even meant for when they were *accidentally* caught. They probably used it to free up Cat's time to do more scripted content.

"That's messed up," I said.

"Thin line between crazy psychopath and genius, right?" Jeremy mused, clearly a philosopher.

"Cat must feel pretty secure in her relationship to put up with a younger version of herself prancing around her husband," I pressed lightly.

I knew I had a limited view of their marriage, one that had been formed by the videos they themselves posted. The little I'd seen of them in person, they seemed in love.

Strangely, the social media content they put up told a slightly different story. He wasn't as lovey-dovey in their videos as he was in person.

But that was part of the tradwife appeal. Husbands were rarely seen. Sometimes they swooped in to taste whatever the wife had spent all day baking, or they rolled in off the range, or were framed in the background of some content. Their interactions were very *Leave it to Beaver*–ish. The welcome-home hug, the hard hand of the law if needed.

Plenty of influencers out there were famous *because* of their marriages, but, almost ironically, that wasn't how it worked with Cat and her ilk.

The point of the content was never to showcase a relationship. It was meant to showcase *a wife*.

While in theory the influencers were aiming to capture the attention of hormonal postpartum women and overstressed mothers, there was a hidden audience out there, one that accounted for a bigger slice of their viewership than people probably realized.

Men.

It made sense once I thought about it. This was *their* fantasy that the women were living out, after all. No informed woman actually wanted to go back to the time when she couldn't drive or have credit cards. Or back before a time when she could make obscene amounts of money off social media content and decide for herself how to spend it.

No, this was all largely done for the benefit of men. Because of that, the husband in the content couldn't be a fully developed person. The men who watched these videos had to be able to project themselves into the life that was presented for their fantasy to work. In these videos, in this life they believed they deserved, there was no burden of childcare on them or even the relationship building that came with real-life marriages. Here was your own personal, beautiful, thin robot, built to cater to you but not ask anything from you.

It was a family the men didn't have to do any work to get or maintain.

Cat was no different with her content, though she did have a few cute relationship-type videos in her archive: Kris twirling her around a kitchen before pulling her into a slow dance; them on an early-morning run together; a silly one of him throwing her into the pond off the dock.

Still, it was his absence that I noted the most.

Nothing about any of that made me think Kris was the cheating type—but nothing suggested he wasn't, either. If there was a twenty-one-year-old version of Cat running around, interacting positively with his children, and being subservient in the way an employee would be rather than a wife who only playacted at it? Was he really immune to that kind of temptation?

"Eh, I'd say Catriona knows she doesn't have to worry about anything happening between her husband and the nanny. Anna has a boyfriend back in Switzerland, and she can't go five minutes without bringing him up," Jeremy said. He tilted his head. "Maybe two."

"Long-distance," I murmured, because that didn't exactly prove anything.

"Girls, though," Jeremy said, like that was a real thought he should express. "They're loyal and shit."

"Sure." Because this wasn't the place or time for a gender studies lesson on stereotypes in relationships.

"Anyway, I'd be looking somewhere else for that," he said, with a little wink.

I wondered if I really had picked up on something with those lingering glances in the entryway. "Mia?"

"I didn't say nothing," he said, putting on a 1930s informer voice. "But I will say the marrieds have been fighting a ton ever since Steffie came to live here."

"And that's been about six months?"

He squinted at me, suspicious despite the fact that he couldn't seem to stop running his mouth. "Are you going to write some exposé on the kid? He doesn't need that."

"No," I said, putting all the conviction I felt into the denial. "I'm trying to understand Cat better. It's easier to do that when you understand all the dynamics at play."

"Well, it's not exactly a groundbreaking story," Jeremy said, relaxing once more. "Stepkid from a previous marriage not fitting in well with the stepmom. Tale as old as Hans Christian Andersen."

"Right," I said. Then decided to fish a little more since we were in these waters anyway. "I still can't believe the mother died in a kayak accident."

"Yeah." He nodded. "Steffie was there, you know. They'd been on a trip to help him clear his head—he'd been having some trouble in school. And this was a day's kayak in already, so he had to hike out and leave his mom's body there."

I blew out an appalled breath, the facts brutal despite my already having heard them. "What were the school troubles?"

"He got kicked out of three fancy private schools in a row," Jeremy said, taking a puff on his vape. "Having a shit dad will do that to you."

"You don't like Kris?"

"It's not about whether I like him or not," he said. "When you act like one of your families is real and the other isn't, that's gonna mess a kid up, for sure."

It was an emotionally intelligent take, which only made Jeremy more attractive, unfortunately.

"Was there any speculation that Steffie . . ." I trailed off and made a face.

He followed. "He didn't kill his own mom. If he was going to kill someone, it would have been Kris."

"Fair point." I decided to take one more swing, since my brain had been fixated on the information since I'd received it. "Do you know anything about this fan who is sending Cat messages? Obsessive messages."

"Uh, yeah?" Jeremy said with a shrug. "Mia sent out a memo to be on the lookout for any suspicious people hanging around. She said there's a chance they could want to talk to us because we work for Cat."

That made sense—any peek behind the orchard's walls would be tantalizing. "And have you? Had any weirdos come up to chat?"

"Vermont is full of weirdos," he said, his voice fond. "None that stood out as dangerous, though."

No one seemed to be taking the threat seriously, which probably meant I shouldn't, either. But it was interesting. If I'd had my phone, I might have gone searching for commenters, people who showed up frequently beneath Cat's videos, even if that probably wasn't enough to narrow anything down. Cat had plenty of fans with alerts set up for her posts just to be the first to like them.

For now, I'd be forced to take my cue from everyone else: It wasn't dangerous until it was dangerous.

I decided that was as good a time as any to drop the interrogation for the night. "So why don't you show me where the magic is made."

Jeremy grinned. "The kitchen, you mean?"

I popped my hip and smirked. "Obviously."

Later, I couldn't help but think about Cat carrying that pot of soup out to the table, a proud smile flitting across her features as she accepted my compliments.

If I hadn't been wandering about when and where I wasn't supposed to be, I might never have stumbled onto Jeremy.

She couldn't hide her nanny, but she could hide her private chef.

We lived in a golden era of grifters. If the snake oil salesmen of the Wild West had become infamous enough to enter our daily lexicon decades later, I wasn't sure what kind of impact this age of hustlers was going to have. But it would be significant.

So many people were trying to make a dollar off each other in ways that, at best, toed the line of unethical. Catriona was selling a fantasy, and maybe everyone knew it was a fantasy, but that didn't make it the right thing to do. I made a living off telling stories about other people, and who said that was much better?

But at least I didn't make a play for the high ground.

These people had invited me into the fantasy and then were going to get resentful if I pointed out that it was all make-believe. I would be the *evil media* out to get them.

The thing about living in the Golden Era of Grifting was that no one really wanted to hear about how they were getting grifted on the daily. They wanted to buy their branded Catriona Bouchard pot and pretend it was something better than what they could pick up at Goodwill for three bucks.

I didn't exist to write articles that people wanted to read, though. I existed to try to find the beating heart of my profile subject.

At one point in my life, I had believed the one that pounded away in Cat's chest was one that was worth something.

Now I wondered if I would walk away from all this knowing that it wasn't.

CHAPTER TWELVE

Holland

Now

I had no interest in actually sleeping in the carriage house with Jeremy. I was too worried that Mia would show up at my door at 5:00 a.m. and find my bed empty.

So, not long after midnight, I heaved myself out of Jeremy's too-comfortable bed.

"Do you guys get a lot of guests?" I asked as I slipped back into my corduroys.

Jeremy was sprawled out in all his naked glory, not even a sheet covering him to provide a wink toward modesty. "Nah. Kris is weird about people coming here. Sometimes Catriona has some of those ladies over . . ."

"What ladies?" I asked, wondering if one of them might be the obsessed fan.

He sighed as if it were too much brain power to come up with the words. "The Stepford Wives."

Ah. That was less interesting. "She hosts influencer weekends?"

"A few times," he said, before grabbing his vape pen off the nightstand.

I pulled my sweater on. "Do they have to give up their phones when they're here?"

Jeremy barked out a laugh. "You'd have to pry those things from their cold, dead hands."

I hummed in agreement. It made sense that Cat had taken mine when she hadn't theirs. Trust in legacy media wasn't exactly high these days. Whereas the influencers she'd personally invited probably would have been far more interested in currying her favor than exposing some silly little behind-the-scenes gaffe. "Was it the kidnapping attempt on Fleur? Is that why Kris is so weird about visitors?"

"You know about that?"

The question stopped me. I had been operating on autopilot, but my brain scrambled to catch up. Was the kidnapping attempt something I wasn't supposed to know? Was that something that revealed just how much I'd researched the family? But, no. I'd been told about it this weekend.

"Mia mentioned it," I said, and then to keep him focused, asked again, "Is that why he doesn't like visitors?"

"Dunno," Jeremy said.

"Insightful," I murmured, and he grinned, seemingly unrepentant in his own stupidity.

"Hey," he said. "I have thoughts. I'm just not going to share them with some nosy reporter."

That hadn't seemed to stop him earlier. But maybe all he'd offered me before was idle gossip, things he didn't actually believe but wanted to shoot the shit about.

"How about you share them with one of Cat's oldest friends," I said, wiggling my brows enticingly.

He shook his finger at me. "I'm not that easy."

I deliberately let my eyes run over his body and then the bed, and he laughed.

"I don't know, Kris likes control," Jeremy said, with a careless shrug. "All those rich guys do. He's not any different from any other multimillionaire prick out there. They don't make that much money by being nice guys."

And wasn't that a cold, hard fact.

"Do you ever get the sense that . . ." I trailed off. "Never mind."

He sat up. "What?"

I shook my head. "Nothing, just a passing thought."

Jeremy chewed on his lip. "That . . . ?"

I could tell he wasn't going to let it go. "I don't know. That some of these things could be, uh . . ." I searched for a delicate way to ask it. "Red flags?"

His eyebrows shot up. "Like that he's . . . ?"

It was stupid to talk around it like this, in half sentences. But I didn't want to poison this well, either. Still, it was late, and I couldn't help but offer, "Well, there's a certain type of man who likes to control his wife's surroundings with things like a huge-ass security gate. And it's not just rich guys."

"No," Jeremy said, the kind of knee-jerk response a lot of dudes made to support their bros. "No, he's not . . ."

"Of course," I said, despite the fact that neither of us had really said anything. That was the best way to test the theory, anyway. There was plausible deniability on both sides. "Anyway, thanks for the entertainment."

He saluted, just as willing to drop the topic as I was.

As I left the carriage house, I tried to temper my suspicion and anger toward Kris.

It was hard, though. I'd had a front seat to Cat being put in the hospital by one boyfriend and making a whole lot of excuses about "accidents" that happened with her next. From things she'd insinuated, neither of them had been the first to treat her like that, either.

I exhaled, my hands trembling at the memory of Benji. Of warm rain, black dresses, and oak branches covered in dripping Spanish moss.

"I trusted you."

A shadow moved in front of me.

I swallowed a startled cry. Kris materialized from the darkness as if my thoughts had conjured him up.

"Are you lost?" he asked, in that soft French voice of his that seemed perfectly pleasant by candlelight but, with the memories of death so fresh, now slithered over my skin.

I forced out a laugh and held up my vape. "Addictions are brutal. Didn't want to stink up your house."

"I appreciate that," Kris said. "But you're headed in the direction of the woods, and that's hardly safe. Let me help you."

His hand found the small of my back, too low, too close to my ass. Too French.

"I trusted you."

"I've read some of your work," Kris said. "I'll admit I was worried about you coming here."

It was interesting that the two people who had told me that were Mia and Kris. Did that lend credence to the idea that they were having an affair? "You do realize that makes me think you have something to hide."

"You're so . . ." Kris trailed off.

"Blunt?" I offered, and a corner of his mouth twitched.

"American," he murmured, and I couldn't exactly argue since they were one and the same.

"And Cat isn't?"

"Catriona," he corrected, absently. And I almost laughed at how perfectly that encapsulated our impasse. Cat was American; Catriona was French, or at least French enough. "I think there's something you should understand."

That sounded dire. "Okay."

He stopped, the moonlight spilling over his face as if he'd scripted the perfect location to stand in to look threatening. "I need you to hear me when I say this. I would do anything to protect my wife."

It should have been one of those ridiculous statements men made that they thought made them sound cool, but they didn't actually mean to do anything about. But for some reason, in this moment, I took him seriously. Perhaps he really had cultivated the exact right tone to have my arm hair standing on end. Or maybe this was the Kristopher Bouchard who had made a hundred million dollars before he'd turned forty.

"That's good to hear," I said, trying to inject some levity for the sole purpose of making myself feel better. "I would hate to see someone hurt Cat."

His mouth tightened but he didn't correct me this time. "I think there is a chance you do not have my wife's best interest at heart."

"I'm not sure why you would think I don't," I said, though something tightened in my belly with the feeling that he could see through time to us standing beneath Spanish moss–draped trees.

"If you'd let me explain . . ."

He studied me. "Why are you two not friends anymore?"

"What did she say to that?" I asked, my heart beating too fast.

"Do you always answer questions with questions?" he asked.

"What do you think?" I tried, but he was not in the mood for humor.

"I think you've been flippant this whole evening," he said. "I think you don't seem to realize that I know the publisher of that magazine you write for, and that he hasn't much cared about the day-to-day workings up until now. But that could change."

Everything steadied, my heart, my breathing. I didn't love confrontation, but I couldn't stand bullies. "Some people might take that as a threat."

"I think you should take it exactly as it sounded," he said smoothly. "And before we say good night, I wanted to offer my condolences on your mother's passing."

The world went quiet around us, my fingers tingling, my head light.

No one knew who my mother was—not that she was famous or recognizable, but I'd done my best to cut her out of my life, both physically and digitally. I left home at eighteen and never once looked back. I'd even officially changed my surname to my middle name. Holly Cielinski almost seemed like a different person to me now.

I hadn't hidden all that, exactly. But it also wasn't easy to find. What Kris was doing was telling me he'd run a background check on me, with some degree of thoroughness beyond just a Google search.

This was the exact kind of behavior I had been trying not to diagnose as anything but rich, entitled prick. But, paired with the threat to my employment, it all felt tinged with violence. Maybe because we were outside at night alone together; maybe because he'd made sure to stand just close enough that, even at his stature, he was able to loom over me. Maybe because as a woman, I recognized the signs of danger even in so-called polite conversation.

Up until now, I'd demanded I give this guy the benefit of the doubt. But in that moment, I stopped caring about that. I wouldn't make up a story about him in my own head, but I wouldn't write off the red flags that I was slowly collecting.

And this place was a fucking compound, no matter how much people wanted to hand wave that away.

"Thank you," I said quietly, as if cowed. Then I locked eyes with him. "I should offer you my condolences as well. For your ex-wife. She died about six months ago, didn't she?"

He didn't seem surprised that I knew about it, and Cat had probably told him that I'd met Steffie. But thunderclouds brewed behind his expression, and I felt like I'd landed at least a soft punch on the jaw after he'd pummeled my solar plexus.

"That must be hard, to parent a child through that," I said, knowing I was pushing it.

His right hand clenched and his eyes went icy; he'd somehow stepped even closer to me, so that now I could smell the toothpaste on his breath. It was such an innocuous detail, but it drove home the physicality of him. The threat of him.

I wondered for a delirious moment if he really was about to hit me for mentioning his son.

Then he exhaled, his fingers uncurling right before he shoved his hand in the pocket of his thousand-dollar pants. "You're playing with fire, Ms. Tate."

"I'm simply conveying my sympathies to you and your family," I said, and it came out just a hair shakier than I wanted it to.

"You're so gracious. How lucky we are to have such a considerate and kind guest," he said smoothly, without a hint of the sarcasm he must've been dying to employ. "And on that, I'll bid you good night."

He gave me a little bow that should have looked silly but came off as a fencer acknowledging his opponent, not with respect but with the muscle memory of courtesy.

I waited until he'd gone inside before I fully exhaled; then I somehow made it to my room before collapsing onto my bed.

Anxiety buzzed beneath my skin, my hands jittery like I'd downed an espresso after a night of no sleep.

I thought about the way Kris's fingers had curled into a fist from the rage I must have sparked in him.

And I wondered if Cat had ever borne marks left by that curled fist.

As I'd thought earlier, it wouldn't have been the first time.

CHAPTER THIRTEEN

Cat

Then

I waited in the coffee shop across from the hospital for an amount of time that might have been embarrassing to someone else. I, an enlightened soul, looked at it as an investment in my future.

And I got to try the brownies one reviewer had called "the best dessert in Savannah."

Spoiler alert, they were not and she was a dumbass.

If the desserts had actually been good, I would have brought Holland back to tell me how much more delicious mine were. But they weren't even worth that effort.

Three hours after I arrived, Benji Croft finally walked out the doors of the hospital.

I didn't have to hurry—I had been ready to jump up as soon as I saw him—but I did add an extra pep to my step as he started down the sidewalk so that I wouldn't lose him.

"Hey," I called out when I was within a few strides.

He turned, surprise followed by a flash of recognition. He'd probably seen hundreds of patients in the two weeks since I'd ended up in the ER, but he remembered me.

"Hey," he said gently, because he thought I was the victim of domestic abuse. He wasn't *wrong* per se, and it was cute, but I didn't actually need him thinking I was made of glass. "How are you feeling? How are the ribs? Did you tweak something?"

Oh. Something warm slipped into my veins at the concern in his voice. That was nice. "No. I thought you might like to take me out to dinner."

There was that same delightful combination of surprise and recognition, made lovelier by the fact that he settled into a smile at the end of it all.

"That's a funny way to tell me you can read minds," he said. We had slowed to a stop, and now had to step out of the way of a couple of tourists.

"I don't like to brag about it," I said, with fake humility.

He laughed and then sobered. "Uh, don't you have a . . ."

He trailed off. I'd told him I'd fallen down stairs, even though we both knew he hadn't believed it. He thought I had an abusive boyfriend.

I tapped my chin in thought. "I did get rid of about 185 pounds of trash a couple weeks ago, if that's what you're wondering."

His eyes lit up. "Well then, I just got off and am starving."

"There's a dirty joke in there," I said. "I'm going to let it go since I'm a lady, but please know I caught it."

"I like dirty."

"Are you always hungry after you get off?" I asked, and then buried my face in my hands. "I did that for the bit. Don't think I'm that kind of girl."

He tugged at my wrists to uncover my face. His hands were so gentle, and I wondered if maybe I *liked* being treated like glass. Everyone always viewed me as so competent and, quite frankly, as a bitch, that few people bothered handling me with any kind of care.

"Hey, I would never," he said, and then glanced around. There was a decent Thai place a few storefronts down. I wasn't going to suggest it because I'd already been so pushy, but his eyes locked onto the sign. "Come on."

He linked his fingers in mine and tugged me into the place. We were greeted warmly and shown a secluded table in the back. Shadows were my friend, as they softened the hard lines of my face and my personality. Less of the *cunt* came across on my features when someone couldn't see every micro-reaction.

Something in my gut told me Benji liked nice girls.

We covered the basics over sweet iced tea. He was from California and had three brothers and parents who were still together. When a position had opened up in Savannah, he'd jumped at the chance to get a change of scenery, and then he'd fallen in love with the city.

I had long ago perfected a glossy version of my life. I had been born and raised in LA, which sounded much cooler than Bakersfield. I had been raised by a single mother and my grandmother, both strong women who taught me I didn't need a man to support me. Which sounded much better than *I was the result of an unwanted teenage pregnancy, and my narcissistic, ruthless grandmother made both our lives miserable in punishment of that fact.* I told people that the exacting standards with which I was raised had pushed me to be the best version of myself, instead of the fact that I had known from a young age I'd need to excel at something to escape the hell that was that household.

"Siblings?" he asked.

"No." Thank god.

He looked sad at that, as many people who had siblings did. As if my life weren't complete without a sister toddling along in my shadow. You couldn't miss something you'd never had, though.

And this way, I had been free of any guilt in leaving my mother and grandmother behind at seventeen, never looking back even once.

Benji ordered one of practically everything off the menu, and we sat for hours talking favorite movies and favorite restaurants and favorite drinks.

He was not my usual type—but my usual type had also just put me in the hospital. So. If ever there was a time to deviate, now was it.

Mostly, I walked away with an impression that he was kind, a trait I had never felt strongly about before. In my experience, kind people tended to be weak and easy to manipulate. In Benji's case, I felt myself altering my behavior to fit what he seemed to want from me, which flipped the script. He might not have been trying to manipulate me, but with his personality, he was doing so.

I could appreciate the skill that took.

Holland was working at the desk overlooking our only tiny window when I got home. I went over to her and leaned my chin on her shoulder, pressing my face to hers, wrapping my arms around her from behind.

She pressed back. "Where were you?"

I paused. But if Holland had wanted Benji, she could have staked out the hospital herself. "Remember that hot guy from the ER?"

"Hmm," she said, and I hated her for a second. She was pretending she could barely remember him, even though he'd checked her out first.

"We went to dinner," I said.

"Oh, fun, what did you get?" she asked, and I straightened.

"Thai."

She craned to look around to see if I'd brought leftovers, which of course I hadn't. Just because I would if I was alone, didn't mean I would ask for a *doggie bag* in front of a date.

"Damn," she said, and stood, stretching. "I don't even know what time it is."

I didn't appreciate how nonchalant she was being about all this. I had well and truly staked my claim, and she should at least be a little annoyed I'd done so. "I think I'm going to marry him."

She stared at me like she was finally listening. "Girl, what?"

That was more like it. I shrugged, adopting my own casual air. "I don't know, we talked for hours. He's just . . . so nice."

She squinted at me. "You don't like nice guys."

"I've changed."

She laughed at that, and headed toward our tiny galley kitchen. The only really fancy things I kept in our home were the dessert holders. That morning I'd put out cupcakes beneath a glass dome that sat atop a pretty pedestal. It always vexed me that I didn't have hundreds of millions of dollars to make the entirety of my life just as beautiful as that one holder.

But it was a start.

One that I wouldn't have thought possible growing up in that shithole house in Bakersfield—

I cut myself off. I should have found a way around talking about my family and my history, but when I did that, men tended to fill in the gaps in weird ways. The rich ones thought I was hiding that I was broke, which I was. The others thought I had Daddy issues or something and then tried to use that in bed.

Holland popped herself up onto the counter and dragged a finger through the icing of one of the cupcakes. Lavender buttercream. The cake was lemon. Simple and lovely.

"I thought you didn't want to get married," Holland said, after she'd sucked her finger clean.

That wasn't . . . untrue. And I'd said the thing about marrying Benji—after a first date, no less—because I'd wanted a reaction from her, not because I actually wanted to marry him.

I had graduated from the CIA less than two years earlier. I was already being talked about as one of the up-and-coming stars in Savannah. I wasn't about to become a child bride and throw that all away for a man.

"I mean, if anyone could understand my weird hours and devotion to my craft, it's an ER doctor," I said, with a shrug, because giving up the game would be silly after such gentle prodding. She'd have to work harder than that.

Holland finished off the cupcake, which she'd already raved about this morning, so I'd excuse her for not lavishing heavy praise on me now, in the middle of a conversation. But she only got a couple of lapses before I would start limiting her cupcake supply.

"He sounds boring," she said with a shrug as she hopped down from the counter. "But I'll start saving for the hideous maid of honor dress I know you'll force me into."

She stopped by me and pressed a kiss to my cheek. "Your cupcakes made my night."

I smiled, though I didn't return her affection. "He's not boring."

"At least he's better than Mark." She shrugged again and then stepped back. She looked fully engaged for the first time since I'd come home, whatever story she'd been working on finally scrubbed clean from her brain. "It's weird he hasn't come pounding on our door in the middle of the night or something, isn't it? Guys like that don't typically just let their girlfriend dump them without a fight."

I didn't shift. I didn't blink. "I broke up with him the day before he had a three-week business trip."

"Oh jeez," Holland said, moving on, satisfied with the answer. "Well, let me know if I should be stocking up on my bear spray."

She was already moving down the hallway to her bedroom, the topic mostly forgotten. "Night, babe."

"Good night," I said. I hadn't moved from my position leaning up against the stove.

Holland liked me. I had a finely tuned sense of that, probably instilled in me from my grandmother. The bitch.

Holland liked me. She thought I was funny and cutting, and she liked not having to be perfectly nice around me. We were simpatico in that regard.

Still, Holland wasn't *like* me. She was mostly good. She thought about other people in ways that didn't relate directly back to herself. She was curious about the world.

She liked me. And she hadn't liked Mark.

If she heard about how I'd handled that particular problem, though, she would like me a whole lot less.

My phone vibrated, as if on cue.

I had a wonderful evening. Can't wait to see you again.

Benji hadn't made definitive plans when we'd parted ways, which had been a knock against him. But this helped.

And when will that be? I wrote back, because this part was easy and mostly scripted.

I pocketed my phone, ready to ignore his response for a good twenty minutes to let him sweat.

I eyed the lavender and lemon cupcakes, the glass dome that was now askew. I crossed over to it, straightening it again.

So few people had appreciation for perfection.

CHAPTER FOURTEEN

Holland

Now

The farmhouse smelled of coffee and bacon and something maple-y, which was exactly what I would have expected when waking up at Cat's orchard.

My alarm clock reported that it was 5:15 a.m., and my body confirmed that unpleasant fact. Usually on Saturdays, I let myself sleep until noon, but that clearly would have been met with horror by the Bouchards.

I stumbled my way down the stairs and into the kitchen. There I was greeted with a scene from a Hallmark movie. The kids giggled and chased each other around; Cat stirred something on the stove, the baby wrapped to her chest; classical music softened the air; and the table offered a feast that was probably typical for this family but I was only lucky enough to experience on the rare years the magazine splurged on a holiday party.

My fingers curled around the recorder I had running in the pocket of my flannel pajama pants.

"Morning," I croaked. Cat didn't startle—she'd probably completely lost her jump reflex from the chaos of her household.

"Holland," she said, with a beatific smile. She was wearing brown linen pants and a creamy blouse, her hair pulled back into a perfect bun. Her makeup was done, but it was of the barely noticeable variety that had men believing women didn't have anything on at all. "Did you sleep well?"

I muttered something that she'd take as an affirmative, my eyes scanning the room for coffee.

She smiled, and this time it was real. "Over there."

I followed where she pointed and found one of those fancy coffee machines on its own island, which was also occupied with handcrafted mugs, a pot of sugar, and an old-fashioned jar of cream. I skipped that—God knew if it had been pasteurized—but gleefully made myself something that smelled divine. When I was done, I hopped up on the counter next to the stove so I could watch her work.

"You always liked counter surfing," Cat commented.

"Mama, she's not allowed up there," Céline said, coming to a skidding stop in front of me. "Papa will be mad."

Something crossed in and out of Cat's expression, something I wished I could capture with a photograph to study. Was it fear? Was it just annoyance? I thought about last night and wondered if Kris got mad often. It would be interesting to see him spend time with the children—they were little barometers when it came to anxiety. But he didn't ever seem to interact with them for very long.

"He won't get mad, love," Cat said, her voice gentle, whatever emotion that had been gone now. "He doesn't like when you're up there because you might fall and hurt yourself. Miss Holland is an adult."

The three-year-old glared at the injustice of that, but then took off running in the next heartbeat.

"Am I breaking a house rule?" I asked, not caring, but curious anyway. Discipline was a fascinating pressure point in marriages, especially for couples who pursued traditional gender roles. Technically,

Cat was in charge of the children and house, so she was in charge of laying down and enforcing the rules. But that was at odds with the idea that she was loving above all else, gentle, and subservient.

The hard hand of the law usually belonged to the husband, but it often came down to the wife directing him on when to be the enforcer.

"As if you care," Cat teased, reading my mind. There was that muscle memory twinge again. She glanced out the window over the stove, a tic almost, and I craned my neck to see what she was looking at.

There wasn't much light, but I could make out the outline of two people talking.

Kris and . . . Mia?

Cat exhaled quietly and shook her head, as if telling herself off.

"They're friendly," I tried, and she shot me a look.

"Don't," she warned, and I raised my hands, the picture of innocence. "Oh, please, I know what you're thinking."

It was the closest she'd sounded to my Cat so far. Pissed off. Calling me out on trying to stir the pot.

"It's nice for everyone in your household to get along so well," I pushed.

She rolled her eyes. But then she put her customer service voice back on. "Mia wants to expand her role in the business, and we have so much to do these days, I'm excited for the extra help."

"And that involves early-morning confabs with just the two of them?" I asked, making an obvious attempt to get another look.

Cat's nostrils flared, but that was the only sign she was upset that I could see.

"How long has Mia been with you?" I asked.

"I'm sorry—is this a profile on my manager?" Cat snapped, and I pressed my smile into nonexistence.

I liked, though, that I could get her to take off the mask. I was guessing not that many people could.

"Nope," I said. "I'm not on the clock yet. This is just me being curious."

She seemed to read what I was saying—that I was asking as a friend. And sent me a somewhat grateful smile, even if it kind of looked fake. "I know I used to be a jealous"—she glanced at her kids and lowered her voice—"bitch. But I was so young. I put that kind of behavior behind me a long time ago." Then she waved at me. "Obviously."

That rankled, because I'd never given her reason to be jealous of me and Benji. I hadn't even liked him as a person, let alone a love interest for myself. But I didn't want to start the fight again right here in her kitchen before 6:00 a.m.

I leaned forward. "I just want you to be happy."

And safe, but I didn't add that part. It had taken a long time last night for the anxiety to ease, for the nerves running beneath my skin to settle. I'd remembered getting that first call from the hospital, when she'd asked in the quietest, most shameful voice if I could come pick her up. She'd been back to her indomitable self by the time I'd arrived, but that didn't erase the fear, the self-loathing, I'd heard.

I had consoled myself over the years that Cat seemed happy enough in this life, even if it wasn't what I would have thought she wanted.

But what if she wasn't? Everyone knew that these kids had tantrums even if Cat never showed it. They knew she had a dirty kitchen after cooking even if they didn't get to see the cleanup.

What if this picture-perfect image was hiding something much darker than that?

I pushed the thought out of my head as Cat rolled her eyes at me.

"What, exactly, about what you've experienced in the past twelve hours would leave you with any doubt that I am absolutely the happiest I could be in the world?" Cat asked, though she didn't meet my eyes.

A lot of things, I wanted to say but didn't. It wasn't my place right now. And just like with Jeremy, I didn't want to speak the words out loud in case I somehow brought them into reality. Like some kind of jinx.

I was here the rest of the weekend. Abusers could cover up their behavior for much longer than that, but maybe not if I kept applying pressure. It didn't seem like it would take Kris much to crack.

How brilliant would that be—if I could press charges instead of Cat?

I was getting ahead of myself again. All I'd seen really was a curled fist, some rage that seemed far and above what the moment had called for. A man who liked to control where his wife was at all times and denied her access to leaving their compound. A man who saw himself as the dictator of the house.

A woman who seemingly had masks to hide her masks.

An ex-wife and a mysterious death.

I wasn't jumping to conclusions, but I was *noticing*.

"Okay, tell me about your life." That was always my first question, the one I would have asked at dinner last night had this been a typical profile piece. It was too broad, I knew that. People didn't know what I meant or which topic to focus on—career, hobbies, political leanings, friends.

But that was why I liked it. I liked hearing what jumped to mind first.

Tell me about your life.

Tell me what's the most important thing to you.

I wondered how I'd answer that.

No one had ever asked.

Cat's forehead wrinkled in a way I was impressed with in this Botox era. "You know the basics."

"Yeah, but we're introducing you to people who still pay for a magazine subscription. A lot of them don't even recognize the names of the apps you're on," I prodded. "Tell me about your life."

She glanced at the children, who, by some unspoken agreement, were finding their seats at the table. Fleur came over to help carry things for Cat.

"It's good and chaotic."

I took a sip of coffee and waited. When she didn't continue, I laughed. "Come on, girl. Give a little."

She didn't relax. "People don't want to hear how good my life is."

"I think you should stop worrying about what people want to hear and just talk to me like a human," I said, interjecting just a tiny bit of bite. It got her attention. "I think you're probably very good at giving people what they want, and less good at just talking about yourself."

"My job is talking about myself," she said, a spark lighting behind her eyes.

"Is it?" I asked quietly, my eyes locked on her face, my gut screaming *dig, dig, dig* and my head trying to pull me back. And my heart said I'd get more out of Cat with a slap than with honey. So I went with that. "Because it seems like your job is filming mini propaganda movies to sell people products they don't need or can't afford. And don't forget acting as a fetishization object to men who want to jerk off to a *Mad Men* exec's idea of a 1950s housewife."

She sucked in a breath, but before she could say anything, the door swung open, bringing in Kris along with a gust of wind.

The light in her eyes extinguished. Her face smoothed out. And she offered Kris the bland, pleasant smile I was starting to hate with a passion.

I stared at him as I stayed rooted on the counter, breaking the rule Cat had refused to call a rule.

Kris greeted Cat with a kiss on the nape of her neck, but he was looking at me while he brushed his mouth against her skin.

Calculating—maybe gauging to see if I'd told Cat about our late-night chat.

Then he smiled that same welcoming and warm host smile from the day before.

"Not a morning person, huh?" he asked with amused sympathy.

I blinked at the whiplash. "Uh."

Cat laughed. "Holland can't form a coherent thought until she's had at least two cups of coffee. And that's if she wakes up at 10:00 a.m."

The information came out like an exhale, without any thought. Like Cat still knew me as well as she knew herself.

Kris laughed, missing the moment. But Cat hadn't.

Her wide eyes met mine, and we were both transported back to our kitchen in Savannah. Benji instead of Kris standing next to her, his hand on her hip.

I cleared my throat and hopped off the counter. "Actually, you know what, I forgot my meds upstairs. I have to take them with breakfast. I'll be right back. Don't wait for me."

"Oh," Cat said, seeming caught off guard. Her eyes slid to Kris and then back to me and then back to Kris.

"Seriously," I said. "I'll be right back."

Before anyone could broach an argument, I was out of the kitchen, the hardwood cool against my bare feet.

Mostly, I was just fleeing a rush of emotions. It was stupid to mourn a friendship from a decade ago, but I had never had a friend before or since like that. I'd felt like we were in a TV show about codependent twentysomethings making mistakes and loving life.

Beneath that was a whisper, one that I knew I shouldn't listen to.

A whisper that said this was one of the few times all weekend that I could guarantee that both Kris and Cat were occupied and in the same place.

I took the stairs two at a time, not even pausing on my floor, but heading straight up to the top level.

To the primary bedroom.

I shouldn't snoop. I never would've dreamed of snooping over the course of a normal interview.

This was Cat, though.

And more than I wanted a story, I wanted her safe. That meant searching for any red flags she would absolutely hide from me if they existed because she knew I wouldn't shut up about them.

Their bedroom door was open, anyway.

Or cracked.

Or closed but unlocked.

Semantics.

I stepped quickly in, shutting the door behind me. It was all as gorgeous as I would have expected. The apple quilt on their bed a little too on the nose for an orchard in my opinion, but everything else fit the style perfectly.

This was one of the few rooms I didn't know well, given that Cat rarely filmed in here, if at all. I couldn't think of a single video with even a glimpse at the inner sanctum.

That was probably a good boundary to draw.

I scanned the room, not really looking for anything in particular. I just . . . I wanted to see past the facade for one brief second.

That wouldn't be in here, where Cat clearly ran an immaculate ship. She'd always been neat to the point of pathological.

Instead, I headed for the bathroom.

It was as polished and pristine as the bedroom, but there was a lot more potential for secrets to lurk in here.

I made my way quickly through the drawers, discovering nothing but spare washcloths and the kind of skin care where they don't even bother to tell you the price because if you have to ask, you're too poor to buy it.

Only the pantry-style door near the shower looked promising.

Here were the basics that weren't nearly as aesthetically pleasing as the rest of the room.

Cat had done her best. The extra toilet paper was stacked in a wicker basket; the containers of toothpaste had been removed from their garish boxes; the mouthwash had been transferred into a pretty glass vial. But you could only pretty up *bathroom supplies* by so much.

On a hunch, I grabbed the basket—wicker, of course—that was packed with tidy rows of tampons. Any woman worth her salt knew it was a place that would be safe from husbands' prying eyes.

And sure enough my fingers brushed something at the bottom that I recognized immediately.

Cash.

I didn't pull it out—there was no time to rearrange the tampons back into order—but I was familiar with the feel of wads of money.

If they were hundreds, there could be as much as three grand tucked away beneath the tampons. That might be pocket change for the Bouchards, but was it for Cat?

Kris had never answered if Cat had access to her own money. Plenty of women out there didn't even know the log-ins to their bank accounts. What if Kris gave her an allowance? What if this was money she'd saved up to . . . what?

She couldn't leave. Not with six kids.

What was the other option, though? Getting Kris out of there. But he'd created a compound in just a way so that she couldn't do that, either.

As I put the basket back, I caught sight of the orange bottles. There were four of them on the very top shelf.

Prescription pills.

Hadn't Jeremy alluded to the idea that Cat was on Valium? It hadn't seemed like Cat at all, but maybe this was proof she was?

I stretched up as far as I could, but couldn't reach the bottles.

Cat wouldn't be able to reach them, either.

Did that mean they were Kris's? Or just that he was the one who could access the bottles?

Kris likes control.

"Shit," I murmured, staring at them, all lined up like little soldiers.

I glanced around, but there was nothing to stand on, and I'd already been away too long anyway.

I stepped away in defeat, but before I could completely retreat, the hardwood in the bedroom creaked out my only warning.

"You're not supposed to be in here."

CHAPTER FIFTEEN

Holland

Now

Steffie stood in the doorway to the bathroom, eyeing me with interest.

"Right," I said, trying to decide how to play it.

You're not supposed to be in here. He hadn't sounded angry—he hadn't even been scolding me, really. It had been more of a comment than anything else.

Finally, I offered a weak "I know."

The kid rocked back on his heels, a piece of dark hair falling over his eyes. He looked almost out of time, but not like the rest of the family. They seemed to have come in from the prairie. Steffie looked like he'd been transported from the early aughts, when Goth kids thought they were counterculture because they wore dark eyeliner and shopped at Hot Topic instead of Forever 21.

"What are you doing?" he asked.

Well, now was the time to test his rebel tendencies. "Snooping."

He barked out a laugh that seemed to surprise him. So maybe emo boy wasn't so scary after all.

"You shouldn't be."

Obviously, I thought but didn't say. "Are you going to tell on me?"

His eyes tracked over my shoulder to the closet. "Did you find anything?"

I thought about the cash, and the prescription bottles, neither of which could be called a smoking gun. "Nope."

Steffie nodded. "All the good stuff's in my dad's office."

I managed to keep my voice simply curious when I said, "Oh yeah?"

"You should go," he said, and for a second, I wondered if he meant now or for good. "Catriona will get suspicious."

He was right. I'd taken way too long, and was going to have to come up with some excuse that likely involved some kind of IBS-related emergency that everyone would be too embarrassed to question. But I didn't want to waste my shot with Steffie.

"How's it been, living here?" I asked.

"You should go," he said again. And then he turned and walked out of the bathroom.

"Okay," I drawled, and followed him.

Only, when I stepped into the bedroom, he was waiting for me. "Later. I'll talk to you later, if you can get away."

"Where?" I asked.

"Head toward the woods," he said. "There's a greenhouse back there. You'll find it. Or you won't."

"Okay," I said again, intrigued by the cloak-and-dagger of it all.

By the time I hustled back into the kitchen, Mia, Cat, and Kris were all regarding me with various levels of suspicion.

Mia, especially, looked like she wanted to staple herself to my side the rest of the weekend.

I gave everyone a bland smile and then took a seat next to Cat. The pancakes and cinnamon buns had already been passed around, and someone had stacked some on my plate.

"Sorry," I said, without bothering to give even a bowel-related excuse. If they weren't going to ask, I wasn't going to offer.

Cat and Kris locked eyes, but they were apparently too polite to push on where I had been.

Kris spent the breakfast regaling me with details about their pots-and-pans collection as if I didn't live in a tiny studio apartment in the city, where I owned approximately two pans, one sauce and one frying.

I mostly tuned him out as I tried to imagine Savannah's Cat smiling like that at the husband who was telling me all about *her* business. And that reminded me that I hadn't really gotten a good sense of the logistics of their businesses.

"Which one of you actually owns the line?" I asked, interrupting Kris's polished marketing pitch.

He stuttered to a stop. "We already answered that last night."

What he'd said was that he was the head of the house. "So your name is on the papers?"

"Yes," he said slowly, like the question was so dumb that he must be missing something. "We don't care about that kind of stuff, though."

"You might not care," I said. "It might matter to Cat if she ever wanted a divorce."

I knew I'd gone too far as soon as I said it.

"Enough," he said, slamming his palm against the table. I inhaled as the plates rattled. The color drained out of Cat's face, and she held herself perfectly still. One of the twins started crying, perhaps sensing the tension in the air or perhaps because they were three years old and a light breeze could set them off.

"You've upset my children," Kris said. "We've welcomed you into our home because you're an old friend. But we will ask you to leave if necessary."

I held up my hands like this was all a big misunderstanding. "You're right, I'm sorry. That was an inappropriate question. I'm too nosy for my own good. Thank God I found my way into journalism or someone would have punched me long ago."

I watched Kris's hand. It didn't curl into a fist, but I didn't need to see much more than Cat's frozen smile to know that this show of temper wasn't new or rare.

"Excuse me one more time," I murmured, and no one stopped me as I stood. I had caused a scene, and everyone wanted me gone.

I stepped into the bathroom closest to the kitchen and splashed some water on my face. I stared down at my shaking hands.

PTSD, I'd come to suspect, though I'd never actually seen a therapist about that in particular. I didn't mind confrontation or raised voices. It was the threat of a hit that had my chest flushing red.

I wanted to take my shaking hands and drag Cat out of there, at least far enough away that she could tell me if I was being ridiculous or not. Obviously, that wasn't a possibility, so I just waited for the hives to go down. Once they did, I stepped out into the hallway, newly collected and refreshed.

Mia was there.

"What are you doing?" she asked.

"You didn't give me any off-limit topics," I said. No one had, which had surprised both me and my editor.

"Because I thought you'd be a respectable professional."

"I promise you, if you thought that was a tough line of questioning, you've never watched a single White House briefing," I said.

"You're not exactly Bob Woodward."

"Ouch," I said, giving her her dues. I settled back against the wall, in no rush to return to the kitchen. "What do you want this piece to be?"

She lifted a perfectly sculpted brow. "Off the record?"

"Sure," I lied. Sort of. I wouldn't put it in the article, but my recorder was still going.

"A slightly lifted curtain," she said, leaning back against the wall, mirroring me. "Show how hard it is to be Catriona Bouchard, because it is hard. Stay-at-home moms work tirelessly and don't get enough credit for it."

"She's not a stay-at-home mom," I almost yelled, feeling a little unhinged about it all. How had these people bought into their own propaganda?

Mia waved it away. "You know what I mean."

"I don't," I said, probably overloud, but oh well.

"She's a part-time stay-at-home mom," Mia corrected.

If I were a cartoon, I'd be tearing out my hair in frustration. "She's not. She's running a multimillion-dollar company and has a nanny and a private chef. She's not a stay-at-home mom."

"I don't know why you're fixated on that," Mia said.

I stared at her. "You just said"—I didn't seem to have control of my hands, which were waving around in front of her face unbidden—"stay-at-home moms don't get enough credit."

"They don't," Mia agreed solemnly.

And it was then I caught the spark in her eye. I slumped back against the wall, partly relieved, if I was being honest. "You're fucking with me."

"Indeed," Mia agreed. "Now don't fucking mention divorce again or you're booted."

I weakly saluted and then eyed the tablet that she carried.

"Hey, I'm jonesing for like, ten minutes of screen time," I said. "Can I borrow that just to check my mail?"

She eyed me with derision. "You've been here all of twelve hours."

More like sixteen, but I saw her point. "What if there was an emergency?"

"You didn't leave a way for someone to contact you on the landline here?" she asked, dubious.

I had, but . . . "Come on. I won't erase anything. You can track exactly what I do—and I'm not going to post about Cat off your device."

She glanced toward the kitchen, then sighed. "If anything goes up about Cat, you're gone the second I get the alert for it."

"I may not be Bob Woodward, but I'm also not some tabloid sleaze," I said, nearly giddy now. The addict tempted with a hit of the good stuff.

"Hmm," Mia said, before handing over her tablet. "Seven minutes, and I'm timing you."

"Why seven?" I asked even as I took the thing out of her hands with an embarrassing lack of couth.

"That's how long the dishes will take," Mia said, her attention now on her own phone.

I sank down on a well-placed wall bench and opened a web browser. I typed in "Stefan Moreau + kayak."

Most of the articles were just the facts of what had happened. Everyone seemed to agree it was a tragic accident. I had to dig three pages into the search results before I found a true crime blog talking about foul play.

The writer was a self-described murder-mystery aficionado. They were clearly looking to become the next hot podcast, but that didn't mean what they were saying was wrong.

Odette Moreau appeared to have been a devoted mother to Stefan. She'd never dated or remarried, and from all accounts, her life had been dedicated to her son—Kris's heir. He'd just gotten kicked out of his third school when Odette proposed a kayaking trip, just the two of them. Three days down their favorite river. At first glance, it might've seemed a bit odd, but apparently Odette had been an avid kayaker—whatever that entailed—so it wasn't out of line with her normal behavior.

On the second day of their three-day trip, Stefan had woken up alone to a note that his mother had gone off ahead to check out a fishing spot. About a quarter mile away, he found his mother's kayak and her dead body tangled up in a downed tree. If I were the cops, I would have found that kind of death suspicious, but experts said that with high waters, it was a common enough accident.

The crime blogger conveniently highlighted frequently asked questions—such as, *Did the cops think Stefan killed his mother?*

Apparently, the detectives had decisively ruled that out through some sort of GPS data.

Of course, the blogger didn't think Odette had died of natural causes. If she had, she wouldn't have featured the case on her site. No, she thought Kris had done it, even though he'd provided a solid alibi.

He'd had help, she theorized. A friend or someone he paid.

No one brought up Cat, interestingly enough.

"And . . . time," Mia said, snatching the iPad from my hands without any chance for me to clear my search history. "Now, you have a walk in the orchard to get to. Catriona doesn't like to be kept waiting."

"Aye, aye, captain," I said, jumping to my feet.

Mia didn't look down at the tablet before shooing me on my way.

I wondered if she would.

CHAPTER SIXTEEN

Det. Jamie Alvarez

Detective Jamie Alvarez watched the woman in the interrogation room from behind the mirrored glass for longer than she should have kept her waiting.

The woman shouldn't be in there. She wasn't a suspect. But their tiny police station had limited options, and Jamie wasn't about to talk to her in front of the three officers who had barely gotten their uniforms dirty yet.

Mia Preston's hands shook where she had them pressed to the table. Jamie watched as she clasped them together, then fiddled with one of her rings before dropping her hands into her lap to hide them entirely.

She hadn't said anything, but Jamie could hear her voice, sharp and panicked.

"Oh, God. Oh my God. He's dead. I think he's dead."

Once the operator had asked Mia questions, she'd snapped back into control, giving quick and efficient instructions about how to reach The Orchard.

But that first moment of stunned panic—that was hard to fake. Not impossible, but difficult.

"Tell me about her," Jamie directed Keller, who was all but bouncing on his toes as he stood beside her. Jamie had only investigated three high-profile deaths in her twenty-five years with the station, and here was Keller, less than five years into the gig, with one that would make national headlines.

"Mia Preston, Catriona Bouchard's manager," Keller said in a rush, as if he'd been holding the words carefully in his mouth for too long. "She's thirty-seven, no kids. She lives with the Bouchards full-time and helps run their business."

"What does that entail?"

"Everything from filming content to arranging contracts." Keller handed her a file. "A few traffic tickets, one of which resulted in a warrant because she didn't pay it on time. Other than that, no record."

Jamie flipped through the thin file. On paper, Mia Preston looked like exactly what she'd presented herself to the police as—a smart, capable woman who had worked her way into a cushy position.

"Does she ever appear in Catriona's content?" Jamie asked.

"No," Keller said. "But she actually has her own account. It's mostly geared toward young professionals looking to get into the business. She gives them tips and advice without ever mentioning who she works for."

"Why would anyone take her seriously, then?"

"I watched a few of the videos," Keller said. "She makes sure that it's obvious she works for someone important, even if she keeps her identity and any obvious references out of shot. There were multiple people in the comments that guessed she worked for the Bouchards."

Jamie looked up at that. If someone had been sending Catriona Bouchard disturbing messages, might they have been able to find Mia's account, too? Especially if the person was local—they would have seen Mia in town on the few occasions she'd come in with Catriona. "Could you give me a list of the accounts that commented frequently on Mia's content?"

Keller's brows rose. "Sure thing."

She cleared her throat and went back to the file. "So, her work is limited to Catriona Bouchard's business and doesn't cross with Kristopher's, correct?"

"Right," Keller said. "Ms. Preston gets a percentage of everything Catriona brings in, but she can't touch the source of most of the Bouchards' wealth."

Jamie popped a mint in her mouth and then gestured toward the door. "Let's go see what she has to say, then."

Mia Preston looked up when they entered, her expression inscrutable.

Before Jamie could get a single question out, Mia held up her hand. "You need to look into what happened to Odette Moreau."

It wasn't until after the interview finished that Jamie remembered the rabbit hole she'd nearly gone down.

Mia was being led away by a uniformed rookie, but Jamie hustled to catch them.

"Ms. Preston," Jamie called out, and Mia turned. She had a tissue in her hand, and her eyes were glassy.

Everything about her had screamed "genuinely upset" throughout their whole conversation, and this did nothing to dissuade Jamie of that opinion.

"Did you need something else?" Mia asked. There was zero defensiveness or fear in her voice.

"Just one small thing," Jamie said, her eyes flicking to the uniform. He took the hint and backed off a few steps, giving them the semblance of privacy. "Was there someone messaging Mrs. Bouchard over the past few weeks? In a way that might read as . . . disturbing."

Surprise flickered across Mia's face. It took her a second, but she did nod. "Yes. I . . . Yeah. I forgot about that, honestly. You don't think that has anything to do with Kris's . . . his death, do you?"

"I'm just crossing *t*'s and dotting *i*'s," Jamie rushed to say. "Did you ever figure out who that was? Sending the messages?"

"Holland . . ." She broke off, pressing her fingers to her lips. "Holland had said something about maybe . . ."

"Are you saying Holland Tate figured something out about who the fan might be?"

Again, she shook her head. "No, no. No. I'm sorry, I don't know why I mentioned that."

"What did she say?" Jamie pressed.

But, again, Mia demurred. "It was just a passing thought."

Jamie recognized a brick wall when she smacked into one. "Okay. You all hired a digital expert to track this *fan* down?"

"Yeah, yes," Mia said, sounding crisper now. She dug in her purse for her phone and then for a pen and something to write on.

After jotting down a name and a phone number, she handed the scrap paper over to Jamie. "I don't think she found anything useful. But . . . I'll send her a text to expect your call."

"Did they ever contact you?" Jamie asked. "Through your social media."

Mia tilted her head. "I didn't even think about that."

"You didn't?" Jamie asked, surprised. She was starting to feel like Holland Tate must have in that conversation in the kitchen. "And the digital expert didn't, either?"

"No," Mia said. "Well, she never said anything if she did."

"And you weren't worried?" Jamie asked.

"I'm sure you think me hopelessly naive," Mia said, looking exhausted all of a sudden. The police station lights weren't kind to the bags under her eyes or the lines around her mouth. Her body curled in on itself, sad and defensive. "Or maybe just numb. Catriona received approximately five hundred hate messages a week. Someone saying kind things just didn't break through."

And wasn't that the whole problem with their social media landscape? At least as Jamie could see it. "Okay, thank you."

Mia nodded and walked off with the rookie. Jamie stared at the empty space she'd left behind.

In different circumstances, Jamie might have pressed her harder. She was one of the few people who lived at The Orchard, and just on that fact alone, she was a person of interest.

The fact that she'd been the one to find his body only added to the intrigue.

But these weren't those circumstances.

Kristopher Bouchard had killed himself. There was nothing more to the story than that.

CHAPTER SEVENTEEN

Holland

Now

"Did you buy an orchard because it rhymes with *Bouchard*?" I asked, as Cat and I started walking toward the trees. She was dressed in boyfriend-fit jeans and a flannel shirt that was more fashionable than functional. Over it, she'd thrown a distressed bomber jacket, which made her look way cooler than I'd ever admit to her.

Cat laughed, a belly laugh, perhaps the first real one I'd heard on this trip. I clutched at the recorder in my pocket, glad I had caught it.

"Not when you say it properly," Cat said, and then demonstrated a nearly perfect French accent. The name became so much softer in her mouth than I'd heard from anyone else.

I snagged an apple from the first tree we passed and slid her a look. "You can send me an invoice."

Cat plucked one for herself. "I think we can afford a sample to someone who has promised us fame beyond our wildest imagination."

"Yup," I said around a bite of the golden. "Your audience of millions is going to seem paltry once I publish this article in *Profile Magazine*."

She laughed again. “I miss your snark. Kris is funny, don’t get me wrong, but mostly it’s observational French humor. He does not do self-deprecation.”

“What do you like most about him?” I asked, hating that I had an ulterior motive to asking. Her answer might be telling, more so than a wad of cash hidden beneath tampons.

Cat bit into the apple, a delay tactic if I’d ever seen one. After a stretched-out minute, she said, “I like that he feels like a warrior, protecting me. Protecting our family.”

I glanced in the direction of the fence we couldn’t see. “You seem very focused on security here.”

“When your child is taken from you, it changes a lot of things,” she said.

“How do you like it, really?” I asked. “Being a mother.”

I half expected her to blurt out some platitudes that she thought her audience would want to hear. But she did actually seem to consider the question.

“It’s different than baking a cake,” Cat finally said, which was actually the most perfectly Cat response of all time.

“I think that might be the headline of this piece.”

Cat tossed the core of her apple, without any regard for where it would fall. I followed suit.

“I think you look at me like I’ve sacrificed something,” she said, and I grunted before I could stop myself. She looked at me, curious. “What? Do you disagree?”

I considered whether I should just say I’d stumbled on a branch and keep her talking. But this wasn’t just any profile subject. It was someone who used to be my best friend.

“I’ve been researching this article for a few weeks now,” I said, not to make her feel self-conscious, but to lay out my credentials. “And something I see and hear over and over is that stay-at-home moms and tradwives—”

This time it was Cat who interrupted with a distressed sound. "I'm not a tradwife."

I sighed, because it was tiresome arguing the point that was so blatant to everyone but her. "Wives and mothers who participate in and extol the virtues of more traditional gender roles," I spelled out. Her mouth twisted, but she didn't argue further. "Anyway, they all say stuff like that. Something that equates to 'you're judging me for my choices.' But that choice they think they're being judged for is literally just them doing something women have done—and have been expected to do—for thousands of years. Why is everyone so defensive about it?"

"Oh, please, save me the innocent act," Cat drawled. "Like you aren't wondering why I'm not the head pastry chef at some Michelin-star restaurant right now."

"I'm wondering, sure," I said. "Because you were wildly talented. But why does that always equate to a defensiveness? Why does that equate to me judging you for choosing not to do it?"

"You don't?" Cat asked, as if the answer was so incredibly obvious, and once again, I tried to swallow my frustration.

I inhaled, and actually gave it some thought. I worried, I supposed. That Kris had stolen her professional dream from her. But at the same time, I acknowledged that she had succeeded in ways my Cat would never have imagined possible. When I'd known her, all she'd had to fill her life with beautiful things was a pretty cupcake holder.

"What I think," I started slowly, "is that you're sensing me grappling with the weight of your talent. I'm not judging stay-at-home moms. I think that's wonderful, if that's what they want. But I want you to picture an athlete at the top of her game right before the Olympics quitting something she worked her whole life toward because she was going to get married instead."

"An Olympic-level athlete." Cat seemed amused. And pleased. "I wasn't that good."

"You were," I corrected. "It's not that you've made a choice to be a mother—it's that you worked really damn hard to do one thing and then seemingly threw it away on a whim. That might be what you're reading off me. But it's not judgment for being a stay-at-home mom. And you know why?"

She crossed her arms. "Why?"

"Because you're not a stay-at-home mom," I said, still amazed that these people had fallen for their own talking points. They played tradwives on TV—or iPhones—but they weren't *actually* tradwives. It felt weird to have to remind both Mia and Cat of that. "How much money did you make last year?"

"I don't have any interest in giving you those specifics," she said, all prim and proper, like we were still operating in Savannah's stuffy society, where talking about wealth was more taboo than having an affair.

"But you get my point," I said. "I don't judge women's choices, but I do judge someone who is selling snake oil and telling me it's whiskey. You sell the image of an impossible life for ninety-nine percent of the women who do want to be stay-at-home moms. You peddle a lie, and most people know it's a lie. But some don't."

"Social media is inherently a lie, though," she said, though she didn't sound insulted. More . . . thoughtful. "Everyone makes their lives seem better, easier, and prettier than they are. Come on, we've had a decade and a half of this. Do you think Janet, a human resource manager, is posting shots of herself on the toilet when she got food poisoning on vacation? No, she's posting the ocean-view pictures from her hotel room."

"How many of your followers are men?" I asked, and her eyes narrowed.

"What?"

I waited, because she'd heard me.

"Why does it matter?" she asked, lifting one shoulder. She started walking again.

"Because you're not selling snake oil to women," I said. "They're the ones who know it's fake, and know if they marry Bob down the street and stay home to raise the children, their life isn't going to be roses and rainbows and sourdough bread. But Bob down the street? He doesn't realize that you're selling an image. He thinks you are the ideal woman. He watches your content and doesn't think about the fact that he doesn't have a hundred million dollars in the bank to support that kind of life. He just thinks that the fact that he doesn't have a woman like you means maybe the world is working against him. And that kind of resentment is what drives men to pick up guns and aim them at the bitches who don't love them like they *deserve* to be loved."

She breathed in through flared nostrils. "This is all very professional, Holland."

I wasn't trying to be professional; I was trying to get a reaction. I was trying to get some *honesty* out of her. And the closest I'd come this weekend was by insulting her.

I rolled my eyes. "You wouldn't have let me in here if you just wanted a journalist who was professional."

She stopped again, right by the fence. She stared up at it for a long while.

"It feels like a snowball rolling down a mountain in the Alps," she said. "This life. I didn't start out trying to radicalize men into thinking of me as the ideal, as something they're owed. If that's what you're accusing me of."

"So you're saying you lack agency in your life?" I asked. "That you don't make your own decisions?"

"Right, because I'm the only thing wrong with the world. Hell, you could take the same criticism you made of me and throw it at a Nancy Meyers film from ten years ago," she said. "Or even the apartments on *Friends*. Only millionaires could have lived in that building in real life."

"But people know those are films," I said. "Five-year-olds can distinguish between fiction and reality. It's social media that blurs the lines between the two. Our brains aren't set up for it. We see movies and know there's a script. We see people and think we're seeing their lives. We think we're seeing *them*."

She looked away at that, and I finally felt like I may have scored a point in our argument.

"Men want to go back to the housewives of the fifties because marketing from that time painted women as essentially lobotomized," I continued. This may have started as a tactic, but just like what always happened with anything involving Cat, I was invested now. "Companies were selling convenience *to* housewives. That's what everyone wanted while they were parenting the ten kids they had during the baby boom. To sell convenience to housewives, companies had to make it look glamorous at the same time. And now, seventy years later, we have women cosplaying marketing stereotypes to market pots and pans to women and market a marketing fantasy to men."

"You didn't even follow that," she accused, and I laughed.

"You are too smart not to get my drift," I countered, and she wrapped her arms around herself.

"It feels like an avalanche," she said again, quietly this time. "You can't stop it once it starts. It just picks up speed."

I stared at the fence, sensing that she wasn't just talking about gender roles right now.

"You can stop it, you know," I said quietly. "Any time. It might seem difficult, but if you want off the ride—"

"I don't," she cut in, sharp and certain.

I choked back my frustration. "So complaining about the inevitability of it all is just to . . . what? Make yourself feel better?"

Cat whirled on me, breathing heavily. For a second, I thought she was going to lay into me. But then she seemed to collect herself. "Oh my god."

I shifted, caught off guard. "What?"

"I forgot how fun this was," she said with a little laugh. Then she shook her head. "I mean, maybe not fun. But exhilarating. I love Kris, but he's boring. All he wants to do is praise me and talk about the business. The kids can barely string more than a couple words together, Anna can't go a full sentence without mentioning her boyfriend, and Mia is . . . well, I pay her. I don't really have anyone to fight with."

I pressed my lips together. "Well, at least I'm good for something."

She giggled at that, and then before we knew it, we were laughing together.

"It must be hard to make friends out here," I commented once we'd trailed off into amused huffs.

"Yeah," she agreed for once. "It is."

A branch snapped.

Cat ducked like a gun had gone off.

Jumpy, my brain supplied, eager to notice things. Because *jumpy* was about a half step away from *living in fear.*

I raised my brows as she straightened, a flush of pink on her cheeks.

In the meantime, Stan the guard stepped out from the shadows. "Sorry, Mrs. Bouchard. Didn't mean to scare ya."

"It's quite all right," Cat said, despite the fact that her knuckles were white where they clutched her arms. This was someone with too much cortisol flowing through their bloodstream on a daily basis.

"I wanted to check on this section," Stan said, nodding toward the fence. "Mr. Bouchard said it was dead on his security system, and we can't get someone out here to check on it until Monday."

Cat glanced over her shoulder. The fence out here was wire and apparently monitored somehow by Kris.

"He did mention something like that," Cat said, sounding absent-minded. But then she looked over at me as if to check whether I was following the conversation. A strange certainty settled in my chest. What were the odds she'd "wandered" to the only part of the fence that couldn't be monitored on a security system? A dead portion that had to be checked in person to see if it was still intact.

I reminded myself that this wasn't a horror movie, simply because it had the ingredients of one.

Yet I couldn't help but wonder about that question that ate at me.

Why had she finally agreed to let me come?

And why had the only option she'd given me been this particular weekend?

CHAPTER EIGHTEEN

Cat

Then

Holland and I loved parties. Not *partying*, like your average twenty-three-year-olds, the ones who slathered glitter body lotion all over their exposed limbs and stumbled around a club looking for a hookup, all the while spilling their dollar Long Islands all over the sticky floor.

No, we loved *parties*.

We were fairly poor, as much as I didn't like to admit it, as was anyone we invited. But we had our apartment and certain standards, and we at least tried to act more civilized than we were.

Those other girls had beer pong.

We had *themes.*

Tonight's was *The Great Gatsby*, which I had worried guests would deem cliché. But who didn't like glam and glitz and flapper dresses and wearing a headband just wrong enough to look like it was out of the twenties?

I dressed as Daisy, because that was who I'd always wanted to be—someone a wealthy-beyond-belief man lusted for above all else. Someone who'd nabbed the rich, if philandering, husband and was still able to drive other men to madness with my beauty alone.

Holland dressed as Gatsby, because she was funnier than I was.

She looked phenomenal, too, in her emerald velvet suit, with only skin beneath. Her hair was slicked back, but instead of making her look masculine, it simply highlighted her cheekbones. She yelled about rotten crowds and fast women and green lights all night long, and everyone found her absolutely delightful.

Including Benji.

"Well, she's getting her MFA. Are you actually surprised she knows quotes from the novel?" I asked, after he repeated for the third or fourth time how impressed he was at Holland's ability to spout passages at will.

He had, of course, come as the Tom to my Daisy, but that was hardly saying anything. The men never committed to the themes as much as the girlfriends did. Benji had done a decent job by breaking out his white linen summer suit and picking up a hat from a thrift store, but I could tell his heart wasn't in it.

That was . . . his heart wasn't in it until he saw Holland, and the flash of belly button she kept giving everyone as she swanned through the room.

Now she stood in front of us, her eyes glossy-drunk as she swayed on her feet.

"Poor kitten," I mused. "You look toasted. You want a nap?"

She giggled and shook her head, her hand waving the plastic cocktail glasses we'd bought for us alone—everyone else had to use red Solo cups. We had taste but it was paired with sense.

"It's too early, Daisy," she said, the words slurring together. I exchanged a look with Benji, who'd gone a bit red at the sight of her.

Holland had learned what many girls did when they had a body like hers. Sometimes, hiding a lot of it and putting only some of it on display was actually more enticing than if she strode in here in a tube top and miniskirt. It was the way the jacket fell open and then closed with the sweep of her arms that made the look interesting.

"I think a nap," I said crisply. I was not drunk in the slightest—nor did I ever plan on imbibing to the point where I would be slurring my words. I typically nursed one cocktail throughout the evening so as not to be deemed a prude, but letting loose was not something I had any interest in.

"Nooo." Holland pouted. But whereas friends in the past would have lashed out at me with anything from *killjoy* to *bitch*, or worse, Holland didn't seem to have it in her. She put up a few more token protests as Benji and I guided her to her room, which was off-limits to the guests.

Her eyes were closed before her head hit the pillow.

A few people asked about her as the night went on, but she hadn't invited anyone she was particularly interested in, and everyone was nearly as drunk as she was, so no one went looking for her.

"The roommate's working out, huh?" Michi asked. I remembered she'd been on the phone with me during that awful day I'd been interviewing applicants.

"Thank god," I muttered. "It could have been bad."

"I can't believe Amanda did you so dirty," Michi said. "Did she ever apologize for leaving you without even paying the next month's rent?"

"No," I said, though, honestly, I wouldn't have known. I'd blocked her on my phone and all my social media accounts. "Doesn't matter. We've moved on to bigger and better things."

"You have," she said, clinking her glass against mine with the enthusiasm of someone who had been overserved. And then she wiggled her brows. "In more than one department."

I followed where she was looking to see Benji talking with a group of beefed-up guys in polos. They hadn't even given the theme the old college try. I wished I could take back the cupcakes they'd already eaten.

"He's not quite as rich as Mark," I said, the taste of my ex's name in my mouth sour enough that it forced me into a sip of my cosmo.

"Yeah, but he's not a pretentious asshat either," Michi pointed out.

"Fair," I said. "So tell me about the new waiter you hate."

Michi readily obliged, as I knew she would. My secret theory was that she wanted to hook up with said new waiter, but it didn't take a genius to guess that. It was the easiest way to distract Michi from any more questions about Mark, and I would leap on it whether I was right about her crush or not.

I didn't actually listen to her. She'd been talking about this man for weeks now, and I was quite bored by the topic.

Instead, I watched Benji. I watched him glance toward Holland's closed door. Once, twice. The third time, he didn't look away.

Finally, he disentangled himself from the group with ease, working his way over to Holland's bedroom, before slipping inside.

Rage surged into my bloodstream, copper and hot and tangy. My hand curled around the stem of my plastic cocktail glass, and I was thankful it wasn't glass. It would have snapped beneath the pressure.

Michi blathered on, unaware that I was counting the seconds that Benji was inside.

Forty-two.

I exhaled as he stepped out and then closed the door behind him, glancing around as he did.

Before he got to me, I quickly turned my full attention back to Michi, laughing—at the wrong spot, given her startled expression. But Michi didn't matter.

I tried to convince myself Benji wouldn't have been able to do anything to Holland in that short amount of time alone with her. But my worst devils were whispering to me. He could have taken a picture. He could have palmed one of her breasts, to get the feel of the weight of it, as opposed to mine, which could never be called a handful. He could have kissed her. Maybe he was obsessed; maybe he was psychotic.

Maybe I was cursed to forever be attracted to the very scum of the earth. How many would that be now? Three? Four? I hadn't even dated all that much, to rack up such a list.

"Hey," he said, as he stopped beside me. He bent close to my ear, knowing I wouldn't care what Michi was saying. "I just checked on Holland to make sure she didn't asphyxiate."

I would have thought that would have extinguished the rage, but it had built too fast and too strong, and it had become a wildfire in me.

Of course he would say he was checking on her. He knew I might have caught him either going in or coming out. He'd want to get ahead of my paranoia.

He hadn't, though. All he'd done was fuel it.

"Fuck me," I whispered back, and his eyes dilated.

"Everyone's here," he said. But it wasn't true. It was late enough that a lot of people were starting to filter out.

"Don't be a pussy," I said, and his hand flexed on my back. "Fuck me so everyone can hear."

He liked when I talked like that. It had surprised me, if I was being honest. I guessed it had something to do with the contrast to my prim-and-proper aesthetic.

"Shit," he said, because he wasn't like me. He couldn't talk dirty. He was a nice boy.

But he liked to pretend he wasn't.

We slinked off to my bedroom, and he had his hands on me before the door even closed. Just what I'd goaded him into.

I didn't try to be quiet.

By the time we made it to the bed, I knew I'd have bruises on my skin—they always showed up so easily. He would look at them later with shame, but then he'd press into them any time he needed to get off. I remembered that first day I'd ambushed him outside the hospital. To him, then, I'd been a domestic abuse survivor. And now he put fingerprints on my body.

I didn't know what that said about either of us, psychologically speaking. I didn't think he actually had any interest in hurting me—it was just the rush of adrenaline he got from it that was so heady.

I didn't know what it said about me that I liked it.

I would never let a man put me in the hospital again, but this? This was *good.*

It chased away the rage like nothing else could.

He pushed into me and I took his hand. He whimpered because he knew what I was about to do.

I put his fingers around my throat.

They flexed and then squeezed, his thumb finding the soft spot right beneath my jaw.

I cried out, which must have covered the sound of the door opening.

Benji froze, but I didn't. I wrapped my thighs up around his ass, and shifted just enough to see Holland standing in the doorway, backlit by our now mostly empty apartment.

"Cat?" she asked, her voice so small and scared, like that of a child.

Benji's hand flexed against my throat, tightening, and I gasped reflexively.

And Holland . . . Holland ran.

CHAPTER NINETEEN

Holland

Now

After the walk in the orchard, Cat and I made pies.

And it felt good. This was what I had been expecting from the weekend, if I was being honest. The kitchen was warm and smelled of spices, the children were all "helping," and soft music was piped in from a sound system that had clearly been wired into the walls.

Cat—wearing the baby, of course—laughed and smiled and directed children in an effortless manner that never veered too sharply into dictatorial.

She had always been good in kitchens, a quirk to her otherwise sharp, demanding personality that won her allies nearly immediately when she worked at The Bistro. Our mutual friend Michi had marveled over it time and again because it had never come across as an act. As long as you were competent at your job, Cat respected your place in her space.

And her children were, of course, incredibly competent.

As I pretended to help—but really just worked on my third cup of utterly divine coffee—I wondered how painful it was to Mia not to be filming all this. It would have made for a perfect video, spliced with shots of the children's hands working the butter into the flour for the crust and slicing apples picked right from their own orchard. They were making the pies in Bouchard pans that were so fall and aesthetically pleasing this really could have been an ad from a big-spend magazine campaign.

Just as I had the thought, Gabriel, the seven-year-old, spilled a glass of milk all over the butcher-block counter. I watched as it rushed toward me, but the soporific vibes in the kitchen had dulled my reaction times.

The milk splattered all over my jeans, the warmth of it an unpleasant reminder that it had probably been inside another creature not too long ago.

Gabriel stared in open-mouthed horror before his lower lip wobbled. Tears came next, and he curled into himself as he wailed his apologies.

Cat rushed to him while shooting me apologetic grimaces. "Buddy, it's okay. It was an accident."

"Papa's gonna be"—big gasp of air—"mad."

Just one more confirmation in a long line that Kris had a temper so volatile that the children had noticed.

Cat wrinkled her nose. "No he's not, sweetheart. It was an accident."

"He was"—gasp—"so mad"—gasp—"I didn't mean to—"

"Darling, that was when you dumped milk on your sister's head on purpose," Cat said, meeting my eyes and shaking her head, as if to say, *Kids, am I right?*

Gabriel continued to wail, and I stood, trying not to let any droplets slide off my jeans onto the floor.

"Hey, I get to do an outfit change midday, like a pop star," I joked to ease the tension. I thought that was what kids liked, though I didn't have enough experience with them to be sure.

Gabriel blinked at me with big, wet eyes. "I don't care about you."

I couldn't help it—I laughed. It was such a Cat thing to say. Even her lips twitched, though she tried to maintain a stern expression.

"That's not nice," she tried.

His lip wobbled.

"Well, pop stars don't care about little boys' tantrums either," I said, to tease him out of it.

The fun part about not having kids was that it was not my problem if it worked or not. I winked at Cat and then exited stage left.

I skipped up the stairs and took the right to my bedroom. Then I had to suppress a surprised—and unattractive—yelp when I opened my door.

Jeremy was sprawled on the bed, looking good and settled, as if he'd been there for hours. He glanced up when I entered. "Finally."

I quickly stepped inside, my pulse skittering against the insides of my wrists. But I covered my shock with an easy "Sorry to keep you waiting, my liege."

His eyes darkened. "I don't know what that means, but it sounds hot."

"Oh my god," I said, the rest of my tension finally dissipating. I shrugged out of my button-up and threw it at him. "Why are you in my room? And, no, we're not hooking up."

He sat up, affronted by the mere suggestion. An affronted labradoodle.

"I'm not here for that," he said, but then sort of shrugged. "I mean, I wouldn't say no—"

"I am. Saying no, that is," I said clearly, even as I shimmied out of my jeans. His gaze tracked down my thighs, and I showed off a little bit because who didn't like hot men checking them out?

"So, you got me thinking," he said, settling back onto my pillow, watching through hooded eyes as I searched my suitcase for a fairly similar pair of jeans to the ruined ones.

"About . . ." I prodded.

"Steffie's mom," he said, and then he grinned and banged his head up and down, singing a few bars of "Stacy's Mom," which made me think he was a little older than I'd originally calculated. "Anyway. I googled it—"

"You have a phone?" I cut in, not sure why I was surprised.

He held it up in victory. "Yeah. Service is shit and I only have Wi-Fi at the carriage house, not here, but we're not Amish."

Debatable, but still intriguing. And I liked the knowledge that I had access to a phone I wouldn't have to beg for.

"Gimme," I said, holding my hand out, and he shook his head.

"Doesn't work well in the main house," he said, and I realized he'd already mentioned that. I'd been too caught up in my joyous haze for that to process.

That was disappointing, but I'd take what I could get. "Okay, so what did you find on the ole Google machine?"

I was guessing it was exactly what I had found, but now I could get him intrigued to dig further, maybe.

"Get this," he said with the drama of a midnight-talk-show host who only reviewed the trashiest of reality shows. "Odette was suing Kris at the time of her freak accident."

I sat down in the chair by the window. "What?"

"Yup," he said, seeming pleased by my surprise. Which he should've been—it was genuine. I had done a ton of research, and I hadn't found that. "It had to do with stocks and Kris's company. I couldn't understand it all, but bottom line was she thought she was owed more money after the divorce. A lot more money."

"Why did it take her so long to file?" I asked.

He shrugged. "It takes time to get your ducks in a row?"

I whistled, low and long. "But Kris had an alibi for that weekend."

"Did Mia?" Jeremy tossed out. "Or Cat—"

I held up a hand. "Cat did not kill her husband's ex-wife."

But Mia was an intriguing possibility. Especially if she was having an affair with Kris. And he was mentoring her on the business side of things—at least according to Cat. If Odette had challenged for a large slice of Kris's profits or even his company, Mia could have felt threatened enough to go along with Kris's plan to get rid of Odette.

"I don't know, man. I could see Catriona doing it easy," Jeremy said, drawing out the *easy* until it had far too many syllables. "She's got ice in her veins."

I couldn't exactly refute that. "Wouldn't she have been in France with Kris?"

"Wait, was that his alibi?" he said, looking back down at the phone as if he could search that.

"He flew out on the red-eye the night before Odette and Steffie left for the trip," I said.

"Huh. Well. I don't remember if Catriona was with him."

None of the articles had mentioned it, either. Maybe that meant she hadn't been.

But they would have asked her for one, wouldn't they have? The current wife seemed like she would be a prime suspect in the ex-wife's suspicious death.

"The police would have checked that," I said. "Anyway, whether or not you believe she could kill someone, Cat is *not* the type to go kayaking. She would have figured out a way to do that without getting in a death trap on water."

Jeremy laughed so hard he had to smoosh his face in my pillow.

"What?" I asked, somewhat annoyed that I had probably said something ridiculous but didn't know what.

He peeked up at me. "You kind of just admitted you think she could have killed someone."

"Don't be ridiculous," I snapped, though he was right, of course. "Anyway, if it was anyone, it was probably Steffie. That makes way more sense than Cat killing her. Or even Mia."

"You really think someone offed Odette?" Jeremy asked, his voice once again slipping too close to a Bugsy Malone impression for my liking. I wouldn't have minded sleeping with him again, and I didn't want to get the *ick* before that happened.

"I don't know. Probably not," I said. I knew we'd had the conversation before, but that had been in half measures. I decided to just go for it. "Hey, do you ever get the impression Kris is . . . scaring the children? Or maybe Cat?"

"Like is he punching walls and shit?"

"And shit, yeah," I said.

"Nah, he's French," Jeremy said.

"Aren't they supposed to be passionate?"

He shrugged. "Whatever kind Kris is, it's like the cold psychopath kind of French guy."

"Oh, jeez." That was more confirmation than I'd been expecting. "You mean he acts like a rich guy."

Jeremy snapped and pointed at me. "That's it."

"Right, let's not malign the entire country of France then," I said, and he grinned, unrepentant.

"I've worked for worse, I've worked for better," he said with the practicality of someone who really did need a paycheck. "He gets real quiet when he's pissed, though. That's all I'm saying."

"Have you ever pissed him off?" I asked.

"I brought a hookup back here once when I first started," he said, and then winced at me like I would care that he had slept with other people before even meeting me. I made a face that I hoped conveyed how ridiculous he was being. "The guy before Stan let us in. Kris was standing in the doorway the next morning when we woke up. It was creepy as hell, dude."

I shivered while picturing it.

"He was chill enough to the chick," Jeremy said. "But he fired the guard who let us both in. And told me about all the people he knew, how I would never find work in this industry if I ever did something like that again."

"That seems like an overreaction."

Jeremy shrugged. "Mrs. Bouchard told me later they'd had an uptick in online threats just before it happened. The chick I hooked up with knew who they were and apparently posted and tagged a picture of their house after we'd hooked up."

"Ew," I said, and he nodded sagely.

"I guess celebs have to deal with that shit all the time," he said. "That's why they're on Raya."

"I don't know what that is," I admitted, and he smirked.

"Exactly," he said, pleased with himself. When I glared, he added, "It's a dating app but for like rich celebrity-type people."

"Also, ew," I said, though that was less gross than someone coming in here to spend the night with Jeremy just so she could share content about Cat's private space.

So in the end, it actually seemed like a somewhat understandable reaction from Kris, if a little extreme.

"Is that the only time?" I asked.

"Yup," Jeremy said, with a grin. "I'm a good boy. He doesn't get mad at me."

I wrinkled my nose, and he straight up laughed.

"For real, though," he said. "I've only seen him like, psychopathic a couple times."

"At Cat ever?"

He considered that. "I don't . . . I don't think so."

"Really?" I asked, because I did *not* buy into the picture-perfect relationship, even if it wasn't abusive per se. Everyone got in fights. "Ever?"

Jeremy tilted his head back and forth, and then his eyes lit up. "Actually, you're right. Once. Oh man, I haven't thought about that in forever."

I couldn't help but lean forward. "Do you know what it was about?"

"She left the orchard without telling anyone," he said. "For a full day, apparently didn't even write a note."

"Was that unusual?"

"Yeah. Kris almost called the cops, except he knew they wouldn't care until she'd been gone for much longer," he said. "But he rounded us all up and questioned us about anything we knew."

"How did she get out?" I asked. Because I was still caught up on the fact that Kris was the only one with the code.

"Oh, that was when we got distributed a security code weekly," he said. "That's when they changed it to daily codes. Now we have to ask if we want to go out."

That distracted me. "Does it bother you? Feeling like an elementary student who needs a pass to go to the bathroom."

Jeremy did some kind of move that meant, *Sort of but eh.* "I like the job too much and am paid too well to care. Which is probably how they keep anyone from having complaints about it."

"Fair," I said. "Did anything happen to Cat?"

"Nah, she came back, and apologized for the trouble. She showed us the note she left—it must have slipped off the oven," he said. "She'd gone for a spa day or something like that, and hadn't had her phone. I wouldn't have remembered it, but I thought he was going to kill us all there for a second."

"But just to put a fine point on it, he *was* angry at Cat?" I asked, because that made a difference. "Not just scared about her whereabouts."

"You know, good point," Jeremy said. "He got a Liam Neeson, 'I'm going to teach you a lesson for taking my daughter' vibe going that whole day. But he didn't yell at her."

"He doesn't yell, though," I murmured. And he'd corrected his error by revoking the security code from everyone. Maybe it had been his wake-up call that Cat could just simply walk off his compound, no one the wiser.

"Right," Jeremy said, though he now seemed a bit confused about everything. I decided to cut him loose before he burned his two brain cells to dust.

"I'm sure there's nothing strange going on," I said. "Odette died in a freak accident, Kris is a faithful, loving husband, and Cat likes a spa day every once in a while."

"Sure," Jeremy said, but something about him had changed. And he was truly invested now. I wondered at the monster I'd created. "I'm gonna keep looking."

I laughed. "You let me know what you find."

"Maybe," he said, bending to kiss the top of my head as he passed. It was sweet. He was sweet. "Or maybe you'll have to wait to read it in the eventual police report."

CHAPTER TWENTY

Det. Jamie Alvarez

Jamie's chair groaned as she sat down at her desk.

Her tongue slid over her teeth as she considered what to do.

It wouldn't hurt to look to see if Mia's suggestion to check out Kristopher's ex-wife had any merit to it.

She pulled up Google first and typed in "Odette Moreau." She could find the police report, she was sure, but she didn't even know what state the death had occurred in, and, honestly, plain written articles were sometimes faster than parsing through police jargon.

The results were all news sites, with headlines including words like *tragic*, *accident*, and *freak drowning*.

It had happened six months ago.

"Jesus," Jamie breathed out and then apologized to her—deceased—grandmother for the blasphemy. She could still feel the echo of the woman's ruler on her knuckles.

Jamie made quick work of finding the official report. She laughed when she saw who one of the officers on the case had been. Fate and the universe were on her side—the man had worked at their station before transferring to North Carolina a decade or so back.

She grabbed for her phone and dialed his precinct. A few minutes later Shawn O'Malley boomed a hello that sent her straight back to boisterous pubs and cold pints and sticky floors.

They shot the shit for a minute, but he must have seen the news.

"You're calling about that Odette Moreau case, huh?" he said, after the first moment of silence.

"I was pointed in that direction, yes." If this were some other detective, she might have worried more about pressuring him into revealing details, but Shawn couldn't have been pressured if there were a gun to his head. "Looks like a freak accident, though, huh?"

He sighed a sigh she recognized from other cops. *Yes,* that sigh said. *But that's not what I think really happened.* "You've read the details?"

"Yeah, the basics," she said.

"Well, here's the thing," O'Malley said. "When the kid woke up that morning? Odette was already gone."

Jamie scrambled to figure out what he wasn't saying, before it hit her. That big sigh. "She left a note?"

"Yup," he drawled. "Now, it didn't say she was about to go off herself. But it was, uh, pretty emotional."

"And by that you mean . . ."

"She signed it, and I quote, 'I love you forever, my baby boy. Never forget that,'" he said, sounding awkward for the first time.

Well, that sucked for the kid. Why hadn't she gone on the trip by herself? Why unleash years' worth of trauma on him when she must have known he would be the one to find her?

"What a shitty way to kill yourself, if you're going to do it."

"Ah-yup," he agreed.

"Is that what you think happened?" she asked. "No chance there was foul play?"

"Always a chance," he said. "But the ex-husband was out of the country. The kid was . . . inconsolable. I'm not sure he would have had the temperament to hold his mom underwater for as long as he would have needed to."

“You never know,” she pointed out.

“True, he might have gone partially catatonic from the shock of it,” he said. “There was also some GPS stuff they figured out that put him at the campsite at the time. Some people said it was imprecise so they can maintain doubt. But honest, it never seemed all that likely that he did it. You would have had to have seen him after to know what I’m saying.”

Jamie trusted Shawn, she did.

But . . .

There was new information now.

The truth of the matter was, Stefan Moreau had been at the scene of both his parents’ deaths.

And that? That trumped gut instinct every time.

The boys from State arrived.

Detective Roland Boyd led the charge. Jamie had worked with him before, liked him as much as she could like any of the boys from State.

Keller hummed at her elbow as the two of them watched the officers head toward the chief’s office. Jamie wasn’t even sure Keller realized he was making the excited sound a puppy did when they saw their owners, but she found it amusing enough that she wasn’t about to be the one to tell him.

“You keep his poster above your bed?” she asked, which was the closest she’d get to it.

Keller scowled theatrically. “Just because you have all the ambition of a lumpfish doesn’t mean we’re all happy languishing away in Bumblefuck, Freezetown.”

“You don’t wear enough layers,” she told him, like she’d been telling him for years now. He never wanted to believe the problem was with his decision-making instead of the “god-awful state” he’d ended up in. “Come on.”

Keller followed her so closely that he stumbled when she paused outside the chief's door. She was the lead on the case, so she should have been invited into the room already. There was no reason to hesitate.

But she did. *Just because you have all the ambition of a lumpfish . . .*

That wasn't true. She did have ambition. But she also had a teenage daughter, who'd had to take priority for the past fifteen years.

This case, though . . . it was big, and it was *hers*, at least for as long as she stood outside the door. The minute she went inside, it might be taken away from her.

Jamie took a breath and entered without knocking. The chief glanced up, but didn't pause as he gave the boys from State a rundown.

When he was done, Detective Boyd looked over toward Jamie. "Any other thoughts?"

"Stefan Moreau," she said. "He's Kristopher Bouchard's son."

"He had quite a few kids, didn't he?" Boyd asked, his eyes back on the file he held rather than her.

"This was from a previous marriage," Jamie said, trying not to rush or sound too eager about her own pet theory. "With a woman who died six months ago."

That got Boyd's full attention, along with the chief's. "Cause?"

"Mysterious kayaking accident," Jamie said, making it sound as absurd as it was. "The lead was an old buddy of mine. He thinks it was suicide, but could never get enough to prove it."

At that, she lost his interest. Boyd went back to the file.

"And Stefan Moreau was the only other person there when she died," Jamie said. The whole room went quiet. "Jeremy Dawson is our next interview. I think we should ask him about Stefan."

"Where's the boy now?" Boyd asked.

"With an advocate at the hotel three blocks that way," she said, tilting her head in the direction, as if it mattered.

"Do you think he had something to do with all this?" Boyd asked, his eyes boring into hers.

"I think once is coincidence," she said. "Twice?"

Boyd hummed. "Jeremy Dawson is the . . ."

"Live-in chef," Keller answered. Eager to add something.

Boyd's eyes flicked to Keller, then back to Jamie. "Do you guys mind waiting in the observation room while we talk to him? We don't want to overwhelm him with people."

Jamie let out a quiet breath, disappointed, a little furious. But the chief was already nodding along with that plan.

Before Boyd went into the interview room, he tapped her shoulder with the folder. "Thanks for the tip."

Keller fumed beside her as they set up shop behind the mirrored glass.

Boyd was overly pleasant to Jeremy, playing up the fact that all they wanted to do was get timelines straight and tick boxes.

Jeremy, meanwhile, was completely relaxed, his bloodshot eyes giving away why that might be.

"Did you ever know Kris to be abusive?" Boyd asked after a few softballs about Jeremy's time working at the Bouchards' orchard.

"I never saw him hit her, if that's what you're asking," Jeremy said, looking a bit more alert than he had before. "But he has this cold rage about him. One time Mrs. Bouchard left for the day, and when she came back, he was furious with her just because she hadn't left a note. He grabbed her and shook her and everything."

Jamie stilled.

The answer scratched at the back of her skull, though she couldn't say why. Something was . . . *off* about it. She glanced at Keller, who, while annoyed at being relegated to the audience, hadn't so much as shifted. If he'd picked up on anything, his expression didn't reveal it.

Boyd nodded and moved the conversation along. Clearly, he hadn't heard anything weird in that answer, either.

Jamie shook her head.

She was probably imagining it. She was as bad as Keller. She wanted the boys from State to take her seriously, and they so clearly didn't.

Detective Boyd didn't mention Stefan Moreau even once during the entire interview.

CHAPTER TWENTY-ONE

HOLLAND

Now

The pies distracted Cat enough that I slipped back into the kitchen unnoticed. By the time she had them all laid out, I was back on my counter, coffee mug in hand, like I hadn't just taken twenty minutes to change into a new pair of jeans.

Cat seemed to be taking the nonconfrontational approach to my disappearing acts, which I appreciated. At some point, I would probably push her too far, but I hadn't yet.

The look-alike au pair—Anna, she had a name—had shown up in the meantime and had the children occupied at the end of the table.

The windows were fogged up a little from the heat, the orchard cool and magical behind them. The air smelled of cinnamon, and Cat hummed to herself as she sliced up the pies.

And in the middle of all that quiet, serene loveliness, I decided to drop a grenade.

"Does Kris know about Fleur?" I asked softly.

Metal hit tile as one of the pans Cat had been working with clattered to the floor. The red mush that had been so beautiful only seconds ago now looked like masticated guts.

Anna was upon us in an instant. “Oh my goodness, Mrs. Bouchard.”

The girl dropped to her knees and tried scooping the pie up with her hands. One of the toddlers started to cry. Mia even peeked into the kitchen from where she must have retreated to her office.

Cat hadn’t moved. She just stood there, staring at me, her face pale.

The baby on her chest *also* started to cry, and that shook her from her daze. In a few efficient movements, she unwrapped Vivienne and handed her off to Anna, who took her despite her messy hands. Once divested of the child, Cat gripped my arm, and pulled me out of the kitchen with a surprising amount of force.

Spurred on by what seemed to be blind rage, she dragged me through the hallway and into Kris’s office.

I hadn’t been one hundred on my guess. I had been pretty sure with the timing of everything that Fleur must’ve been the baby Cat tested positive with the day Benji had died. But the stress of all that could have triggered a miscarriage, and then she could have gotten pregnant again quickly after marrying Kris. Like he probably believed had happened.

And Fleur looked exactly like Cat.

Cat’s reaction was confirmation enough, though.

Most of me was thrilled by the reaction I’d finally managed to yank out of Cat, but a smaller part of me started immediately cataloging the forbidden inner sanctum. I wondered if she’d even thought much about where she was going—probably operating on pure instinct and the need for privacy.

Everything about the space screamed masculinity in the same way the rest of the house whispered how feminine it was. The chairs were dark leather, the bar cart gold and loaded down with heavy crystal decanters, the photography on the walls black-and-white landscapes.

Cat stared at me, her arms wrapped around herself, her knuckles white and her breathing labored. And it hadn't been the exertion of pulling me along that had done that. She was visibly shaken.

Never had I been more sure not only that Fleur was Benji's but that Kris did not, in fact, know.

"That was completely inappropriate to bring up in front of my kids," Cat said, her voice tight as a wire.

"They didn't hear me," I reassured her, though I didn't think she was angry because of that. There had been no way that could have been a concern, considering how quietly I'd asked and how far away they'd been, none of them paying us an ounce of attention. But it let her be mad at me for something.

"You don't know kids," she said, and that was true, I didn't. "They hear everything."

"I'm sorry," I said. "But I thought . . . well, Kris must have done the math? It can't actually be that big of a secret?"

She inhaled so her nostrils flared. It was an unattractive quirk she had, and I kind of loved seeing it because it reminded me she was human.

"We had a whirlwind courtship," she got out through gritted teeth.

"So Kris doesn't know that Fleur—"

Cat cut me off. "She's his daughter."

Her eyes were fierce, all the uncertainty gone from her face. Again, she said, "She's his daughter."

I held up my hands. "Okay. Sorry, I was just—"

Again, she cut me off. This time it was with razor-edge precision. "You were just what, Holland? A concerned friend?"

I stared at her, because we both knew what the obvious answer was. I was a journalist. I wanted the story. Even if that wasn't the full story, it would be easy for her to assume.

"Right," she said and huffed out a breath as she looked away. "I don't know why I keep thinking this is anything other than some opportunistic vulture come to pick apart my life."

I had pretty thick skin, but I had to admit that stung. "I'm not a vulture, Cat."

"It's Catriona," she said.

I didn't know why I was resistant to calling her that, other than that if I called this woman, this woman who was so clearly Catriona Bouchard, Cat enough times, maybe I'd get my best friend back.

That was silly. She was no more her twenty-three-year-old self than I was mine.

"Look, I don't want that to be the story," I said. "I'm not going to put information about Fleur in the article."

Just like I wouldn't put Steffie in. Part of me kind of wished I cared just as little about her as she thought I did.

She didn't relax at all, and I had to admit I wouldn't either, in her position. "And I should trust you why?"

That was fair. The last time we'd talked, she'd thought I had betrayed her—that had been ten years ago, and she had no reason to think I'd matured into anything but . . . well. A vulture.

"You don't have to trust me as a person," I said slowly. "But we wouldn't run that kind of story in *Profile Magazine.* The only people interested in that would be tabloid trash."

"Yeah, but you could sell the information. Or make some viral video spilling all the tea on me," she said, and her chin went up. "You've always been jealous of me."

I laughed, and it landed heavy in the silence between us. "You don't even believe that."

Her mouth pursed, and I could tell I was right. She'd liked me back then because I *hadn't* been jealous of her. She would have found that boring. If anything, I had the sense she'd been envious of me sometimes.

"Look, I'm not trying to be mean," I said. "But it doesn't seem like you have friends."

"I have friends," she snapped reflexively, like she'd banged an elbow.

"Okay," I said, trying not to make it sound like I didn't believe her, even though we both knew I didn't. "Okay. But you don't seem to have friends to whom you would tell a secret. Or with whom you'd share your hardships. And I know I'm a journalist here to write a profile on you, but once upon a time I was that person. For you. I was that person."

That muscle memory of *us* twinged again. It was so strange how much leeway society gave us to mourn romantic relationships but then acted like breakups between friends just never happened or never affected anyone if they did. They could be just as—or more—devastating.

"I *was* trying to surprise you a little," I admitted, because even a little truth always made everything else seem more believable. "I think you've gotten really good at presenting yourself to the world in a certain way. But that means you've built up thick walls, and I'm struggling to see inside them. And that's kind of a requirement of the job."

"So you went with the shock jock route," she said, but I could tell the ice had started to thaw.

"Thick walls sometimes require battering rams," I said, with a shrug. Coming off too apologetic wouldn't work—she knew me too well for that. I had to nail this ending.

Cat bit her lip as she assessed me. "Kris doesn't know. If that wasn't obvious."

"Okay," I said, hardly able to believe we'd emerged unscathed from my grenade. "She looks just like you."

"Thankfully," Cat said, though I wasn't sure it would have mattered. People tended to see what they thought they should.

"I take it Kris wouldn't react well," I said, tiptoeing toward what I really wanted to know.

"He would be . . ." She trailed off, shaking her head, her eyes going distant. "He can't find out."

"Okay," I said again. "Will you ever tell Fleur?"

"Kris is her father," Cat said. "That's all that matters."

I tried to figure out a way to press harder, but we were interrupted by a knock on the door.

Cat tensed, seeming to realize we were in Kris's office for the first time. "You're not supposed to be in here."

"Right," I said, and felt magnanimous in not pointing out that she'd been the one to choose the location for this particular conversation.

Cat shook her head again and called out, "Come in."

It was Mia, because of course it was Mia. The shadow hovering at the edge of Cat's life.

She eyed us both before turning her full attention to Cat. "Are you all right?"

I wanted to drop another grenade right there, just to blow everything to shreds. *Are you sleeping with Kris?*

It would at least be interesting to see what reaction would slip out from behind that cool disdain.

"Yes, thank you, Mia," Cat said, back to completely composed. If Mia and Kris did have something going on, it wasn't affecting the way Cat treated the woman.

The Cat of old, I was pretty sure, would have found a way to poison her soup by now if that was a thing that was really happening and not just in my and Jeremy's imaginations.

"The children are a little restless," Mia said.

"I'll get back to them, thank you," Cat said, but in a way that made it clear it was *her* decision.

"Could I grab Holland real quick?" Mia asked, and Cat smirked, because she knew Mia was about to read me the riot act.

"Of course," she said. She squeezed my arm as she passed, though, so she couldn't be too angry.

I took the moment to plop down in the chair behind Kris's desk. Mia didn't seem pleased with the choice, but there wasn't much she could do about it. She took the seat across from me.

"What did you say to Cat?" she asked.

"Believe it or not, just because you're her manager, that doesn't make you privy to every conversation she has," I said sweetly, half annoyed at the gall of her question and half impressed. I wanted to be Mia when I grew up.

"It matters when it's a journalist doing the provoking," Mia countered.

"Oh, well, then let me put your mind at ease," I said. "It had nothing to do with the article, so there you go. Not your business."

Mia stared at me for a long minute but then sighed and sat back. "I wish I smoked."

I enjoyed the fact that I was stressing her out. "Your lungs don't."

"No, I know." Mia pressed a hand to her face. "What were you doing last night? Vaping? Isn't that just as bad?"

"Does everyone know everything that goes on in this house?" I asked.

"Yes, Cat does know you slept with Jeremy, if that's what you're wondering," Mia said, sounding amused more than anything.

I didn't let myself get embarrassed. "Hey, can I ask you a question?"

Something about my tone must have put her on edge. "You can ask it."

Which didn't mean she'd answer. "This is just me asking, not reporter Holland Tate."

"Okay," she said, though we both knew she wasn't about to say anything that could make it into a profile, promise or not.

"Do you ever feel weird peddling this content? Considering that you're a"—I waved at her incredibly put-together persona—"badass professional lady?"

She opened her mouth but I stopped her, anticipating her first argument. "And I know Catriona does not call herself a tradwife. She thinks she's above all that. But we both know exactly what her content is. I've watched it all."

"Really? All of it?" Mia asked, her head cocked to one side as she appraised me anew. "That's dedication."

I shrugged, my cheeks hot now when they hadn't been before. "Everything available, I guess. I wasn't sure you'd agree to let me come out, but I wanted to be prepared if you did."

Mia sighed. "There aren't that many influencers who need a full-time manager. It's not like I can choose someone who only posts videos I agree with."

"Yeah, but you could be running a Fortune 500 company," I pointed out, and she flushed with pleasure. "You could do whatever you want. And you're helping post content that moves the needle toward a world where you wouldn't have the choice to work."

"People marketed cigarettes, too," she said with a carelessness that grated on me, considering how much thought she clearly put into everything she did, everything she wore, and everything she said. "They market opioids and fast food and fast fashion and, and, and . . ."

"So you just don't care," I realized. "That's certainly more honest than I expected you to be."

"I have a lot of freedom in this position. I have a good salary, and I like Catriona, as well as Anna and Jeremy." Which was essentially what Jeremy had said, too. The Bouchards paid too well for any of their employees to be bothered by the quirks of the position. "I like my life."

And she didn't care about the big battles going on in the world outside the compound, apparently. "You're not worried about us ladies losing the vote, huh?"

"I think the horse is out of the barn on that one," she said with the laugh of someone who'd lived too comfortably with the belief that progress only marched forward.

There had been plenty of people who had thought that throughout history, too. But I'd gotten my answer. I didn't know how I felt about Mia now, but I did still find her very interesting.

"So, does Cat get a ton of threatening messages?" I asked, shifting the subject to something that had been in the back of my mind since my first conversation with this woman.

Mia tilted her head, considering. "It depends on how broadly you want to define 'threatening.'"

I waved a hand to get her to elaborate.

"Well, there's the men. The dick pics, the propositions. They like to neg her." She stopped there as if to check that I knew what *neg* meant.

Unfortunately, I did. At some point, men had bought into the idea that if they insulted a woman in some way, it would undermine their confidence and make them more receptive to being hit on. "Yeah, I've existed as a woman on the internet my whole life."

She laughed at that. "Right. So multiply what you get by about a hundred thousand. I call it the 'sex pest' category. They get nasty—she gets threatened with rape multiple times a week—but in terms of urgency, it's pretty low."

"Keyboard rapists," I said, nodding. The type was all too common.

"We get a lot of concern-trolling, too," Mia continued. "That's usually just obnoxious—they can't believe she lets her kids eat . . . name your food. We've seen it all. Someone should call CPS on her, according to these people."

Again, a common type of social media lurker. They let their own anxieties, insecurities, and irrational fears tell them that they were the only safe and responsible people on the planet.

"One or two of them have escalated into obsession," Mia said. "On a family vacation, the person tracked down where they were staying through pictures and then contacted the company they rented the house from to inform them of all the ways the kids would ruin the place."

"Who has that much time?" I asked.

Mia rolled her eyes. "Too many people, apparently. Those, I escalate to our digital expert, since it crosses the line into—"

"Crazy-town?" I interrupted.

"I probably wouldn't phrase it that way, but it does seem to carry a little more physical threat than just rude DMs."

"Okay," I said. "And then you have the people like your current obsessed fan?"

"That type scares me the most," Mia said, and then held her hand up. "I know, I said I wasn't worried. I don't think she'll turn violent, or anything like that. But she isn't a keyboard-anything. She's close by. She's followed Catriona in person. That is a little dicier."

"Thank you," I said, with a little laugh. "I felt like I was the weird one for being nervous about it."

"You're right. I probably should take it more seriously." She paused and ran a hand through her hair. "I think she just seems lonely, though. Maybe I was letting that color my perspective—especially considering the rest of the messages we get."

"That makes sense," I admitted. "When you see a hundred 'I hope you die in a fire after being showered with acid,' 'I like your hairdo' probably doesn't hit as hard."

Mia huffed out a laugh. "That's very true."

I went to leave, but Mia stopped me. "Can I ask *you* a question?"

"Sure."

"How can you write a profile on Catriona and not let your . . . dislike, shall we say, of tradwives color it?"

That was fair, especially coming from Cat's manager. "Because I think the world is complicated and interesting and layered. And I think Cat is as well."

Mia sat with that for a moment, as if weighing the words to test out their mineral makeup. "You really do seem to know her."

And to be honest, even if I'd convinced Mia of that, I wasn't sure I did anymore.

I knew Cat's base notes. Who was she now? I wasn't so certain.

But I did know something. "I'll say this. She's really good at making people think they do."

CHAPTER TWENTY-TWO

Cat

Then

The day after the Gatsby party, Holland watched me carefully all morning.

I finally broke around our third episode of *Vanderpump Rules*. Holland and I had discovered a shared love of trashy reality TV shows four days after she moved in, and we spent most of our "hangover days" camped out on the couch, working our way through dozens of episodes of rich people behaving badly.

And Holland was ruining this one for me.

"Babe, I don't know how to explain this to you, if you don't already know," I said, right before she clicked play on the next show. "Just because you like boring vanilla sex, doesn't mean everyone does."

She sputtered, her face flushing. "I don't like boring sex."

Her eyes flicked to my neck again, for perhaps the thousandth time. And so, okay, there were bruises there, but they were light, fingerprint-shaped ones that only existed because Holland had scared the shit out of Benji while his hand had been in a vulnerable position.

"What were you even doing walking into my room in the first place?" I asked, because I was feeling defensive. I shouldn't have been, but something about Holland's sad eyes made me bristle. They were the same ones she'd watched me with when she met me in the ER that one day. And while I appreciated her concern, this time, I really was fine.

"I didn't think you guys would be, uh, going at it. There were people still here," she said, so obviously trying not to sound like a scandalized prude that it made her sound exactly like one.

"If they were as drunk as you, they wouldn't have even noticed if Benji and I had started having sex in front of them," I lashed out. Holland was a drinker, but she *hated* being called a drunk. Maybe she had a parent who'd been an alcoholic and didn't want to be accused of going down that path. Or maybe she just prided herself on being able to hold her liquor—which, to her credit, she was usually able to do better than she had last night. Either way, she despised the idea that any of her behavior could ever be attributed to too many glasses of wine, and that included tripping, spilling a beverage, laughing too loudly or too long, et cetera et cetera.

Predictably, her blush deepened, anger spurred on by embarrassment. "I mean, can you blame me for being worried?"

"Date one abusive man and get labeled a survivor the rest of your life?" I asked.

And . . . okay. She wasn't necessarily wrong. It hadn't just been Mark who had crossed the line in my dating history.

There had been Theo, too. He'd been my high school boyfriend, back in Bakersfield. But he'd never really hurt me—he just liked to yell a lot. Punch a wall or two, throw a lamp. Near my head, though not at my head. That seemed an important distinction for some reason.

He hadn't fit the mold for an angry man, either. He'd been a stoner, a rock climber who liked to spend weekends driving out to Joshua Tree, taking mushrooms, and having trips under the great expanse of stars.

I was the uptight overachiever who had been attracted to his mellow, affable demeanor in a way I have never been able to explain.

I learned a lot from dating Theo—including how to extricate myself from men like him. And Mark.

I wasn't going to tell Holland all that, though. She wouldn't understand.

"Was Mark really the first?" she asked quietly, as if she could read my mind. And the terrible truth was that I liked her ability to do so. I liked that she could see I was keeping secrets, even if she didn't know just how bad those secrets were. I liked that I finally had someone who knew me that well.

My boyfriends never did. I didn't even think they liked me very much, if I was being honest, which I tried to be. I was too ambitious, too focused, too cutthroat. I had opinions and shared them. I had been told by both men and women that doing so would mean I'd never catch a man.

Maybe that was why I was trying so hard with Benji, who was dedicated to his own career, too.

"He was the last," I finally said, and something about my tone must have hit home for Holland. She studied me for a minute, then relaxed for the first time all morning.

"Okay," she said, pushing play on the next episode. "Sorry for barging in on you."

I tossed my hair. "All good. Maybe it'll inspire you out of your missionary funk."

"Oh, fuck *off*," she said, but she was laughing as she tossed a pillow at my head.

Maybe it had been a little awkward to clear the air, but it turned out to have been the right thing to do. Because from then on, Holland became a different person around Benji. Before she had been cold and unfriendly, barely tolerating his presence if the three of us were hanging out. I hadn't minded it, because it read as protective and perhaps a little jealous, and both reactions were pleasing to me. But now when Benji was over, she acted just like she did when it was the two of us alone.

Benji, in turn, relaxed, too, and it was really only then that I realized he had always been a little bit tense around Holland. Their energies had been feeding off each other in a vicious cycle.

Now they seemed to genuinely appreciate the other's role in my life, even if they weren't ever going to be fast friends themselves.

I didn't necessarily *love* this development. There had been part of me—a large part, if I'm being honest—that liked that they hadn't gotten along.

I would never forget that first moment in the ER when Benji had looked at Holland before he'd noticed me. I knew I should be the bigger person and let that go, but never in life had I been the bigger person, and so far it had worked out for me.

Holland dated, but she hadn't had a steady boyfriend in the seven months I'd known her. Or girlfriend, for that matter, though I'd never seen her show any interest, surreptitiously or not, in the same sex. And Holland was the type to have announced that kind of preference to the world.

So part of me—a large part, if I'm still being honest—worried about my gorgeous, single friend laughing along with my boyfriend.

But another part of me was relieved Holland no longer searched my arms and face for hidden bruises.

"What is that about?" I asked about a month after the Gatsby party. We were sitting on the roof of our building, passing a bottle of wine between us as we so often did. The sun was setting over the skyline, turning the Spanish moss on the magnolias across the street gold and shimmery. We were celebrating. *Savannah Scene* had just written a profile on me, and Holland had a short story accepted by her favorite hipster literary journal.

The world was our oyster.

Except . . . I had read the story she'd submitted. I'd realized the obvious brilliance of it once I finished, but at first it had seemed like cliché-ridden drivel.

Or, not drivel. Holland couldn't write drivel if she tried. She wrote as well as I baked, and that was a compliment I hadn't ever lavished on anyone else. It was why we got along. Neither of us could stand being around people who didn't excel at their talents. No matter what those talents were.

But she'd written about an abused woman—it had been a brilliant story, of course, a deep dive character study about a flawed, complex person who made bad choices yet still deserved dignity and safety. I had read plenty of stories about domestic abuse before. And I could always tell the authors who had personal experience with it.

Holland had personal experience with it. But for some reason, I didn't think she had been the victim.

Obviously, she hadn't followed my non sequitur and was now watching me with raised brows. "What are you talking about?"

"Was it your mom? Did you watch her get abused?" I wasn't exactly what one would call skilled at sensitive conversations. But I was going to give it my best effort. Helped out by the fact that this was our second bottle of wine for the night.

Holland shook her head because of course now she knew what I was asking. I knew it was front of mind for her, always.

She took another deep swallow of the wine, then huffed out a resigned breath. "My sister."

I nodded and splashed the last of the bottle into my glass. "Okay."

"She died," Holland said, and my drink wobbled in my hand with my surprise. "She was pregnant with my niece. He killed them both."

"Jesus," I whispered, all out of pithy comments.

"She was only eighteen," Holland said, her voice hollow.

"How old were you?" I asked, because as sad as the story was, I didn't really care about Holland's sister.

I cared about Holland.

"Fifteen." Holland scrubbed her hands over her face. It was a rare moment of vulnerability. Perhaps one of the few I'd seen from her. "The wild thing was that I had been friends with him. Or I thought I was. I mean, it was a faux big brother–style relationship for us, but I thought it was real. He would like, buy me teenybop magazines if we ever stopped at the gas station when they were driving me somewhere. Stuff like that. And then he beat my sister to death because she got pregnant."

"Yikes," I said, and even as it came out, I realized it might not be the most considerate reaction I could have had.

But it actually wiped some of the despair off Holland's face. "With people skills like that, it's amazing you haven't taken over Michi's job as hostess."

"When you're as good at things as we are, you don't have to be nice to people," I said, just to make her laugh.

She obliged and leaned her head against my shoulder.

"I guess I should stop bleeding my heart onto the page," Holland said. "I'm getting obvious."

"You get one pass, and that's it—otherwise you're going to get pigeonholed," I said. "This was your story about domestic violence. Now you can't ever write about it again."

I could almost feel her smile. "As long as you don't give me a reason to."

I held out my hand. "Deal."

CHAPTER TWENTY-THREE

Holland

Now

We ate a lunch of perfectly gooey grilled cheeses and rich tomato soup on the back patio. The air was probably too crisp to do so, but Cat had prepared for that. Each of us got a cozy blanket to keep us warm as we devoured a plate of the sandwiches—on homemade sourdough bread, of course.

Mia and Anna joined us, and I actually got to ask Anna a few questions. All her answers led back to her boyfriend in Switzerland, proving Jeremy had an accurate read on that particular situation. I dismissed her from my mind after the third monologue about his Alps-hiking prowess.

Cat had been watching us with a smirk, and I could now appreciate why she felt so calm about a look-alike running around her house. Not only was Anna boyfriend-obsessed, she was truly so obnoxious about it, her attractiveness diminished to the point that I almost found her ugly.

Overall, that about summed up the level of chatter for the entire lunch. There was no way around the fact that it was bland.

Part of the problem was that I didn't think any particular line of questioning was going to center my article. If I came out with anything, it would be based on my observations, not what media-practiced answers Cat and Kris doled out. But that realization left me strangely uninterested in quizzing them all about the daily minutiae of their lives just to get the writing equivalent of B-roll.

As if summoned by my boredom, Steffie rounded the corner of the house. No one else noticed the angry figure heading at a fast clip toward the forest beyond the carriage house, but I couldn't help but track his path.

He had said he'd talk to me. *Later*. Now could be later just as well as any other time.

I'd stashed my vape pen in my pocket for just this reason. I slipped it out now, and leaned over to whisper to Cat.

"Excuse me for a second?" I asked, holding the thing up, but also obscuring it from the children like I thought it was a dirty habit. I *did* think it was a dirty habit, but I also didn't think the children would start saving their chore money to buy one simply from seeing it, either. When Cat rolled her eyes, I offered, "I know, I'm trying to quit."

Then, in a few slick moves, I disappeared myself around the carriage house.

The land stretching back behind the farmhouse was immense. There were rows upon rows of apple trees, plus two more outbuildings along with the barn—and while they weren't currently bustling, they seemed like they would be during the week.

Sometimes it was hard to think about this place as a functioning business, but it must have been, especially during the fall. Not that the Bouchards needed it, but they could have made a lot of money charging tourists twenty-five dollars a bushel to come pick their own apples.

Thankfully, Steffie stayed in view and cut away from the orderly rows of trees, where he could have easily escaped my notice.

I prided myself as a New Yorker. We were some of the fittest people on the planet—at least, that was what we liked to tell ourselves. But

I was breathing hard and clutching my side by the time he slowed to a stop.

"Thank God," I whispered, though I did *not* bend in half. I was not that out of shape, even though I was rethinking my diet of mac and cheese, Cheetos, and the occasional fancy salad forced upon me only when the magazine ordered delivery and I was too ashamed to go with my preference of chicken fingers and fries.

I looked up to see where Steffie had stopped and found myself staring at a greenhouse, one that looked a little run-down but that might have been plucked off an English manor's lawn.

Without thinking too hard about it, I stepped inside.

He was up in my face in an instant. "Are you fucking following me?"

While I hadn't assessed him as dangerous, I realized I had been downplaying his height and overall size in my head, while picturing him as an emo boy. Now he loomed over me, his fists curled.

No longer just a pimply kid in an oversize sweatshirt but a teenager on the cusp of adulthood, with the strength to show for it.

I didn't take a step back even though I wanted to.

My hands wanted to shake. I didn't like angry men. I didn't like men who thought they could intimidate women, who thought they could hit women just because they were bigger. And at the same time, they always made me want to cower, as if my loved ones' trauma lived in my body instead of their own.

When I saw curled fists, I saw the ones that put Cat in the hospital.

The ones that put my sister and unborn niece in the ground.

Up until now, I had felt bad for Steffie. He reminded me of myself, actually, in that year after my sister had died. I had been so angry at the world that anyone coming within a five-foot radius of me was going to become a casualty of the nuclear blast of rage I was pumping out at any given time.

But with Steffie, I had done what I almost never did with full-grown men.

I had given him the benefit of the doubt.

Now I wondered what had really gone down on that kayaking trip. Because maybe Odette had made him mad like this. Maybe he had swung, probably he hadn't *meant* to, but she'd driven him to it.

Wasn't that how it always went?

"Yes, I was obviously following you," I finally said, keeping my voice as unruffled and breezy as possible. We were all just bantering, weren't we? "You said you would talk to me. Later. And now's later."

He stood frozen, breathing through his nose like a linebacker told just before he was about to tackle the other team that he had the wrong opponent.

Then, as if the air had been let out of him, he deflated. "What do you want to talk about?"

"First . . ." I said, as I stepped around him to create more space between us. He no longer seemed like he was going to push me through the glass walls, but I'd long ago realized precaution was best. "Why didn't you snitch on me?"

"Who would I have told?" he asked as he retreated to his own corner. I breathed easy for the first time since stepping into the greenhouse. "Ice Bitch Elsa or . . ."

I waited to see what his moniker for Kris was, but apparently it was worse than words could sum up.

"You don't like Cat?" I asked, though of course that was a dumb question and he treated it as such.

He barked out a laugh. "I love how you call her Cat. She hates that."

It's Catriona.

I was fairly convinced she didn't actually hate it—that it just didn't sit quite right with her new persona. Maybe she pretended to hate it so much because it reminded her of who she really should be. Not Catriona, not a shell, not someone who catered to the masses, but Cat.

Cat, who'd had Savannah's culinary scene at her feet, begging for literal crumbs.

She didn't hate the nickname; she hated the reminder that she could have still been that person if only she'd made different choices.

"Whatever," Steffie said at my silence. "I just can't wait till I can get away from her. My grandparents are trying to get custody of me, but it's a 'long process.'"

He said the last part with air quotes—something he must have been told time and again and only partly believed.

"Your father wouldn't mind that?"

"Why would I care if he did?" he asked, all but daring me to push and push and push.

"I take it you're not a fan of his, either?"

"Would you be a *fan* of your father if he killed your mother?" he spat out.

He watched my face as if hungry for a shocked expression. I gave it to him because I wanted him to keep talking. "What?"

I even added a little gasp into the appalled question.

His smile turned smug and self-satisfied. He was testing out his manipulative skills. Paired with his generally angry demeanor, I didn't like what the future held for Stefan Moreau.

Of course I felt bad for him. He was a product of his environment, but I could see the calculation in his eyes, and I couldn't help but wonder if this was the birth of a serial abuser.

Perhaps the apple didn't fall far from the tree.

"He comes off as so nice, so welcoming," Steffie said, venom laced in the words. I didn't contradict him, but I did silently question the assessment of Kris. He hadn't come off that way to me. "No one thinks of him as a killer."

"You father has a pretty solid alibi for that day," I said gently.

He looked away. "Kris might not have held her under the water, but he drove her to it."

Which was quite a different accusation to *he's a killer*. I didn't point that out, though. "How did he do that?"

"He made her life hell." Steffie ran his hands through his hair, the floppiness of the locks reminding me that he was a teenage boy. "He fucked with her money."

"You want to be more specific?"

Steffie shrugged. "He hid a lot of his assets from the court, so she got way less than she deserved in the divorce. He put her on an allowance. Made her beg for money if she wanted to buy anything bigger than a loaf of bread."

"That's . . . rough," I said, but it also sounded like any rich man. They were always going to protect their money, even if in unethical ways. That was how they got so wealthy in the first place.

"It was more than that, though," Steffie continued. "I didn't realize it when I was young, but he . . . he kept her isolated. Just like with Catriona. Made sure she didn't have any friends. Kept her lonely."

That . . . that resonated.

It doesn't seem like you have friends.

I have friends.

But Cat didn't. The closest person she interacted with on the daily—Mia—seemed to be far too cozy with Kris. Maybe she even informed on Cat, kept Kris apprised of every decision, every move she made.

I already knew he liked control—men didn't make themselves the sole holder of gate codes if they didn't want to have the final say in what everyone on the compound did.

It was plausible he'd made life unpleasant for Odette. I still didn't see him—or Cat, if I was being honest—kayaking down a river to kill her, either.

Steffie rubbed his hands over his face. "When my mom died, I was her best friend. I shouldn't have been her best friend."

Misery poured off him, and it was thick in the air. I could taste it in my mouth.

Like rotten meat.

I didn't want to say *I'm sorry.* Too many people had told me that. Instead, I asked a question I thought might jolt him out of his memories. "What are the prescription bottles in the bathroom?"

It surprised him, as intended. He'd wanted me to wallow with him, to wade into his mess and try to yank him out even as he took me down right alongside him.

But I'd learned to swim a long time ago.

"Uh," he said, on unsteady ground. It took a minute for him to center himself in the present. "They're Kris's."

"How do you know?" I asked, because I wanted to be sure. I didn't think Kris was drugging Cat. That would be absurd. As absurd as his ex-wife dying in a freak kayaking accident in the middle of a court battle that might have awarded her a good portion of his holdings.

"I looked," he said, meeting my eyes defiantly. "Just like you were trying to do. It's phenobarbital and codeine."

A barbiturate and an opioid. Mixed together they increased the chance of death by, well, a lot. I wasn't sure of the exact statistic, but it wasn't good.

"I think he broke his ankle a year or so ago," Steffie continued. "And the phenobarbital he uses for his insomnia."

"There were four bottles," I said.

Steffie shrugged. "Two each, maybe? According to the dates I saw, they're both old prescriptions, so maybe he's filling them and not taking them."

I nodded. The responsible person disposed of their unused drugs at some pharmacy drop point. There was an opioid crisis in this country, and oftentimes kids got started off drugs in their relatives' medicine cabinets.

I didn't think Steffie cared about proper disposal techniques. Except it was notable that Kris—might have—refilled those prescriptions while saying he'd gone through the first bottle.

My breath hitched as I considered the reasons for that. There were plenty of legit ones, I was sure. Maybe? He wanted to make sure he had extra in case some emergency happened?

That was weak.

But what was the other reason? I rubbed my sweaty palms against my thighs.

"Do you know if he has a safe in his office?" I asked, knowing I was pushing it. But Steffie didn't like Kris and didn't seem to have any morals tied to privacy, so I wanted to take advantage of the situation if I could.

"Oh, yeah he does, a hundo percent," Steffie said, reminding me once again that he was just a kid. "I haven't cracked the combo yet. But I think he has cash, some personal papers, and a gun in there."

I ran my tongue over my teeth. "A gun? Really?"

He rolled his eyes. "Yeah, welcome to Vermont."

"I'm trying to picture your dad with a gun," I said, even as the sirens sounded in my head. I knew the statistics on guns. A weapon like that increased the odds of murder in a domestic abuse situation by . . . again, a lot. I wasn't sure of the exact number, but it was high. This time, I shoved my shaking hands in my pockets.

Guns didn't always spell death. Sometimes curled fists were enough.

"He's actually good at shooting," Steffie said, though I could tell he was growing bored of this conversation. He'd wanted me to act this scene differently, and since I hadn't, it was less fun. "Stress relief or something."

"Or something," I murmured. "Will you live in Vermont when your grandparents come?"

"No, they have a house in Miami," he said. "They're Kris's parents, and they don't like him, but they have money."

I nodded. "That sounds nice."

What it sounded was far away from Kristopher Bouchard, which seemed like the optimal outcome for this kid.

Steffie tensed, his eyes locked on a point behind me.

It was the only warning I had to the door opening. My pulse kicked up in my throat, but I kept my face neutral as I turned to find Kris standing there.

"There you two are," Kris said, his pleasant voice not matching his blank expression. "We were so scared you'd fallen into some old well, Holland."

"Because I bear such a striking resemblance to Baby Jessica?" I asked, because I was known to bluff my way through stressful situations.

Both Steffie and Kris stared at me like I'd spoken Greek, and I realized the reference was too old for Steffie and too American for Kris. "Uh, I don't usually just walk into wells."

"We have several out around here," Kris said after a confused beat. "They're dreadfully dangerous and unassuming at the same time. We've been meaning to fill them in before the children are old enough to go exploring by themselves."

It took a moment for what he was saying to sink in. On the surface, it seemed pleasant enough. A warning, a weird one at that, but a warning from a host to be careful where I stepped.

But I put it together with our conversation the night before. The way he'd made sure that I knew he'd tried to unearth all my secrets. I put it together with the rage he'd so obviously felt as he'd attempted to tower over me. I put it together with the jealousy that must be powering that rage, at the idea that I had known Cat before him. That I'd known her previous partners as well. I put it together with the way Cat had ducked at a branch snapping, like she'd been braced for a pan flying at her head. I put it together with a gun and a security fence and the need for control that must be screaming at my mere presence.

I held my breath as I met his cold eyes.

"It would be a shame, wouldn't it?" Kris all but purred. "If someone fell down one of those wells. And then no one could hear them scream."

CHAPTER TWENTY-FOUR

Holland

Now

Cat was waiting for me with a glass of wine when I returned from the greenhouse.

It was strange to see her offering something so normal, so fitting to the beautiful aesthetic right after her husband had threatened to throw me down a well. Now he hovered at my elbow, a heavy presence I couldn't ignore.

The wild thing was that he'd actually been perfectly pleasant on the walk back—talking me through the production process for the orchard. But wasn't that how these men all acted?

Perfectly pleasant until they shattered your jaw.

Cat asked Kris to join us on the porch and I wished I had less control of my face. Because maybe if Cat had seen my flash of fear, she might have paused for just a second.

I had no faith in her caring about her own safety. But I thought she might care about mine.

Still, I was a master at controlling my expression—at least when I put thought into it. So I did. Despite the fact that being this close to Kris gave me heartburn.

I didn't think he would do anything in this setting, though. So I curled myself up in an Adirondack chair as Cat and Kris took the porch swing.

As I gathered my thoughts, I took a sip of the hundred-dollar-a-bottle wine, and looked out over the orchard.

This really was a beautiful life, filled with beautiful things and beautiful moments.

And I had to acknowledge that it was a lot of what Cat, who'd prided herself on her fancy cupcake holder, had dreamed of. Maybe she hadn't envisioned the husband and kids, but looking at it objectively—she had her own business, she created what she considered art, and she had a house filled with pretty things.

She'd gotten what she'd wanted.

Maybe her husband was more controlling than I would personally like. But she'd always seemed to accept that side of men more than I had been able to.

"I want to hear more about how you two met," I said, because there was only one way to get to the end of this and that was *through*.

"There was that chocolate cake . . ." Kris said, draping an arm around Cat's shoulder. It seemed like such an act to me, but she cuddled into his side.

I took my recorder out and made a show of "turning it on." "You don't mind if I record this?"

"No, go ahead," Cat said, though she'd tensed at the sight of it. My inclination to keep it hidden most of the time had been the right one. The two of them were media trained, and there was a big difference between a printed quote that they could claim was taken out of context and their voices saying the words.

"So," I said, leaning forward, "Kris was only in Savannah for a few days on business, right?"

"Yes," he said. "But I knew the moment I saw her in the kitchen that we would marry one day."

"It seems like it was more like, you would marry a few days later," I commented as lightly as I could.

Cat laughed. "You aren't wrong. But I was the same as Kris. I looked up one day and my soulmate was just standing there. And I'd never even believed in soulmates." She looked at me. "You know that."

"I do, yeah," I said, trying to tiptoe around the next part so as not to put Cat on edge about Fleur. "That must have been only a few days after I left Savannah."

Her brows dipped. "Yes. And honestly, between your departure and, well. The accident. I had thrown myself into my baking to forget all of it. In theory, it was the worst time for someone to come into my life."

My eyes slid to Kris, wondering how much he knew about Benji's accident. Had he even known about their relationship?

"That's probably why that cake tasted so good," she said. Kris picked up her hand and kissed her knuckles. "I was baking like my survival depended on it."

That was a good line. I made a mental note to pull it for the article.

"Your work always tastes that good," Kris said.

She didn't demur. "So Kristopher talked his way back into the kitchen to compliment the baker."

Cat had always pretended to hate when someone did that, but in truth she must have loved it. She loved praise.

"And this man who had incredible taste," she said with a little smile to signal she knew she was being arrogant, "was gorgeous and lovely and funny and kind. I realized all of that out of, I don't know, a five-minute chat."

"Five minutes," Kris agreed in that way couples did when one was telling a story.

"But more than that . . . I had been so miserable," Cat continued. "There was Benji's death, and then we had our . . . well." She grimaced, searching for the right word. "Falling-out."

I made a face at that gentle descriptor and she shrugged.

"On the walk to work that day, I'd seen this big, beautiful blue butterfly," she continued. "And I couldn't help but think it was Benji, you know? Visiting me. Comforting me."

Kris said his lines. "That very night, I told her about the restaurant I owned in France at the time and how I would have killed to have her as the pastry chef there."

Cat laid her hand on his knee. "And guess what the name of that restaurant was."

I tried not to cringe as I answered. "The Butterfly?"

"*Le Papillon*," Kris said in agreement. They beamed at each other.

The story was cute on the surface, but it also seemed out of character. Cat had never believed in signs in the year plus change that we'd lived together. This was either a story she told herself or, most likely, him. Especially if, at the time, she'd wanted to convince him she wasn't an opportunistic gold digger.

If the Cat I had known had seen a butterfly that reminded her of Benji—which seemed unlikely in the first place—she probably would have thought, *I'm going to kill that motherfucking butterfly for cheating on me with my—*

And then stomped the shit out of it.

It felt so strange, always trying to fit my idea of my Cat onto this version.

It was like one of those clear overlays that had outfits printed on them so you could "dress" different dolls up in the same skirts and blouses. Only this overlay had the picture-perfect Catriona Bouchard on it, which completely covered up Cat Vandale. I knew my Cat was under there, but I couldn't see her.

The feeling bothered me more than it should, eating at the edges of a wound that was still bleeding.

I thought back to what had made me pitch this article in the first place.

If I was being honest with myself, at the core of it all had been my mother's death. It had been a reminder of the people I had cut out of my life—or in Cat's case, who had cut me out of theirs.

There were differences, of course. I'd loved Cat more than I'd loved my mom when I cut her off. That was a strange thought, but my mother had become a husk of her former self after my sister died. And since that happened when I was fifteen, I'd been too young to really know her as a person before she'd completely given up.

And if we were being honest, the biggest difference had been who had done the leaving.

With my mother, I'd left and never looked back.

With Cat, in theory, it had been me packing my bags and heading out of town. But she had been the one to dictate our goodbye.

She had been the one who hadn't wanted to talk to me "ever again."

I think that would have changed if not for a handsome French financier walking into her restaurant only a few days later.

"What happened next?" I asked.

Kris glanced at Cat, looking as smitten as if this had happened yesterday. "I extended my stay in Savannah for two weeks. We spent every day together."

"Every hour," Cat interjected with a laugh.

"I didn't want to be apart from you for even a second," Kris said, looking down into her eyes. "About twelve days after we met, we booked flights to Aruba and got married there."

I wanted to ask if he'd had any fears she was a gold digger—as all multi-multi-multimillionaires must have—but I couldn't figure out a way to do so delicately. And, anyway, it would have been a question designed to sate my own curiosity. Maybe some nosy nellies would want to read about the business side of their romance, but most people would care more about what type of dress she wore.

I wouldn't be writing either of those stories, but out of the two, I'd lean more toward asking about the gown.

"Your family must have been . . ." *Horrified* was what I wanted to say. Instead, I finished, "Thrilled?"

And made it a question.

"Well, I'm not close with my parents," Kris said. It threw me back to the greenhouse with Steffie, who so desperately wanted to leave his father's mansion and live with his grandparents. That had to be saying something, given that most teenagers probably would have preferred this lap of luxury and the relative autonomy that came with quiet neglect instead of living with what he would probably think of as dinosaurs.

If there was a war between the factions, that was a damning condemnation of Kris's side.

"Cat's not close with her mother," Kris said, as if that would be something he needed to tell me.

"I know," I all but snapped.

"Well, anyway, it was nice, you know?" Kris recovered easily. "My first wedding was that huge, fairy-tale kind of affair, and I hated it. It wasn't me at all, and then I was miserable in that marriage."

I almost raised my brows at the way he was talking about his now dead ex-wife. I would have thought he'd have feigned it a little out of respect for the deceased.

"Our wedding was so different," he went on, squeezing Cat again. "And I knew our marriage would be, too."

Cat smiled up at him adoringly. I didn't know what kind of wedding my Cat would have dreamed about, considering she didn't dream about such things. But she had picked up a few wedding cake jobs along the way to earn some extra money. And the ones she'd talked about hadn't been the small events in front of the justice of the peace. They'd been the big splashes with budgets in the six figures. I couldn't imagine what she'd thought when she'd picked up a multimillionaire and gotten a tiny wedding to show for it.

Maybe she'd just been happy that he hadn't seemed to notice that she wasn't walking down the aisle alone.

"When we conceived our first night together, it just felt like God had a hand in everything," Kris said, trying to stick the landing. It would have been more effective had I not known Cat had already been pregnant when she'd married him.

"So sweet," I murmured, and while I thought Cat might have heard the sarcasm, Kris did not.

"It was," she said, her chin tilted up like she wanted a chance to refute all the thoughts I was trying so hard to keep off my face. "And then we got this fresh start. I can't imagine my life turning out more perfect than this one."

"You went back to Aruba for your fifth anniversary, didn't you?" I asked, wondering if that was a cute detail or not.

Kris's brows went up. "You did your research. Yes, we renewed our vows, this time with our kids there."

Those posts would have been old, but I remembered impossibly blue water and white sand and children in outfits that coordinated with their parents' fancy attire. I wanted to ask why they'd felt the need to renew their vows only five years in, but I refrained.

"And you had only moved to New York a few days before Cat and I met, right, Holland?" Kris asked. "You and I were passing ships."

We were indeed. "Yup. My internship wanted me local. Mostly because 'internship' in magazine speak means picking up dry-cleaning and coffee orders." I took a sip of the wine. "But I will say, it was hard to leave Savannah."

"Was it?" Cat asked, icy now.

It had been strange the way that summer had worked out, how I had been offered an escape hatch from a terrible situation just when I'd needed it.

"Yes," I said, and I wasn't lying. The months I'd spent living with Cat had been some of the best of my life. Even now, ten years later, I still felt that way.

I'd never had a friend like her—or even a friend at all. That was sad to admit, I supposed. But it had been the same for her, too.

We were special to each other in ways that no one else in our lives had ever been.

I wondered how everything would have turned out had I not left. We would have made up—we had been too close not to. Then she would have come home one day and told me about the pretentious asshole who'd had the audacity to come back into the kitchen, and we would have laughed about him over a bottle of wine on the rooftop. Maybe she still would have gone on a date with him, but she would have had my laughter in her head. Kris probably would have sensed that she wasn't all in, and then he would have just gone back to France, or wherever his businesses had been located at the time. We would have made a trip to the abortion clinic, and I would have held her hand the whole time.

But I had applied to *Profile* thinking I could easily talk Cat into moving to New York City with me. She was never going to elbow her way into Savannah society, even if she didn't want to admit it out loud. She didn't have old money and she was a West Coast gal, both strikes against her. In New York, there was plenty of fun to be had with the new-money set. While Cat didn't actually have the bank account to hang with them, that was fine. People appreciated talent in New York, whatever the kind. It became a sort of currency. Bills were picked up for you, clothes were given, experiences comped.

She would have had the city eating out of the palm of her hand.

What would our lives have looked like?

Talk about butterfly wings.

CHAPTER TWENTY-FIVE

Cat

Then

Benji had a birthday coming up. It was earlier in our relationship than I normally would have baked a cake for someone, but Benji deserved one. He was so sweet. And so caring.

He was by and far the best boyfriend I'd ever had, if I were being honest.

I knew when talking about our relationship, I should have demurred and wondered how I could have possibly snagged such a man. But that wasn't my style.

Anyway, I knew.

I had thought Benji liked nice girls—he did have an aversion to meanness that I would've liked to chip away at—but mostly he liked take-charge women.

That had always been a pitfall of mine when it came to men, so I had been thrilled to realize I didn't have to dampen that part of my personality.

He actually liked it when I gave him orders.

It felt like fate that we had found each other.

Now Holland sat cross-legged on the counter, practically inhaling her coffee, as she watched me flip through my recipe binder.

"So you *don't* want to throw a party for him here?" she asked. Her surprise was understandable. We threw parties, it was what we did. They were rarely on Friday or Saturday nights since I worked in the restaurant industry, but that didn't seem to matter to any of the acquaintances and friends we invited. They always came because they knew it would be a good time.

"I think we should do something, just the two of us," I said, pausing over a pumpkin cheesecake that I had been told was better than the best sex in the world. I pursed my lips and then slid one of my bookmarks onto the page. I wanted to narrow the recipes down to a few options and then pick from there.

Holland made some doubtful sound as she stretched her neck. It was an absent-minded grunt, but it still got me looking up. "What?"

"I don't know. You guys both love parties, why wouldn't you want to do a party?"

"We have parties all the time," I said, pausing once more, this time at a German chocolate cake. It wasn't a difficult recipe, but for whatever reason, mine always made people fall in love with me. Maybe it was the simple things that really showed how much better I was than everyone else. You can't screw up a basic item, people say, but then they try my "basic item" over someone else's and realize you might not be able to screw it up but you sure can make it amazing. "I want this to be special."

Holland waggled her brows. "Oh la la."

I rolled my eyes and went back to my recipes.

"Oh, hey, do you want to do a double date next week if you and Benji can get the same night off?" Holland asked.

I looked up at that, annoyed that she'd kept something from me. "Excuse me, who are you dating?"

"Just a guy who has asked me out a bunch," Holland said with a careless shrug, oh so irritated to be found attractive by a man. "I figure a double date will be less pressure."

"For your first date?" I asked, skeptical. I did *not* want her foisting her bad time off on us.

"We've done coffee a few times. He's funny in the way we are." Holland batted her lashes at me. "Please, please, please."

I rolled my eyes again, but we both knew I'd say yes.

And I did. A few days later, we hit up our favorite seafood joint. It was dirt cheap, had phenomenal plates, and was three blocks away from our apartment.

Benji kissed my cheek when he met us outside the restaurant, then hugged Holland. Their embrace lasted the perfect amount of time, neither of them lingering.

Jake, Holland's date, was a model. Or he could have been one, with his chiseled face, thick, dark hair, and swimmer's physique. They were beautiful together, and I couldn't figure out why Holland seemed more bothered by his attention than normal.

Jake and Benji got along immediately, but Holland was quiet most of the night.

I asked her about it when we went to the bathroom.

"If you don't even want to be here, imagine how little I do," I said, as I watched her reapply her lipstick.

"I know, sorry," she said, with one of her patented careless shrugs. "He just likes me too much. It's making me itchy."

Now, I had never experienced this phenomenon, but I'd had other girls tell me about it. And it sounded like bullshit to me. "Then break up with him or get over it."

"I know," Holland said, dragging it out. "But you and Benji are getting serious . . ."

"Wait, what?"

She pinned me with her all-seeing eyes. "You're baking him a cake. You said you've never done that before a relationship is older than a year."

"Well, I know he's going to do something really nice for my birthday," I said, feeling defensive, even though there was no reason to.

"And you don't want to have a party—you want it to just be you two," she continued. She looked down at the floor. "Before you know it, you'll be moving in together."

My face did something unpleasant, I was sure. But the thought was nearly repellent to me. "You know I'm not settling down for at least another fifteen years."

"Does Benji know that?" she asked, and she had a good point. He fit so comfortably into my life in ways other men hadn't. He might have gotten the impression from that alone that we were on the same page in terms of commitment levels.

"Yes," I said, but we both knew I was lying. Holland was kind enough not to call me on it—any further, at least.

She ended up going home with Jake because while she might be emotionally complicated, she was pretty simple when it came to her body count.

Benji walked me home, his fingers tangling with mine.

"Holland was weird tonight," he commented idly. I was glad that he did it unselfconsciously, that I didn't react so violently when he mentioned other women to me that he thought he couldn't. It felt like a real theatrical act on my part, but also worth it so I could get his unfiltered thoughts.

"She's feeling like the third wheel," I said, swinging our joined hands.

He raised his brows. "Huh."

When he didn't expand on that, I pushed. "What does that mean?"

"It means 'huh,'" he said, with that stupidly pleased grin he got when he thought he was being clever. I pinched the delicate skin between his thumb and finger and he cried uncle. "How do I say this . . ."

"You put words together to form a sentence," I said, overly sweet because it sounded like he was about to drop something on me that I wasn't going to like.

"You guys are really close," he said slowly. "I would say almost codependent, if I had to."

That wasn't . . . wrong. Holland and I spent most of our free time together, helped each other with major life decisions. But . . . "We're best friends."

"Right," Benji agreed quickly. "Only . . . and don't get mad at this. But. Have you ever had a best friend?"

My hand twitched in his, but he wouldn't let me drop it. "No, of course not."

He huffed out an amused—and dare I say, fond—breath at that. "I'm guessing she hasn't, either."

That struck me as a surprising observation. "But it's Holland."

"Right," he said. "Okay, but do you notice how, at your parties, you guys don't actually have any friends there?"

"Of course we do," I said, feeling like I was having a different conversation than he was. "What are you talking about? Michi comes to most of them."

"What's Michi's boyfriend's name?" Benji asked gently.

I licked my lips. "That's hardly fair. It's a rotating cast."

"She's been dating the same guy since I've met her," Benji pointed out. "And I'm thinking Holland has a similar experience with her 'friends' from her graduate program. Everyone has a great time, but you guys don't actually care about any of those people."

I exhaled. "So what's the point of this observation, Dr. Freud?"

"I'm not psychoanalyzing you, I swear," he said, and sounded genuine. "I just find it sort of amazing, the two of you. Neither of you really likes other people, yet you immediately liked each other."

"I thought I did a better job of hiding that side of my personality from you," I admitted, and he laughed again.

"I like it, though," he said. "You're like this feral alley cat who bites and scratches anyone trying to get near you, but for some reason you let me pet you. It's a cool feeling."

"I think that's either very sweet or very enraging, and you better hope I settle on the former."

He stopped us by my stoop and cupped my face in my hands, kissing me. "It feels like an honor."

"Okay, sweet," I mumbled against his lips. "Is Holland an alley cat, too?"

"Mm-hmm," he said. "And you guys are somehow sharing the cardboard box that either of you would have killed others for even looking at before."

I did fancy myself introspective. I had a laundry list of flaws, but also a binder full of strengths. I thought I knew myself pretty well. Yet this descriptor felt new and surprising. And it fit.

For both Holland and myself.

"So, what you're saying is that I shouldn't be annoyed she's dragging us on double dates because she's upset that I want you to come into the box as well," I said.

"Right, because that's how you view it," Benji said. "How she probably sees it—reasonably or not—is that you're kicking her out of the box and out of the alley because you found a nice Labrador retriever to settle down with."

"Ew, never," I said, and he threw back his head and laughed at that.

Later that night, after Benji had passed out in his usual post-sex near coma, I grabbed for my phone.

Holland and I had been friends for less than a year. I didn't even know her mother's name or where she'd grown up. *I should probably ask her for a few of those details.* But, still, we fit in a way I never had with anyone else, including Benji.

You know we're ride or die, right? I texted her.

The typing bubbles popped up and went away, popped up and went away.

Are you trying to ask me to help hide a body?

Girl, we wouldn't be doing that over text, I wrote back.

The typing bubbles popped up and went away, popped up and went away.

Finally, she sent the text. I love you, too.

CHAPTER TWENTY-SIX

Holland

Now

"Why aren't you two friends anymore?"

It was Mia. Of course it was. She was sitting on the floor outside my room, waiting for me.

Cat, Kris, and I had finished a few glasses of wine on the porch, chatting about Kris and Cat's magical love story until I wanted to vomit. But there were probably some decent quotes in there, which was what mattered.

Now I was trying to change for dinner. Over the course of only twenty-four hours, I'd switched clothes more than I had on weeklong vacations.

"It's a long story," I said, even though it probably wasn't. Girls get in fight over boy. Boy tragically dies. Girls let all their guilt and anger and fear get tangled up in that. Girls are no longer friends.

"I have time," Mia said, pushing herself, fairly gracefully, to her feet.

I hesitated, but Mia was probably the most interesting person in the house now that Cat had fully adopted her tradwife persona. I wouldn't mind trying to get more information out of her, even if she thought she was the one doing the investigating.

I waved her into the room, and she took one of the fancy chairs by the window.

"We got in a fight," I finally said, stepping out of my pants without much regard to my audience. She didn't bother to look away, either. "Over a guy. And then life intervened, and we never got a chance to make up."

"That's not a long story," she pointed out, as I pulled off my sweater. I had a fall dress and boots I was planning on wearing for dinner, and I bent to rummage in my bag for the outfit.

"I think the long story comes into play after," I said. "We should have made up. But we both hold grudges like mean alley cats."

Mia huffed.

"What?" I asked.

"When I was asking about you, about what the two of you were like, Catriona said, and I quote, 'We were like alley cats.'"

I smiled, pleased. That old muscle memory of knowing someone so well twinging again.

"It was one of those friendships you have when you're young and your atoms just kind of fuse together," I said.

Mia shook her head. "I don't think I've had one of those."

"It's . . . addicting, I guess?" I tried, before stepping into my dress. "That might sound weird."

"No, I get it," Mia said, and she rose again to come help me zip it up. "To be known, that's all we ever really want, isn't it? As humans."

I chewed on the inside of my cheek. "Yeah."

"I guess that's your entire job," Mia said, stepping back once more.

"Yeah," I agreed, before sitting on the bed to get my boots on. "So tell me your story. How'd you end up here?"

"I'm not the interesting one."

"I think you are," I said honestly, though I tried to play it off as if I weren't curious. "You don't want a family of your own?"

"No," Mia said. "Don't get me wrong, this isn't my forever job. I don't actually like living all the way out here with no visitors."

This time, I laughed out loud. "You mean you don't like pretending you're one of those sentient furniture items in *Beauty and the Beast*?"

"Technically, they were people," Mia corrected, amused. "But that is the vibe we sometimes get around here."

"You have other workers come in, though, right?" I crossed to the mirror to try to salvage my makeup from that morning. Redoing it all felt like a daunting task.

"Sure, and there's Anna—"

"The brain-dead nanny?" I shot back.

Mia smirked, reminding me a little of Cat as she did. "That's mean."

Apparently that was where the similarities died.

"She's not a nanny. She's an au pair," Mia finished her own joke, and I spun around, a little delighted. "And of course Jeremy likes to bake his last brain cell out of existence, so . . ."

"Cat's good company," I pointed out.

"You're not wrong," Mia admitted. "But she'll always be my employer."

"And landlord," I said. "Why *is* Kris so weird about visitors? I swear, it's off the record."

Before Mia could say anything, I held my hand up. "And don't tell me it's because of a kidnapping that happened when Fleur was a baby. Or some recently obsessed fan. From all accounts the Bouchards' behavior predates that."

Mia made a face. "I mean, I had never really thought of it as weird. But I see it now."

I sank into the chair facing hers and crossed my legs. I studied her, gauging how she'd take my own personal theories. For some reason, I thought maybe . . . well? "Listen, this is off the record, too. But Cat has a . . . shall we say history . . . with choosing guys who aren't very nice."

Mia's eyes went wide. "That surprises me. She doesn't seem the type."

I chewed on my cheek instead of asking who exactly was "the type" to get beaten up by their boyfriends.

"At least three that I know of," I said.

Mia clicked her tongue. "Is that why you were looking up Odette Moreau on my tablet?"

"Where there's smoke . . ." I said, weakly. "I'm probably barking at shadows. They seem disgustingly in love, more so, even, than in her videos."

Mia hummed. "I don't know."

I remembered in that moment that Jeremy thought Mia could be having an affair with Kris. "What do you mean, 'you don't know'?"

"You got me thinking with that Odette thing," Mia said, looking antsy all of a sudden. "Catriona has . . ."

Mia broke off and heaved a sigh. I waited.

"She has bruises sometimes," Mia finished, looking guilty as hell for even mentioning them.

"I know lots of people who bruise easy."

Mia nodded. "Yeah, that's what I always thought. She explains them when they're obvious. The orchard—sometimes she actually pitches in. It can get physical."

"Makes sense," I said. We were both being so reasonable.

"Right," she said. "But I guess that's what victims do, too, don't they? They explain them all away."

I didn't say anything, and she reached into her pocket to pull out her phone.

I stared at it longingly, very aware of my problem.

She ignored my obvious drooling and pulled something up. "This is a video we filmed three weeks ago. We couldn't post it."

I took the phone, eager to watch content that no one else had seen. The video was like so many of Cat's posts. It was an early-morning scene, and she was about to head out on a run around the orchard. She was stretching, going through some poses that were obviously second nature to her. And her shirt gaped to reveal a large bruise along her collarbone.

It was only a quick glimpse, but it was impossible to ignore.

"What did she say?" I asked, watching it again. And then once more.

"That she smacked into one of the machines in the dark," Mia said. "It's actually believable. Sometimes she heads out there way earlier than anyone else. And she can be clumsy."

"She always had excuses," I said, staring at the screen, where I'd frozen the video. Proof, finally. I could hardly believe it.

Not that it really mattered.

I shrugged and handed the phone back. "You can't make someone admit when they need help."

I knew that all too well. I thought about that time I'd walked in on Benji and Cat, his hand around her throat. She'd played it off so well that I'd ignored my instincts even as she wore his fingerprint bruises on her skin.

It hadn't taken long to learn that Cat could and would lie with ease when it came to her boyfriends. It was why I hadn't been able to give Kris the benefit of the doubt. Now it wasn't just me who was worried, though.

Mia thumbed at the screen, pulling up another video. She showed me three more, all of which were unusable because of large, visible bruises.

"You weren't suspicious?" I asked, wondering again at the theory she was sleeping with Kris.

"I wouldn't want to be married to him," she said, seeming to put it to rest. "But Kris has always been a perfect gentleman. Cat doesn't seem scared of him or even timid or jumpy. And I've seen her run into things that result in bruises that big. But, I don't know, people know how to hide things pretty well. Then everything with Odette's death is so shady . . ."

Mia was staring at the screen, where the latest injury was frozen, on display. "I just don't know."

We met each other's eyes. Two women who cared about Cat a decade apart, still wondering if she was wearing the violence of the man who was supposed to love her.

I wasn't new to the idea of spending time with Cat and a man I thought might be hurting her. I also wasn't unaware of the fact that the man I thought might be hurting her was the only person at the table with a code to get out of this place.

Unless I wanted to wire-cut through a fence, which I wasn't quite ready to do yet.

So, while it was hard to stomach the lovey-dovey routine, I could sit across from him at the dinner table and make pleasant conversation.

If I was plotting his ruin the entire time, that was between me and the glass of wine I *wasn't* sipping.

"Can I ask more about the kidnapping?"

We had finished dinner, which I suspected Jeremy had cooked despite the fact that Cat had once again brought it out like she had done the preparation.

Anna had shepherded the kids inside, and it was just the Bouchards, Mia, and me left. They were all sharing their second bottle, but I didn't want to lower my guard at all, so I'd sipped about half of one glass.

Cat reached out and tangled her fingers with Kris's. "Okay."

"You don't have to," Kris told her, bringing their joined hands to his lips. It was one of his favorite moves, I'd noticed.

"No, I want . . ." Cat paused, gathered herself. "I want people to know why we do some of the things we do. It's important. And maybe it will serve as an important reminder to people posting their children online."

As the Bouchards did frequently. I kept that thought to myself.

"Okay," I said, pulling out my recorder, which had been whirling away anyway. I set it on the table. "The police weren't able to arrest anyone, but did they have any interesting leads?"

Cat nodded. "They found a few social media accounts that had been following and reacting to my content in suspicious ways. They didn't have the means or personnel to follow up on it, but we hired a digital investigator to do a private investigation."

"Oh," I said, leaning forward. That sounded like what was happening right now as well. "What was that like?"

"She was excellent," Kris said, and Cat nodded.

"She found that two of those three burner accounts were actually connected and were probably the same person," Cat said.

"Based on?"

"Digital forensics, I was told," Cat said, shrugging. Neither of us were technophiles, so I sympathized with the generality. "And posting behavior."

"Fascinating." My heart beat against my chest, because it was slightly terrifying to face the fact that the internet wasn't as anonymous as it seemed. I knew social media companies tracked us across sites and eavesdropped on conversations. But there was something—wrongly—sanitized about the idea of that being done by a huge organization. They were faceless in my mind, not really interested in the fact that I looked up how to get rid of zits and more interested in the fact that I liked skin care ads.

A person, a real live individual person, being able to suss out what I was like via my social media likes, follows, and comments was disturbing.

"She was never able to take it any further, sadly," Cat continued. "But it did seem to confirm that this person had become obsessed with me, Kris, and Fleur via the content I had posted. Honestly, none of their messages were even threatening. They just seemed like they were a really lonely person who wanted to be a part of the family they watched on their phone."

Parasocial relationships. It was a buzzword that floated around the office. They'd existed long before social media, but that was certainly exacerbating the problem.

"Did any of your investigators figure out what had triggered the suspect into taking action?" I asked.

"No, but the cops guessed the person probably approached me once or twice beforehand," Cat said, with a little shiver. "To be honest, it gave me a touch of agoraphobia hearing that."

"That's creepy," I said, before clarifying, "Knowing they talked to you first. Why do the police think that?"

"Because of how much of an escalation the kidnapping was from the online behavior," Cat said. "It's quite unusual to go from commenting online to breaking into someone's house."

"The police had the audacity to suggest the person was offended by Cat's attitude when trying to talk to her," Kris said, and I could tell from Cat's expression she hadn't wanted that part recorded.

"I'm often rushed when I'm in town," Cat explained to me. "If someone stopped me at the grocery store or dry cleaner, I might have seemed like I brushed them off. Which, since we were close friends in their mind, would have felt very painful."

"You would think you would have remembered running into some woman multiple times," I said.

"We never said it was a woman," Kris pointed out, and I shrugged.

"If the motive was as personal as the cops seem to think, then that fits with a female suspect," I said, though he was right. Most kidnappers were men. Still . . . "Nothing about this screams 'random male intruder.'"

"No," Mia agreed, chiming in for the first time. "Everyone working the case believed it was a woman. Just for the sheer fact that she left Fleur well protected against the night weather."

Shadows covered much of Mia's face, and I considered her more closely. "Were you here for that?"

"That was just a little before my time," she said.

For some reason, it seemed like she had been here for a shorter time period than that, though I wasn't sure why I thought that.

This time, when Cat reached out, it was to Mia. "I can hardly believe there was a time before we had you as part of our family."

Mia squeezed her hand in return. "Can you believe you survived without me?"

Cat and Kris laughed lightly, then agreed heartily.

I smiled at the scene, but all I could think about was that when I had asked Mia her story, she'd never really answered me.

CHAPTER TWENTY-SEVEN

Cat

Then

I was covered in scars.

Burns and bruises and knife marks.

Someone might look at the patterns on my skin and think I was the victim of a tortured mind.

In all honesty, I was just a baker who worked in a busy kitchen.

I was used to pain—it came with the territory.

That was why I didn't scream when Benji spilled scalding-hot water right out of the kettle all over my arm.

He didn't make a sound, either. He just stared at my skin as it puckered into angry welts.

"What the hell?" Benji yelled just as Holland stepped into the kitchen.

"Oh my god," she said, shoving him out of the way to cradle my arm in her hands.

I still hadn't mustered up even so much as a good yelp, though I wanted to milk the horrified sympathy in Holland's eyes and the horrified guilt in Benji's for all they were worth. Still, I was a top pastry chef who had made it through the CIA. I was too well trained to panic.

"Get me to the sink, please," I said, my voice devoid of anything—pain or fear or annoyance even, though I was certainly feeling all three.

Holland guided me gently, keeping her body angled between me and Benji, who was still sputtering about how I'd been in his way, so how was he to blame, really? It was a common enough reaction to something like this, driven by guilt, so I tuned it out.

Holland's shoulders were so tense they were nearly at her ears.

"Cool water, not ice," I said, because that was one of the first things you learned at school. Holland nodded and guided my arm under the blessedly lovely tap water.

I tipped my head back and nearly moaned, the relief so sharp it felt like pleasure.

We all stood there in silence for seven to nine minutes of awkwardness as my arm went from a four-alarm fire to a too-sunny day at the beach.

"Okay, shit," I said, finally sinking into one of the kitchen chairs. "I think I'm going to keep the arm."

Holland laughed, but I could tell it was her anxiety coming out more than actual amusement.

"Cat, Jesus, why did you do that?" Benji asked, still so flustered. He was apparently not good in a crisis despite working in the ER. Except that wasn't fair. It was different when it was a loved one who was hurt, and even more different when you were the one who'd—inadvertently—caused the injury.

Holland, who saw domestic abuse in every banged elbow, whirled on him. I was more surprised that I hadn't seen it coming than surprised at the reaction itself.

"Don't you fucking blame her," Holland spat, her finger all up in Benji's face like we were on some kind of soap opera.

"Holland—" I tried, and she spun toward me.

"No," she said. "I don't want to hear excuses for his behavior."

I shrugged, because honestly I was in too much pain and didn't really have it in me to battle Holland at the moment.

Benji, meanwhile, had gone sheet white, possibly remembering finally the way he'd met me.

"No, no, no," he tried. "She tickled me and I didn't realize she was there . . . It was an accident, I'm not blaming—"

"Get out of here," Holland all but roared. I had to admit that as wrong as she was right now, I did like the feeling of being protected.

Benji's eyes cut to me. "You can't think—"

"Get the fuck out of here," Holland said, and she started pushing at Benji, hard.

Benji kept trying to explain, and I talked over both of them. "Babe, can you run down to the drugstore and get me something to put on this? Thanks."

But Benji had finally had enough of the pint-size Bratz doll beating up on him. He grabbed at her fists. "Hey, cool it."

That, of course, enraged Holland, who just went in harder.

"Can you just—" I tried again.

"Goddamn it, get off me," Benji snapped at Holland, trying to ward her off without hurting her.

"Or you'll what? Pour boiling water over me?" Holland asked, though she'd stepped back, hands on her hips. "Or will it be acid next time. Because I did something you didn't like?"

Benji stared at her, and I tried to imagine the highs and lows of the emotional roller coaster he'd just ridden. But I did wince when he called her some name and tacked on something that sounded like *psycho* to the end of it before he stormed out of the kitchen.

I huffed out a breath. He was in the right—in what world would a normal person jump to acid—but he could have handled that better.

"Cat," Holland whispered, taking the chair opposite mine, leaning forward and cupping my wrists in her hands. Everything done so gently, the fight completely gone. "What happened?"

And here was the difficult thing.

I would say, *It was an accident, I startled him, it was my fault, and I'm not even hurt that badly.* Which was, of course, all true.

She would hear an abuse victim making excuses for a violent man who had lashed out and then blamed the victim for making him do so.

There was simply no answer that would satisfy her.

All the goodwill that Benji had built up slid off her onto the floor with a disappointing plop.

I sighed and let myself think what I had so studiously been avoiding thinking: Holland could be exhausting.

She might have reasons to be exhausting, especially in this particular way, but that didn't make it any easier to live with.

It seemed . . . disloyal to feel that way. We had been in lockstep for so much—almost everything. Except for this, and I knew it had the power to drive a wedge between us. One I would never want to be there.

I wasn't emotionally intelligent enough to handle this, though.

So I tried to ignore it.

I thought maybe she would get over it.

But only a week later, I rebroke the wrist Mark had injured, fate's funny way of laughing at me.

At all of us.

Benji had spent most of our relationship trying to get me to Rollerblade, and I had, of course, refused. Rollerblading made you look dumb, especially if you didn't know how to do it.

He finally succeeded in bribing me with a trip to one of my favorite expensive restaurants in the city plus tickets to the ballet.

Three minutes in, I wiped out because it was a dumb fucking sport, and I got the tiniest fracture in my wrist.

"Oh my god," Holland said, when she saw my wrapped arm.

"I broke my wrist," I admitted, because I wanted to be babied a little.

Holland's eyes flew to Benji, who was a half step behind me, carrying my pain meds. "How."

Not even a question mark there, just straight up accusation. "Rollerblading."

As soon as the reason was out of my mouth, I was mentally back in that ER room meeting Benji for the first time, saying I'd fallen down a flight of stairs.

I didn't Rollerblade. I was not even the type to try it.

But Holland didn't press. She just watched us for a long minute and then asked, "Are you going to be okay?"

"Yes," I said, hesitant.

"Okay," she said. "Good night."

I stared at her retreating back, annoyed. I wanted to be fussed over. I wanted her to coo and bring me my favorite bag of chips and settle in on the couch beside me.

"I'll get your snacks," Benji said, pressing a kiss to the top of my head as if I were a child. He waggled the bag from the pharmacist. "And the good stuff."

I didn't bother to say thanks, just stepped out of my shoes and collapsed onto the armchair so Benji couldn't cuddle up next to me. I didn't think I could stand his touch at the moment.

My phone dinged.

You'd tell me if we needed to hide a body, right?

I rubbed my fingers into my eyes. It was funny how people said things like that so carelessly over text. If this really was what she was imagining, and she really wanted to do something about it—something more than a restraining order someone could just walk right through—she never should have sent that.

That was how I knew that if I actually did need to hide a body, I wouldn't call her.

She could never cross that line, didn't know what it would take to do so.

You'd be my first call, I lied.

Four days later, the doorbell of our place chimed.

Holland was closer to the door and didn't have flour on her hands, so she got up and then peered through the peephole.

The line of her back went tight, and my stomach clenched against the nothing I'd eaten all day.

And I knew I wasn't going to like whoever was at the door.

Her throat bobbed as she dropped back onto her heels and reached for the handle.

"It's the police," she said quietly, the only warning I got before she opened the door to them.

My feet wanted me to run for the hills. My gut wanted me to run for the toilet. My head told me to stay perfectly still.

"Catriona Vandale?" a voice asked.

Holland hesitated, and I swore she almost lied for me. But there was no reason to do that.

"She's my roommate," Holland said, without indicating that I was home.

"Is she available?" the voice asked, starting to get annoyed.

"May I ask what this is about?"

Another voice chimed in, this one male. A baritone. "We'd just like to ask her a few questions about, uh, Mark. Mark Sinclair."

I really did run for the sink then, retching and praying to God my years of bulimia as a teenager would give me the gift of silence now.

"Mark? Her ex-boyfriend?" Holland asked, sounding more relaxed and confused now than anxious. "What the hell did that asshole do now?"

It was the original voice that answered. "He died, ma'am."

CHAPTER TWENTY-EIGHT

Det. Jamie Alvarez

Detective Boyd from State had taken over the investigation—even though there really wasn't much of one to take over.

Jamie was left to sit at her desk with not much to do. But she did have a scrap of paper given to her by Mia Preston. The digital investigator's number.

Beatrice Daccord.

It was a long shot, but Jamie punched in the number below the name.

Beatrice answered like she'd been waiting for the call. And it turned out, she pretty much had been. She didn't need to be caught up to speed.

"I've spent the past couple hours scouring my case file on this obsessed fan," Beatrice said. "But I've hit a brick wall."

"Why didn't the Bouchards go to the police with this?"

"Nothing had happened," Beatrice said. "And honestly it wasn't that out of place. Influencers with that many followers get death threats all the time. This was just someone who seemed to love Catriona a bit too much."

"Did you narrow it down at all?" Jamie asked.

"Just that it was someone in the area," Beatrice said. "They used the local library's computer several times over the past few months, but I was limited with the amount of information I could get from there, since, well, a crime hadn't been committed."

Yet, Jamie could all but hear. "That sounds like they weren't too tech savvy."

"You'd be correct on that one," Beatrice said. "I didn't work on Fleur's kidnapping case, but the person who was contacting them back then was a lot better at hiding their tracks. Given a little bit of legal leeway, I could probably eventually find out who this fan was—not so with Fleur's kidnapper."

So, not the same person. There went Jamie's theory.

"You might not have an answer to this, but did it seem like the fan was escalating with their messages?" Jamie asked.

"To the point of killing Kristopher Bouchard?" Beatrice asked, putting the subtext into words. "No, not at all. They never even mentioned him. I've had plenty of cases where I've alerted police right before something bad was going to happen. I would have said we were months away from that, if at all."

This was all exactly what she'd expected. "Okay, if you remember anything else, even if you don't think it's connected, can you let me know?"

"For sure," Beatrice said. "Oh, hey, can I ask a question?"

"Shoot."

"Is Mia Preston . . . is she . . . okay?" Beatrice asked, sounding hesitant.

Is she alive. "Yes, she's the one who gave me your number."

"Oh, thank god," Beatrice breathed out. "It's just, she's the person I worked with most closely."

"How was that?" Jamie asked, not sure why, but listening to her gut.

"Amazing," Beatrice gushed. "She's so smart. So loyal. She was the right amount of concerned about those messages—you know, aware but not overly panicky."

Beatrice paused and Jamie let her have her silence.

"You know, I kind of worried about her up there," Beatrice said. "They were a little cult-y, that family."

Jamie's brows shot up. It was exactly what that young uniform had said. "Did you ever visit in person?"

"No, thank god," Beatrice said. "But I know Mia didn't get out at all. She didn't have any friends. It was kind of sad."

Jamie thanked Beatrice again, made sure the woman had her phone number, and then hung up.

She was quietly glad no one had overheard her make that call. She didn't want to have to explain why she was wasting her time on something that likely had no bearing on the case.

Keller dropped into her visitor's chair not more than a minute later.

"How do you handle those arrogant bastards with such grace?" he asked, as he eyed Boyd and the boys from State across the room. He sank down behind his coffee cup, so that she could mostly just see his thick—yet manicured—brows pinched menacingly.

"I look up their solve rates," she said. "They're nothing to be arrogant about."

Keller huffed out an annoyed breath. "But if no one cares, they still get to act like hot shit."

"Hot shit is exactly what they are," Jamie muttered, and Keller hooted, delighted.

"I thought you were above it all," he said, now sitting up straighter.

She shrugged. "He killed himself. They'll close this case in the next couple hours. Practically, at least, even if the paperwork takes forever."

"You don't think it should be closed?" Keller whispered, intrigued.

She shrugged again. "Dunno. Probably it should be."

He licked his lips. "What can I do?"

"Keep your ear to the ground," she said. "See what Boyd and his boys are saying."

Given a task, Keller was rejuvenated. He saluted with his cup of coffee and bounded over to the cluster of state police officers like he hadn't just been calling them names five seconds earlier.

Meanwhile, Jamie pulled up the nationwide database they had access to.

She searched "Catriona Bouchard."

Nothing but the reports about Fleur Bouchard's kidnapping came up.

She shook her head, and glanced at the file on her desk.

Then she typed in "Catriona Vandale."

And she got results.

CHAPTER TWENTY-NINE

Holland

Now

It was time to talk to Anna.

From all that I'd heard about and experienced with the girl, I didn't have a strong interest in having a prolonged conversation. But she was clearly a part of the household.

I cleared it with both Mia and Cat, because I would have leaped at the excuse not to do it if they had said no. Both agreed, of course. It was the easiest thing I'd arranged since coming to the orchard yesterday.

They directed me to Anna's suite, which was on the same floor as mine.

Anna opened the door nearly before I finished knocking—one of the others must have texted her that I was coming.

"Hello," Anna gushed, grabbing me by both hands and pulling me inside. The room was beautiful in a different way from Cat's rustic chic. The decorations leaned toward jewel colors with heavy, romantic furniture.

She perched herself on a chair that wouldn't have looked out of place in a French palace, and I followed suit. I've never understood why people would choose such uncomfortable seating for their own living room.

"I've never been interviewed before," Anna said, with the nervous excitement of someone who found my job much more important than it was.

"I'll be gentle," I teased, and she flushed.

"I have a boyfriend," she said, as if I'd been flirting with her instead of just putting her at ease.

There really was no reason for Cat to worry about this younger version of herself.

It was funny: If Cat had acted like this when she'd been that age, I wouldn't have had any trouble picturing her married with a bushel of children.

"I'd heard," I said, and took out my recorder. I'd also brought my notebook and a pen, but I didn't think I'd find them necessary. I started with some softballs, and she proved to be just as dull as expected in answering them.

Although, *dull* was perhaps too harsh. She was simply a young woman, who seemed to live most of her life online, in conversation with her boyfriend, or around six children nine and under. She wanted to move back to Switzerland eventually, marry her partner, and have the life Cat lived, pretty much.

I wanted to ask her about money, but that felt too personal—as in, I would just be asking the question to sate my own curiosity. I wanted to know what someone who idolized Cat really believed about having this life as a real possibility without the hundred million dollars that came with it.

"How do you feel about appearing in Cat's social media?" I finally asked, when she'd redirected my fifth question about her to her boyfriend. "As her double?"

Anna's brows wrinkled. "Oh, that's harmless. It's only if I'm caught in the frame."

"So you don't mind?" I asked.

"No." Anna laughed. "Neither does my boyfriend."

"He knows about it?"

Anna tilted her head, like that was the strangest question she'd ever heard. "Of course. Catriona asked me about the possibility in our interview. I had to consult with Luca, but we both agreed the request seemed reasonable."

"All right then," I murmured, because I wasn't sure I agreed with them. But if someone made the decision with her eyes wide open, who was I to judge? "What is it like working for Cat?"

"Catriona," Anna corrected. "I believe you've been told multiple times that she prefers Catriona. Or, of course, Mrs. Bouchard."

I blinked, taken aback by the newly sharp tone and attitude. It was something I would have expected from Mia, but not from this bubblegum version of Cat.

"What is it like working with . . . Mrs. Bouchard?" I tried, though it sat sour in my mouth. The previous Mrs. Bouchard had died tragically, and I wasn't so sure Cat wasn't on her way to that same fate.

But it worked to appease Anna, who grinned. "She's a bit demanding, but she's my very favorite boss I've ever worked for."

For the second time in as many minutes, I was surprised into silence for a beat. Although maybe I shouldn't have been. Like I'd thought earlier, Cat respected talent. As long as someone was good at their job, they could expect to be treated well.

Anna leaned forward, pouncing on the moment. "Can I ask *you* a question?"

"Sure," I said, expecting to be quizzed on whether I had a partner.

"Why do you care?" she asked instead, her blue eyes wide and unblinking.

"About . . . you?" I clarified. "I'm mostly trying to understand Cat better through the people she surrounds herself with."

"Mrs. Bouchard," Anna corrected, almost absently. "No, why do you care about *her*? You clearly don't follow her content because you enjoy her or learning about her kind of lifestyle."

"And that lifestyle is . . . rich?" I interjected. "Yeah, you're right."

"I know I'm right," Anna said. And gone was the girl who could barely concentrate on a question for figuring out how it related back to the incomparable Luca. In her place was a guard dog. Fierce, loyal. I had heard women like Cat amassed armies of a sort, online warriors who went to bat for her in the comment sections. It seemed like Anna was one of them in real life, too. "So why do you care?"

The wild thing was that I actually wanted to give her an answer.

"Because knowing Cat ten years ago—" I held up my hand. "She was Cat back then. Knowing her ten years ago helped me define who I was."

And it had. I was nicer than Cat, quicker to forgive. But she was kinder than me in ways I'd found interesting. I was charismatic, and people usually liked me immediately. But Cat, she was *magnetic*. For some, their polarization didn't work with hers, which meant she forced them away with an ease that could make her look bad. For others, it just clicked in ways that I don't think even she realized. Either way she was a force. That was different from being charming at a party, which was what I had going for me.

She was ambitious, which in turn made me realize how much I was, too. I had applied at *Profile* because I'd thought it was something Cat would do. At the same time she was weak. She cared what people thought of her; she wanted—yearned—for the approval of rich folks, who I would have gladly told to go fuck themselves; her high evaluation of herself, combined with pernicious doubt, gave her both a superiority and an inferiority complex, which battled it out to see which could turn the most people off.

It made me more secure in myself, in turn. It also helped reveal how much I liked getting to know people.

Some of what Cat was now was a maturation of the things she'd been then. She had to be ambitious to create her business and her following, even with her husband's money. The biggest influencers were always magnetic more than charming, because even people turned off by them still wanted to *watch* them. Maybe having an obscene bank account had quieted those voices in her head seeking society's approval, but even if it hadn't, she could just buy and sell all her haters.

I couldn't tell if she'd weaned herself off her complexes, but being able to hide them better was probably a step in the right direction of personal growth.

And thinking through all that, I realized I didn't want to figure out the ways that Cat had changed—because maybe, fundamentally, she hadn't. I wanted to figure out if *I* was different than I had been ten years ago.

This wasn't about Cat; this was about me.

I had been in a slump recently. I was plateaued at work, budget cuts always creeping in on the edges. I'd struggled to make any real friends in the city. I got invited to holiday parties and girls' nights, but I had never found that connection like I'd had with Cat again, the way we'd felt like platonic soulmates.

I couldn't remember the last relationship I'd had. There were just a string of Jeremys in my rearview window. I had never wanted kids, and that hadn't changed. But I was lonely and probably bordering on depressed, if I was being brutally honest with myself.

Which I wasn't actually a huge fan of these days.

Then my mother had died. We hadn't been close. When my sister, Francesca, was murdered, my mom just gave up trying to be a functioning adult. She pretty much wilted away, refusing to move from her chair, which she'd set up in Francesca's bedroom.

My mother's death should have been uneventful, a blip in my own life. But it sent me back into the darkness that had taken over both of us in the wake of the tragedy. I found myself gravitating toward Cat's account more often.

I might have convinced myself it was research for an article I hadn't come up with yet, but I had always checked in on Cat via her socials. Of course, I used the account I'd long ago created for my research—one that didn't have my name linked to it in any fashion—because I hadn't been assured of my welcome.

I still didn't feel certain of that. Maybe Cat had learned to forgive people right along with learning to love having children.

"So, you're using her to figure your own shit out? That's not a fair way to tell her story," Anna said, after giving me a minute to sit with my thoughts. "You should have realized that before coming here."

"I think it's the fairest way, actually," I countered. "No one else sees all her layers like I do."

Anna's head tilted again, like that was the oddest thing she'd ever heard. "Kris does."

I wanted to roll my eyes.

But before I could say anything, she continued. "He does. And before you say you knew her when she was young, that's when he met her, too."

That was all well and good to say, but Anna didn't know how Cat had worn personas before—she'd done it for Benji. She just seemed to have accepted it as her personality now. So, no, Kris didn't know Cat like I did.

I knew the real her, while he got the overlay.

I wasn't going to sit here and argue with the au pair, though—especially one who had a little more bite than I had been expecting.

"Okay, thank you for your time," I said, standing.

She stopped me, though. "Holland, you seem like you mean well."

I didn't just keep walking, but I was tempted. "Okay."

"When Catriona told us that you were coming, she said you were her roommate for a couple months ten years ago," Anna said. "That you weren't very close back then, but that you're a good writer and that it should be good for her business."

Anna said this to hurt me, I knew. But what she didn't understand was that I had known plenty of women like her.

Cat didn't want people to know we'd been close because they might guess I held some of her secrets.

Who Fleur's real father was, for one. And I guessed anything that related to Benji came along with that.

"That's so interesting, Anna," I said, in a way that conveyed that it was not. "I wonder . . ."

She bit, because she was that type of person. "You wonder what?"

"I wonder how exactly she would describe you," I said softly, letting my eyes trail over her, and then her silly, romantic room, which clashed with every single fiber of Cat's being.

I left the rest unsaid.

Anna could fill in the blanks.

She was smarter than she seemed.

CHAPTER THIRTY

Holland

Now

Anger nipped at my heels, chasing me through the hallway outside Anna's suite.

My heart beat erratically in my throat, in my pulse points, and I wanted to stop, lean against the wall, and calm down.

I didn't usually have a hair trigger—I couldn't. The number of ways my interview subjects had found to insult me were both legion and creative. My skin might as well have been hide for how thick it was.

But something about Anna's smug expression as she played gatekeeper to Cat had made my skin prickly and blood hot.

She thought she knew Cat.

My feet carried me down the stairs and headed toward the back of the house before I'd consciously thought through where I was going.

Kris, Cat, and Mia would think I was still chatting with Anna—they would never have guessed that I would bail on the interview in less than ten minutes, deeming it unworthy of my time.

They would never expect me to slip into Kris's office. The door wasn't even locked. Three minutes after I'd left Anna's room, I was in.

The dark slid over me not only like a blanket but like a tonic. My anger melted away into the breath I exhaled, gone as quickly as it had come on.

I shook my head, mad at myself now. This wasn't high school. Anna's mean-girl roleplaying couldn't affect me if I didn't let it.

I turned my attention to what the hell I was doing in Kris's office. There was only a night-light plugged into the far wall, but it created shapes out of the furniture instead of just a void. At least I wouldn't run smack into anything—or anyone.

Turning on one of the standing lights might give me away, but there was another option. Kris was apparently one of the few people left who had a giant desktop monitor for his computer. I woke it up, getting the log-in screen I'd expected—a photo of him and Cat on their wedding day.

The sight of the old version of her stopped me.

Cat.

I was struck again by the thought that this was more about me than Cat. I wanted to be who I had been then, when we knew everything and the world was ours and every other cliché of what it felt like to be young and happy and alive. Before the disappointments, the rejection, the universe showing you that it didn't give two shits about you.

Kris was staring at her as if that Cat gave him the same feeling. Like he would never let her go now that he'd caught her.

His hand curled tight against her hip, his fingers gripped her arm.

This was supposed to be a great, whirlwind love, and yet all I could see was obsession.

I looked away.

The safe, I was guessing, was behind one of the paintings or photographs that hung on the wall. I went around to each, tipping them to the side only to find nothing underneath.

I chewed on my lip. What was I even trying to accomplish with finding it?

"It's behind the books."

I nearly screamed, but managed to hold it back in time.

Steffie leaned against the wall right by the door. I didn't know how long he'd been watching me or, really, how long I'd been in here.

"What?" I managed, though I wondered if he could hear the question over the sound of my pounding heart.

"You're looking for his safe. It's behind the third bookshelf," Steffie said. "*Moby Dick* pulls out as a secret lever."

"Oh my god," I muttered, but crossed over and found the volume. It gave easily when I tugged. The bookshelf slid easily to the side after that, revealing a fancy black safe tucked behind it.

At some point Steffie had joined me. "That's as far as I got."

I nodded, staring at the keypad. I had actually expected some biometric lock—requiring Kris's fingerprint or retina. But like with the gate, he'd gone the simpler route. I wondered if he was a technophobe, which would make a lot of things make sense.

"You're not going to try to crack it, are you?" Steffie asked, and there was nothing but unbridled curiosity and excitement in his voice. He didn't seem even a little appalled at my blatant invasion of privacy.

"No," I said, though my eyes drifted back to the background on his father's desktop.

I typed in their wedding date and held my breath.

Nothing.

"Who's your dad's favorite?" I asked Steffie.

He laughed. "He's not going to use one of our birth dates, if that's what you're thinking. I'm not even sure he can tell the twins apart."

No, he was right. It would be about Cat, if it was personal at all.

I scoured my memory for any important dates, and thought about the conversation on the porch this afternoon.

"The day they met," I murmured, and typed it in.

The light glowed red.

I wondered if I had limited opportunities or if it was a free-for-all.

"What did you try?" Steffie asked.

"Their wedding and the day they met," I said, staring at the keypad, willing it to give up its secrets.

"Whoa, how did you remember those?" Steffie asked, but then nudged me aside before waiting for an answer. "You're American."

"So?" I asked.

He shook his head. "What are the two dates?"

I gave him the wedding one, and nothing happened. "I already tried it."

"Not with the right day-month order," he said, sounding disgusted despite the fact that he'd grown up in the States. "What's the day they met?"

I told him and held my breath as he punched it in.

The pause between the last number and the light blinking green felt like a lifetime.

But the door clicked open.

As softly as possible, I cheered and bumped into Steffie with my shoulder.

"I didn't think he'd go for sentimental over what he should," Steffie muttered, but he looked quite pleased with both himself and the situation. "Which is a string of random numbers, of course."

"Of course," I said, but my eyes were locked on what the safe had revealed.

A gun. And in some gangster-movie cliché, it sat on stacks of money. Beneath those were a few file folders that would only be interesting if they had something to do with Kris's divorce from Odette. I had no interest in his various business dealings as long as they didn't involve the women in his life.

Steffie's hand twitched upward, as if he wanted to reach for the weapon, but knew he shouldn't.

Guilt and dread slipped in behind my excitement. Here was a troubled boy, one who hated his father, and I had just essentially provided him with a gun.

Shit.

I stood there, paralyzed with indecision. This horse couldn't go back in the barn unless I told Cat and Kris what I had done. I obviously couldn't change the code.

The only thing I could do was pray that he wouldn't come back for this after I went to bed.

Or . . . I could take the gun myself.

How often did Kris check his safe? Judging from the contents, I guessed not often. There wasn't anything in there that he would need on a daily basis. If he checked it in a week and found the gun missing, he would probably connect the stolen item to me, but it wouldn't matter at that point. I would be out of the house, my article already in my editor's hands.

And Steffie wouldn't have access to a dangerous firearm that no one realized he had access to.

I stared at him staring at it. Did I really think he would do anything with the gun?

I didn't know. I didn't know how to read him. He'd been terrifying in the greenhouse, looming over me with clenched fists. But his temper had cooled almost as quickly as it had come upon him. The other times I'd dealt with him, he'd seemed fairly chill.

There was also an anger in him that I recognized, though. It was the kind that had lived in me like a wild thing in the aftermath of my sister's murder. I would have, with my bare hands, ripped apart the man who had done that to her if I could have reached him.

Steffie blamed Kris for Odette's death, even if he thought it was because his father had driven his mother to suicide. That would be enough to plant a seed.

And all a gun needed was that seed, that anger, that twitch of a finger.

I hated myself in that moment, because my own stupid anger had brought me in here, and now I had put us into a no-win predicament.

There was nothing else to do, though. I had to take the gun.

"I think we better get out of here," I said quietly, making sure to keep my voice as upbeat as it had been when we'd been partners in crime.

"Yeah," he said, still not taking his eyes off the weapon.

"You leave first," I said. When still he didn't move, I placed the most careful hand on his elbow. "Steffie."

He flinched and then shook his head, finally breaking eye contact with the gun. "We can leave together."

I'd known he was going to suggest that. "I'm going to make sure everything's in place."

"I'll do that," he said, stubborn now. I wondered if he was aware of the fact that he wanted to take the gun or if his subconscious was just directing him to stall.

"You don't know everything I touched," I said, and this time when I touched him, he reared back, gripping his arm.

"Don't put your hands on me," he said, a bit too loud.

I held up my palms to show I meant no harm. "Let's be smart, Steffie."

His eyes were wild, darting in the dark corners and back to my face. "Why were you even in here? You're not supposed to be in here."

I had already been told that. But I didn't need him to start questioning me. I shifted so that my body blocked the safe, hoping to break whatever spell he'd fallen under.

"I know," I said. "I'm trying to get out of here, but I need your help. Why don't you go watch in the hall to make sure no one is coming? They won't wonder what you're doing down here, but I could get in trouble."

Steffie drew in a breath, seemingly coming back to himself. It had been a good idea to give him a task. And he would be able to see that I left only a couple of minutes after him. In theory, he could check if I'd taken the gun.

He exhaled and finally nodded. In the end, I was an adult and he was a teenager. Even if he was "troubled," it was still more likely that he would listen than not.

With one last longing glance in the direction of the safe he could no longer see, he turned and left.

Once I was sure as I could be that he wasn't peeking in, I grabbed the gun and pulled my sweater up. The fabric was bulky and would do a good job covering the weapon. I finagled the weapon so that my bra strap held it tight against my chest. It wouldn't last long that way, but it would hold until I got past the boy.

Then I covered our tracks as best I could.

A minute later, I was at the door. "All clear?"

"Yeah," Steffie said, assessing me.

"I didn't take anything," I assured him, lifting the hem of my sweater to show him that I hadn't stashed the weapon in the waistband.

He seemed genuinely surprised and pleased. He nodded, and I wondered when he would discover the thing was missing. He'd probably at least wait until everyone was asleep.

At the latest, he would know by the next morning.

I didn't think he would rat me out—that would involve him knowing that the gun had been in the safe in the first place. Plus he'd shown me the hiding place for it. But I wouldn't put it past him to try to find it in my things.

Perhaps when the rest of the family left the orchard for the church.

"Come on," I said. Just because I didn't think he would go right back in didn't mean he wouldn't. "Let's get out of here."

To my pleasant surprise, he went willingly.

"I've been thinking," he said quietly. "When we were on our camping trip?"

Him and his mom. Odette. I nodded to get him to keep going.

And he did. "I didn't remember until you asked, but I think . . . that night before she . . . did it?"

"Yeah?" I prodded.

"We both heard someone outside of our tent."

I stopped, nearly mid-stride. "What?"

He nodded, turning to me. His eyes were big and dark and glassy. "We laughed it off as a bear, or something. But what if . . . what if someone had followed us?"

My breath hitched. "It was just the sound? You didn't see anything else?"

Probably he was misremembering now, filling in details that hadn't been there in reality.

He made a dejected face. "No. I wish I had gone to look."

His eyes slid back to the office. He wanted his past self to have a gun, ready and willing to go out and brave whatever that sound had been.

"Okay," I said, and anger slipped into his expression.

"You don't believe me," he said, his dark brows knitting together. "No one ever believes me."

"I didn't say that." I didn't actually know what I believed at the moment. Odette Moreau's death had been strange, but so was remembering a crucial detail like this six months after it had all happened.

"See, this is why I haven't told anyone," he said. "No one ever believes me."

"That's not—"

But I couldn't even get the reassurance out completely before he stormed up the stairs, making sure each footfall was loud and pointed.

"Wow, I'm impressed," Mia said from behind me. "That level of tantrum is usually reserved for Catriona."

I spun to find her standing in the door of her own office, her arms crossed, her eyes sharp.

The gun was suddenly hot against my chest, and I resisted the urge to fidget with my sweater. That left me very unsure of what to do with my hands.

"Anything I need to know about?" she asked, and for a brief moment I thought she was talking about the gun. But her eyes were on the stairs.

"I guess my not-great-with-kids vibe extends to teenagers," I said, with a casual shrug. A bead of sweat had formed beneath the metal and now it slid down my belly.

"Hmm," Mia hummed, sounding dubious. Her eyes shifted to the hallway. "Did you find what you were looking for?"

The world went silent around me before a loud buzzing filled my ears. "What?"

She looked at me. "From your conversation with Anna. Did you find what you're looking for?"

I exhaled as quietly as I could so that it didn't expose the rush of nerves fluttering beneath my skin. I was going to be caught out. Mia was simply too clever not to notice something was off.

Anna.

"Actually," I said, slowly, hesitant. "How long . . ."

"How long what?" Mia prompted, and I could tell I'd piqued her curiosity.

"How long has Anna worked here?" I asked. I might have been told this information at some point, but it didn't matter if I was supposed to know or not. The point was to get Mia thinking about it so that she wasn't wondering what was shoved beneath my sweater.

"Four years or so," Mia said. She cocked her head. "Why?"

"The obsessed fan," I said, again, like I was feeling out a new theory and not deliberately trying to distract her. "Is there any chance she lived in this area before she was hired? A few years before?"

Mia rocked back on her heels, but she didn't burst out with a denial. "Did she say something that made you think . . . ?"

I pictured our interview, how she'd been far more aggressive than I could have ever expected. How she had an idea of Cat built up in her mind and my very existence challenged it. This had started as a tactic, but honestly, it wasn't far-fetched. "She seems quite devoted to Cat."

"A lot of people are," Mia mused.

"She said Cat is her favorite employer she's ever had," I said.

"That doesn't mean she's sending Cat these messages."

"No," I agreed quickly, because I knew Mia and I thought on similar wavelengths. And she would be able to hear the *it doesn't mean she's not* in the silence.

"Well, thank you for your observations. I'll take them into account," Mia said, not sounding particularly convinced. But she no longer looked suspicious, so I counted it as a win. "Are you going to church with the Bouchards in the morning?"

"Yup," I said, and once again I could feel the gun pulsing against my skin. I forced a yawn. "Well, I think I'm going to turn in."

Mia nodded. "Okay."

Before she could comment any further, I dashed up the stairs and didn't stop running until I got to my room.

I'd never locked a door so quickly in my life. I leaned against it and pulled out the gun, which had been barely hanging on to the band of my bra. I tried to imagine what would have happened if it had fallen to the floor between us.

Maybe she would have kicked me out on the spot.

Or maybe she wouldn't have said anything.

Maybe she would have understood that it wasn't exactly the best strategy for the same person who was the only one who knew the gate code to also be the only one in the house with a weapon.

Along I came, then, one of about three people who would have known to try that date.

And suddenly, the equation had completely changed.

CHAPTER THIRTY-ONE

Cat

Then

The taste of bile lingered in my mouth, so I grabbed a Diet Coke from the fridge before stepping into the living room. It had the extra benefit of making me look casually curious about who was at the door rather than already knowing it was a cop who stood there.

Holland stepped back to let the detective who'd come asking about Mark into our apartment.

I was furious with her for doing so—she wasn't a Boomer who would just appease the cops' every whim. She was young, she knew her rights. She should have made them come back with a warrant.

But Holland wasn't trying to hide anything.

The tall, slim woman who stood just on our side of the door stared at me with hard eyes. She was young and so held herself in a way that demanded everyone take her seriously because no one instinctually would.

"I'm Detective Silvia Rodrigues," the woman said, and then gestured to a portly man behind her. "And this is my partner, Detective Bart Hetrick."

The name was so absurd it knocked some of the fear out of my system. "Can we help you?"

"You're Catriona Vandale?" Silvia Rodrigues asked, checking her notebook as if she couldn't remember a simple name. It was all part of the show, I knew. To unsettle me.

"Yes," I said. Then I asked again, "Can I help you?"

"You knew Marcus Sinclair," she asked.

My grip tightened on the Diet Coke can. "Yes. I dated him a few months ago."

She nodded. She'd known that. "I'm sorry to have to tell you this, but he was found dead this week."

I didn't know what to do with my face. My honest reaction upon hearing the news had been to vomit. But I didn't think it would go over well if I tried to replicate that. I probably ended up with some expression that looked like I'd smelled rotten meat. I nodded. "Oh."

Silvia Rodrigues was watching my face closely. "Oh?"

I nodded again and then silently sought help from Holland. She burst into action.

"Officers, perhaps we could have this conversation another time?" she suggested. "Cat's obviously received a bit of a shock here."

"It's just a few questions," Silvia Rodrigues said, and the ingrained need to bow to authority proved too strong for Holland. She shot me a helpless look and then waved toward the living room.

"Then perhaps we could all sit down?"

I was caught between thinking that was a good suggestion and thinking that was a terrible suggestion. It would buy me a few minutes, at least. But then the cops might not ever leave.

I reassured myself that I had done nothing wrong. Technically.

Ethically? That might be a different story.

Silvia Rodrigues, of course, jumped at the chance to come in farther. She made herself comfortable on one of the two chairs facing the couch. Her partner took the other, while Holland and I sank, in unison, onto our well-loved sofa.

I wanted to grip her hand, but she would feel how clammy mine was.

"Did he kill her first?" I couldn't help but ask, all my walls crumbling under the weight of this young police officer's eyes.

Because that question was what had sent me hurtling toward the sink, bile already in my throat, and the words rushed out just as easily.

She exchanged a glance with her partner and then pulled out a notebook. "Did he kill *who* first, Catriona?"

"It's Cat," I corrected and then shook my head. "Sorry, what did you want to ask us?"

"Did he kill who first, Cat?" Silvia Rodrigues asked again, and I wanted to slam my hand very hard in a door as punishment for letting the thought slip out.

Holland didn't seem to know what to do; she was stuck looking between me and the detectives. "Um, how did Mark die?"

With that, I forgave her for letting them into the apartment in the first place, because that actually got Silvia Rodrigues to take her attention off me.

"He was shot," she said. Then immediately her eyes tracked back to me. "Who were you worried about, Cat?"

Holland laid her hand on top of mine and squeezed.

I took a breath and decided the truth was best. I could dance around this. I was smart as hell and I hadn't done anything wrong.

And I wanted that fucking answer.

Shot could mean self-inflicted. Though perhaps the fact that they were sitting here meant that it hadn't been suicide.

"His girlfriend," I said, and Holland's thumb stilled. I hadn't even realized it had been drawing circles on my skin until it stopped.

The girlfriend he'd probably put in the hospital. Men like Mark didn't change.

"Did you think he had a girlfriend?" Silvia Rodrigues asked, her pen hovering above her notebook, her eyes on me. She posed the question like a therapist would. Like there was no wrong answer—the right one was whatever I believed.

But this wasn't a shrink's office. This was the real world, and there was an actual answer here. "The last I'd heard, yes, he was dating someone."

Holland had sat back, taking her hand away completely, probably surprised that I had followed up with Mark after dumping him.

"And when was that?" Silvia Rodrigues asked. "That you knew he had a girlfriend."

"I don't know," I said, my chest tight. "Three or four months ago?"

Some of the tension Silvia Rodrigues had been holding in her body melted out. The answer disappointed her, I could tell. It had also brought Holland back to me.

Her hand covered mine again, and she was sitting forward, engaged in the conversation.

"Could you tell us what happened, Detective?" Holland asked, nonthreatening. Almost pleading.

Silvia Rodrigues and the partner exchanged glances. "First, Cat, could you tell us about your last interaction with him?"

Of course, I wasn't about to tell them my actual last interaction with the man. But I could give them something.

"It was when I broke up with him," I said. "A year ago now, maybe?" I took a deep breath. I didn't want to admit to the next part, but it would distract them, and maybe even make them take it easy on me. I was a domestic abuse survivor, after all. I rubbed a knuckle at the corner of my eye as if there were a tear there. "He put me in the hospital and it was my last straw."

Understanding dawned on the detectives, and I could see them replaying my frantic question: *Did he kill her first?*

I glanced at Holland and could see her doing the same.

Of course, Holland didn't need me to help her get to that thought; it was always hovering in the corners of her mind.

Silvia Rodrigues closed her notebook. "Are you dating someone?"

I reared back. "What does that have anything to do with anything?"

She sighed. "Marcus Sinclair was found stuffed in the trunk of a stolen car in the alley behind a strip bar."

"Oh Jesus, what a fitting end," Holland muttered.

"It was clearly a crime of passion," Silvia Rodrigues said without reacting to that. "Maybe a boyfriend seeking revenge on an ex who hadn't treated his girlfriend right?"

"Oh God no," I said on a rush that must have sounded as authentic as it felt because Silvia Rodrigues looked like she immediately believed me. "In no universe would my boyfriend . . . No. His name is Benjamin Croft, but just, no. I don't even think he knows Mark's full name."

Silvia Rodrigues looked at Holland, who made a face. "He's not my favorite person, but no, I couldn't see him hunting down Mark and shooting him. Plus we met him when Cat was put in the hospital. If he'd been going to do something drastic, it would have been a while ago."

The detectives nodded in unison and then stood. "All right, thank you. We're chasing down any lead we can, so if you think of anything . . ."

Just as Silvia Rodrigues stepped into the hallway, she paused. "Oh. Do you know the name of the girlfriend? Or ex? The one he was dating?"

My heart raced again, and I tried to ignore the gray at the edges of my vision that came from the whiplash. "No, I'm sorry. I just heard he'd started seeing someone through a mutual friend."

Silvia Rodrigues nodded, then smiled at both of us tightly. Then she—blessedly—walked out of my life.

I sank back onto the couch, my hands shaking from the excess adrenaline.

Holland was by my side in a second, rubbing my arm soothingly. "Jesus. I mean, I'm kind of glad that scumbag is dead, but . . ."

She didn't finish her thought, just shook her head, disbelieving.

"Yeah," I said, and then stood. "I need alcohol."

"Amen," she said.

Once I'd poured us hefty doses of wine, she pulled her legs up beneath her and studied my face. "How did you know Mark was seeing someone? And don't give me that mutual-friend bullshit. You guys didn't have any mutual friends."

I could lie. It would be easy enough. Michi from The Bistro knew the girl he'd been dating. But I was feeling off-kilter, and honestly, the confession was burning a hole in my tongue. I couldn't keep it in any longer.

I exhaled, and told her the reason I had been so terrified at the news of his death. "Because I introduced them."

CHAPTER THIRTY-TWO

Holland

Now

The knock on my door came at 2:00 a.m.

I stared at the drawer where I'd stashed the gun for now. It wasn't a good hiding spot. If that was Kris out there, I'd be screwed.

But as long as someone didn't outright search my room, it should be okay for the night.

My palms broke out in a sweat, even as I told myself it was probably Jeremy looking for a booty call.

I crossed the room and tried to listen for any sign. The only sounds in the night were produced from an old Vermont farmhouse settling in for sleep, and the forest beyond doing the same.

I had expected Jeremy.

I had braced myself for Kris.

I had been hopeful for Mia.

And I'd been dreading Steffie.

The one person I hadn't anticipated, though, stood there.

Cat was dressed in an old-timey sleeping dress, her hair in a loose braid. The look was so compelling, I would not have been shocked to learn she'd been taking pictures and videos of herself just now to post later.

The light behind her gave her edges a gauzy look, and if I had been in a different state of mind, I might have thought her a ghost come to visit.

"Did I wake you?" she asked.

"No, come in," I said, eager now. Even when we'd been alone before, it hadn't felt that way. On our walk in the orchard, Stan had been not far behind us. Mia had been lurking outside during our conversation in the office. Cat's children were always about a half step away, a second from barging in.

But right now, it felt like the world was built to hold just the two of us.

Cat didn't hesitate. She simply climbed onto the foot of my bed and curled herself against the post.

I hopped up, leaning against the headboard as casually as I could. My recorder was on my nightstand, but for once, I didn't want this conversation on tape. So I let it be.

Cat watched me until I was settled in. "Can I ask you about you?"

"Uh," I said, stumbling at first. "Yeah, of course."

She nodded. "I know this is all about me, but I really do want to know what's been going on in your life."

"Not a whole lot," I said.

"Yeah, you keep trying to downplay it," she said, serious now. "But I do want to know. Are you dating anyone?"

I hated that people always started with that question. No, I was never dating anyone. But if I said that, I would get the sympathetic head tilt. So I made someone up instead. "Max. I met him in an adult softball league, of all places."

She wrinkled her nose, and I loved it. I loved when I could see the old Cat, even for a second. "You're in a softball league."

It wasn't even a question, just a statement of disbelief coated in disdain.

I laughed so hard I almost pitched forward. "I was in it exactly long enough to meet Max. Who does boring work with computer things, but also always goes and gets my favorite bagels every Saturday morning even though they're an extra three-block walk."

Cat smiled and I couldn't tell if she actually believed me or just wanted to. "I'm glad. You deserve to be happy."

I didn't know if I wanted to go there or not. But it was late, and I was going to leave on Monday and would maybe never have this opportunity again.

"Do you really think so?" I asked.

Cat inhaled and brought her legs to her chest, hugging herself tight. "You were young."

That wasn't forgiveness. It wasn't even acknowledgment that she'd made a huge fucking assumption that had led her to believe I needed forgiving in the first place.

"I didn't sleep with Benji," I said, perhaps for the four hundredth time. Only, I'd uttered the last three hundred and ninety-nine ten years ago. The one before this had come when we were both standing over his freshly covered grave.

She inhaled and looked away like she was talking herself out of engaging in the argument.

"I didn't," I repeated.

I could practically see the debate going on behind her eyes. But why else would she have come here tonight?

"Why were you with him that night he died? Without me there?" Cat asked.

And this was what I hadn't been able to tell her before. I wasn't sure why the words had never come out; I didn't remember why a lie had seemed easier at the time.

"I found your pregnancy test," I finally said.

Cat exhaled like she'd been punched in the solar plexus. "What?"

I swallowed hard. "I had to go into your room for some reason or other, and . . . I found it. And I couldn't let Benji do what he'd been doing to you to a kid. I couldn't."

She opened her mouth, then closed it. She had never wanted to admit back then to what had been going on between them. I didn't expect her to change her story now, either, even after all these years. She was stubborn.

But her silence was acknowledgment enough.

"I went over to his place," I said. "I just . . . I wanted to tell him I knew what was going on. How he was hurting you."

"He wasn't hurting me," Cat said, throwing her limbs, all exasperation. "You misunderstood a series of mishaps."

"Okay," I said slowly, because I didn't want to argue. One or two mishaps, sure. But there had to have been a half dozen incidents, and those were the ones that I'd known about. "I thought he was hurting you. And I knew you wouldn't leave him unless he put you in the hospital, which meant you could lose the baby."

Her hand went instinctively to her lower belly, as if Fleur weren't safely sleeping down the hallway, nearly ten years old now.

"I wasn't going to tell him about the pregnancy," I rushed on. "You hadn't even told me. I didn't know if you wanted to keep it, and . . ."

This was the hard part.

"And what?" Cat asked, gentle as anything.

"That's why my sister's ex killed her," I managed to get out. "Because he found out she was pregnant. She wouldn't get an abortion, either. I think he wanted to beat the baby out of her."

"Goodness," Cat murmured. I'd told her about Francesca, but I didn't think I'd been so graphic.

"Benji was already wasted when I got there," I said. "I'd never seen him like that before."

He had been able to hold his alcohol, so it had been surprising to find him like that.

"He was kind of belligerent," I continued, lost in memories of that night. That terrible, god-awful night. "And I knew I'd made a mistake the second I'd walked in."

"But you stayed," she said softly.

I had, which had proven to be the ultimate fault line in our friendship. Cat had called and Benji had answered. He'd acted like the two of us were hanging out for fun, not like I was trying to keep him from passing out and then asphyxiating on his own vomit. I didn't even remember what he'd said to her, but I'd been trying to get him to drink some water.

Cat, though, she wouldn't have needed any other detail beyond the fact that her best friend and boyfriend were hanging out together. The green-eyed monster that lived in her chest was perpetually just one tiny poke away from roaring awake.

"He started talking about going to see you," I said. "So I took his keys. I knocked on his neighbor's door and asked the old guy who answered to return them in the morning."

That was all in the police report, if she'd have thought to look at it. The neighbor had been elderly but very kind. He'd been an alcoholic in his younger years, he'd told me, and he understood how people could get sometimes. He'd thanked me for looking out for a friend, then promised to return the keys to Benji after he'd sobered up.

"Why didn't you call me?" Cat asked. "I could have come to stay with him."

I met her eyes, and it only took a second for her to answer her own question.

"He was being belligerent," she said, understanding coating her voice. "You didn't want to put me in that situation."

I shrugged. "I guess I wish I had. But I also don't know what would have happened to you had you gone over there."

Cat stared at a spot on the wall behind me, unblinking, unmoving. I let her sit in her memories.

Finally, she looked back at me. "I'd told him about the baby that day."

He had mentioned that. I nodded.

But she didn't see because she was staring at a spot over my shoulder, lost in memory. "He got wasted because of me. I told him about the baby and he hung up on me. I guess it was too much for him to handle."

"He was coming for you," I whispered. "That's why he got behind the wheel that night."

"Maybe," Cat admitted. "He always kept an extra set of keys because if he got called in to the hospital on an emergency, he didn't want to waste time looking for his."

"I didn't know that." A half hour after I'd left Benji on his couch, he'd wrapped his car around a telephone pole. He hadn't been wearing a seat belt. The only silver lining had been that he hadn't hurt any bystanders.

Tears slipped down Cat's cheeks. "Why didn't you tell me any of this?"

I tried, I wanted to say. But was that true?

Profile Magazine had brought in a memory expert one time. This had been back when the company was still interested in making a good product. But Dr. Bhatt had told all of us what psychological thrillers and true crime TV shows had been preaching for decades: Human memory was completely fallible. It was actually more likely to misremember something than to remember it with pinpoint accuracy.

Dr. Bhatt had said that people viewed their memories like files on a computer, as though you could just click into a video and watch exactly what had happened on any given day and then close out. The next time you looked, even if it was five years later, it would be the exact same video.

But that was not how brains worked. Instead, people should think of memories like particularly malleable Play-Doh. When we held the memories in our hands, we inevitably changed them. We left our fingerprints all over them, we dented them, we smoothed them out in some places and created divots in others. And then we put them back in the drawer thinking that the latest version was the original one.

The days after Benji had died had been chaotic, painful, and traumatic. The memories created during that time couldn't be trusted.

I had known Cat was furious at me for being with Benji alone when she'd called. I had known she had taken his death incredibly hard. I had known she was pregnant and hadn't wanted to upset her, given the fact that she was carrying her dead lover's baby.

Still, I'd thought I'd made my case. Maybe not as clearly and concisely as I had just now, but I had tried to tell her: I hadn't been sleeping with her boyfriend.

Now, though, I realized something else.

She had blamed herself.

She hadn't wanted to hear the truth because doing so would mean that *she* was the one who'd dropped the news on him, that *she* was the one he'd been trying to come see. She'd needed to be angry at me so she couldn't be furious at herself.

If that was what she'd needed to keep her going, I couldn't even regret all the years that the misunderstanding had kept us apart.

Cat was full-on crying now.

"You didn't need the truth back then, Cat," I said quietly, finally answering her question. "You just needed to find a way to survive."

I held out my arms, and she came easily into them. She was taller than me, but she tucked her head under my chin and sobbed as if Benji had died just yesterday.

She wasn't loud at all—Cat was, if nothing else, always aware of her surroundings—but her body trembled, and I smoothed a palm up and down her back.

I didn't believe in the whole detox fad, but it felt like Cat was releasing something poisonous, something that had infected her bloodstream for ten years.

I wasn't sure how long we stayed that way. Cat had long ago stopped crying, but she hadn't removed herself from my embrace.

In the quietest voice, she finally said, "I'm going to tell Kris about Fleur."

I stiffened, as fear slipped into every part of my body. "Cat, no."

She nodded against my chest. "I am. I'm sure he's suspected over the years. He must have done the math before and found it too close for comfort."

I kept rubbing her back, but my mind was turning over everything from this weekend. It kept getting stuck on Odette Moreau and the videos Mia wouldn't post because the bruises were too obvious.

"Just don't do anything rash," I said, terrified now. I wouldn't have brought this up had I known what it would make her consider. "Don't turn your life upside down after one emotional evening."

Cat was quiet for a moment, and then she sniffed. "I'll pray on it tomorrow."

And maybe, for the first time in years, I would join her.

CHAPTER THIRTY-THREE

Det. Jamie Alvarez

Catriona Bouchard née Vandale didn't have a record. She'd never been issued so much as a speeding ticket.

But she was one of those women who trouble seemed to follow around.

Jamie's grandmother had talked a lot about women like that, mostly because Jamie's mother had been one. These women, they had the boyfriends who were arrested for mob-related activity; the kids who got hauled in on a drug lab bust; the friends who would snitch anyone out to the cops for a dollar. Jamie's kid would lecture her if she ever said anything like that out loud—it wasn't the woman's fault, it was the circumstance and the system and the patriarchy all conspiring against her.

It wasn't that Jamie didn't think all that was true; it was that she was a practical person. There was a type of woman who trouble followed around, and naming that phenomenon was just stating the facts.

Nothing showed up in the database since Catriona had been married—other than her daughter's kidnapping case.

The first mention of her was in a police report from ten years ago.

Benjamin Croft had drunk himself into a 0.23 blood alcohol level and then gotten into a car to drive. As too often was the case in that scenario, it had not ended well for him. Jamie was just glad to see no one else had been injured.

He had been Catriona's boyfriend at the time.

But people drank and drove all the time. People died from drinking and driving all the time. It was sad, but not exactly a red flag.

Catriona was also listed in another case, as an interviewee. The case had been a homicide, which had Jamie raising her eyebrows.

Marcus Sinclair had been found, shot dead, in the trunk of a car. No security cameras, no witnesses, no usable forensic evidence. No obvious motive. He hadn't been involved in drugs or gangs or even white-collar crime. There were conflicting reports about a girlfriend—some of his friends said they'd broken up, while others said they had an on-and-off-again thing.

Catriona had been interviewed as a known associate of the victim. Ex-girlfriend, if Jamie was reading between the lines correctly.

Detective Silvia Rodrigues had noted that both Catriona and the on-again, off-again—Tamara, according to the case file—had hospital visits on record during the months they'd been dating Sinclair.

She'd tried to pursue that line of thought, but it hadn't led anywhere. Tamara *did* have a new boyfriend who had seemed like he could get access to an unregistered gun and had the demeanor to stuff a dead body in the trunk of a car, but without any proof that he'd done so, the case had died in a cold file drawer.

Jamie glanced up to see the boys from State all clustered in the chief's office. Maybe they were preparing for the press conference they'd called. Maybe they were measuring each other's dicks. She didn't care. What mattered was that she wasn't being given anything to work on, so she might as well waste time on a wild-goose chase.

It took a couple of tries to get Detective Silvia Rodrigues on the phone, but after about twenty minutes, Jamie managed to track her down.

After a few explanations, Jamie said, "Can I ask you about the Marcus Sinclair case?"

"Shoot," Rodrigues said. "I might be hazy on the details and the file isn't in front of me, but I remember it decently well."

"Who did you make for it?" Jamie asked. Plenty of investigations went to the cold case drawer even when the cops knew who'd done it. Jamie was guessing Rodrigues at least had an idea.

"Tammy's new boyfriend," Rodrigues said without missing a beat. "Sinclair was abusive and a pest about it."

Most of them were. "Not taking the breakup well?"

"At all," Rodrigues corrected. "He'd show up at her work, show up at her apartment, wait by her car. She tried to file a restraining order, but the Sinclairs are popular in town here. It's why I remember the case so well, actually. It had all the makings of Tammy ending up dead instead of him."

The story was so common it was almost boring. Or it would have been without the twist.

"And what did you make of Catriona Vandale?" Jamie asked. "The ex-girlfriend before Tammy."

"I would have made her for it had she not looked like a light breeze would blow her over at the time," Rodrigues said.

Jamie had been rocking back in her chair, but that made her sit up. "What?"

"I scared the shit out of her by showing up," Rodrigues said. "I swear she puked right before the interview."

"Because you were there?"

"Don't know, but I could smell it on her," Rodrigues said. "She was pale and shaking."

"Yet you don't think she had anything to do with it?" Jamie asked.

"No, and you know why?" Rodrigues said. "Because she asked a question first, pretty much before I could say anything."

It had to be a doozy for Rodrigues to write off such suspicious behavior. "I'll bite."

"She said, 'Did he kill her first?' Gave me goose bumps, I'll never fucking forget it."

Jamie nodded, though Rodrigues couldn't see her. "Well, that would do it."

"Yeah, pretty much ended the interview there," Rodrigues said.

A commotion caught Jamie's attention. The boys from State were on the move, all bustle and fluster. Keller was headed in her direction.

"Hey, I gotta go, thanks for the info," Jamie said, and hung up right after Rodrigues offered her a "no problem."

"What is it?" she asked, already on her feet. Keller had that too-excited look again that she was going to have to warn him about.

"The dogs. They found a body," he said. "Near the woods, out by those abandoned wells."

All Jamie could do was stare at him as a small clip from the Tate recordings played in her head.

We were so scared you'd fallen into some old well, Holland.

CHAPTER THIRTY-FOUR

Holland

Now

I didn't sleep the rest of the night.

I had been the one to find my sister. It was a terrible thing that I could only remember her with her face crushed in, a doll broken because of some little boy's tantrum.

And wasn't that the biggest issue I had with all this tradwife nonsense? Our world was set up to cater to little boys, their wishes, their needs, their lives. Yet they were never taught how to handle emotions, either. Rage, humiliation, shame—they rarely turned inward. Instead, they came out as violence. When you were catered to by society, it felt like when you didn't get something, it was society's fault for not giving it to you.

How many times could we call a mass shooter a "lone wolf" because we couldn't admit that we had created a pack of boys throwing tantrums with deadly weapons?

How many women had to be killed before we no longer considered each instance like a one-off?

How could I look at the tradwife movement and not see the boys who were watching these tradwives and deciding *that* was what they were owed?

They were going to lash out in rage, in humiliation, in shame when they realized it was all just a fantasy.

And women would have to bear the brunt of their anger because people like Cat wanted to make a few more dollars.

Maybe that was victim-blaming when it came to Cat, or maybe it was realizing that women, even ones who had been hurt themselves, had always played a crucial role in upholding the patriarchy. Without them, it would crumble.

I couldn't stop picturing my sister's body, her limbs at odd angles. But it wasn't her face that I saw. It was Cat's. And I lived in fear of being the one to find her. Tomorrow maybe, after she'd told Kris about Fleur.

I was pretty sure that would destroy me. I'd come into this weekend wanting to write a profile, but that was so far down on my list of concerns, it barely registered anymore.

What I wanted to do was make sure Cat was safe. I had no interest in reading about her name in the headlines as just another victim, another cautionary tale.

I watched Cat all through the morning, which was essentially a duplicate of the day before.

Coffee and cinnamon rolls and waffles and bacon and eggs straight from chickens that squawked around the backyard. As cynical as I was about the tradwife con, I could absolutely see the appeal of this kind of life.

Even the children were aesthetically pleasing. They wore matching clothes for church, the boys in pants and vests, the girls in dresses.

Cat was in some designer outfit that had been made to look simple. Meanwhile, I had trotted out my corduroy-and-cable-sweater combo once again.

I had a moment of fear when Cat informed me I'd be riding to church with Kris, but half the kids came with us, too, offering a buffer.

The only time I even spoke directly to him was when I asked a question that had been eating at me.

"I've noticed you're not big on new technology," I said as we drove away from the orchard.

He sent me a questioning look.

"Well, you know people obsessed with security tend to love cameras and biometric locks," I said. "Things out of a Tom Cruise movie. But you guys have gone the more basic route."

"You know how easy all of that *technology* can fail?" he asked. "It's fantastic until it's not."

That was fair enough. There were plenty of times I'd been amazed by some gadget or gizmo only for it to fritz out three times out of four or right when it really mattered.

"Keep it simple, stupid," he said, with a shrug. "I believe that's the phrase. It may be vulgar, but it's true."

After that he dropped silent, and I followed suit, as the children filled the space with idle observations and singing and infighting.

Cat smiled at both of us when we met up in the parking lot.

"I wanted to give you a chance to get to know him better," she whispered to me, and I nodded like I gave two shits about her abusive, gun-toting, controlling husband.

The church was small and the Bouchards were clearly the stars of the show. Some people tried not to stare, but most gave up on any attempts at decorum. I scanned their faces from the end of the pew, thinking about that obsessed fan who had been sending Cat messages.

Not threatening, everyone had rushed to assure me. Perhaps that was why they hadn't bulked up their security. If it had been me, I'd have used some of my obscene wealth to pay a bodyguard to accompany me to a church where anyone could come in and get close to me.

It took forty-five minutes to find her.

She stood in the back, her thinning brown hair pulled into a low chignon, her dress long and covered with a cardigan buttoned up to her neck. I must have dismissed her on the first few passes, but something in my hindbrain picked up on the bad vibes. By the time I fully noticed her, I realized she hadn't seemed to take her attention off Cat's face since we'd walked in.

I swallowed hard, my pulse ticking up a beat. There were three children between Cat and me, but they were little. I leaned in, the motion catching Cat's attention.

"Do you recognize her?" I asked as softly as I could. "Back corner, blue sweater."

Cat was smart enough not to whip her head around. But she eventually was able to sneak a peek over her shoulder.

The woman looked away quickly, confirming my guess that she had been watching Cat's every move.

"Mary Jane Sitwick. She's a librarian in town," Cat said, earning herself a reprimanding glance from Kris, who was apparently quite devout. Cat pressed her lips together and faced front once more.

I looked back one more time, only to find Mary Jane Sitwick staring at me, her eyes narrowed, assessing.

A chill stole over me, because that wasn't curiosity in her expression.

No, it was pure, unbridled, jealousy-fueled rage.

People swarmed Cat when the service ended. She and her children were so obviously celebrities here, and I was able to fade into the background once more. I glanced to where Mary Jane had been stationed, but she was gone now.

And she hadn't joined the gaggle surrounding Cat, either.

Maybe I was wrong about what I'd read on her face, but I couldn't help but think about the fact that when people escalated into violence, it usually required some kind of trigger.

Those messages hadn't been threatening . . . yet.

But I was a new entity. Even if she didn't know who I was, I was someone who'd been immediately welcomed into the inner circle of a woman she idolized.

Telling stories, I chided myself. Always getting ahead of myself.

Still, it wouldn't hurt to look around. No one else seemed to be taking this threat seriously. And I had always been more protective of Cat than she had been of herself. Why would that change now?

Kris was taking the boys to the hardware store, so I didn't have to worry about him. And the locals were keeping Cat busy while Anna minded the children.

It let me slip out one of the side doors.

Mary Jane wasn't hiding. Instead, she was lurking in the lobby, possibly biding her time to try to get Cat alone rather than jockeying for attention.

I cleared my throat, and her eyes snapped to me.

Without thinking too hard about it, I spun and started down the hallway. When I got to what looked like the pastor's office, I stepped inside. Maybe I had been making all this up in my head, or maybe Mary Jane would follow me, demanding answers on who I was and what I was doing with Cat's family.

It took about thirty seconds to prove my theory correct.

Mary Jane stepped into the bright, airy office behind me, shutting the door as she did.

I raised my brows as she just stood there staring at me.

"Can I help you?" I asked, as if I hadn't just orchestrated this confrontation.

"What are you doing here?" she asked.

"Um, how is that any of your business?"

"You're not supposed to be here," Mary Jane said, ignoring me. Her voice came out hollow and strange, and for the first time, I began to doubt this impromptu plan. She didn't seem the type to carry a weapon, but she was tall and strong—taller and stronger than me, at least. And I'd let myself be cornered by her.

"I needed a moment by myself," I lied.

"No," Mary Jane said. "What are you doing *here*? You live in New York."

So, she really was creepy. "How do you know that?"

She blinked at me. "You're Holland Tate, Catriona's friend from Savannah. Of course you live in New York, because that's where you work."

Right. I wanted to force her to realize how strange it was she was talking to me like this. I wasn't as convinced as everyone else seemed to be that those messages—and she, by extension—were harmless. But I could see a lonely person getting caught up in a parasocial relationship, and simply getting in too deep because no one forced her to take a hard look in the mirror. Or the direct messages inbox.

"Okay, but how do you know all of that?"

The question seemed to stump Mary Jane. Like I'd asked her why the sky was blue. It just obviously was. "Does Catriona know—"

The door opened, cutting Mary Jane off mid-thought. I cursed the interruption, because it felt like I had been on the brink of getting somewhere with her.

"Holland?" Cat asked, peering around the door. "Are you in here? Someone saw you go this way."

I winced. I didn't want Cat confronting Mary Jane. I didn't think that would go well—and if I was being honest, it made me worry about her safety. Mary Jane didn't exactly look like a threat, but obsession could do strange things to a person.

Cat didn't wait for an answer, just stepped inside and closed the door behind her. With more warmth than I would have expected, she greeted Mary Jane. "How lovely to see you, Mary Jane."

Mary Jane's entire demeanor shifted, her face brightening, her posture softening, leaning toward Cat like a sunflower. "You remembered my name."

Cat tilted her head, seeming confused. "Of course. How are you?"

The smile that spread across Mary Jane's face was almost painful to look at directly. She glanced at me. "She's so kind. So wonderful."

If I hadn't been in this exact situation before, that might have thrown me. But I'd seen fans treat celebrities like this—as if they weren't standing there, able to hear everything being said.

"She is," I agreed. I considered bailing on my plan. But I had a strong sense that Mary Jane was our girl, and if I didn't push now, she might go home and delete everything. And then next time she made a move, it might not be as innocuous as a social media comment. "Mary Jane, have you been messaging Cat on her social media pages?"

"Who is Cat?"

"Catriona," I corrected gently. "Have you been sending her private notes?"

Mary Jane looked between us. "Plenty of people do."

Which was a yes. "But you've told her you like her outfit choice, or that you'd like to have the same coffee as she ordered?"

Her nostrils flared. Some part of her must have known that she shouldn't have been sending things like that, because she was starting to look trapped. And guilty as hell.

"That's normal," Mary Jane said.

Cat's eyes widened. She clearly hadn't thought Mary Jane would admit to it—or maybe she doubted that I'd been able to pick her stalker out of a crowd after spending only an hour in town. This, though, was why they should have gone to the police with the messages in the first place. Mia didn't go to church with them, and Anna was distracted by the children.

And Cat and Kris? They were so used to being stared at, they hadn't been able to pick her predatory eyes out from the rest.

"It's normal," Mary Jane said, looking between us. When we both remained silent, her expression went tight, panicky. "I just wanted to talk to you."

That seemed to shake Cat from her surprise. "We're talking now."

"No, you're always talking to everyone else," Mary Jane said, and my radar pinged. There was real distress in her voice. And the second Mary Jane let herself feel anger toward Cat, a light switch would flip. In dating terms, it was called getting the *ick.* The person became so revolting to you that you couldn't even imagine ever having liked them in the first place. I didn't know what it would be called in stalking terms, but I did know the results wouldn't be pretty. "You say hello to everyone but me."

Cat took a step forward, and I honestly didn't know if that was the right move. "I appreciated your compliments, Mary Jane. I'm sorry you felt like I was ignoring you."

I nearly winced. *I'm sorry you felt . . .* was practically the worst way you could apologize to someone.

Mary Jane's eyes narrowed. "You do ignore me. And after everything I've done for you."

"Uh," I said, because that sounded interesting, but I also didn't want this to spin out of control. "I think we should probably take this outside."

Cat went from consoling to indignant, though. I would have appreciated seeing my Cat, if the stakes weren't so high right now. "What you've done for me? What on earth are you talking about?"

"I know where you were when Odette Moreau died," Mary Jane said. "I know where you were and I didn't tell a single person. And this is how you treat me."

My heart stuttered in my chest, as my eyes slammed into Cat's. She had paled, but otherwise maintained her composure. "I have no idea what you're talking about. I do know that if you try to spread whatever these lies are, I'll go to the police with your messages."

Mary Jane's fingers tangled together, her eyes darting wildly. If I had been advocating for her, I would have told her she hadn't done anything criminally wrong with those messages. That Cat might try to spin whatever evidence Mary Jane had against her as an obsessed woman, but they still wouldn't be able to charge her with anything.

But I had no interest in advocating for Mary Jane.

I thought about all those times Cat and I had texted, each in our separate bedrooms after a long night.

You know we're ride or die, right?

Are you trying to ask me to help hide a body?

Somewhat shockingly, I realized that hadn't been hyperbole. What I wanted right now, more than breaking some story about Catriona Bouchard and her husband's ex-wife, was to get the hell out of this room and get Mary Jane to shut the hell up about whatever she thought she knew.

I started drafting plans in my head, but they ended up being unnecessary.

Mary Jane slumped, a sad balloon with its air let out. "I'm sorry. I'm sorry. I know you don't mean to ignore me. I just lost my temper. My mother says I do that too much."

"It's quite all right, Mary Jane," Cat said, back to her warm, soothing voice. She stepped closer to Mary Jane, wrapping an arm around her shoulder. "None of us are perfect. Including me."

Mary Jane nodded, but continued to stare at the carpet.

"Why don't I give you my phone number?" Cat said. "Then you can text me instead of messaging me on social media. You know how many DMs I receive, they can get lost so easily."

"Maybe you shouldn't—" I started, but Mary Jane whipped around.

"You shouldn't be here," she said. "Why are you here?"

"She's writing a profile on me," Cat answered, but Mary Jane didn't blink, didn't look away.

"She shouldn't be here," she said again, and I decided not to press my luck.

"You're right, I'll leave," I said, skirting around the two of them. "Cat, we should be getting back, right?"

"Yeah, unfortunately. The kids, you know?" Cat squeezed both of Mary Jane's shoulders. "It was so good to see you."

And then we stepped out into the hallway without Mary Jane ever realizing that Cat hadn't given her that phone number.

"Holy"—I dropped my voice to a whisper so the girls wouldn't hear me curse—"shit."

Cat shook her head as she peeled out of the parking lot. "That was scary."

"Yeah," I said, slumping against the van's front seat. "You should talk to the cops about it."

"I will," Cat agreed easily, which was nice. I'd thought it was going to be a battle. "They're not going to be able to do anything, but they should know."

I nodded, then slid her a look. "What was that about Odette?"

Her eyes tracked up to the rearview mirror, likely checking to see if Anna had overheard. But the girl was lost in her phone. "I don't know."

"Obviously, I don't believe that."

She laughed. "You saw her, she was crazy. Talking nonsense."

Mary Jane had been emotionally volatile, but she'd also made sense. Even telling me I shouldn't be there made sense. In her mind, I used to be Cat's friend, but I no longer visited her. I was no longer in her inner circle. So I shouldn't be there.

"Where were you, Cat?" I asked quietly.

She didn't answer.

I wasn't sure I'd actually wanted her to.

"I'm going to change out of these clothes," I announced to a kitchen full of noise and laughter and chatter. Mia was at the table with her computer open in front of her, Anna was doing finger painting with some of the younger kids, and Cat stood by the stove, the baby strapped to her chest.

No one looked up, but I'd tried, at least. I wondered if that meant Mia trusted me now, since she was no longer acting as my guard.

I *had* been telling the truth. I changed into jeans and shoved my hair into a bun on top of my head. But when that was done, I eyed the dresser, where I'd stashed the gun. It had been calling out to me the entire night, like a siren's song, begging for attention. I had wondered if Cat had noticed my eyes flicking in that direction several times the night before.

I couldn't resist checking in on it.

I crossed the room and pulled out the drawer.

My breath caught as my fingers turned frantic, sweeping along the bottom of the drawer over and over and over again.

But no amount of searching was going to change the fact that the gun was gone.

CHAPTER THIRTY-FIVE

HOLLAND

Now

Steffie.

Or Mia.

Or Jeremy.

Those were the three most likely options for who had taken the gun while the rest of us were at church. I suppose it could have been Anna, Kris, or Cat sometime between when I'd left my room and when we'd all headed out, but that provided a tighter—though notably not impossible—timeline.

Steffie, Mia, or Jeremy, I repeated to myself.

Jeremy was the least likely of the three, but he had barged into my room without an invitation before. Maybe he had come up, not realizing I was going to church with the family. He'd thought to wait for me, see if he could talk me into a quickie. He'd gotten bored and started snooping.

But why would he have taken the gun, even if he'd found it?

The best way to get to the carriage house would be to retrace my steps down the stairs and out the back door. That would take me through the kitchen again, though, and I didn't think an announcement that I was headed outside would be met with the same sanguinity as my previous one.

So I found a less direct path that took me out the front door. I rounded the house on a run.

If I eliminated Jeremy—which I had a feeling I could do—then the next two likely suspects were Steffie and Mia.

I knew which of the two had probably done it. I knew which of the two scared me more.

They were one and the same.

Once I got to the carriage house, I pounded on the door. I wanted to yell, but that would have drawn attention from the kitchen.

It took a solid minute of knocking for Jeremy to open the door, bleary-eyed, his hair sticking up every which way.

If I'd had any doubt that he hadn't been the one to do it, the sight of him blinking against the sun, scratching at his naked lower belly, and shuffling his large bare feet on the concrete would have eliminated it. This was a man who had been woken up by someone banging on his door. He hadn't been in the main house riffling through my things.

"Did you go to my room today?" I asked anyway.

He blinked at me, his brain clearly not online yet. He smacked his lips together, his jaw working like a cow's while eating cud. In that moment it felt very upsetting that I had slept with this man.

"Hmm? Coffee?"

I almost laughed, but instead I snapped my fingers. "Jeremy. Focus. Did you go into my room?"

"Only yesterday," he said and then turned, heading back up to the loft. He flipped the light on when he got to the top, further corroborating the idea that I'd dragged him from bed. He could've been lying, but it wouldn't make sense for him to.

He got coffee started, then turned to lean against the counter, one eye closed, the other assessing me. "Start again?"

I could've lied, but he was the one who'd started looking into Odette's death. He didn't trust Kris any more than I did.

So I told him everything that had happened with the safe.

"Why did you go in there in the first place?" he asked, which was a good fucking question that I didn't really have an answer to.

I'd been angry at Anna. But underneath that was a fear for Cat's safety that I just couldn't shake. Before I'd come, no one here had known about Benji and Mark and the boyfriends before them. They didn't know that Cat was drawn to men who put her in the hospital. And those were men she'd been dating for a short amount of time. What would her husband do? When he could so easily control her with her own children?

What I'd really been looking for was a leg up on Kris. Leverage, maybe? Or . . . hell. Maybe I had been looking for the gun. To make sure he didn't have it.

The statistics didn't lie when it came to gun ownership numbers and the deaths related to domestic violence.

"Doesn't matter," I said, because going into all that was just a waste of time. "What does is that Steffie—angry, bitter-at-his-father Steffie—might now have the gun. Which was the whole reason I took it in the first place."

He rubbed his fist into his eye. "Or Mia."

"Yeah," I agreed. "She saw me coming out of the office yesterday."

Jeremy nodded like that didn't surprise him. "I don't know, man. I think she's sleeping with Kris. Could give her a reason to shoot the wife."

I shook my head, mostly because I was pretty sure Kris and Mia weren't having an affair. But also: "In no world does that make any sense."

"Hey." He straightened, insulted. "Jealousy is a powerful motivator. So is over a hundred million dollars in a bank account if she thinks she can get Kris to marry her."

"But that's what I mean," I said. "If she shot Cat, she'd just go to jail."

He deflated. "Yeah, I guess. Jealousy's more a crime-of-passion sort of killing. Not a find-and-hold-on-to-a-gun sort."

"Right, and you'd expect it to go the other way around, wouldn't you?" I asked. "Cat finding Mia in bed with Kris."

We both wrinkled our noses at that. I for one had no interest in thinking about what Kris was like in bed.

He stretched and yawned, clearly not as concerned as I was. "Maybe she wants it for a different reason."

"Or maybe it's the most obvious choice," I said, and when he stared at me blankly, I rolled my eyes. "Steffie."

"Oh, huh," he said, and then turned to fetch mugs.

I felt like I was going to lose it. I wasn't sure why I came out here, except that Jeremy had one thing I didn't.

Internet.

"Let me see your phone," I said, and he pointed to the bedside table, offering up a string of numbers as he did.

I punched them in and pulled up a search page.

Unfortunately, Mia Preston ended up being too common a name to find anything useful. The only result that came up that was directly connected to her was a LinkedIn page—which ended up being mostly just full of her accomplishments with Cat.

"I know all this," I muttered, scrolling. Mia had started off as a personal assistant, mainly helping with video production.

Jeremy peered over my shoulder. "I didn't realize she didn't come in as Cat's manager."

"Hmm," I hummed, scrolling the rest of the page. "Yeah. Cat used to do more behind-the-scenes content than she does now. She'd talk about Mia in them."

"Huh."

"Quite the contribution," I said. Mia had worked in low-level jobs at a couple of the most popular social media sites and then with a couple of big influencers from back in the day. But all of it looked pretty standard.

"When did she post all that behind-the-scenes stuff?" Jeremy asked, adding cream to a mug and handing it over. "She would never do something like that now."

He was right. Cat was well into her Wizard of Oz phase now. There was no man behind the curtain, just a magical being who had perfect hair and perfect children and a perfect life that she somehow managed when no one else could seem to figure out how to *have it all*.

"Must have been a while ago," Jeremy commented when I didn't immediately provide an answer.

"Yeah," I agreed absently, and wondered if it had coincided with Mia's promotion. Maybe she had wanted to keep everything beautiful, seamless, perfect. "None of this matters. It's Steffie who took the gun. Probably. Maybe."

"Then why'd you come out here?" he asked, scratching at his tummy again and staring longingly at the bed. "I mean, I'm all for the hot sleuth-y thing you've got going on, but if you think it's the kid, go confront him."

I was half impressed he'd come up with *sleuth-y* and half outraged at his suggestion.

"Go confront an unstable teenager who has recently acquired a deadly weapon?" I asked. "What fantastic advice."

He laughed, as if all this were a joke. "I'll keep digging on Mia, see if there's any dirt. But I'll have to start dinner prep in an hour or so . . ."

"Thank you," I said, sincerely.

"Want backup for talking to the kid?" he asked, sounding like he actually would pull on a shirt and shoes if I said yes.

"No, I'm sure you're right—it's nothing," I said, not believing myself.

When I got back outside, I tried to put myself in Steffie's shoes. He might be in his bedroom, but if he was, I was somewhat screwed. Surely someone would be looking for me by now, and if I went into the house, I'd be stopped.

But if Steffie had taken the gun, if he was planning . . . something . . . he wouldn't be doing it anywhere someone could stumble upon him.

The answer, of course, was obvious.

The greenhouse.

Out near the wells where a body could be thrown and never found again.

I took off at a run and wondered if I was being foolish. Jeremy wasn't concerned, even if he'd bought into the theory that there might be more to Odette's death than first appeared.

I know where you were when Odette Moreau died. I couldn't shake Mary Jane's voice from my head. What if Cat had played a role in the death of Kris's ex-wife? I had a hard time believing that. But could Mary Jane have made a convincing argument? One that if Steffie heard, he might snap?

Maybe I was just being paranoid. But if Steffie did something with the gun—the blood would be on my hands. That was different than just theorizing in bed or over coffee.

Those were real-life consequences.

I was panting by the time I hit the tree line, so I slowed to a fast walk, my palm pressed to the stitch in my side.

I paused when I got near enough to the greenhouse to see movement.

Steffie.

I had never wanted a phone more in my life than in that moment.

If I walked into that greenhouse, and he was erratic, angry, and waving a weapon around, I wasn't sure I could talk him down from something he'd regret.

Honestly, I wasn't sure I could walk out of that situation alive.

You're being dramatic, I told myself.

I was doing with Steffie what I did with everyone: I was writing his story even before it had happened.

A bitter kid who had been kicked out of multiple schools, who was treated like Cinderella by a father he blamed for his mother's death and a stepmother he viewed as cruel and cold. He was forced to watch his siblings be showered with love and affection while he was scorned. He lived in the dark shadows of his own life, growing ever more resentful at having been put there.

Presented with a weapon on a silver platter—why would he not take the shot?

I couldn't muster much concern for Kris. It was Steffie I was worried about.

He reminded me of myself at his age. There hadn't been anyone in my life, either, who had wanted to offer a hand to guide me out of the dark shadows I'd been forced to survive in.

My mother had been a husk of herself following Francesca's murder. I didn't even know my father. Teachers never had enough patience—they knew that my anger, my temper and bad behavior, stemmed from unimaginable grief and pain and loss, but they could only be slapped so many times before their skin became too tough to care about a stupid kid who was making their lives so much harder.

I had been Steffie. And if someone had given me a gun at that age, I'm not sure I wouldn't have hurt someone with it.

Actually, I know I would have.

I didn't think I could be the hand that would guide Steffie into the light. But maybe I could be a nudge in the right direction.

I took a deep breath.

And then I walked into the greenhouse.

CHAPTER THIRTY-SIX

Det. Jamie Alvarez

The boys from State requested that Jamie and Keller stay behind when they went back to the orchard.

Keller seemed so devastated that she volunteered to hold back alone, so that he could go observe.

Detective Boyd hesitated, but an overeager ride-along was a lot different from having the locals mess up your crime scene.

So Jamie was left to do the only thing she'd thought to do before.

Research the bodies that lay in the wake of Catriona Bouchard née Vandale.

Because there was one more attached to her name beyond Marcus Sinclair and Benjamin Croft.

For the third time that day, Jamie found herself dialing an out-of-state police station.

It took only five minutes, though, to get Savannah Detective Martha West on the phone.

"Do you remember a missing girl case from about eleven years ago?" Jamie asked after introducing herself. "Her name was Amanda Cooper."

West hummed, and then Jamie could hear typing. "Sorry, just reminding myself."

Jamie waited, not surprised that a city cop wouldn't remember every missing persons case that had ever crossed their desk.

"Right," West finally drawled out. "Mandy. It was one of those situations where her parents were adamant that something terrible had happened to her, but she was an adult and there was never any evidence of foul play."

The basic details of the case were available to Jamie, just as they were now to West.

Twelve years ago, Amanda Cooper had left Missouri and the only home she'd ever known to follow a boyfriend to Savannah. Her parents had begged her not to go, but she'd been twenty-two, and there hadn't been much they could do about the plan.

According to them, the boyfriend had dumped her immediately once they'd gotten there. She'd managed to find an apartment and planned on getting a job. If she couldn't find something in three months—the amount of savings she had—then she promised she'd come home.

Amanda had gotten a waitressing position, though, and ended up staying for a year.

One night, the parents got a text from her that she'd gotten back together with her boyfriend and they were going to head down to check out a job offer in Florida.

That was the last they ever heard from her.

"Honestly, I feel bad, but no one here took them seriously," West said. "I was eventually given the case a couple months after they first contacted us. But we can't make grown adults talk to their parents."

"You never found her?" Jamie asked just to make sure. "Or the boyfriend?"

"We never got more than a nickname for the boyfriend," West admitted. "The parents had never met him—they hadn't approved of the relationship, apparently, so Amanda had been cagey about it.

Since they broke up immediately when they got to the city, none of her friends had met him, either."

"An impossible case," Jamie murmured. "Were you ever able to get phone records? Anything?"

"No, the judge never deemed it worthy of a warrant," West said. "We talked to all her coworkers and friends and the person she'd rented a room from. All of it checked out as a flighty young woman who took off after a guy."

Jamie nodded. She would have thought the same thing an hour ago if she'd heard all the details.

She thanked West as she hung up the phone, staring at the name of Amanda Cooper's last roommate.

Catriona Vandale.

One death could be written off as an accident.

Two could be a coincidence.

Three, though?

Three was a pattern.

CHAPTER THIRTY-SEVEN

Holland

Now

Steffie looked up when I walked into the greenhouse.

He was sitting on one of the counters reading a book.

The wind was knocked out of my sails a bit, and I faltered, coming to an awkward stop in front of him.

I readjusted the story in my head, not really sure what I'd expected to find. Maybe him practicing with the gun? Nothing about this scene meant he hadn't taken it.

But I did relax slightly. At least he wasn't about to walk into the house and start shooting.

He raised his brows at me, and I decided to just come out with it, hoping the element of surprise worked in my favor.

"Did you take the gun?" I asked.

"No," he drawled out. "You did."

Well, there went the pretext that I had just been straightening up last night. "Are you lying to me?"

He squinted like I was a complete idiot, and perhaps I was. "Why would I tell you that I was lying to you if I was lying to you?"

"Okay, right." But that didn't mean he wasn't lying. The thing was, I wasn't some cop; I wasn't even a plucky sleuth, like Jeremy had suggested. I was just a writer, someone who had never even covered the crime beat. In shows and movies, they always made it seem like you could just *tell* if someone was lying to you, or at least the protagonists could. Sometimes I could sense it, especially if the interviewee actually wanted to tell me what they were hiding. Some were like that, after all. They just needed a little coaxing. A lot of people lied by omission or sidestepped the truth, and in the past I had been able to call some on that.

But how did I know my success rate?

What if everyone was lying to me and I was just really shitty at spotting it?

Steffie seemed to be telling the truth—his expression a mix of bored and confused. What if he was a sociopath, though? Couldn't they lie with ease? If I really thought he was going to use that gun, didn't I also have to consider the fact that he might not immediately reveal with some flush of shame that he'd taken it?

I wasn't a human lie detector. So I was just going to have to trust my gut, which said he was telling the truth.

"Did you lose it?" he asked, that *are you stupid* now thick in his voice.

"I would not call it 'losing,'" I muttered, and he raised his brows at the confirmation that I both had taken it and no longer had it.

He whistled. "Kris found it."

I wondered if it mattered that he was calling his father Kris, psychologically speaking. "No, he didn't have time. He went to church with us."

"But didn't you have breakfast with *Cat*?" he asked, clearly delighted to use the nickname she apparently no longer liked. "He could have gone in and gotten it then."

I hated that I was about to use this vulnerable kid as a sounding board, but I couldn't help but ask, "How much do you know about Mia?"

He reeled back. "Why would she take the gun?"

"I don't know," I admitted. "I haven't gotten much further than compiling a list of suspects."

"Which includes everyone in the house?" He was so clearly not impressed with my detective skills, I almost felt bad about them.

"Apparently."

He went back to reading his book. *Atlas Shrugged.* Of course. "Kris has it. He's just waiting for the perfect time to back you into a corner with it."

I rubbed my sweaty palms against my jeans, wondering if he was speaking metaphorically or literally.

"Oh," he said, looking up from his book again. "I nabbed these."

And before I could ask what *these* were, he tossed me two little orange bottles that I only caught by the grace of god.

I cursed as I stopped one of them from rebounding into my face. "What the hell?"

"They're the pills Kris had in the closet," Steffie said, like it was no big deal. "I checked them when you guys were out. He's got two more full bottles of those things."

The barbiturates and the painkillers. I'd thought it was bad that Steffie could have a gun. But these seemed almost more dangerous for an emotional teenager. I could have easily walked in on him dead, these bottles beside him.

He must have read something in my expression because he rolled his eyes. "I'm not going to *take them*, take them." He stopped and started over. "You know what I mean. I'm not going to *consume* them."

"We should put these back," I said, the bottles too warm in my hand. I didn't like this turn of events.

Steffie waved at me. "Go ahead. You're the one who wanted to see what they were in the first place."

Yeah, but this drastically increased the likelihood that Kris would suspect something was off. The gun he might not have noticed for a while. These pills, though? How long would that take?

But I wasn't about to argue with the kid, so I pocketed the bottles. "Sorry I accused you of stealing the gun."

He lifted one shoulder, back to his book now. "I would have if I'd been able to find it."

I barked out a laugh. "Fair enough."

Steffie looked up. "What are you going to do?"

I pressed the heel of my hand to my forehead. I should have stayed out of Kris's office last night in the first place.

That milk was spilled, though.

"Ignore it?" I suggested. "I'm leaving in the morning."

If Kris had it—and Steffie was right, that was the most likely scenario now—then I would have to face whatever consequences he wanted to enact. But at the end of the day, the gun was back in the hands of its rightful owner.

If Mia had it . . . well, that wasn't any of my business.

For a moment, I thought about Odette Moreau and wondered if Cat had the gun.

But I shook my head. Cat wasn't a murderer; she hadn't killed Kris's ex-wife. She wasn't built for that.

I was writing stories again.

Anyway, why would she want a gun now?

"Goodbye then, I guess," Steffie muttered, sounding almost disappointed.

I didn't give myself too much credit. It had probably just been nice for him to have someone who didn't ignore or get bothered simply by the sight of him.

"Keep your head up," I said, before slipping back out of the greenhouse.

I felt for him, I did. But right now there were bigger problems to worry about.

As I walked away, all I could hope was that I hadn't just been played.

Mia stared me down when I finally found my way back to the kitchen.

Cat was set up at her butcher-block island, doing something with dough and a cheese strainer; Anna had the kids at the table; Kris was still nowhere to be seen.

I tried to wander over to Cat, but Mia grabbed my arm, directing me to the far side of the kitchen, far enough away from everyone else that they wouldn't overhear us. "Where did you go?"

"To talk to Jeremy," I said, having realized that was the best excuse to head off any further questioning and explain why I'd disappeared for so long. "We became, shall we say, fast friends on Friday night."

I let the innuendo slip into my voice so she would know exactly what I was talking about. She nodded for me to continue.

"I . . . didn't want to leave without saying goodbye," I said, over-innocent, to make it seem like we'd had a nooner. "I wasn't sure when we'd see each other again otherwise."

Mia could have offered that I would be there another night, but she didn't seem like she wanted to think about any of it too much.

"Just the model of professional behavior, aren't you?" she murmured, though she didn't seem like she was about to call my editor, nor like she was about to kick me off the property, so I counted it as a win. I could not have cared less about what Mia Preston thought about my character.

I shrugged. "I wanted tips for making my own pumpkin soup."

Mia laughed, her stony facade cracking. It had been a good excuse, even if it made me look unserious.

She tipped her head. "So, I guess you have enough from Cat to write this piece?"

My eyes drifted toward the island. Cat was bathed in light, the baby for once not strapped to her chest but puttering away in an old-fashioned high chair. For some reason, she looked all the more vulnerable without the child attached to her.

Apparently, I was not immune to fetishizing mothers' strength.

I shook that off and thought about Mia's question.

I could write about the darkness lurking behind picture-perfect social media pages, but that felt *done*. Everyone knew the couples who posted too much about their love usually were the ones headed for divorce three months later.

I could write about Cat as a mother, but as much as she spent time managing the children, it didn't actually seem like that was at all her identity. I would never go as far as to think she viewed them as props, but they were more like precious kitchen tools. Beloved and simply *there*.

I could write about her as the mother of the tradwife movement, but again I tried testing the depths of such an article and found it shallow. The phenomenon deserved to face a harsh spotlight, but framing Cat as the face of it, when she was so much more interesting than just that alone, seemed a waste of knowing her personally.

Cat glanced up, as if she could feel my attention. She smiled, and I thought of the night before. And so many nights that we'd spent staying up too late, swapping confessions. Our promises to help bury bodies if needed, passed champagne bottles, shared sunrises on rooftops listening to playlists made just for us.

And I realized in that moment what this story should be about.

There were so many people our age who complained about how hard it was to find adult friends. They yearned for the bright obsession of youthful relationships, which at times could feel even bigger and better and more dazzling than romantic love.

We'd had that. A codependent, toxic, and brilliant kind of friendship. We'd been soulmates, in the truest sense of the word.

And then a boy had come between us. A tale as old as time, but not in the expected way. There were too many stories out there of girls fighting over boys' romantic attention.

I found them pedestrian and, more often than not, written by men.

Women didn't love the way they thought we did.

We loved with our veins cut open.

"I think I do," I finally answered Mia's question.

"Oh yeah?" Mia asked, brows raised. "You figured out what it's going to be about?"

Coming into this weekend, I hadn't known how much of myself to insert into the article, but the answer was now so blindingly obvious I knew I had subconsciously been working toward it the whole time.

"Us," I murmured, my eyes still on Cat. "It's going to be about us."

CHAPTER THIRTY-EIGHT

CAT

Then

The first time it happened, it was an accident. Sort of.

I was so young. Sixteen.

I didn't understand obsession back then. I didn't understand the ways I provoked that in people.

I still don't understand why some people latch on to me like that. I'm not kind; I'm not particularly funny; I can tell a good story, but I rarely listen to other people's. I'm generous to people I like, but those are few and far between; I'm arrogant and also insecure, creating a lethal combination that has driven plenty of friends and coworkers away.

But something about me must be magnetic to at least a handful of men and women.

Leo was a stoner I'd met in Santa Monica. I'd just gotten off the Ferris wheel and puked in the trash can next to where he'd been sitting, idly rolling his skateboard back and forth.

I had been horrified beyond belief, contemplating changing my name and flying off to Russia. But he'd just laughed and run to get me water and napkins from the nearest hot dog stand.

He wasn't my type at all, except that he did have money. He dressed like he bought his clothes from charity stores, but they were all actually expensive, because he was that breed of rich Californian who didn't want to look like he was a rich Californian. That was fine by me, mostly because my clothes *did* come from charity stores. He paid for all our meals, and I ate the best I ever had in my life. Up until then, if I had gotten anything other than ramen or mac and cheese, it had been other people's leftovers from the restaurants I'd worked in since I was fourteen.

I thought I'd gotten the best of both worlds: a chill skater boy and a dude with deep pockets. Then I "made him angry" and he proved that he was a rich Californian in more ways than one. For anyone who hasn't had the privilege of meeting one of that particular breed, they tended to be entitled douches who thought they could do anything they wanted to their girlfriends and get away with it.

Leo'd had a friend at the time, a girl who was so obviously in love with him it had been glorious to watch whenever I rubbed her face in our relationship.

I knew if I tried to leave Leo, I'd end up as a character in a Lifetime movie, portrayed by some blonde who would be way prettier than me as one final insult that would reach me in my grave. He had that obsession with me that I was only starting to recognize as dangerous and powerful back then.

So I helped the girl finally catch Leo's eye. I took her shopping, I got her a haircut. She'd been pretty beneath all that basic neglect.

When we hung out, I laughed at her jokes. I helped her tell stories that I knew Leo would find interesting.

I set her up with a guy, so that we could go on a double date and Leo would be forced to wonder if he was missing out on something that he hadn't seen before.

Our whole group spent a weekend at his parents' beach house, and I made sure to get the girl drunk and shove them both into a hot tub together.

At the same time I was doing all this, I strove to become the most boring version of myself. I got an unflattering haircut. I stopped sharing every witty remark that popped into my head, and I started telling dull, meandering stories about celebrities and their pets. I made sure Leo's friends didn't like me by nagging at them, and being a general wet blanket.

I almost couldn't believe it took as long as it did for Leo to break up with me for the girl.

But, in the end, I walked away from that relationship without a scratch.

It had felt as easy as playing a Get Out of Jail Free card, and I never forgot that lesson.

I hadn't had to use it often, but I did use it enough that I'd racked up some guilt along the way. At sixteen, I hadn't given two shits about the other girl.

I didn't even think about her until I attended the CIA.

Everything was more intense at the institute, and perhaps that was why it had finally blown up in my face.

Stu had never hit me, but he had been cruel. When I tried to put distance between us, he could sense I was pulling away. He started doing weird stuff, like showing up outside my apartment at 3:00 a.m. and following around any guy he thought had looked at me twice.

Gloria was the sweetest girl in our graduating class, but she also struggled with the actual work.

Stu wanted to be thought of as brilliant and loved being asked for advice.

It was a match made in heaven.

Then Stu put Gloria in the hospital. She lived, but she lost partial vision in her left eye, which sent her fleeing to whatever flyover state she'd come from in the first place. She was probably working in some chain restaurant on a bypass next to a gas station and a nail salon now.

I'd promised not to try that ever again.

But then Mark had come along.

I'd helped set him up with Tamara, and now I really hoped she'd had him killed. Because if she'd been dead right alongside him—a victim of some horrific murder-suicide—I wasn't sure I'd be able to live with that on my conscience.

It was why I had thrown up when that cop knocked on our door to tell us Mark was dead.

And it was what had me telling all this to Holland after Silvia Rodrigues left our apartment.

I expected recrimination. I expected anger and disgust.

What I didn't expect was a placid expression, as if she'd already known all my deepest secrets.

"What was the girl's name?" she asked.

I stared at her, unsure. "What do you mean?"

"The first girl," she said, patiently, as if she would repeat it as many times as I needed. "What was her name?"

I searched my memory. At the time, I'd had an obsession with those yellow disposable cameras, and I'd taken dozens of pictures of our group of friends. The girl had featured in so many. I was kissing her cheek in one as she grinned into the camera. I probably still had it in a shoebox in my closet.

She had looked like Holland, actually.

Now that I thought about it.

I still wasn't sure why Holland wanted to know, but I could give her the name easily. Far more easily than I had given her my confession.

"Francesca," I said. "Her name was Francesca."

CHAPTER THIRTY-NINE

Holland

Then

The first time I saw Cat Vandale, she was laughing, her head thrown back, her blond hair streaming over her shoulders, catching the sunlight. She wore a bikini top and short-shorts showing off miles of golden skin in the process.

California personified.

"Bitch," Francesca murmured as we both stared out the window. Francesca hated Cat because she was Leo's new obsession.

Francesca wanted Leo for herself, but I knew that wasn't going to happen. Francesca was funny and smart and kind, and attractive, when she put in an effort. But Leo didn't look at her that way. I wasn't really experienced with boys at that point, but I knew they didn't slot you into the category of "best friend" if they wanted to date you.

So Francesca was left to be miserable over Leo's rotating cast of girlfriends, while she played the cool, understanding bestie along for the ride. She'd been holding out hope for a while that he'd eventually have some kind of revelation—considering how often she was the one who remained at the end of the day when Leo moved on from his latest love interest. That hadn't happened, and now Cat seemed to be sticking.

I wanted to be on Francesca's side, because she was always on mine. But personally, I thought she should find a new crush and become best friends with Cat Vandale instead of mooning over Leo any longer.

"She's mean," Francesca told me when I gently suggested doing just that.

All teenagers were mean, though. All *kids* were mean. Had Francesca not come home crying three times the previous week because the cheerleaders had been calling her pimply and fat?

Francesca just hated Cat because she was biased against her.

I wasn't.

It was about that time that I started collecting facts about Cat Vandale, relayed to me by Francesca. She liked french fries with salt and vinegar, no ketchup. She ordered lattes but never drank them. She smoked exactly one cigarette a weekend, but reasoned she couldn't have any more than that because she wanted to keep her skin beautiful. She said her favorite movies were obscure French films no one had ever heard of, but Francesca was pretty sure it was really *Center Stage*, a soap opera–y, cult-classic dance movie.

The details accumulated over the weeks that summer and eventually formed a character in my journals. And that character went on to star in some of my earliest attempts at storytelling.

I had been left alone a lot those days. My mom had three jobs and zero time for anything other than paying bills and keeping cereal stocked in the pantry. Francesca was supposed to be watching me, but I was fourteen and mostly self-sufficient. I couldn't blame her for running off with the cute boy she liked and the rest of his friends.

But it meant I was lonely.

Cat helped fill my afternoons.

I wasn't . . . weird. I knew I didn't *know* the real Cat Vandale. I almost felt like I had another sister, though. Or a friend. Even if she didn't know my name.

Francesca also started to like the real-life Cat more, which meant that I could include all three of us in my stories.

We had so much fun in between those pages.

I stopped telling stories after Francesca was killed.

I had found her. I'd guarded her body like a dog did their master. I didn't remember that, but a cop told me after. That I'd growled, my hand on her belly where my niece had slept.

It took weeks before I would talk to anyone, and I didn't mean that figuratively. I simply didn't talk for two weeks after.

The police referred me to a psychologist, who referred me to a psychiatrist because they deemed whatever was wrong with me serious enough I might need medication.

If I had been talking at the time, I would have told them that *whatever was wrong with me* was finding my beaten-to-a-pulp sister dead on the floor of our living room when I was fifteen years old.

Leo got two life sentences for murdering Francesca and my would-be niece. My mother had taken the same path as I had and decided life in a nearly catatonic state was preferable to the unending grief.

So I'd been left alone again.

Except I had Cat. Well, the Cat in my journals.

When I read the stories I'd written about her, I noticed something. Many of them were fictionalized adventures, silly things written by a girl whose imagination had been both too big and too limited by her circumstances.

But there was another pattern emerging from the facts I'd sprinkled in.

That year, Francesca had told the story to herself, to me, to the world, that she'd snagged Leo from Cat Vandale. It had made her feel better about herself. She was irresistible.

That wasn't what had happened, though.

Cat had seen the darkness in Leo before any of us had. That made sense—she'd been the one who'd seen him in the most intimate moments of his life. He could hide that monster from everyone else.

Instead of shining a light on that monster, though, she'd simply foisted him off on Francesca, without once looking back to see the devastation in her wake.

It wasn't just my gut saying so, either. Once I knew what to look for, I found all the evidence I needed in the long thread of text messages between Cat and Francesca.

The handoff of a death sentence, caught in teenage-speak for all of time.

The rage and grief that had turned me mute braided together to form a whip I could lash out with.

Cat was the one responsible for Francesca's death.

When I told my psychiatrist this, she'd stared at me with dismayed eyes and tried to walk me back from that conclusion.

I'd stopped going to her and instead focused on getting to Cat.

She was in New York City then, and I had been very poor and living in California, but that hadn't stopped me. In fact, it had given me a purpose. Social media was starting to take off, but a lot of it was locked down to friends. Cat kept her social media private, so I could only see what she was doing on the off chance someone with lax settings posted a picture of her.

Watching from afar wasn't enough. What if she did to some other girl what she had to Francesca? What if I wasn't there to prevent it from happening?

I had stopped caring about school after Francesca died, but I rededicated myself to it completely, all so I could get into NYU. I knew how to work, how to save money, so I didn't need a scholarship. I just needed to get in.

And I did.

Soon I was back in the same city as Cat. The girl responsible for my sister's death.

I didn't have a plan in New York. I did go to class—I wasn't an idiot. I had worked damn hard to get to a good school, to get myself away from my mother and our tiny, broken house. I'd even changed my surname to my middle name so I could get a fresh start.

But Cat became my . . . hobby. I didn't *stalk* her. I simply followed her.

To make sure she wouldn't do what she'd done back in California.

To make sure no other girls would die because of her.

It became easier to keep track of her after she accepted a friend request from me from an account I'd made sure didn't give any clues to who I really was. She posted a lot—parties she was going to, under-twenty-one nights at bars, bowling alley meetups.

I never talked *to* her. I wasn't really sure what I would say. *You killed my sister?*

She hadn't, of course. No court of law would hold her responsible. She probably wouldn't even care.

But it wasn't just about Francesca.

It was about the other girls. I could hear my psychiatrist's voice sometimes. *You're projecting, you're fixating. This is an unhealthy coping mechanism that lets you avoid processing your sister's death.*

I was proven right, though, when Gloria ended up in the hospital.

I'd known *of* her. She'd tagged along a few times to Cat's get-togethers, but she'd seemed much too sweet for the crew Cat hung out with.

Then she started dating Cat's ex.

I should have done something then, but I was too slow to put the pieces together. I was operating at a distance, after all.

On my desk, there was a stack of journals full of details I'd learned about Cat, and yet I'd failed to do the one thing I'd come to New York to accomplish.

It was foolish to visit Gloria in the hospital. She didn't know who I was, and showing up would confuse and frighten her more than anything, probably.

But the guilt was fierce and demanding.

So I went.

I just never made it inside.

CHAPTER FORTY

Holland

Then

I had been dead-set on visiting Gloria in the hospital. I'd even bought a stuffed capybara for her.

But as I approached, I caught sight of blond hair.

Cat.

She was leaned up against the wall of the hospital, mascara smeared all under her eyes.

I stopped and watched as she scrubbed at her face with her palms. She stared at her hands then, as if they'd betrayed her.

She took deep, gulping breaths of air as she tried to get a hold of herself, but couldn't seem to.

And I realized in that moment that she was visiting Gloria.

That she felt guilty about what she'd done.

The remorse I'd been convinced she could never show for Francesca was here, on full display.

Something in my chest unlocked, shifted. I pictured myself sitting guard over Francesca's body, rabid and wild like a grieving dog.

I pictured Cat there, too. But she was no longer standing over Francesca, grinning. She *was* the body on the ground.

Someone bumped my shoulder and broke the moment.

By the time I looked back, Cat had composed herself. She gave a sharp little nod, then bent to pick up the flowers I hadn't even noticed. In the next minute, she disappeared inside the hospital.

I went home and wrote a story about a sad little girl who had no way out but to hope that other girls were stronger than she while she cast them into the fire.

From then on Cat became my protagonist once again. My professors and critique partners were always so complimentary of how well rounded my characters were, but that was what happened when you spent years conducting a character study that could flesh out a thousand stories.

As I wrote her, I realized that she wasn't heartless and selfish and cruel. She wasn't a vessel for me to pour my grief and rage into.

Instead, she was complex. Lost. Maybe a little weak, but weren't we all?

I forgot about visiting Gloria.

I forgot about stopping another tragedy from happening.

I thought about how Cat might be handing these men off to others, but she was dating them in the first place.

She was a victim, just as much as Gloria or Francesca had been.

It was the men who were the problem.

I didn't need to protect other girls from Cat.

I needed to protect Cat from herself.

Sometimes I tried to imagine what my psychiatrist would say about that. But she didn't know what she was talking about. She'd never sat like I had, my hand on my dead sister's belly. She didn't know how vulnerable a woman could be at the hands of men. Not personally.

The universe tried to throw a wrench in my plan. Cat graduated and took a job in Savannah, somewhere I'd never even considered living. If I wanted to write professionally—and at that point, I had been told enough times that I was good that I believed it—New York was the place to be.

But . . . there was a college in Savannah that offered an MFA program. It wasn't highly ranked, but it wasn't a scam, either. I easily got in.

The relief I'd felt opening the acceptance letter had been overwhelming.

Savannah was different from New York, though. It was smaller, harder to slip into the shadows and go unnoticed.

And I had been watching from a distance for a while now. That no longer seemed the best course of action—nor was it proving satisfying.

I needed more.

I wanted to be able to protect her better.

She'd moved into the cutest apartment with two bedrooms. Becoming her roommate seemed like the best and fastest way to earn my way into the inner sanctum. After all, I knew she would love me once she got over the fact that I was pretty. I had spent years learning her sense of humor, the types of people she gravitated toward, her preferences in TV shows and movies. We would be besties by the first day.

But she already had a roommate.

Amanda Cooper.

The girl had been easy enough to befriend. She was hungry for company—her boyfriend had moved her to the city and then dumped her, the asshole. We had commiserated over way too many drinks, and that became our thing. We'd hit up the happy hours and she'd bitch to me about all her problems: her parents, who were suffocatingly protective; her roommate, who was snobby as hell—I didn't bother to correct her there—the whole city, which she was really starting to despise.

I knew I shouldn't, but I took some inspiration from Cat. Amanda wasn't happy in Savannah anyway. I hadn't realized she was going to join some cult, fall off the grid, and then never talk to her parents again, simply because I made a few suggestions.

All I did was nudge her toward a meeting of like-minded souls. It wasn't my fault she became a missing person. Just like it wasn't Cat's fault Francesca died.

The next week, she was gone in the wind, and I got to become Cat's knight in shining armor.

It was everything I had ever dreamed of. I had been right, back in New York. Cat was snarky and casually cutting, but she wasn't cruel. If she had realized what had happened with Leo and Francesca, I was positive she would feel guilty.

I knew her so well, after all. Better than anyone else, I was sure.

I didn't want to ruin what we had, though, so I never mentioned Francesca's name or where I was from, and Cat never asked. The vague details I'd offered were always enough for her.

Everything was perfect. Until Benjamin Croft entered the picture.

The first time I saw him, all I could think of was how much he reminded me of Leo. The floppy hair, the gentle personality. Cat obviously attracted the type of men who liked to take their fists to their girlfriends, and I had been all but waiting for the first incident to happen.

When I'd walked in on them, his hand on her throat, I'd nearly passed out, but I hadn't been surprised. And then the hot water he'd thrown on her—of course, her fault. The broken wrist that had been a result of "Rollerblading," as if that were any more believable than Cat falling down a flight of stairs. I had been tracking Cat's life since I was fourteen. She had never once Rollerbladed, nor would she have been caught dead doing so.

The excuses were so flimsy they had to be a signal to me about what was happening. She didn't want to admit it out loud, I understood that. She'd be embarrassed that she got caught in the same situation twice . . . three or four times, really, though she didn't know I knew about the other ones.

I could read between the lines she laid down.

The pregnancy test was the final straw for me.

All I could see was Francesca's broken face, her broken body.

I wasn't about to let Cat suffer the same fate.

Getting Benji to join a cult wasn't going to work as well as it had with poor Amanda, who had been primed since birth to end up with that fate.

No, this was going to take more extreme measures.

I thought I'd be terrified to do what needed to be done, but my hands were steady as I headed to his apartment, a fifth of vodka clutched under my arm.

He was surprised to see me, but I made up some lie. I was in the area with an hour to kill.

It was clear Cat had told him about the baby, so we turned it into a celebration.

Then Cat called, and instead of lying like most boyfriends would, Benji had to go and tell her I was there. Which meant she would know. She would ask me about it.

She got pissed, of course. I wasn't sure why Benji hadn't predicted that. But it just led to him downing a few more shots, never noticing that I hadn't bothered to keep up since the first one.

When he was nice and wasted, I started knocking on neighboring doors. An elderly man answered, and I very clearly told him my name, handing over Benji's keys. Just in case someone asked.

Then I returned to Benji's apartment and hunted down the spare ones I knew he kept on hand for hospital emergencies.

I didn't *do* anything. I simply suggested he might want to go talk to Cat in person.

It was just like what Cat did, with the girls. She gave a nudge to the universe and let the rest fall into place.

I had truly just been hoping he'd end up with a DUI, lose his medical license, and have to flee the city in shame. Cat wouldn't need much convincing in that case to get an abortion. She was a generational talent, on the cusp of superstardom. Or as much stardom as a pastry chef could receive, but that was still something.

She didn't have any interest in starting a family.

And maybe nothing at all would happen. Maybe he'd pass out on the couch, or pass out in the driver's seat. Maybe he was a skilled drunk driver and he'd get there in one piece. This was just plan A.

It wasn't my fault he got in the car.

Life was about choices, and he made his.

I hadn't realized he would die.

But was I really going to tear myself up over the death of one more abuser? I hadn't done anything wrong.

Cat, of course, was more mad at me that I'd been there than she was sad that he was gone, even if she would never admit it.

She would have gotten over it, though.

Had it not been for Kristopher Bouchard.

CHAPTER FORTY-ONE

Holland

Now

Kris was distracted when he returned from the hardware store with the boys.

The ladies were all in the kitchen still, of course, Cat prepping and idly answering questions I pitched her way as I scribbled the outline of the profile that had come nearly fully formed into my head—the story of *us*.

Mia had her laptop out and was working alongside Anna and the girls.

Everyone looked up when Kris walked in, but he was staring at his phone, his brows pulled together in a deep vee. His eyes lifted to mine, his head tilting.

It was as if he were seeing me for the first time.

The world around us stilled, and a warning bell rang deep in my chest.

"How was the store?" Cat asked, but Kris just kissed her cheek, his attention back on his phone.

There was no reason to think his behavior had anything to do with me. Perhaps he was just always dismissive, the lovey-dovey act difficult to keep up for an entire weekend.

Anyway, the only thing I'd done wrong was sneak into his office. Honestly, they really had to realize that putting a giant keep-out sign on a door made it all the more tempting.

"Kris?" Cat called after him as he left the kitchen. Mia and Anna had both looked up, too, first at Kris's disappearing back and then to Cat, who shrugged. "Probably a business call."

That settled both of them down, and Cat went back to the pot on the stove.

I didn't think it was a business call, though.

The next few minutes were torture as I waited for everyone to forget what had just happened. I asked Cat some inane timeline questions even though I knew the answers to them. I'd watched all her videos, after all. Even the deep cuts that her employees had forgotten apparently. I knew the day she'd met Kris, the day they'd married. I knew when she'd hired Mia, and every time she'd decided to refine her aesthetic.

In my head, I was counting the seconds until it wouldn't look like I was following Kris.

That turned out to be three hundred and twenty-six, though I was probably cutting it close, given the look Mia sent my way.

But I'd started to wonder if her allegiances had shifted away from Kristopher Bouchard. Because she pointedly looked back at her computer even as I slipped out of the room.

I checked Kris's office first, expecting to find a closed door. It was open, though, and the room was empty.

I chewed on my lip, trying to figure out where he would go if he wanted privacy. It turned out I didn't need to figure it out—a flash of color caught my attention. Outside.

Kris was back in the driveway, pacing, clearly agitated.

I stepped into the front room to my right and crossed to the window. I debated lifting it—in fear it would protest, giving me away immediately. But this was the Bouchards' house. Everything would always be in pristine operating order. My guess proved correct, and I was able to silently ease it open.

Kris was a good distance away, but I caught snippets of the conversation.

". . . digital investigator . . ."

". . . not her real last . . ."

My fingers clenched. There was nothing wrong with changing your surname. I'd wanted distance from my mother, and her deep depression. I hadn't intended to hide anything.

". . . no, Catriona doesn't need . . ."

". . . I'll wait for confirmation . . ."

A long silence. Kris paused his pacing, shaking his head.

Then he swiveled to face the house.

I inhaled, taking a step back so that he wouldn't be able to see my outline through the glass.

"No, the morning's fine," he said. The scuff of boot on gravel. He was back to pacing.

I shifted just enough to catch sight of him again. It was just in time to watch his entire body stiffen.

Of course I had assumed the call was about me. But why? Simply because he'd locked eyes with me in the kitchen? I barely knew this man. I couldn't read his expressions with any certainty.

But I could watch his hands curl into fists.

I could watch him look back at the house.

I could watch his face distort into a mask of rage when he said her name.

"Fleur."

My body recoiled from the anger I'd seen in Kris, and before I'd really considered moving, I had already made it back to the kitchen. My mind was filled with mostly static, but somehow I managed to relaunch my interview with Cat.

Kris knew. He'd somehow found out that Fleur wasn't his before Cat had managed to tell him. How, though?

But of course the answer came easily.

I had started this chain of events. I had put it into motion with my attempt to see Cat again.

I could tear myself up over coming here, but the truth of the matter was that Cat had needed my help before and she needed it now. I didn't view myself as some vigilante. I wasn't going to be able to stop all the bad men in the world. I probably wouldn't even be able to make a dent. I could be a brave friend, though. I could be courageous.

And sometimes that called for doing something other than smiling politely and hoping the next time you got a call from that friend it wasn't from a hospital room.

Or a morgue.

I glanced around the kitchen, so full of laughter and sunlight and music. Everything good and bright in the world, so easily corrupted by the darkness that lived at its core.

Cat smiled over at me, and in that moment, I knew what I had to do.

For our last meal together, Jeremy had made a gorgeous lobster bisque that would be perfect for my plan.

I stopped Cat in the kitchen as the rest of the family went out onto the patio. I made sure my tape recorder was running as I leaned in.

"Have you made a decision? About telling Kris Fleur isn't his biological child?" It came out slightly awkward, but I needed to make sure anyone listening could follow the conversation.

Cat's brows pinched as she glanced around to make sure no one could hear us. She nodded. "I'm telling him tonight. After the children go to bed."

I breathed in. It was the perfect answer. I squeezed her arm. "If you're sure."

"I am."

We settled in around the table just as we had the previous two nights. I had been worried whatever rage I'd caught a glimpse of earlier in Kris would spill over and consume all of us. But he put on a perfectly pleasant mask.

The ability with which he played the doting husband and warm host despite whatever he must have found out only made me more convinced that there was a monster lurking beneath his skin.

I made a show of asking all the questions—any one that popped into my mind came out of my mouth.

They, in turn, leaned heavily into their romance.

"Do you remember that song you loved?" I said to Cat, hoping it would be as easy as this. "That one from Adele. You were obsessed—you played it on repeat for hours until it drove me crazy."

Her eyes went a little dreamy. "'When We Were Young.'"

I nearly laughed at how it could apply to us, too. "Yeah, that's the one."

Kris took out his phone, as if they were acting out a script I'd written. He tapped away at the screen until the opening bars broke the quiet of the night.

He pushed his chair back and held out his hand. Anna actually whooped in delight.

Cat buried her face in her hands for one second, but then she let Kris pull her to her feet.

They fell so easily into a slow rocking dance, the fairy lights behind them, the velvety blue sky as the backdrop behind that. The singer beseeched an ex-lover to remember how good they had been.

Their love had been like a movie.

This was like a movie.

My chest ached with how beautiful every part of this scene was.

Everyone watched them because it was impossible not to.

Which let me, in one quick move, dump the crushed-up pills directly into Kris's half-eaten soup.

CHAPTER FORTY-TWO

Det. Jamie Alvarez

Jamie mulled over the puzzle of Catriona Bouchard née Vandale as she stepped out into the hallway of the police station in search of a cup of coffee.

She happened to run straight into Jeremy Dawson as she did.

And that itch came back, the one that had started when she'd watched Detective Boyd from State interview him.

Jamie was tired, though. And she couldn't figure out what had stuck out to her from his answers.

"Mr. Dawson," she called, and he whirled around.

He looked tired, too—exhausted, even. But his eyes were wide, puppyish and eager to please. She loved talking to people like him, people who still viewed law enforcement as important authority figures to be listened to.

"I was told I could go," he said, bouncing on the toes of his shoes. "Do you need more from me?"

"No, sorry," she said. "I just wanted to make sure you were okay."

She hadn't cared if he was okay or not, but she wasn't sure what to ask him to force that itch to make sense. "Did you drive here?"

He shook his head.

"Are you staying at the hotel?" The orchard was an active crime scene at the moment, so they weren't about to let him go back and sleep in the carriage house.

"My buddy has a couch for me to crash on," he said, sagging. It seemed like now that he knew she didn't need anything official from him, the brief surge of adrenaline that had come with the sight of her fled once more.

"Let me give you a lift?" she offered, and they went back and forth for a few minutes on whether she was putting herself out by doing him this favor.

In the end, she got him to agree, because it was the smart thing and there was no point in trying to order a car and then falling asleep on the sidewalk while waiting for it.

"So, are you really holding up?" she asked as she pulled out of the parking lot.

He'd leaned his forehead against the window. "No. I can't . . . I mean, I can believe it. Kris was . . . not a good guy. But still it's shocking, you know?"

She nodded.

"I guess I'm one of those dumb neighbors who get interviewed on the news when the unassuming dude next door turns out to be a serial killer and they all thought he was normal," Jeremy said, sounding disgusted with himself.

And there was the itch again. Jamie chased it. "You said . . . you said he was not a good guy."

"Yeah." That came out emphatic.

"But you also feel like one of the dumb neighbors who thought he was normal," Jamie continued.

"Right." That came out less certain.

It was properly dark now, and Jamie's headlights did their best to cut through it. She prayed a deer wouldn't jump out at them.

"When did you realize he wasn't a good guy?" she asked. "This morning?"

"No." Back to emphatic. But then he seemed to think about it. "No. Before that."

Jamie nodded. "When?"

"I guess . . . Odette was the first sign," Jeremy said.

"So, six months ago," Jamie said before the itch was finally scratched. Because she'd read Odette Moreau's file. The detective had interviewed Jeremy; he'd interviewed everyone in the household.

And Jeremy had attested to Kris's character. The statement had been glowing, in fact.

"No," he said again. Jamie got the sense that she was taxing the two brain cells he had to rub together. "I kind of went down a rabbit hole this past weekend, I guess."

Jamie nodded. "What did you find?"

"That he was in a legal dispute with his ex at the time of her death," he said, eager again. That was interesting information. But Jamie believed her former colleague that Odette's death had been suicide.

That itch, though, it was almost completely scratched. "What made you go down the rabbit hole?"

The question seemed to stump him for a moment, and he tilted his head. "Huh."

Jamie's fingers tightened on the wheel. "Huh, what?"

"Well," he said drawing out the word as if he'd never said it before. As if he were testing the strength of it. "I guess it was because of Holland."

Jamie watched Jeremy until he was safely inside his friend's place as she thought about the fact that Holland Tate had convinced this kid that Kristopher Bouchard was a dangerous man.

She rubbed at her eyes now, too exhausted to figure out if that meant anything.

Her phone rang, jostling her out of her contemplation. She hadn't saved the number, but she recognized it as one of the many she'd called that day.

Beatrice. The digital investigator.

"This is Alvarez," Jamie said.

"I found the obsessed fan," Beatrice offered without any preamble. "Well, I think I have."

Jamie's breath caught. "Name?"

"Mary Jane Sitwick," Beatrice rattled off. "I've been watching for accounts posting today in particular, and it helped me unlock the final step to identifying her."

Jamie was relieved Beatrice didn't feel the need to explain her entire process. It would have pushed Jamie's headache into a migraine.

"She's local?" Jamie asked.

"Yup," Beatrice said. "I don't have an address, but I'm sure you can get that yourself."

"Yup," Jamie echoed. And then added, "Thank you."

"For what it's worth, she doesn't seem the violent type," Beatrice said. "But be careful anyway."

Jamie thanked her one more time before hanging up. She called into the station to get an address for Mary Jane, and then headed in that direction.

All the officers from State were up at the orchard, as was Keller. She could call in a uniform for backup, but that seemed excessive. Especially considering she was probably chasing a wild goose here.

She ended up thankful she hadn't brought anyone in on this with her when Mary Jane Sitwick opened the door before Jamie even knocked.

The middle-aged woman looked so perfectly pleasant, Jamie almost walked back to her car without asking any questions. This woman hadn't done anything wrong—she'd simply sent some overeager messages to

Catriona Bouchard. Millions of people did the same every day to their favorite influencers.

But before Jamie could retreat, Mary Jane spoke. "Oh, thank God you're here."

Jamie raised her brows. "Uh . . ."

"She shouldn't have been here," Mary Jane said. "She should never have been welcomed there."

"Who?"

"Holland Tate," Mary Jane said like it was obvious, and Jamie's pulse skittered. "She's the one who tried to kidnap Fleur Bouchard."

CHAPTER FORTY-THREE

Holland

Now

Cat was upstairs with the children, as was Anna.

Mia was nowhere to be found, at least on my cursory search.

Kris . . .

Kris might've already been passed out. I wasn't a doctor, and I didn't have my phone to research it, but I had given him a fairly large dose of those crushed pills and he'd washed them down with several glasses of wine.

It was time to make my move.

I wished that I still had that gun, wished that I had thought to hide it in a better place than just my drawer.

But I hadn't planned on this being how this weekend ended.

Didn't you? a voice whispered in my head. It sounded a lot like the one that had told me to befriend Amanda Cooper, and then told me to go to Benji's apartment, and then told me to—

I shook my head, even though it was right. Maybe I had planned all this.

Why else would I have recorded the whole weekend? Or at least the bits that proved how dangerous Kris was? The ones that proved Cat was about to trigger a rage-fueled attack by revealing the true paternity of the beloved daughter he'd thought was his?

Why else would I have searched Odette Moreau on Mia's tablet even though I'd already known everything about Odette Moreau, including that police strongly suspected she had, in fact, died by suicide. Why would I have gotten Jeremy involved in the hunt as well?

The truth was, I had been planting seeds. Ones that might forever lie inert beneath the ground. Or ones that could be watered at just the right time to bloom beautifully.

I liked telling stories, and this one would be so easy for the police to follow.

Mia would suggest the cops look into what happened to Odette Moreau. She hadn't thought much of the accident at the time—beyond caring about what a tragedy it had been. But now, as new information came to light, wasn't it curious that Kris's ex-wife had died in such a strange way? Jeremy would answer the same questions, mentioning that he found out that Odette had been in a legal battle, that she wanted more money, *a lot* more money.

Mary Jane's threat to Cat threw a tiny wrench in the plan, but she was so unhinged, she could easily be discredited. And even if Cat had lied about where she'd been, it had been to cover up Kris's bad behavior. At most they'd give her—a newly bereaved widow—a slap on the wrist for that.

Steffie would mention the gun. He might even say I'd taken it out of the safe. But his father had found it—he'd been adamant about that theory. Kris was going to use the weapon against me, Steffie had even *warned* me of that. He'd found the pills that were so suspicious. Why did Kris have prescription pills that could be used to drug his wife?

Mia would show the police the videos of Cat, of the abuse she'd tried to hide from everyone.

Cat was on tape telling me that she planned to reveal her secret to Kris. It would be easy to point to that as the trigger for his violence.

Even the drugs in his own system could be explained as something Kris had taken to make killing his wife—and then himself—easier.

Everything would point to a man who had been shot in an act of self-defense, before he could execute a murder-suicide plot against his wife.

And Cat . . . Cat wouldn't have to worry about trying to escape with the children. She wouldn't have to worry about the one area of unmonitored security fencing, wouldn't have to make any kind of sacrifice—like leaving alone.

She might not understand at first. But she would see the beauty of my plan.

I knew she would.

Because why else would she have invited me here?

She remembered. She remembered how good I was at reading the signs. She knew I *knew* her, better than anyone else.

She knew I would do what needed to be done.

The last gasp of my psychiatrist's worried voice tried to creep in. She had tried to warn my mother back then about my potential for erratic behavior following Francesca's death.

She doesn't seem to be handling it well.

My mother had nodded and then gone and swallowed some more pills to ease her own pain.

Maybe back then, when I'd been a teenager, I hadn't handled it well. Now I realized that just meant I hadn't handled it within the limits of acceptable behavior. But when did we ever stop men like Kris and Benji and Leo from acting beyond the bounds of acceptable behavior? We didn't, until a woman ended up dead.

That psychiatrist could go fuck herself.

My hand was on the doorknob to Kris's office, turning it before I really even realized I'd gotten there.

The room was dark, but it was easy to find the bulky shape on the sofa.

I flipped the light on, and he turned toward me, though he was slow and uncoordinated about it.

"You," he said, and it sounded like a struggle to get that out. "What did you do to me?"

The words slurred together, none of them fully stopping before they tripped into the next one. His breathing was labored, his eyes glassy.

I crossed the room and grabbed the chair from behind the desk, dragging it over to sit in front of him.

"Where's the gun?" I asked. Because maybe Cat had it, and maybe Mia had it. But I was starting to think Steffie had been correct: Kris was the one who'd found it in my drawer.

He didn't answer, but his eyes slipped to his desk like a dog who'd hidden a bone somewhere and couldn't help but give away the location when asked about it.

"Thank you," I said, heading toward the desk. "Wanted to keep it at hand for some reason?"

"Yeah, because you're a psycho bitch," Kris managed to get out. He tried to stand, but didn't have full control of his legs. Or the rest of his body, for that matter. He fell back on the couch, even as his desperation tried to get him to keep moving.

His eyes were wide now, and terrified.

I wanted to bask in his fear—the fear he tried to make other people feel, turned back on him. I was so tired of these men who preyed on women because they could. My whole life I'd been watching them get away with it, and I was done with that now.

"You took . . ."

"The gun, yeah," I said, distracted, pulling open drawers. I was careful, though. Just in case anyone would wonder why Kris had been frantically searching for his own weapon.

"No," he said, sounding weak. "You really did do it, didn't you? I could hardly believe it . . ."

Again, he faded. This time I looked up, thinking about that call. "Could hardly believe what?"

He laughed. "That you were the one who took Fleur."

I looked away.

Taking her had been a mistake. I had realized that immediately, of course.

Or, almost immediately.

But, at the time, I had thought Kris was using the baby to keep Cat in Vermont. If I could have gotten her out safely first . . . then Cat could have followed. She could have escaped without having to worry about the kid.

It was what these kind of men did—they used their children to control their wives.

I had just removed Kris's leverage.

The baby hadn't even woken up.

I had stood outside that church staring down at the little bundle and wondering if my niece would have slept so peacefully, or if she would have wailed, arms waving and face red.

I went back to searching. "How did you know?"

Because if he knew, someone else did.

"You mean does Cat know?" he said with a laugh. "Your precious Cat. That's all you care about, you fucking psycho."

I didn't say anything—of course he was going to lash out at me. He was an asshole. I ran my hand along the underside of his desk until my fingers touched metal. I grinned.

"Not bad," I said, once I had the gun freed and gripped loosely in my hand. I walked over to him and pressed the muzzle against his forehead. "How did you know?"

I needed to figure out if there were loose threads here.

Kris's breathing was ragged now. He had a while to go before he actually succumbed, I'd imagine. Especially considering he was talking. "I have a private investigator. He gives me a report on everyone who is invited to stay with us."

"Excessive," I murmured.

"Apparently not," he shot back.

"What did he find out about me?" I asked. He wouldn't have been able to figure out I'd taken Fleur. I was certain about that. Kris had been the one to put it together.

His eyes were full of venom now. "He found a list of burner accounts associated to your name."

I had deleted most of the ones I'd used to follow Cat back then. Some of the fog in my head had lifted that night, some of my rage toward Kristopher Bouchard clearing.

I had found a psychologist in the city—not a psychiatrist, as I didn't want to be on drugs.

She specialized in trauma related to domestic violence. I didn't tell her all I'd done to protect Cat, but I had let it slip that I'd probably crossed a line with a friend or two.

I told her about being found sitting next to Francesca, and she asked if I had seen it happen.

It was the first time anyone had asked that. Maybe the cops had and I'd forgotten. But my mother hadn't even guessed I could have.

I didn't know. I'd written a statement for the cops saying I hadn't, that I'd come home to her body. But what if I'd been hiding in a closet when Leo beat her to death? Wouldn't that explain some of the boundaries I might have tested with my friends?

I'd liked that psychologist. She'd understood that all I wanted to do was protect people.

After my ill-fated trip, Kris had put up his security fence. The family had stopped even going into town, and the glimpses I could get of Cat were limited to the content she posted.

I couldn't protect someone who didn't want protecting.

But then my mother died.

I stopped seeing my psychologist the day after. She might have told me that I felt like a failure from not being able to protect my mother from her grief.

That was the first time I reached out to Cat. Because I couldn't protect someone who didn't want protecting, but that didn't mean I shouldn't try.

I should have tried with Francesca, and I should have tried with my mother.

I wasn't going to regret not trying with Cat.

"I recognized one of them," Kris spat out now. "It was one our digital investigator found seven years ago."

"Did you tell him?" I asked. It sounded like right now Kris was the one person who could link me to Fleur's kidnapping. The investigator only knew that I had a burner account—which wasn't exactly suspicious.

Kris swallowed heavily, and I could see the calculation in his eyes. He wanted to tell me the version that would most likely keep him alive.

"The truth," I said, even though that was a lie.

He breathed out. "No. But it doesn't matter. You're going to jail for so much more than just—"

"Right," I said, relief flooding me. I had one more question I wanted an answer to, though. "Did you kill Odette?"

Kris blinked at me, surprised. "What?"

"Did you kill your ex-wife and make it look like a freak accidental death?" I asked. "And then make Cat lie to cover for you?"

"You are a psycho bitch," Kris muttered.

"We've established that," I said, and waved the gun a little bit. "Look, I'm probably going to kill you. But I might not. Your best chance for getting out of this is telling me the truth."

Fear flashed across his face. "No. We went to talk to Odette the night before she and Steffie left for their kayaking trip. But it was to try to work out a settlement. If the cops knew about it, though, they would have tried to pin it on one of us."

I know where you were . . .

"For what it's worth, I believe you."

He closed his eyes in seeming relief. "Like I fucking care."

"You should," I murmured, but then tuned out anything else he had to hurl at me.

I was done worrying about Kristopher Bouchard.

I didn't know where Mia was, though, and I didn't want him calling out to her for help.

Luckily, this was part of the old farmhouse, and as such had a door that locked with a key. If I could just find it . . .

I'd done a thorough job of searching the room the night before. Nothing had stuck out to me, but I'd been looking for a safe.

The walls were decorated with a chaotic wallpaper that somehow looked amazing. But because of that there were only a few decorations on them. By the door was an old chain, and at the bottom of it hung a gold key.

I laughed at my good luck—and hoped the thing was actually in workable shape.

Again, I reminded myself, I was at the Bouchards'.

"Now, you just wait here," I told Kris, before stepping out into the hallway and locking the door behind me.

I tried the knob.

It didn't budge.

Perfect.

I headed for the kitchen, shoving the gun in the back of my waistband as I did.

My hands were shaking, but that didn't matter.

Everything was coming together.

Now I just had to let Cat know the plan.

I realized she might be . . . resistant. I had known that ever since she'd convinced herself it would be safe to tell Kris about Fleur.

But I knew deep down she wanted to be saved.

That was why I was here, after all.

I grabbed a bottle of white wine from the refrigerator, then jogged up the stairs.

I sat on the landing, where I had a view of the front staircases as well. There was only one way for Cat to come from the children's wing, so there was no chance she'd be able to slip by me.

I'm not sure how long I sat waiting—ten minutes, an hour.

But it seemed like all of a sudden I blinked and Cat was there.

She smiled down at me, and I smiled up at her, and everything was right in the world.

"Any interest in rooftop wine?" I asked, because that's what we'd always called going somewhere pretty and splitting a bottle even if we just stayed inside while doing it.

Cat grinned, but then sobered. "Kris is waiting for me. I told him there was something big I needed to share with him."

I inhaled. "Can he wait? Just another half hour?"

She seemed like she wanted to come with me but was torn.

"I'm leaving in the morning," I pressed. "And Vermont isn't very far, but I don't know when the next time we'll see each other is."

Cat stared at me, a curious expression flickering across her features. It was gone before I could identify it. She blew out a breath and then she smiled again. "I guess a half hour couldn't hurt. Neither will some liquid courage."

I had no interest in pointing out that she'd already had a couple of glasses of wine at dinner.

"I should just let him know that I'll be a little," she said, starting down the stairs.

My heart jolted, the bottle slipping in my sweaty hand. "I actually already told him. Ran into him while getting the wine."

"You were pretty sure you'd be persuasive, huh?" she teased, but when she continued on down the stairs, she headed for the kitchen rather than Kris's office. "We don't have a rooftop available, though."

"I was thinking . . . the greenhouse?" I offered. "Similar vibes."

She paused as she considered, but she nodded. "Steffie wouldn't be pleased, but he's currently locked in his room playing video games, so . . . yeah, that sounds great."

Cat grabbed a flashlight and then we headed off toward the woods.

"You don't think you'll come back here to visit?" she asked.

"I . . ." That was impossible to answer. I didn't know how the next hour would even go. "I don't know. Do you want me to visit?"

"Of course," she said, smiling down at the ground.

"I'm not sure Kris would want me here," I said, gently broaching the topic. "He doesn't seem too fond of me."

She slid me a look, and I realized that more than anything it was confusion tugging at her features. "Why do you say that?"

"Uh . . . he told me he was going to push me down one of the wells and no one would hear me scream," I said, a little fed up with Cat's innocent act.

She laughed until she realized I wasn't joking.

"I refuse to believe that," Cat said. "What exactly did he say to you?"

"It doesn't matter—"

"It actually does, Holland," Cat said, stopping and turning toward me, her face righteously angry. It was okay, I had braced for this. "Did he tell you he was going to throw you into a well?"

My skin felt itchy beneath her scrutiny. "He implied it."

She rolled her eyes. "Was he literally just warning you to beware of the wells?"

I gaped at her. "No."

Cat huffed an exasperated sigh. "Holland . . . you do tend to see monsters in shadows with some frequency."

I didn't say anything. I knew she was going to resist at first—it was just frustrating that she was going to be so stubborn about it.

She continued in silence as well until we got to the greenhouse.

I leaned forward to open the door and then glanced back.

Cat was frozen, staring at me.

Something had spooked her.

I immediately tensed, looking around, but I couldn't find any threat. "Are you okay?"

"Hmm?" she asked, her eyes looking glassy now. Then she shook her head, and everything about her sharpened. "Oh, sorry. Um."

She walked past me without any other explanation.

I followed her in, handing off the wine. My newly freed hand instinctively touched the gun in the back of my waistband to make sure it was secure.

Not that I needed it now. It was a comfort to have, though.

"Look, Cat," I said, as she fiddled with the screw-off top. She handed it over to me after taking a swig. I knew I shouldn't drink, but if I didn't take the bottle, she might get suspicious as to why. And right now, I wanted to ease her into my plan. So I took a sip. "I know you love Kris."

"I do," she said, emphatically. She took another quick swig and then immediately handed the bottle back. I stared at it, not thrilled about the pace. "I really, really love Kris. Because he's a good man."

At that, I took a long swallow. "Right."

"A really good man," she repeated, and I couldn't help but drink again. "He treats me so well. Practically worships the ground I walk on."

"I get that you have to say that," I said. "And I understand it's hard to ask for help."

"I don't need help," she said, and all of a sudden the bottle was somehow back in my hand. Had she even taken a turn with it?

"I get that you believe that—"

"Holy fucking shit," Cat burst out. She stared at me with something I'd never seen aimed in my direction before. Contempt. "I don't even care. You know, I wanted to give you another chance. I really did. I went into this weekend thinking, *Man, wouldn't it be great to have Holland back as a friend? She's probably even matured a bit.*"

"I wanted that, too," I said, not sure what to do with that last part.

"But my god," she kept going as if I hadn't said anything. "My. God. Holland. You are so fucking exhausting."

I gritted my teeth. She had never wanted to admit . . .

"You showed me the fence," I pointed out.

"What the hell are you talking about?" she asked, all exasperation.

"When we walked in the orchard, you were planning something," I said. "You showed me where we could escape from the compound this weekend if we needed to."

She could've looked no more stunned if I had punched her in the face. "Holland, you need help. We went on a fucking walk. This isn't some postapocalyptic TV show where we're cutting through fences."

"He built it to keep you in."

"Oh my god, Kris wanted to protect our family," she said, jabbing her finger at me. "He's not abusing me."

I looked away and she nearly screamed.

"I can watch your messed-up brain telling yourself a ridiculous story about how I don't know what I'm saying," she said. "That I love you and hate Kris and poor little me, I can't help but hook up with men who want to hurt me."

"That's how abuse works, Cat," I said, though I could feel my heart in my jaw, in the softness of my wrists. I wanted to touch the gun again, but I didn't.

This time, Cat did let out a guttural scream. "Kris isn't hitting me. He would never lay a hand on me. And news flash, you psycho, Benji wasn't, either. He was the best boyfriend I ever had until Kris. Which you refused to fucking believe."

"Stop trying to gaslight me." A bead of sweat slid from the nape of my neck down my back. "I know what I saw."

"You saw what you wanted to see," Cat said, slumping back. "I get it, you're traumatized. You lost your sister. It's all very sad."

My breath caught in my throat.

I tried to remember Cat crying outside the hospital. Flowers for Gloria at her feet. She would have felt guilty if she'd known what happened to Francesca. Cat didn't know it was Francesca who had been her first patsy—she didn't know what had ultimately happened to that first girl. I had never told her the truth about just who my sister was. She would feel guilty if she knew, if she knew Francesca had been murdered, she would feel guilty—

"Poor you," this Cat said, her face a mask of pity and rage and disdain. "But, God, Holland that was so fucking long ago. Are you really so pathetic you haven't gotten over it? That you need to ruin my life because you're stuck on something that happened to you as a teenager?"

"Get over it," I repeated softly.

Cat would feel guilty if she knew . . . she would . . .

"Yes." She threw her hands in the air. "I don't know what fucked-up fantasy you've told yourself here. But guess what, baby doll? I want to live in a multimillion-dollar compound where I don't have to deal with idiots like you all of the time."

"Idiots like me." Idiots like Francesca. Like Gloria. The girls who were too dumb to realize they were being played by Catriona Vandale.

"You know what's wild?" Cat stepped closer to me, hatred and frustration all but pouring off her. "You say you want to save me from bad relationships, but *you* are the bad relationship. You are the abusive boyfriend who just won't leave me the fuck alone."

That struck me like a fist. I stepped back, and shook my head. None of this was right. I was different. I *knew* Cat. I was different from everyone else in her life, I was special to her. "I'm not. I'm not like them."

"You are," Cat said, and it seemed like it was a revelation even to her. "Oh my god, you are so like them." She laughed, high on her own realization. "I've been with a guy that put me in the hospital, and honestly I'd take that over you."

Her voice trailed off at the end.

And, finally, she saw me.

She saw the gun in my hand.

Aimed directly at her.

CHAPTER FORTY-FOUR

Cat

Now

The bloodletting had been so cathartic that it took me far too long to notice the gun Holland held.

I had seen it on the way into the greenhouse, and maybe I should have turned around just then and headed straight back to call the cops. But I had a feeling if I had tried that Holland would have taken it out and shot me on the spot.

I had gotten the sense that something was a little off with her. But it hadn't been until that moment that I realized how unhinged she was. I'd had to act fast, shaking off my shock, pretending I hadn't seen the huge-ass weapon sticking out of the back of her jeans, and trying to proceed as normal while at the same time crafting a plan to extricate myself from the situation.

And then, because I'm weak, I'd gotten caught up in my own spiel. It wasn't my fault that Holland, more than anything, really was fucking exhausting beyond belief.

I'd loved her back then, of course, when we'd been living in each other's pockets. I'd been young and never had a friendship that intense and codependent before. I hadn't realized why people called them unhealthy.

Then Holland had left Savannah and it had felt like a breath of fresh air. There had been way too many months where I'd felt her eyes on me constantly, trying to look for bruises, trying to save me from some abusive relationship she'd made up in her own mind.

It had been such a relief to start my relationship with Kris without her hovering in the background, rushing to put space between Kris and me with every bruise on my arm or rolled ankle or, god forbid, raised voices in a fight. I could bump into tables and fall over when I got too tipsy and even throw a book in the vicinity of Kris's head and no one would sulk in a chair and watch me with dark eyes, judging me as if I were letting down all of womankind.

I was already a head case. I was self-aware enough to realize that. Adding in Holland's shit hadn't been good for me.

Maybe I hadn't seen that clearly back then, in the haze of friendship so intense it felt like drugs sometimes. Blue skies weren't as exciting as thunderstorms, but you also didn't worry you were going to get struck by lightning every few minutes.

And here she was proving me right.

The lunatic was holding Kris's gun on me like she was actually going to use it.

"Put that down," I said, using my most bored voice. Like she'd accidentally picked up a weapon without realizing it, and I was simply pointing out the error.

"Get over it," she repeated. Her eyes were wild, but her hands were steady.

I shouldn't have invited her to The Orchard. I'm not even sure why I finally said yes, except that Mia had been making noise about getting some good publicity ahead of the launch of my app. I realized I hadn't even mentioned the thing to Holland all weekend—I must have sensed that she was not the right person to write about my beloved project.

Now that I thought about it, it was strange how little Holland had talked to me this weekend. She'd been busy flitting around with Mia and Jeremy. She'd spent several hours in the kitchen with us, but her eyes had been unfocused, as if she hadn't been present.

At the time, I'd just thought she might regret signing up to write about how glamorous my life was while hers was kind of shitty.

I realized now that she'd apparently been having a complete and total mental breakdown right in front of me.

"What was the name of the girl?" she asked, sweat beading on her upper lip.

If I didn't do something soon, she was bound to shoot me. She looked well and truly like she was losing her tether to reality.

I really should have noticed something was off before spotting the gun in her waistband. And I would have had I not been worried she was going to unmask me as a total cunt to all my followers. Holland was the only one who knew what kind of person I'd been before the screens and the pretty filters. So, all weekend, I'd been more focused on keeping my face pleasant than watching for signs of truly psychotic behavior emerging from my once best friend.

"I don't know what the fuck you're talking about," I said. "You lunatic."

Probably, it wasn't the best choice to antagonize the girl with a gun. But it wasn't like I was known for making the best choices.

"The girl you pawned your first boyfriend off on," she said. Her voice was hollow now, scarily so.

Honestly, I knew it. I did. I just . . . was blanking on the name. I had a gun pointed at my face. Could anyone really blame me? I swallowed. "What does it matter?"

"What was her name?"

"I don't know," I yelled. "She was just some girl. Who cares?"

Even as the words came out of my mouth, I realized my huge error.

If Holland was asking me her name while pointing a weapon at me—and looking very much like she could pull that trigger—then I had an answer to that question.

Holland. Holland cared.

I searched my memory and it came up blank. "Look, I know it, I'm just . . ." I waved to the gun. "Fucking stressed."

"Her name was Francesca," Holland said, with that same dead voice. "And she was my sister."

I stared at her as the truth knocked the breath out of my lungs.

Francesca. I tried to picture her, but her face was hazy—I got a blur of dark hair, braces, and freckles. Someone a little awkward in their body.

She'd been in love with Leo, and he'd laughed at her behind her back.

Or he had until I'd started nudging him in her direction.

I remembered . . .

I remembered the rooftop, when I'd finally asked Holland why she was so fixated on domestic violence. Her sister had been beaten to death by her boyfriend after he found out she was pregnant.

My stomach clenched. Francesca had been so jealous of me, and all I'd wanted to tell her was to run. But that wouldn't have saved me.

I remembered . . .

I remembered the day that cop had come knocking on our door. I'd thrown up in the sink, wondering if there was a way I'd be charged as an accessory to murder.

I might not have meant for the girl to die, but I had known it was a possibility that she'd get hurt.

Holland had listened to my confession that day. She hadn't judged me.

The only thing she'd asked was . . .

What was the girl's name. I pressed my hand to my mouth, the memory nearly taking me out at the knees. I had been so self-centered. I had thought she was worried about me. She had been so kind and understanding as I'd told her my deepest secret.

And all this time . . . Holland had been . . . what? Stalking me? Enacting some fifteen-year revenge plan that involved becoming my best friend and then not talking for a decade?

Out of all the questions, one thought crystallized.

She was so fucked up about her sister's death, and she blamed *me* for it.

I was not getting out of here alive.

Before when she was holding the gun on me, I could tell myself that she didn't really have a reason to pull the trigger.

Now she did.

But . . . the gun wavered. Just a fraction.

"I'm sorry, Holland," I said, trying to recover from calling her . . . well, whatever names I'd hurled out in the past five minutes. They'd been ugly, I was sure, but I hadn't exactly kept track of them. "I do remember her. I'm just not great under pressure."

She scoffed, and I rushed to correct myself so I didn't get caught lying right away. "This kind of pressure."

I nodded to the gun, and noticed it wobble again. I exhaled, trying not to let any kind of relief show.

"Babe, don't listen to me, I'm being a total nutjob," I said, realizing, probably too late, that I needed to sweet-talk Holland and not yell at her. "I'm so glad you're here. I'm so glad you came. Let's talk this out."

Holland swallowed, looking unsure now. Unsteady.

Maybe I was getting through to her.

Or maybe it was the drugs I'd dumped into the wine.

CHAPTER FORTY-FIVE

Holland

Now

I wanted to press my fingers into my eyes for just a moment. Or sit down.

Sitting down sounded so nice.

But Cat wasn't *my* Cat right now.

Right now she was every inch of Catriona Bouchard. Even when she'd tried to alter course, when she'd tried to act like she hadn't meant any of the insults she'd lobbed so precisely in my direction, I could only see Catriona in front of me.

She said she remembered Francesca's name, and maybe if I could still see her as Cat, I'd believe her. But this was someone completely different, someone I didn't trust at all.

"You're lying," I said, though my tongue felt heavy when I did.

I squeezed my eyes shut for just a moment, trying to get the world to come back into sharper focus.

I hadn't had that much wine.

"You're right," Cat said, prowling toward me now. "I've been putting on a persona for ten fucking years, and I couldn't even keep up the pretense that you aren't crazy for three minutes. And you're pointing a gun at me. Imagine how nuts that makes you."

I couldn't follow what she'd said.

"I'm sorry your sister dated someone who beat her," Cat said. "I'm sorry she died. But I didn't kill her."

My grip tightened on the gun. "You might as well have."

"No," Cat said. "That's not how it works."

She sounded so reasonable, I thought, for a second, that I should agree with her.

"And Kris is going to come looking for me any minute," Cat continued.

"No," I said, mimicking her tone. I steadied myself. "He's not."

Cat's eyes flicked down to the gun, and I watched her face lose all color. "You killed him?"

"Not yet," I said. The world tipped sideways again, and when I tried to blink, I couldn't open my eyes.

Cat was in front of me, reaching for the gun, when I finally unstuck my lids.

The adrenaline rush made everything come into focus. I stepped back and steadied my grip. "No. Get back over there."

"What are you going to do? Shoot me?" Cat asked, but she listened, retreating.

I didn't say anything and she didn't say anything for a long time.

"How are you going to get out of this?" she finally asked. "I don't know exactly what the charge would be, but it would probably warrant jail time."

"You were supposed to accept my help," I said sadly, and she nodded.

"But I never needed it," she said, quiet now. The arrogance gone.

We both knew there was only one way out.

I had written the story before I'd even stepped foot in their house.

A flaw of mine, really.

The world blurred again, and I drew in a shaky breath.

Because Cat smiled.

I *knew* Cat.

She wasn't meek. She wasn't deferential. She was arrogant, and would be until she was dead in the ground.

She hadn't retreated.

She'd created space for me to stumble.

I had underestimated her.

Cat's very best and very worst trait were the same—she was endlessly clever. If there was a way to save her own skin, she would figure it out. She'd gotten women killed over it.

I rewound the past half hour in my head until I found the moment.

Just outside the greenhouse.

Cat had frozen, startled and fearful.

Because she'd seen the gun.

I hit play on the memory.

Right after that I'd handed her the wine. And I'd been agitated, drinking half the bottle even though I knew I shouldn't.

I was no lightweight. Wine alone wouldn't have done this to me. It was easy to make the next leap in logic, considering that I had just done the same thing to Kris.

I met her eyes. "Why did you have those drugs on you?"

"Kris noticed two of the bottles were missing," she said, not even attempting to pretend she didn't know what I was talking about. "We thought it was Steffie."

She reached into her cardigan and held out an orange bottle. "I was holding on to it until we decided what to do about him taking the pills."

I nodded. I didn't know how much I'd consumed—*she* probably didn't, even. But they were affecting me.

Soon, it wouldn't matter that I had the gun. She would be able to catch me unaware.

I would be like every antagonist who monologued too long and ended up dead.

And Cat knew it.

Even though I had the weapon, she looked poised and in control. Like all she was doing was waiting for me to fall down so that she could step over my prone body. A minor inconvenience on her way to live her best life.

Just like Francesca had been.

"You didn't even remember her name," I said softly, mostly to myself, because I needed the reminder. I had seen her as Cat ever since I'd watched her break down outside that hospital going to visit Gloria. I'd thought that had revealed something about her character, but all it had done was let me tell myself a story.

I had started seeing her face on Francesca's broken body. But this was a cold dose of reality. This was her once again standing over my sister, standing over me, grinning as she surveyed the pain she had wrought.

"I remembered, I did," she said. "I promise I did. You know me. You know I did. I told you, way back then, I told you her name. On the roof, right?"

Maybe she had.

But that was a long time ago. And this was no longer Cat.

She was well and truly Catriona Bouchard.

I just wished I'd seen it sooner.

I raised the gun, and desperation finally slipped into her expression.

"Come on, we can be friends again," she said, pleading. "Holland, you were my best friend." Her eyes filled with tears. "I loved you. *I love you.*"

"See, here's the thing," I said. I swayed again, and I saw her knees bend as if she might throw herself at me. "I don't believe you, Catriona."

And with that, I pulled the trigger.

CHAPTER FORTY-SIX

HOLLAND

Now

I had thought it would be difficult, but it came as easy as writing *The End*.

Catriona's body hit the ground, and I moved quickly. A little worried about the drugs and wine, and a little worried that I wasn't sure where Mia was.

I considered just leaving Catriona in the greenhouse. That would be the most efficient option, but I liked the idea of the wells. I liked that Kris was on tape talking about them.

The greenhouse had all sorts of helpful tools, like a tarp, which I rolled the body up in. There was a moment when her eyes seemed to loll open that I'd almost frozen—and when I thought about what I'd actually done, the black started to creep in at the sides of my vision. But for the most part, it was simple to drag her by the feet toward one of the stone circles that marked a well.

Dumping her down one of these also meant that investigators would waste time searching for her rather than preserving evidence in the crucial first few hours of the case. Not that I thought I'd left any behind, but it was good to give them something to keep them occupied.

The hardest part was hefting her up onto the stones. One strand of hair came out from the tarp, the blond shining nearly silver in the moonlight. I swayed, and swallowed hard against my nausea. That song played in my head, the one Catriona and Kris had danced to. A sweet, melancholic ballad about what used to be. About, just for a moment, seeing the memory of a person in the changed one standing in front of you.

Even in death, the memory of Cat was beautiful.

I reached down and grabbed her feet once more. Her body resisted for only a moment.

Then it went easily into the darkness of the well.

Actually, everything was easy after that.

Getting the angle right for Kris to "shoot himself" was probably the most difficult part, considering he was half dead already. But that was good because he didn't put up a fight. I wouldn't have to explain any scratches, bruises, or wounds to the police.

I was worried about the noise of the shot, but it was somewhat muffled by the gun going off *in* Kris's mouth. The renovated farmhouse was huge, though, and the Bouchards must have invested in good insulation, because no one came running in the seconds right after.

I thought about leaving a note, but that seemed like it could cause more problems than it would solve.

Right now, the story was so easy to follow. Even the local police wouldn't be able to screw it up, despite the fact that this area probably hadn't seen many homicides.

A note would be overkill.

I wiped down the key I'd used to lock Kris in the study and then rehung it. I left the light on and the door wide open so that he would be easy to find.

Then I went up to my room. I showered, scrubbing every part of my body no fewer than four times. I got under my nails for no reason other than extreme caution. I shoved the clothes I'd been wearing into the bottom of my duffel.

The memory cards were dated and somewhat time-stamped—Day One, hours one through seven—which would make it easier for the detectives. I had made sure not to record anything I didn't want someone else to hear, so I didn't have to worry about editing them. That would make it all seem more authentic to the investigator, anyway. God knew what kind of ideas they would get if they thought I'd digitally tampered with the recordings.

Once done organizing those into an envelope, I finally sat on my bed, staring at the wall.

There were no cameras that I had to worry about. And I knew for a fact neither Anna's nor Steffie's windows overlooked the path we'd taken to the greenhouse. I didn't have my phone, so they wouldn't be able to do any fancy GPS location tracking on it.

Of course, there was a chance I wouldn't get away with this.

I had known that, though, coming in. No use borrowing worry from the future.

Now, all there was left to do was wait.

And try not to think.

I had just killed—

No. I hadn't just killed two people. What happened was that I had finally gotten full justice for my sister. For my niece.

And that could only ever be a good thing.

The house really did have good insulation, because I didn't hear Mia scream, though surely she must have.

The first sign that anyone had discovered Kris was the banging on my door.

I opened it to find Mia, her face a mess of tears—which, if I was being honest, surprised me. She hadn't seemed like the type to fall apart at the sight of a traumatic crime scene.

"Kris—" She broke off, swallowing hard. "He killed himself."

I had practiced for this. I made sure my face arranged itself into *stunned confusion*. "What?"

"And Catriona's missing," Mia said, the grim certainty on her face the result of a weekend of hard work from me.

"Oh my god," I said, making myself sound angry and scared and sad, but not too much of any one thing. "I told her not to tell him. I fucking told her."

"Tell him what? Tell him what?" Mia asked, her eyes wild. If I had suspected her of being anything but who she presented herself to be, this reaction certainly proved me wrong. She was genuinely distraught. "Did she tell him something that would have made him . . . ?"

Her eyes went wide. She didn't want to say it. That was the beauty of this plan. I had led her to the edge, but she would make the jump herself and think she'd come up with the idea on her own.

"She told Kris Fleur's not his daughter," I said, whirling around to shove myself into a pair of jeans. All frantic motion, incredulous and angry and a little righteous. That was quite easy to fake. "I knew he was going to . . ."

Neither of us was going to say it. You didn't say it if you didn't want it to be true. I knew that much.

"Should we go look for Catriona?"

I didn't say *her body*, but Mia so clearly heard it in the silence. "I don't know. I called the police, they said not to leave."

"Okay," I said, shoving my hands through my hair. I was so much less woozy, and wondered how long I'd sat here, sobering up. Not thinking. "Maybe we go stand outside to wait for them? So we don't contaminate anything."

"Yeah, yes, I think . . ." Mia stared at the floor. "Yeah, I think that's good. Let's let the children sleep for now."

There was a pang there, at the thought of them. At the thought of the baby Catriona had worn all weekend, like it was part of her.

I pushed that aside. There was no undo button here. There was only forward movement.

"Let's go," I said, grabbing her by the hand and all but dragging her down the stairs. We went out the back way, and Mia didn't seem to think it strange I knew how to avoid Kris's body despite the fact that she hadn't told me it was in the study.

By the time we heard the sirens, I had Mia wrapped up in a tight hug. I hadn't expected her to cry like this, but it wasn't every day you found your employer dead.

I liked this side of her, though. The one that needed comfort.

It was perhaps what I'd liked most about Cat as well. She'd needed my praise, my approval, even though she didn't want to appear to be seeking it.

Maybe Mia would move to the city. Why wouldn't she? She wouldn't want to live out here any longer, and I was sure Cat had left her with enough money that she'd be able to afford an apartment in Manhattan.

She would need a friend when she got there.

Someone to look out for her.

She was tough, of course. But sometimes it was the most fun to take care of someone like that.

I tightened my grip on Mia, who sniffed into my shoulder.

"It's going to be okay," I promised.

I would make sure of it.

CHAPTER FORTY-SEVEN

Det. Jamie Alvarez

When Jamie left Mary Jane Sitwick's house, her phone dinged.

It was from Keller.

> Found Catriona Bouchard's body dumped in a well. Shot through the heart.

And there it was. This case was exactly what it had looked like. Exactly what Holland Tate and Mia Preston and Jeremy Dawson had all said it was.

Kristopher Bouchard was just another man who had finally snapped and killed his wife before killing himself.

Jamie glanced back toward Mary Jane's house. The woman was watching her from the window. At first, Jamie had been thrilled that following this wild-goose chase had panned out with a real lead. And then she'd talked to Mary Jane, who had been distraught at the rumors of Catriona Bouchard's death.

Jamie half considered sending a social worker out to do a wellness check on her. She was nearly incoherent, showing Jamie a board that essentially looked like that one conspiracy theory meme with red thread and a wild-eyed man who thought he was making some kind of sense.

The "evidence" she'd collected against Holland Tate essentially added up to Holland not posting her normal amount of social media content on the weekend Fleur Bouchard had been kidnapped. And a post that included a coffee cup that could be traced to a shop on the route between Burlington and New York City. And the shop hadn't even been in Vermont.

All Jamie could see when Mary Jane wrapped up her spiel was a woman incredibly jealous of a close friend of her favorite influencer. Which had all been exacerbated by the rumors of Catriona's untimely death.

Kristopher Bouchard had killed his wife after finding out that she'd lied about her daughter being his for nearly a decade. Both Mia and Jeremy had given statements that they'd been worried for Catriona's safety. Even if Jeremy had changed his tune on that once Holland Tate entered the picture—well, sometimes it took the stress of a new person to reveal secrets that had been well hidden.

Maybe Jamie still felt a little restless about how easy the story was, but that was stupid.

She contemplated for another second before swinging her car around in the direction of the hospital.

Holland Tate, it had been discovered, had been dosed with some of the drugged wine Kris had meant for him and his wife. So, while she'd been declared fine at the scene, out of an abundance of caution, the first responders had sent her to the hospital.

When Jamie approached the nurse's desk, the woman on duty protested weakly that visiting hours were over. Jamie was feeling particularly stubborn, though, and the woman was clearly at the end of a shift with no interest in dying on any hills.

So she'd coughed up a room number for their intrepid journalist.

It seemed like a waste that Holland had been admitted just because she'd consumed trace amounts of barbiturates and painkillers, but who was Jamie to decide that?

The door to the room was open, so Jamie took a second to peek in before announcing her presence.

Mia Preston was sitting in the visitor's chair, chatting with Holland, who was laid up in the bed.

This was Jamie's first glimpse of the woman whose interviews had filled her head hours earlier. She was one of those people who matched their voice—thick auburn hair and eyebrows, freckles and big eyes, a pout of a mouth that probably had men lining up at bars to talk to her.

She was pale, her hair a little frizzy, and seemed generally tired, but beneath all that it was easy to see she was gorgeous.

It was so strange that she'd come back into Catriona Bouchard's life on such a tragic weekend.

It also made sense. Holland had been the catalyst, after all. Jamie could tell from listening to the recordings that Holland had given them that she had been the one who'd set the confrontation about Fleur's paternity into motion.

Jamie would never say that to her, though, of course. She wasn't exactly Ms. Sensitive, but she knew not to blame the victim's former best friend for something she might feel guilty about the rest of her life.

Still . . . just an odd little happenstance. Because while Catriona had been linked to those deaths in her past, an argument could be made that Holland Tate had been as well.

Amanda Cooper had been Cat's roommate prior to Holland.

Mark Sinclair had been Cat's boyfriend when Holland met her.

Benji Croft had been Cat's boyfriend just before Holland left Savannah.

And now Holland had witnessed two more deaths.

It was Mia who noticed Jamie first, and Jamie watched the woman's face for any signs of distress upon seeing her. But all she offered was a hesitant, though not unfriendly, nod of greeting.

Holland followed Mia's gaze, and once again Jamie looked closely. She just needed a single ounce of guilt to flash into the woman's eyes, for the bob of her throat to reveal that she'd swallowed too hard, for her fingers to tangle together atop the sheet. But all Jamie could see was the slight concern of someone who'd just survived a traumatic experience and wasn't quite sure they were safe yet.

"I'm sorry to bother you ladies," Jamie said, feeling stupid and big and unnecessary, loitering there in the doorway.

"It's no problem," Holland said. "Can we help you with anything? I probably don't even need to be here if you want me to give my statement again at the station."

She was earnest, but not overly so. Nothing in her demeanor screamed that she was lying.

Jamie shook her head. The woman had just lived through a murder-suicide involving someone she'd once been close to, and here Jamie was harassing her.

Jamie had extremely limited experience with homicides. She wasn't someone from State who dealt with this kind of stuff all the time. All she had was some niggling doubt that this investigation felt like a script they were all following too easily without pausing to take in any other options.

There was no reason to look for zebras, though, when the horses were trampling over you.

This kind of crime happened every day. Hell, her daughter had just done a report on the fact that, worldwide, every ten minutes a woman or girl was killed by an intimate partner or loved one.

"No, it's okay," she said, but then curiosity got the best of her. "Hey, you were friends with Catriona back in Savannah, right?"

"We lived together, yes."

"Did you know the roommate before you?" Jamie asked. "Amanda Cooper, I believe was her name."

And there it was.

Surprise and something else. Where Holland had so carefully crafted her expression when talking about Catriona, here she slipped. But the curious mix of emotions was gone before Jamie could really pin it down.

Holland frowned in thought. "I know Cat hated her because she left without warning. But no, nothing more than that. It was before my time."

Jamie nodded, like that was all perfectly understandable. "How about Marcus Sinclair?"

"Oh, I was around for him," Holland said, sounding genuinely angry, and Jamie began to doubt herself again. Had she really seen surprise a minute earlier? And if she had, so what? Holland couldn't have been expecting to be asked about Cat's former roommate. "He was a preview for, well, all this, I guess."

"Oh, that's so sad," Mia murmured, though both Jamie and Holland ignored that.

Jamie tried one more shot across the bow. "And Benjamin Croft?"

"Benji." Holland's eyes went a little soft. "Now, he was a good guy. Well, until he drank himself into a telephone pole, I guess."

"Right," Jamie said, shoving her hands in her pockets and rocking back on her heels. "That is what the police report said."

Holland nodded, brows raised politely, as if she would answer Jamie's questions all day long if she wanted to throw them at her.

"It's interesting," Jamie mused. "How much death you've experienced. At such a young age."

It was Mia who answered, all tart and vinegar now. "'Interesting' isn't exactly the word I would use."

"No, of course, you're right," Jamie said, eyes flicking to the woman. It was *interesting* that Holland had gotten herself such a fierce defender in such a short amount of time. "But that does seem like some bad luck."

"I'm not sure how much luck had to do with it," Holland said, sadly. "Cat had a pattern. This kind of felt inevitable."

Inevitable.

"Yeah," Jamie said softly, realizing it really was just that.

She was probably trying to make a sad story into one that wasn't so goddamn tragic for her, for her daughter, for women in general.

Jamie silently cursed at herself. She shouldn't be here, she should be home, and these women should be left alone. When she excused herself, they both offered polite, but firm, goodbyes.

She did make one last stop at the police station to check in with Detective Boyd. She didn't have to search—he was in the parking lot, leaning against his cruiser, scrolling on his phone.

"So, you found Catriona Bouchard," Jamie said, sidling up to him. "Is the case essentially closed?"

"ME will examine both bodies," Boyd said, with a shrug. "We'll do our due diligence, but yeah." He studied her. "Is there a reason you think this is something other than a domestic violence case?"

Jamie considered telling him about Mary Jane, but then she pictured the messages the woman had shown her between her and Catriona Bouchard. The endless thread of one-sided desperation to connect.

That coffee you were drinking looked delicious.

Your hair looked beautiful today.

They were borderline inappropriate, and probably not even borderline. Jamie thought the woman probably needed a friend and some professional help, not Boyd from State dragging a statement about Holland Tate's empty coffee cup out of her.

She would follow up with the woman in a week or two, make sure she was all right.

"Did you interview the nanny?" she asked, mostly out of curiosity. She hadn't made a big appearance on the tapes.

"Yeah, she's a piece of work," he muttered, something he probably wouldn't have if this day hadn't been so long. "Going on about how Catriona and Kristopher were deeply in love, just like her and her boyfriend."

Jamie couldn't help the disbelieving sound that came out of her. "She talked about her boyfriend?"

"Yeah," Boyd said, amused as well. "They're long-distance, he's a rock-climbing instructor. I know more about this guy in Switzerland than I do about my own kid."

"What's her theory on who did it?"

"The stepkid," Boyd said, with a shrug. "But it's not like she's the brightest bulb in the box."

Jamie raised her brows. She could excuse one of those—she worked with mostly men, and they rarely had good impressions of their female witnesses. Or victims, for that matter. But only one.

He winced. "Sorry, sorry. And I know you flagged him, too. But he was live streaming a video game when it all went down. There's video of him and everything. Time-stamped. There were other kids participating, too. He's alibied up to his elbows."

Jamie nearly slumped at that. This was why she wasn't a homicide detective. Her instincts were all off. To be fair, she'd never asked to be one. She liked her mostly quiet life of neighbors arguing over someone's dog that just wouldn't shut the hell up.

"Any news on what's going on with the kids?" she asked.

"Apparently the grandparents were already working on getting custody of the oldest boy," Boyd said. "They were happy to take the rest in."

"Even Fleur?" Jamie asked. "Do they know?"

"Yeah. And they seem like decent folks," Boyd said. "I only talked to them on the phone, but they didn't even hesitate when her paternity came up."

"They must have been so shocked," Jamie murmured. And then rushed to clarify: "About the murder-suicide. Not the daughter."

"They were and they weren't," Boyd said. "They didn't have a good relationship with Kristopher. He cut them out of his life for the most part after his first divorce. And Stefan had been pretty harsh about how terrible Kristopher and Catriona were."

Jamie nodded, and then because she was a stubborn old bitch who couldn't let things lie, she asked, "Did you run a background check on Holland Tate?"

Boyd had returned his attention to his phone, but at that he glanced up. "The journalist?"

"Isn't it strange that she came into town and then, boom, her best friend and her best friend's husband are killed?"

Now she worried she sounded like Mary Jane, but it would have eaten her alive if she hadn't said something.

He made a considering face. "Nothing red-flaggy came up for her. She's worked at *Profile Magazine* for ten years, has won some awards."

Boyd punched her lightly on the shoulder, in a patronizing manner. "I like where your head's at. Asking all the right questions. But it's most likely that her presence simply set all of it in motion because, well, she was the one person who knew Catriona's secret."

Jamie *knew* that, she did. She'd had the exact same thought in the hospital room. But if Catriona Bouchard had been so scared of her husband, why had she let herself be convinced to tell him about Fleur? The question itched at her the same way Jeremy Dawson's change of mind had. And both had been because of Holland Tate.

Boyd smiled when she didn't say anything to that. "Hey, thanks for all your help with this. You were instrumental in this case."

He said it like she was some junior officer who needed praise for watching the perimeter of a crime scene. In the next moment he sauntered away, up the steps of the police station.

Jamie officially washed her hands of the case.

She said goodbye instead of "fuck off," like she wanted to, and left it all behind her.

Her daughter was still awake when she finally arrived back home, all but waiting by the door for details of the death of a quasi-celebrity in their backyard.

"I cannot believe it," Maria said, mostly chattering at Jamie rather than asking her questions. "The Bouchards were *goals*. They seemed so in love, so perfect."

"Come on, bug," Jamie said, tapping her lightly on the head. "You know better than to believe that everything posted on the internet is real."

"I know," Maria drawled out, overdramatic. "People are going back to find all the weird things he did in some of the videos."

Of course they were. Hindsight being twenty-twenty and all that. "Stop watching that shit, bug."

Maria was already back on her phone, though. "It's all so tragic, isn't it?"

"No," Jamie said, sinking into her recliner, completely unsatisfied with the entire day. "It's just a tale as old as time."

"Yeah," Maria said softly, yearning in her voice now. "But for a moment it was beautiful."

ACKNOWLEDGMENTS

This book wouldn't exist without my fabulous editor Megha Parekh asking if I wanted to write a stand-alone thriller in between series. I am forever grateful to you for your trust in me, and for letting me push myself creatively at just the right moments.

As always, a thank-you that is never big enough to Charlotte Herscher—the most brilliant editor, who has been pushing me for ten years now to get the best version of each book I write out there. The woman who makes sure at every turn to advocate for the reader in a way that—as a reader—I find extremely reassuring and comforting.

My gratitude to agent-extraordinaire Abby Saul is boundless, but it is especially profound during projects where I leap off a cliff and drag her along with me. Thank you for diving into the abyss with me every time.

A huge thank-you to the best team in the world at Thomas & Mercer, who makes sure every step of the process is smooth sailing as they get my books into the hands of readers.

Much love must go out to Hannah Vaughn, my film agent, for always advocating for me at every turn.

To my family, friends, and neighbors who have showered me with support and love—I truly don't know how I got so lucky to have you.

And you, my dear reader: Every time I thank you. Because it takes trust and hope and love to open a book and fall into its world not knowing what you're going to get. Thank you for wanting to come along for the ride, even when it's a wild and weird one.

ABOUT THE AUTHOR

Brianna Labuskes is the *USA Today*, *Wall Street Journal*, *Washington Post*, and Amazon Charts bestselling author of *The Lies You Wrote*, *The Truth You Told*, and *By the Time You Read This* in the Raisa Susanto series; *See It End*, *What Can't Be Seen*, and *A Familiar Sight* in the Dr. Gretchen White series; and *Her Final Words*, *Black Rock Bay*, *Girls of Glass*, and *It Ends with Her*. She lives in Pennsylvania with her puppy, Jinx. For more information, visit www.briannalabuskes.com.